CROCODILE CREEK: 24-HOUR RESCUE

**A cutting-edge medical centre.
Fully equipped for saving lives and loves!**

**Crocodile Creek's state-of-the-art
Medical Centre and Rescue Response Unit is
home to a team of expertly trained medical
professionals. These dedicated men and
women face the challenges of life, love and
medicine every day!**

Two weddings!

Crocodile Creek is playing host to two weddings
this year, and love is definitely in the air! But…

A cyclone is brewing!

As a severe weather front moves in,
the rescue team are poised for action—
this time with some new recruits.

Two missing children!

As the cyclone wreaks its devastation, it soon
becomes clear that there are two little ones
missing. Now the team has to pull together like
never before to find them…before it's too late!

**Meredith Webber's
THE NURSE HE'S BEEN WAITING FOR
is the second of four continuing stories
revisiting *Crocodile Creek*. Look out
for two more books from Marion Lennox
and Lilian Darcy.
Join them every month in
Mills & Boon® Medical™ Romance**

He put his arms around her and tucked her body close to his.

Grace knew this wouldn't do much for her keeping Harry at a distance plans, but surely a woman was allowed a little bit of bliss. She slid into his arms and put her arms around his back.

It's just pretence, she told her head. After all, she could go back to distancing tomorrow. It was heaven.

The band was playing a slow waltz and she and Harry were at the edge of the dance floor, barely moving to the music, content, as far as Grace was concerned, just to be in each other's arms.

Outside the wind had gathered strength again, and rain lashed the garden and flung itself against the windows. It was definitely 'snuggling closer' weather. If she moved just slightly she could rest her head against his chest, and for a little while she could dream.

Later, she couldn't remember whether she'd actually made this daring move or not, but what she did remember was that the lights went out, then Harry spun her around and bent his head.

And kissed her.

THE NURSE
HE'S BEEN
WAITING FOR

BY
MEREDITH WEBBER

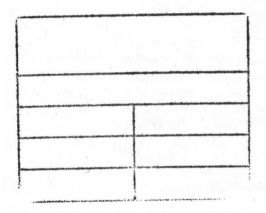

MILLS & BOON®
Pure reading pleasure

First published in Great Britain 2007
Large Print edition 2008
Harlequin Mills & Boon Limited,
Eton House, 18-24 Paradise Road,
Richmond, Surrey TW9 1SR

© Meredith Webber 2007

ISBN: 978 0 263 19945 1

Set in Times Roman 16½ on 20 pt.
17-0408-46877

Printed and bound in Great Britain
by Antony Rowe Ltd, Chippenham, Wiltshire

Meredith Webber says of herself, 'Some years ago, I read an article which suggested that Mills & Boon were looking for new medical authors. I had one of those "I can do that" moments, and gave it a try. What began as a challenge has become an obsession, though I do temper the "butt on seat" career of writing with dirty but healthy outdoor pursuits, fossicking through the Australian Outback in search of gold or opals. Having had some success in all of these endeavours, I now consider I've found the perfect lifestyle.'

Recent titles by the same author:

HIS RUNAWAY NURSE
THE SPANISH DOCTOR'S CONVENIENT BRIDE
A FATHER BY CHRISTMAS
BRIDE AT BAY HOSPITAL
THE DOCTOR'S MARRIAGE WISH*

*Crocodile Creek

Dear Reader

Writing is such a solitary pursuit that to be involved in a series with other people is really special. To be involved in a series with three good friends—Marion Lennox, Lilian Darcy and Alison Roberts—is extraordinarily special. More than that, it's tremendous fun. Although we live far apart, three of us in different states in Australia and Alison in New Zealand, we do manage to get together most years at the Australian Romance Writers' Conference.

It was at one of these conferences about four years ago that the idea for the *Crocodile Creek* series was born. The four of us spent more time in various hotel bedrooms plotting out our masterpiece than we did listening to conference speakers. Then we had to sell the idea to our editors, which took a little time and quite a lot of work on their part and on ours, but in the end we got the go-ahead and suddenly Crocodile Creek became as real to us as our home suburbs, and the people who worked in the hospital and Air Rescue Service became our friends.

I was very fond of Harry, the policeman, so was delighted when I could match him up with Grace in this book. Grace's sunny nature and helpful personality make her the ideal woman for Harry, but she fears she is unlovable and he just flat-out fears love. But as a cyclone whirls above their heads, things change.

And now? Well, while we might have sorted out the love-lives of some of our friends in this second series, several new people have appeared who might also need some loving. I hope so, as being involved in the series has been special—almost as special as being in love.

Meredith Webber

PROLOGUE

As a cyclone hovered off the coast of North Queensland, threatening destruction to any town in its path, several hundred miles away a small boy sneaked on board a bus. Terrified that his father, who was arguing with the bus driver, would discover the dog he'd threatened to drown, Max ducked between the two men and climbed the steps into the warm, fusty, dimly lit interior of the big vehicle. Mum would sort everything out when he got to Crocodile Creek—the fare, the dog, everything.

Mum would like a dog.

'Don't call her Mum—she's your flippin' sister! Or half-sister, if you really want to know.'

Echoes of his father's angry rant rang through

Max's head, but Georgie hadn't ever minded him calling her Mum, and it stopped kids at school teasing him.

The kids that had mums, that was.

Mum would love Scruffy.

He shifted the backpack off his shoulder and hugged it to his chest, comforted by the squirming of the pup inside it, checking out the passengers as he made his way up the aisle. He'd been shunted back and forth across Queensland often enough to be able to pick out who was who among his fellow travellers.

The bus was nearly full and all the usual ones were there. A group of backpackers chattering away in a foreign language, a fat woman in the seat behind them—bet she'd been to visit her grandkids—bloke on the other side of the aisle—he'd be late back on the bus at all the rest stops—an old couple who looked like they'd been on the bus for all of their lives, and a tired, sad-looking woman with a little boy.

Max slipped into the seat behind them. He'd

never told Mum and certainly wouldn't bother telling Dad, but scary things could happen on a bus, and he'd worked out it's always best to stick with someone with a kid, or to sit near a youngish couple, so he looked like part of a family.

Though with Scruffy to protect him…

He slid across the seat to the window, looking for his father, wondering if the argument was over—if his father had actually paid to get rid of him this time.

Wanting to wave goodbye.

The footpath was deserted, the bus driver now talking to someone in the doorway of the travel office. Twisting his head against the glass, Max could just make out a shambling figure moving through a pool of lamplight well behind the bus—walking away from it.

So much for waving goodbye.

'It doesn't matter!' Max told himself fiercely, scrunching up his eyes and blinking hard, turning his attention to the zip on his backpack before thrusting his hand inside, feeling

Scruffy's rough hair, a warm tongue licking his fingers. 'It doesn't matter!'

But when you're only seven, it did matter…

CHAPTER ONE

MIDNIGHT, and Grace O'Riordan lay on one of the examination couches in the emergency department of the Crocodile Creek Hospital and stared at an amoeba-shaped stain on the ceiling as she contemplated clothes, love and the meaning of life.

In truth, the meaning of life wasn't overtaxing her brain cells right now, and she'd assured herself, for the forty-hundredth time, that the dress she'd bought for the wedding wasn't too over the top, which left love.

Love, as in unrequited.

One-sided.

Heavens to Betsy, as if she hadn't had enough one-sided love in her life.

Perhaps loving without being loved back made her unlovable. In the same way old furniture, polished often, developed a rich deep shiny patina, so loved people shone and attracted more love.

What *was* this? Sensible, practical, Grace O'Riordan indulging in wild flights of fancy? She'd be better off napping.

Although she was on duty, the A and E dept—in fact, the entire hospital—after a particularly hectic afternoon and early evening, was quiet. Quiet enough for her to have a sleep, which, given the frantic few days she'd just spent checking on cyclone preparations, she needed.

But she needed love, too, and was practical—there was that word again—enough to know that she had to get over her present love—the unrequited one—and start looking to the future. Start looking for someone who might love her back, someone who also wanted love and the things that went with it, like marriage and a family. Especially a family. She had been family-less for quite long enough…

This coming week would provide the perfect opportunity to begin the search, with people flying in from all over the globe for the weddings of Mike and Emily tomorrow and, a week later, Gina and Cal. Surely somewhere, among all the unattached male wedding guests, there'd be someone interested in a smallish, slightly plump, sometimes pretty, Irish-Australian nurse.

She pressed her hand against her heart, sure she could feel pain just thinking about loving someone other than Harry.

But she'd got over love before, she could do it again.

'Move on, Grace!' she told herself, in her sternest voice.

'Isn't anyone on duty in this place?' a loud voice demanded.

Harry's voice.

Grace slid off the table, pulled her uniform shirt straight, wondered, briefly, whether her short curls looked like a flattened bird's nest after lying down, and exited the room to greet the man she was trying to get over.

'If you'd come in through the emergency door, a bell would have rung and I'd have known you were here,' she greeted him, none too warmly. Then she saw the blood.

'Holy cow, Harry Blake, what have you done to yourself this time?'

She grabbed a clean towel from a pile on a trolley and hurried towards the chair where he'd collapsed, one bloody leg thrust out in front of him.

Wrapping the towel tightly around the wound to stem at least some of the bleeding, she looked up into his face. Boy, was it ever hard to get over love when her heart danced jigs every time she saw him.

Irish jigs.

She looked at his face again—as a nurse this time. It was grey with tiredness but not, as far as she could tell, pale from blood loss.

'Can you make it into an examination cubicle or will I ring for help?' she asked, knowing full well he was so stubborn he'd refuse help even if she called for it. But when he stood he wobbled slightly, so she tucked her shoulder into his armpit to take some of his weight, and with her arm around his back for added support she led him into the room.

He sat down on the couch she'd occupied only minutes earlier, then, as she pushed at his chest and lifted his legs, he lay down.

'What happened?' she asked, as she un-wrapped the towel enough to know there was no arterial bleeding on his leg, then wrapped it up again so she could check his vital signs before she examined the wound.

'Carelessness,' he muttered at her. He closed his eyes, which made her wonder if his blood loss was more serious than she'd supposed. But his pulse was strong, his blood pressure excel-lent and his breathing steady. Just to be sure, she slid an oxygen saturation meter onto one of his fingers, and turned on the monitor.

'What kind of carelessness?' she asked as she

once again unwrapped the towel and saw the torn, bloodstained trouser leg and the badly lacerated skin beneath the shredded fabric.

'Chainsaw! Does that stain on the ceiling look like a penguin to you?'

'No, it looks like an amoeba, which is to say a formless blob.' She was using scissors to cut away his trousers, so she could see the wound. Blood had run into his sock, making it hard to tell if the damage went down that far. Taking care not to brush against his wound, she took hold of his boot to ease it off.

'You can't do that,' he said, sitting up so quickly his shoulder brushed against her and his face was kissing close.

Kissing Harry? As if!

'Can't take your boot off?' she asked. 'Is there some regulation about not being a policeman if you're not wearing both boots?'

He turned towards her, a frown pleating his black eyebrows, his grey eyes perplexed. 'Of course not. You just wouldn't get it off.' He tugged and twisted at the same time and the elastic-sided boot slid off. 'I'll get the sock, too,' he added, pulling off the bloodstained wreck, but not before Grace had noticed the hole at the top of the big toe.

In a dream where Harry loved her back, she'd have mended that hole—she'd like doing things like that—the little caring things that said *I love you* without the words.

'Lie back,' she said, dream and reality coming too close for comfort with him sitting there. 'I'll flush this mess and see what's what.'

She pulled on clean gloves and set a bag of saline on a drip stand. She'd need tubing, a three-way tap, syringe and a nineteen-gauge needle to drip the liquid onto the wound while she probed for foreign particles.

Packing waterproof-backed absorbent pads beneath his leg, she started the saline dripping onto the wound, a nasty contusion running eight inches in length, starting on the tibia just below the knee and swerving off into his calf.

'The skin's so chewed up it's not viable enough to stitch,' she told him, probing a few pieces of what looked like mangled treetrunk, or possibly mangled trouser fabric, from the deepest part. Organic matter and clay were among the most likely things to cause infection in tissue injury. 'Ideally it should be left open, but I guess you're not willing to stay home and rest it for the next few days.'

'You *are* joking!' Harry said. 'I need it patched up now, and maybe in three days' time, when we know for sure Cyclone Willie has departed, I can rest it.'

'Harry, it's a mess. I'll dress it as best I can but if you don't look after it and come in to have it dressed every day, you're going to end up with ulceration and needing a skin graft on it.'

She left the saline dripping on the wound while she found the dressings she'd need and some antibiotic cream which she would spread beneath the non-adhesive dressing once she had all visible debris removed from it.

Harry watched her work, right up until she starting snipping away torn tatters of skin, when he turned his attention back to the penguin on the ceiling.

'Would you like me to give you a local anaesthetic while I do this? It could hurt.'

'It *is* hurting,' he said, gritting his teeth as a particularly stubborn piece of skin or grit defied Grace's efforts to be gentle. 'But, no, no needles. Just talk to me. And before you do, have another look—maybe the stain looks like the little engine on a cane train.'

Grace glanced towards the ceiling but shook her head as she turned back towards him.

'Since when do a penguin and a cane train engine share similarities in looks?'

'It's a shape thing,' he said, grabbing at her hand and drawing the shape on the back of it. 'Penguin, blob, train engine, see?'

'Not even vaguely,' she told him, rescuing her hand from his grasp then changing her gloves again before she continued with her job. 'And I can see right through you, Harry Blake. You're babbling on about penguins and cane trains to keep me from going back to the question you avoided earlier.'

She stopped talking while she spread cream across his leg. He didn't feel much like talking either.

Grace sealed the wound with a broad, long dressing, and bandaged over it with crêpe bandages, then pulled a long sleeve over the lot, giving it as much security and padding as she could because she knew he'd be putting himself in situations where he could bump it.

'That should give it some protection from physical damage, although, with the cyclone coming, who knows what you'll be called on to do? Just make sure you come in to have it checked and re-dressed every day.'

'You on duty tomorrow?'

Grace smiled sadly to herself. Would that he was asking because he was interested!

'You already know the answer to that one. I

finish night duty in the morning and have three days off so I can cope with the wedding and the cyclone preparations without letting any one down here at the hospital.'

Harry sat up and swung his legs over the side of the bed, ready to leave.

'Not so fast,' she warned him. 'I need to check your tetanus status and give you some antibiotics just in case there's some infection already in there.'

She paused and her wide blue eyes met his.

'*And* you're not leaving here until you tell me how you did it.'

Harry studied her as he debated whether to tell her. Tousled curls, freckled nose—Grace, everyone's friend.

His friend, too. A friendship formed when he'd been in need of a friend in the months after Nikki's death. True, he'd had friends, good friends, among the townspeople and the hospital staff, but all the locals had known Nikki since she'd been a child while the hospital staff had all drawn close to her as they'd nursed her through the last weeks of her life.

And though these friends had all stood by him and had wanted to offer support, he'd avoided them, not wanting sympathy, needing to be left alone to sort out the morass of conflicting emotions warring within him.

Grace had arrived after Nikki's death, so there was no connection, no history, just a bright, bubbly, capable young woman who was willing to listen if he wanted to talk, to talk if he needed conversation, or just to share the silence when he didn't want to be alone.

A true friend…

'I'm waiting!'

She had her hands on her hips and a no-nonsense look on her face, but though she was trying to look serious a smile lurked in her blue eyes.

A smile nearly always lurked in Grace's eyes…

The thought startled him to the extent that confession seemed easier than considering what, if anything, noticing Grace's smiling eyes might mean.

'I hit my leg with the blade of a chainsaw.'

'And *what* were you doing, wielding a chainsaw, may I ask?'

'A tree had come down, out along the Wygera road, but part of the trunk must have been dead because the saw bounced off it when it hit it.' He waved his hand towards his now securely bandaged leg. 'One wounded leg.'

'That wasn't my question and you know it, Harry. It's one o'clock in the morning. You're a policeman, not a rescue worker. The fire service, the electricity workers and, or when requested, the SES crews clear roads. It's what they're trained to do. The SES manual has pages and pages on safe working with chainsaws.'

'I've been using chainsaws all my life,' Harry retorted, uncomfortably aware this conversation might not be about chainsaws but uncertain what it was about.

'That's not the point,' Grace snapped. 'What if

the accident had been worse? What if you'd taken your leg off? Then who's in charge here? Who's left to co-ordinate services to a town that could be struck by one of the worst cyclones in history within the next twenty-four hours?'

'Give over, Grace,' he said, standing up on his good leg and carefully putting weight on the injured one to see how bad it felt.

Very bad. Bad enough to make him feel queasy.

'No, I won't give over.' No smile in the blue eyes now. In fact, she was glaring at him. 'This is just typical of you, Harry Blake. Typical of the stupid risks you take. You mightn't care what happens to you, but you've got family and friends who do. There are people out there who'd be deeply hurt if you were killed or badly injured, but do you think about them when you pull on your superhero cape and go rushing blindly into danger? No, you don't! You don't think of anyone but yourself, and that's not noble or self-sacrificing or even brave—it's just plain selfishness, Harry.'

Harry heard her out, growing more annoyed every second. He'd had a shocking day, he was tired, his leg hurt and to accuse him of selfishness, well, that was just the last straw.

'And just what makes you think you have the right to sit in judgement on me?' he demanded, taking a careful stride towards the cubicle curtain so he could escape any further conversation. 'What makes you think you know me well enough to call me selfish, or to question my motives in helping people? You're not my mother or my wife, Grace, so butt out!'

He heard her gasp as he headed out of the cubicle, across the deserted A and E waiting room and out of the hospital, limping not entirely because of his leg but because he was only wearing one boot. The other he'd stupidly left behind, and that made him even angrier than Grace's accusation. He looked up at the cloud-massed sky and wanted to yell his frustration to the wind.

Perhaps it was just as well there was no one around, although if he'd happened on someone he knew he could have asked that person to go back in and retrieve the boot for him. The hospital was quieter than he'd ever seen it, with no one coming or going from the car park.

He was contemplating radioing the constable on duty to come over and collect it for him when he heard the footsteps behind him.

Grace!

Coming to apologise?

'Here's your boot, and some antibiotics, directions on when to take them on the packet. And in answer to your question about rights, I thought, for some obviously foolish reason, I had the right of a friend.'

And with that she spun on her heel and walked briskly back into the hospital.

Wonderful! Now Grace had joined the throng of people he'd somehow managed to upset, simply because they refused to let him get on with his life his way.

Alone! With no emotional involvement with anyone or anything.

Except Sport, the three-legged blue heeler cattle dog he'd rescued from the dump one day.

And his parents—he liked his parents. And they'd known him well enough to back off when Nikki had died...

He climbed into his vehicle and slumped back against the seat. Was the day over? Please, God, it might be. On top of all the damage and power disruptions caused by the gale-force winds stirred up by Cyclone Willie, he'd had to handle traffic chaos at the fishing competition, an assault on Georgie Turner, the local obstetrician, Sophia Poulos, mother of the groom at the next day's wedding, phoning every fifteen minutes to ask about the cyclone as if he was personally responsible for its course, and to top it all off, he'd had to visit Georgie again.

She was still shaken from the assault by a patient's relative earlier that day, and nursing a hairline fracture to her cheekbone. Now Harry had to tell her there was a summons out for her stepfather's arrest—her stepfather who currently had custody of her little brother Max.

Did Georgie know where he was?

She hadn't known where the pair were, and he'd hated himself for asking because now she'd be even more worried about Max, whom she'd loved and cared for since he'd been a baby, bringing him up herself—except for the times when the worthless scoundrel who'd fathered him swooped in and took him away, no doubt to provide a prop in some nefarious purpose.

Max was such a great kid, growing up around the hospital, loved and watched out for by everyone in the close-knit community.

So Harry had been driving away from the doctors' house, seething with frustration that he couldn't offer anything to help the white-faced, injured woman, when the call had come in about the tree coming down to block the Wygera road. His chainsaw had already been in the vehicle so he'd decided to take out some of his anger and frustration on a tree.

None of which was any excuse for being rude to Grace…

Not wanting to think about Harry or the crushing words he'd used, Grace retreated to cubicle one once again and climbed back onto the examination couch. She stared at the stain on the ceiling, trying to see a penguin or a cane train engine but seeing only an amoeba.

Was it because she lacked imagination?

Not that she couldn't see the penguin but that she couldn't let Harry alone to get on with his life his own way.

Did her lack of imagination mean she couldn't understand his grieving process?

Hurt enveloped her—that Harry could say what he had. And while she knew she should have welcomed his angry comment because now she knew for sure she had to move on, such rational reasoning didn't make the pain any less.

She studied the stain.

'Is this place totally deserted?'

Another male voice, this one deep and slightly husky. Grace sprang off the couch and was about to emerge from the treatment cubicle when the curtain opened.

Luke Bresciano, hunky, dark amber-eyed, black-haired, Italian-Australian orthopod, stood there, smiling at her.

'I always napped on examination couches when I was on duty in the ER, and for some reason it's always treatment room one,' he teased.

He had a lovely smile but it didn't reach his eyes—a tortured soul, Dr B. And although, this being Crocodile Creek, stories about his past abounded—a woman who'd left him, a child— no one really knew any more about him than they had the day he'd arrived. Age, marital status and qualifications.

'You're here late. Do you have a patient coming in?' Grace asked, being practical and professional while wondering if she remembered how to flirt and if there was any point in trying a little flirtation on Luke. Although was there any point in swapping one tortured soul for another?

'I find sleep comes when it wants to and it wasn't coming so I drove up to see a patient I'd admitted earlier. I looked in on Susie while I was here—'

'Susie? Our physio Susie? In hospital? But she can't be.' Grace was stumbling over her disbelief. 'She's Emily's bridesmaid tomorrow. Mrs Poulos will have a cow!'

Luke offered a kindly smile—much like the one Grace usually offered drunks or people coming out of anaesthetic who were totally confused.

'You obviously haven't heard the latest. Susie had a fall and sprained her ankle earlier today— or is it yesterday now? But the bridesmaid thing's been sorted out. Her twin sister Hannah is here— they're identical twins—and she's going to do bridesmaid duties so the photos won't—'

'Be totally spoilt by Susie's crutches,' Grace

finished for him, shaking her head in bemusement that such a wonderful solution—from Mrs P.'s point of view—had been found. Grace was quite sure Emily wouldn't have minded in the least.

Nodding agreement to her ending of the story, Luke finished, 'Exactly! So after visiting Susie, who was sound asleep anyway, I was taking a short cut out through here when I realised how empty it seemed.'

He smiled at Grace but although it was a very charming smile, it did nothing to her heart. She'd really have to work on it if she wanted to move on from Harry. 'I thought I'd better check we did have someone on duty.'

'Yes, that's me. I can't believe how quiet it is. All I heard from the day staff was how busy they'd been and I was busy earlier but now…'

She waved her arms around to indicate the emptiness.

'Then I'll let you get back to sleep,' Luke said.

He turned to depart and she remembered the stain.

'Before you go, would you mind having a look at this stain?'

The words were out before she realised just how truly weird her request was, but Luke was looking enquiringly at her, so she pointed at the stain on the ceiling.

'Roof leaking? I'm not surprised given the rain we've been having, but Maintenance probably knows more about leaking roofs than I do. In fact, they'd have to.' Another charming smile. 'I know zilch.'

'It's not a leak. It's an old stain but I'd really like to know what you think about the shape. You have to lie down on the couch to see it properly. Would you mind checking it out and telling me what it looks like to you?'

'Ink-blot test, Grace?' Luke teased, but he lay obediently on the couch and turned his attention to the stain.

'It looks a bit like a penguin to me,' Luke said, and Grace was sorry she'd asked.

She walked out to the door with Luke, said goodbye, then returned to the cubicle.

It *must* be lack of imagination that she couldn't see it. She focussed on the stain, desperate to see the penguin and prove her imaginative abilities.

Hadn't she just imagined herself darning Harry's socks?

The stain remained a stain—amoeba-like in its lack of form. She clambered off the couch, chastising herself for behaving so pathetically.

For heaven's sake, Grace, get over it!

Get over Harry and get on with your life.

She stood and stared at the stain, trying for a cane train engine this time…

Trying not to think about Harry…

Failing…

It had come as a tumultuous shock to Grace, the realisation that she was love with Harry. She, who'd vowed never to risk one-sided love again, had fallen into the trap once more. She'd fallen in love with a man who'd been there and done that as far as love and marriage were concerned.

A man who had no intention of changing his single status.

They'd been at a State Emergency Service meeting, and had stayed behind, as they nearly always did, to chat. Grace was team leader of the Crocodile Creek SES and Harry, as the head of the local police force, was the co-ordinator for all rescue and emergency services in the area.

Harry had suggested coffee, as he nearly always did after their fortnightly meetings. Nothing noteworthy there—coffee was coffee and all Grace's defences had been securely in place. They'd locked the SES building and walked the short distance down the road to the Black Cockatoo, which, although a pub, also served the best coffee in the small community of Crocodile Creek.

The bar had been crowded, a group of young people celebrating someone's birthday, making a lot of noise and probably drinking a little too much, but Harry Blake, while he'd keep an eye on them, wasn't the kind of policeman who'd spoil anyone's innocent fun.

So he'd steered Grace around the corner where

the bar angled, leaving a small, dimly lit area free from noise or intrusion.

The corner of the bar had been dark, but not too dark for her to see Harry's grey eyes glinting with a reflection of the smile on his mobile lips and Harry's black hair flopping forward on his forehead, so endearingly her fingers had ached to push it back.

'Quieter here,' he said, pulling out a barstool and taking Grace's elbow as she clambered onto it. Then he smiled—nothing more. Just a normal, Harry Blake kind of smile, the kind he offered to men, women, kids and dogs a million times a day. But the feeble defences Grace O'Riordan had built around her heart collapsed in the warmth of that smile, and while palpitations rattled her chest, and her brain tut-tutted helplessly, Grace realised she'd gone and done it again.

Fallen in love.

With Harry, of all people...

Harry, who was her friend...

CHAPTER TWO

GRACE fidgeted with the ribbon in her hair. It was too much—she knew it was too much. Yet the woman in the mirror looked really pretty, the ribbon somehow enhancing her looks.

She took a deep breath, knowing it wasn't the ribbon worrying her but Harry, who was about to pick them all up to drive them to the wedding.

The hurtful words he'd uttered very early that morning—*you're not my mother or my wife*—still echoed in her head, made worse by the knowledge that what he'd said was true. She *didn't* have the right to be telling Harry what to do!

It was a good thing it had happened, she reminded herself. She had to get past this love she felt for him. She'd had enough one-sided love in her life, starting in her childhood—loving a father who'd barely known she'd existed, loving stepbrothers who'd laughed at her accent and resented her intrusion into their lives.

Then, of course, her relationship with James had confirmed it. One-sided love was not enough. Love had to flow both ways for it to work—or it did as far as she was concerned.

So here she was, like Cinderella heading for the ball, on the lookout for a prince.

Harry's a prince, her heart whispered, but she wasn't having any of that. Harry was gone, done and dusted, out of her life, and whatever other clichés might fit this new determination.

And if her chest hurt, well, that was to be expected. Limbs hurt after parts of them were amputated and getting Harry out of her heart was the same thing—an amputation.

But having confirmed this decision, shouldn't she take her own car to the wedding? She could use the excuse that she needed to be with Mrs P. Keeping Mrs P. calm and rational—or as calm and rational as an over-excitable Greek woman could manage on the day her only son was married—was Grace's job for the day.

A shiver of uncertainty worse, right now, than her worry over Harry feathered down Grace's spine. Mike's mother had planned this wedding with the precision of a military exercise—or perhaps a better comparison would be a full-scale, no-holds-barred, Technicolor, wide-screen movie production.

Thinking now of Mrs Poulos, Grace glanced towards the window. Was the wind getting up again? It sounded wild out there, although at the moment it wasn't raining. When the previous day had dawned bright and sunny, the hospital staff had let out their collective breaths. At least, it had seemed, Mrs P. would get her way with the weather.

But now?

The cyclone that had teased the citizens of North Queensland for days, travelling first towards the coast then veering away from it, had turned out to sea a few days earlier, there, everyone hoped, to spend its fury without any further damage. Here in Crocodile Creek, the river was rising, the bridge barely visible above the water, while the strong winds and rain earlier in the week had brought tree branches crashing down on houses, and Grace's SES workers had been kept busy, spreading tarpaulins over the damage.

Not that tarps would keep out the rain if the cyclone turned back their way—they'd be ripped off by the wind within minutes, along with the torn roofing they were trying to protect—

'Aren't you ready yet?'

Christina was calling from the living room, although Grace had given her and Joe the main bedroom—the bedroom they'd shared for a long time before moving to New Zealand to be closer to Joe's family. Now Grace rented the little cottage from Christina, and was hoping to discuss buying it while the couple was here for the birth of their first child as well as the hospital weddings.

'Just about,' she answered, taking a last look

at herself and wondering again if she'd gone overboard with the new dress and the matching ribbon threaded through her short fair curls.

Wondering again about driving herself but thinking perhaps she'd left that decision too late. Harry would be here any minute. Besides, her friends might think she was snubbing them.

She'd just have to pretend—she was good at that—only today, instead of pretending Harry was just a friend, she'd have to pretend that all was well between them. In a distant kind of way.

She certainly wasn't going to spoil Mike and Em's wedding by sulking over Harry all through it.

'Wow!'

Joe's slow smile told her he meant the word of praise, and Grace's doubts disappeared.

'Wow yourself,' she said, smiling at him. 'Christina's pregnant and you're the one that's glowing. You both look fantastic.'

She caught the private, joyous smile they shared and felt it pierce her heart like a shard of glass, but held her own smile firmly in place. She might know she'd lost her bounce—lost a little of her delight in life and all the wonders it had to offer—but she'd managed to keep it from being obvious to her friends. Still smiling, still laughing, still joking with her colleagues, hiding the pain of her pointless, unrequited love beneath her bubbly exterior.

Pretence!

'And you've lost weight,' Christina said, eyeing Grace more carefully now. 'Not that it doesn't suit you, you look beautiful, but don't go losing any more.'

'Beautiful? Grace O'Riordan beautiful? Pregnancy affecting your vision?' Grace said, laughing at her friends—mocking the warmth of pleasure she was feeling deep inside.

Harry heard the laugh as he took the two steps up to the cottage veranda in one stride. No one laughed like Grace, not as often or as—was 'musically' the right word? Grace's laugh sounded like the notes of a beautiful bird, cascading through the air, bringing pleasure to all who heard it.

Beautiful bird? Was all this wedding business turning him fanciful?

Surely not!

While as for Grace…

He caught the groan that threatened to escape his lips. He was in the right—he had no doubt about that. What he did and didn't do wasn't Grace's business. Yet he was uneasily aware that he'd upset her and wasn't quite sure how to fix things between them.

Wasn't, for reasons he couldn't fathom, entirely sure he wanted to…

At least it sounded as if they were ready. He'd offered to drive the three of them, thinking his big four-by-four would be more comfortable for the very pregnant Christina than Grace's little VW, but now he was regretting the impulse. With the possibility that the cyclone would turn back towards the coast, he had an excuse to avoid the wedding altogether, which would also mean not having to face Grace.

Although Mike had been a friend for a long time…

A sudden gust of wind brought down a frond from a palm tree and, super-sensitive right now to any change in the atmospheric conditions, Harry stopped, turned and looked around at the trees and shrubs in the cottage's garden. The wind had definitely picked up again, stripping leaves off the frangipani and bruising the delicate flowers. He shook his head, certain now the cyclone must have swung back towards them again, yet knowing there was nothing he, or anyone else, could do to stop it if it continued towards the coast this time.

They would just have to check all their preparations then wait and see. Preparations were easy—it was the waiting that was hard.

'You look as if you're off to a funeral, not a wedding,' Christina teased as she came out the door, and though he found a smile for her, it must have been too late, for she reached out and touched his arm, adding quietly, 'Weddings must be hard for you.'

He shook his head, rejecting her empathy—not deserving it, although she wasn't to know that. Then he looked beyond her and had to look again.

Was that really Grace?

And if it was, why was his body stirring?

Grace it was, smiling at him, a strained smile certainly, but recognisable as a smile, and saying something. Unfortunately, with his blood thundering in his ears, he couldn't hear the words, neither could he lip-read because his eyes kept shifting from her hair—a ribbon twined through golden curls—to her face—was it the colour of the dress that made her eyes seem bluer?—to her cleavage—more stirring—to a slim leg that was showing through a slit in the dark blue piece of fabric she seemed to have draped rather insecurely around her body.

His first instinct was to take off his jacket and cover her with it, his second was to hit Joe, who was hovering proprietorially behind her, probably looking down that cleavage.

He did neither, simply nodding to the pair before turning and leading the way out to the car, trying hard not to limp—he hated sympathy—opening the front door for Christina, explaining she'd be more comfortable there, letting Joe open the rear door for Grace, then regretting a move that put the pair of them together in the back seat.

Mental head slap! What was *wrong* with him? These three were his friends—good friends— Grace especially, even though, right now, he wasn't sure where he stood with Grace.

Very carefully, he tucked Christina's voluminous dress in around her, extended the seat belt so it would fit around her swollen belly, then shut the door, though not without a glance towards the back seat—towards Grace.

She was peering out the window, squinting upwards.

Avoiding looking at him?

He couldn't blame her.

But when she spoke he realised just how wrong he was. He was the last thing on Grace's mind.

'Look, there's a patch of blue sky. The sun *is* going to shine for Mike and Emily.'

Harry shook his head. That was a Grace he recognised, always thinking of others, willing the weather to be fine so her friends could be blessed with sunshine at their wedding.

Although that Grace usually wore big T-shirts and long shorts—that Grace, as far as he'd been aware, didn't have a cleavage…

Christina and Joe had both joined Grace in her study of the growing patch of blue sky, Christina sure having sunshine was a good omen for a happy marriage.

'Sunshine's good for the bride because her dress won't get all wet and her hair won't go floppy,' Joe declared, with all the authority of a man five months into marriage who now understood about women's hair and rain. 'But forget about omens—there's only one thing that will guarantee a happy marriage, and that's a willing-ness for both partners to work at it.'

He slid a hand onto Christina's shoulder then added, 'Harry here knows that.'

Grace saw the movement of Harry's shoulders as he winced, and another shard of glass pierced her vulnerable heart. She hadn't been working at the hospital when Harry's wife, Nikki, had died, but she'd heard enough to know of his devotion to her—of the endless hours he'd spent by her side—and of his heartbreak at her death.

You're not my wife!

The words intruded on her sympathy but she ignored them, determined to pretend that all was well between them—at least in front of other people.

'What's the latest from the weather bureau, Harry?' she asked, hoping to divert his mind from memories she was sure would be bad enough on someone else's wedding day. 'Does this wind mean Willie's turned again and is heading back our way, or is it the early warning of another storm?'

He glanced towards her in the rear-view vision mirror and nodded as if to say, I know what you're doing. But his spoken reply was crisply matter-of-fact. 'Willie's turned—he's running parallel to the coast again but at this stage the bureau has no indication of whether he'll turn west towards us or continue south. The winds are stronger because he's picked up strength—upgraded from a category three to a category four in the last hour.'

'I wouldn't like to think he'll swing around to the west,' Joe said anxiously, obviously worried about being caught in a cyclone with a very pregnant wife.

'He's been so unpredictable he could do anything,' Harry told him. 'And even if he doesn't head our way, we're in for floods as the run-off further upstream comes down the creek.'

'Well, at least we're in the right place—at a hospital,' Christina said. 'And look, isn't that sunshine peeking through the clouds?'

Harry had pulled up in the parking lot of the

church, set in a curve of the bay in the main part of town. Christina was right. One ray of sunshine had found its way through a weakness in the massed, roiling clouds, reflecting its golden light off the angry grey-brown ocean that heaved and roared and crashed into the cove beneath the headland where Mike's parents' restaurant, the Athina, stood.

He watched the ray of light play on the thunderous waves and knew Joe was right—omens like that meant nothing as far as happiness was concerned. The sun had shone on his and Nikki's wedding day—for all the good it had done.

Grace felt her spirits lift with that single ray of light. Her friends were getting married, she was looking good, and so what if Harry Blake didn't want her worrying about him? This was her chance to look at other men and maybe find one who might, eventually, share her dreams of a family.

Unfortunately, just as she was reminding herself of her intention to look around at the single wedding guests, Harry opened the car door for her, and as she slid out a sudden wind gust ripped the door from his hands and only his good reflexes in grabbing her out of the way saved her from being hit by it.

It was hard to think about other men with Harry's strong arm wrapped around her, holding her close to his chest. Hard to think about anything when she was dealing with her own private storm—the emotional one—raging within *her* chest.

You're not my wife.

He's done and dusted.

She pulled away, annoyed with herself for reacting as she had, but determined to hide how she felt. He'd taken her elbow to guide her across the windswept parking lot outside the church and was acting as if nothing untoward had occurred between them. He was even pretending not to limp, which was just as well because she had no intention of asking him how his leg was. Because, Mr Policeman, two could play the pre-tend game.

She smiled up at him.

'Isn't this fun?'

Harry stared at her in disbelief.

Fun?

For a start, he was riven with guilt over his behaviour the previous night, and on top of that, the person he considered—or had considered up until last night—his best friend had turned into a sexpot.

That was fun?

Sexpot? Where on earth had he got that word?

He cast another glance towards his companion— golden hair gleaming in the sunlight, the freckles on her nose sparkling like gold dust, cleavage…

Yep. Sexpot.

'You OK?'

Even anxious, she looked good enough to eat. Slowly…

Mouthful by sexy mouthful…

'Fine,' he managed to croak, denying the way his body was behaving, wondering if rain had the same effect cold showers were purported to have.

Although the rain appeared to have gone…

Bloody cyclones—never around when you needed them.

'Oh, dear, there's Mrs P. and she looks distraught.'

Grace's voice broke into this peculiar reverie.

'Did you expect her to be anything but?' he asked, as Grace left his side and hurried towards the woman who was wringing her hands and staring up towards the sky.

'I'm on mother-in-law watch,' Grace explained, smiling back over her shoulder at him. Maybe they *were* still friends. 'I promised Em I'd try to keep Mrs P. calm.'

Harry returned her smile just in case the damage done was not irreparable.

'About as easy as telling the cyclone not to change course,' he said, before hurrying after Christina and Joe.

Grace carried his smile with her as she walked towards Mrs Poulos, although she knew Harry's smiles, like the polite way Harry would take someone's elbow to cross a road, were part of the armour behind which he hid all his emotions.

And she was through with loving Harry anyway.

Mrs P. was standing beside the restaurant's big catering van, though what it was doing there when the reception was at the restaurant, Grace couldn't fathom.

'What's the problem, Mrs P.?' Grace asked as she approached, her sympathy for the woman whose plans had been thrown into chaos by the weather clear in her voice.

'Oh, Grace, it's the doves. I don't know what to do about the doves.'

'Doves?' Grace repeated helplessly, clasping the hyperventilating woman around the shoulders and patting her arm, telling her to breathe deeply.

'The doves—how can I let them fly?' Mrs P. wailed, lifting her arms to the heavens, as if doves might suddenly descend.

Grace looked around, seeking someone who might explain this apparent disaster. But although a figure in white was hunched behind the wheel of the delivery van, whoever it was had no intention of helping.

'The dove man phoned,' Mrs P. continued. 'He says they will blow away in all this wind. They will never get home. They will die.'

'Never get home' provided a slight clue. Grace had heard of homing pigeons—weren't doves just small pigeons?

Did they home?

'Just calm down and we'll think about it,' she told Mrs P. 'Breathe deeply, then tell me about the doves.'

But the mention of the birds sent Mrs Poulos back into paroxysms of despair, which stopped only when Grace reminded her they had a bare ten minutes until the ceremony began—ten minutes before she had to be ready in her special place as mother of the groom.

'But the doves?'

Mrs P. pushed past Grace, and opened the rear doors of the van. And there, in a large crate with a wire netting front, were, indeed, doves.

Snowy white, they strutted around behind the wire, heads tipping to one side as their bright, inquisitive eyes peered out at the daylight.

'They were to be my special surprise,' Mrs P. explained, poking a finger through the wire to stroke the feathers of the closest bird. 'I had it all arranged. Albert, who is our new trainee chef, he was going to release them just as Mike and Emily came out of the church. They are trained, you know, the doves. They know to circle the happy couple three times before they take off.'

And heaven only knows what they'll do as they circle three times, Grace thought, imagining the worst. But saving Em from bird droppings wasn't her job—keeping Mrs Poulos on an even keel was.

'It was a wonderful idea,' Grace told the older woman. 'And it would have looked magical, but you're right about the poor things not being able to fly home in this wind. We'll just have to tell Mike and Emily about it later.'

'But their happiness,' Mrs P. protested. 'We need to do the doves to bring them happiness.'

She was calmer now but so determined Grace understood why Emily had agreed to the plethora of attendants Mrs P. had arranged, and the fluffy tulle creations all the female members of the wedding party had been pressed into wearing. Mrs P. had simply worn Em down—ignoring any suggestions and refusing to countenance any ideas not her own.

'We could do it later,' Mrs P. suggested. 'Maybe when Mike and Emily cut the cake and kiss. Do you think we can catch the doves afterwards if we let them out inside the restaurant? All the doors and windows are shut because of the wind so they wouldn't get out. Then we could put them back in their box and everything will be all right.'

Grace flicked her attention back to the cage, and counted.

Ten!

Ten birds flying around inside a restaurant packed with more than one hundred guests? A dozen dinner-jacketed waiters chasing fluttering doves?

And Em was worried the sea of tulle might make a farce of things!

'No!' Grace said firmly. 'We can't have doves flying around inside the restaurant.'

She scrambled around in her head for a reason, knowing she'd need something forceful.

More than forceful…

'CJ, Cal and Gina's little boy—he's one of the pages, isn't he?' She crossed her fingers behind her back before she told her lie. 'Well, he's very allergic to bird feathers. Think how terrible it would be if we had to clear a table and use a steak knife to do an emergency tracheotomy on him—you know, one of those operations where you have to cut a hole in the throat so the person can breathe. Think how terrible that would be in the middle of the reception.'

Mrs Poulos paled, and though she opened her mouth to argue, she closed it again, finally nodding agreement.

'And we'd get feathers on the cake,' she added,

and Grace smiled. Now it was Mrs P.'s idea not to have the doves cavorting inside the restaurant, one disaster had been averted.

Gently but firmly Grace guided her charge towards the church, finally settling her beside her husband in the front pew.

'Doves?' Mr Poulos whispered to Grace above his wife's head, and Grace nodded.

'No doves,' she whispered back, winning a warm smile of appreciation.

She backed out of the pew, her job done for now, and was making her way towards the back of the church, where she could see friends sitting, when Joe caught her arm.

'We've kept a seat for you,' he said, ushering her in front of him towards a spare place between Christina and Harry.

Sitting through a wedding ceremony beside Harry was hardly conducive to amputating him out of her heart.

Although the way things were between them, he might shift to another pew. Or, manlike, had he moved on from the little scene last night—the entire episode forgotten?

Grace slid into the seat, apprehension tightening ever sinew in her body, so when Harry shifted and his sleeve brushed her arm, she jerked away.

'Problems?' Harry whispered, misreading her reaction.

'All sorted,' she whispered back, but a flock of doves circling around inside the restaurant paled into insignificance beside the turmoil within her body. Remembering her own advice to Mrs P., Grace closed her eyes and breathed deeply.

Harry watched her breasts rise and fall, and wondered just how badly he'd hurt her with his angry words. Or was something else going on that he didn't know about? He glanced around, but apart from flowers and bows and a lot of pink and white frothy drapery everything appeared normal. Mike was ready by the altar, and a change in the background music suggested Emily was about to make an appearance.

So why was Grace as tense as fencing wire?

She'd seemed OK earlier, as if determined to pretend everything was all right between them— at least for the duration of the wedding.

So it had to be something else.

Did she not like weddings?

Had something terrible happened in her past, something connected with a wedding?

The thought of something terrible happening in Grace's past made him reach out and take her hand, thinking, at the same time, how little he knew of her.

Her fingers were cold and they trembled slightly, making him want to hug her reassuringly, but things were starting, people standing up, kids in shiny dresses and suits were scattering rose petals, and a confusion of young women in the same pink frothy stuff that adorned the church were parading down the aisle. Emily, he assumed, was somewhere behind them, because Mike's face had lit up with a smile so soppy Harry felt a momentary pang of compassion for him.

Poor guy had it bad!

Beside him Grace sighed—or maybe sniffed—and he turned away from the wedding party, sorting itself with some difficulty into the confined space in front of the altar, and looked at the woman by his side.

'Are you crying?' he demanded, his voice harsher than he'd intended because anxiety had joined the stirring thing that was happening again in his body.

Grace smiled up at him, easing the anxiety but exacerbating the stirring.

'No way,' she said. 'I was thinking of the last wedding I was at.'

'Bad?'

She glanced his way and gave a nod.

'My father's fourth. He introduced me to the latest Mrs O'Riordan as Maree's daughter. My mother's name was Kirstie.'

No wonder Grace looked grim.

And how it must have hurt.

But her father's fourth marriage?

Did that explain why Grace had never married?

'His fourth? Has his example put you off marriage for life?'

No smile, but she did turn towards him, studying him for a moment before replying, this time with a very definite shake of her head.

'No way, but I do feel a trifle cynical about the celebratory part. If ever I get married, I'll elope.'

'No pink and white frothy dresses?' he teased, hoping, in spite of the stirring, she'd smile again.

Hoping smiles might signal all was well between them once again.

'Not a froth in sight! And I think it's peach, not pink,' she said, and did smile.

But the smile was sad somehow, and a little part of him wondered just how badly having a marriage-addicted father might have hurt her.

He didn't like the idea of Grace hurting…

Handling this well, Grace congratulated herself. Strangely enough, the impersonal way Harry had taken her hand had helped her settle down. But just in case this settling effect turned to something else, she gently detached her hand from his as they stood up. And although he'd put his arm around her shoulders and given her a hug, it was definitely a friend kind of a hug and had reminded her that's what she was to him.

Now all she had to do was close her mind to the words being spoken at the front, pretend that Harry was nothing more to her than the friend she was to him, and keep an eye on Mrs P. in case she thought of some new reason for panic.

Fun!

It *was* fun, Grace decided, some hours later.

True, Harry had excused himself and left the church not long after the ceremony began, but whether because he couldn't bear to sit through it or to check on the latest weather report and weather-related incidents, she didn't know. Something had certainly happened—tiles or something coming off the roof—because there'd been loud crashing noises then the minister had insisted everyone leave through the vestry, disrupting the wedding party to the extent Grace had to calm Mrs P. down once again, persuading her the wedding was still legal even if the happy couple hadn't left as man and wife through the front door of the church.

Grace had driven to the restaurant with Mr and Mrs Poulos so hadn't caught up with Christina and Joe until the reception.

People milled around, sipping champagne, talking and even dancing. Luke Bresciano came up to her, took the champagne glass out of her hand, set it down on a handy table, and swept her onto the dance floor.

'I was looking for you,' he said, guiding her carefully around the floor. 'Have you heard the ink-blot joke? I remembered it after we looked at the stain last night.'

Grace shook her head, and Luke launched into the story of the psychologist showing ink-blot pictures to a patient.

'So the fellow looks at the first one, and says that's two rabbits having sex. The psychologist turns the page and the fellow says, that's an elephant and a rhino having sex. The psychologist is a bit shocked but he offers a third. That's three people and a dog having sex. Floored by this reaction, the psychologist loses his cool. "You've got a dirty mind," he tells his patient. "Me?" the patient says. "You're the one showing filthy pictures."'

Grace laughed, looking more closely at this man she barely knew. The lines around his eyes suggested he was older than she knew he was. Signs of the unhappiness she'd heard was in his background?

She asked about his early life but somehow the questions ended up coming from him, so by the end of the dance she knew no more than she had at the beginning.

Except that he had a sense of humour, which was a big point in his favour.

But when she glimpsed Harry across the room, bending down to speak to Charles, the excited beating of her heart told her she had a long way to go in the getting over him stakes. Fortunately the best man—some friend of Mike's who'd come across from New Zealand—appeared and asked her to dance, so Harry was not forgotten but tucked away behind her determination to move on.

The dance ended, and she noticed Harry heading in her direction. Dancing with Harry was *not* part of the plan, so she picked up her glass of now flat champagne and pressed into an alcove of pot plants, hoping to hide in this corner of the greenery festooning the restaurant.

Could one hide from a policeman?

'You know I can't dance with my leg!'

It wasn't exactly the greeting she'd expected. In fact, the slightly petulant statement made no sense whatsoever.

'What are you talking about? What do you mean?' she demanded, looking up into Harry's face, which seemed to be flushed with the same anger she'd heard in his voice.

'That I can't dance with you,' he said, his words as cross as his first statement had been.

'Then it's just as well I'm not your mother or your wife,' Grace retorted, unable to keep up the 'friends' pretence another second. 'Because if I was, you'd be expected to dance with me.'

She tried to turn away but the greenery defeated her—the greenery and Harry's hand on her shoulder.

'I shouldn't have said that to you,' he said, tightening his grip when she tried to shrug it off. 'I'm sorry.'

Grace looked at him for a long moment. The flush had faded, leaving his face pale and so tired-looking she had to sternly stem the flash of sympathy she felt towards him.

'No,' she told him, knowing this was the perfect time to begin to distance herself from Harry. 'I think it needed to be said. You were right, it's not my place to tell you what to do or what not to do. I overstepped the boundaries of friendship but it won't happen again, I promise you.'

Harry stared at her, totally befuddled by what had just occurred. Hadn't he apologised? Said what had to be said to make things right again between himself and Grace? So why was she rejecting his apology? Or, if not rejecting it, turning things so it had been her fault, not his?

He opened him mouth but what could he say? *Please, keep telling me stuff like that? Please, stay concerned for me?*

Ridiculous!

He should let it go—walk away—and hope everything would come right between them in time.

Hope they could go back to being friends.

But if he walked away she'd dance with someone else, and seeing Grace in that Italian doctor's arms, laughing up at some funny thing he'd said, had made Harry's gut churn.

'I can shuffle if you don't mind a shuffling kind of dance,' he heard himself say, and saw astonishment similar to what he was feeling reflected on Grace's face.

Her 'OK' wasn't overwhelmingly enthusiastic, but he was happy to settle for even grudging acceptance. He put his arms around her, tucked her body close to his, and felt her curls tickle the skin beneath his chin.

Grace knew this wouldn't do much for her distancing-Harry plans, but surely a woman was allowed a little bit of bliss. She slid into his arms and put her arms around his back—allowable, she was sure, because it was going to be a shuffling kind of dance.

You are stupid, the sensible voice in her head muttered at her.

It's just pretence, she told her head. Everything else seemed to be about pretence these days so why not pretend, just for a short while, that they were a couple? After all, she could go back to distancing tomorrow.

It was heaven.

The band was playing a slow waltz, or maybe a slow two-step. Dancing was something she did naturally but had little knowledge about, and she and Harry were at the edge of the dance floor, barely moving to the music, content, as far as Grace was concerned, just to be in each other's arms.

What Harry was thinking was a mystery but, then, Harry in a social setting—apart from coffee at the pub— was something of a mystery as well.

No matter—he had his arms around her and that was enough.

Well, nearly enough. Outside the wind had gathered strength again and rain lashed the garden beyond the restaurant and flung itself against the windows. It was definitely 'snuggling closer' weather. If she moved just slightly she could rest her head against his chest, and for a little while she could dream.

Later, she couldn't remember whether she'd actually made this daring move or not, but what she did remember was that the lights went out, then Harry spun her around, into even denser blackness in a corner of the restaurant.

And bent his head.

And kissed her.

Harry kissed her…

Folded in his arms, her curls tickling at his chin, Harry had ignored the cleavage as much as possible as he'd shuffled back and forth with this different Grace on the corner of the dance floor. But when the lights went out, he lost the slim reins of control he'd been clinging to and whisked her into the shadows of one of the palms that dotted the restaurant.

He bent his head, and kissed her, curls first, then her forehead, finding the salt of perspiration on her skin and a sweetness he knew by instinct was pure Grace.

His lips moved to her temples, felt the throb of a vein, then claimed her mouth, more sweetness, but this time mingled with heat as Grace responded with a fire that lit his own smouldering desire, so need and hunger fought common sense and a determination to not get involved.

A losing battle—as useless as trying to stop the wind that now raged again outside—as useless as trying to stop a cyclone…

He clamped Grace's curvy body hard against his leanness, and drank in the taste of her as his mouth explored and challenged hers. She met his challenge and responded with her own, so he was lost in the wonder and sweetness and fire that was this new Grace.

Gripped in the toils of physical attraction, a voice whispered in his head, but he ignored it and kept kissing the woman in his arms.

Lamplight. Flickering candles. Maybe the voice wasn't in his head. Someone was calling his name.

Urgently.

'Harry Blake.'

CHAPTER THREE

CHARLES WETHERBY, the wheelchair-bound head of the hospital, was illuminated by candelabrum, held aloft by a young policeman, Troy Newton, the newest member of Harry's staff.

'Charles?'

Harry eased Grace gently away, tucking her, he hoped, into deeper shadows, and took the two long strides needed to bring him close to Charles.

'Bus accident up on the mountain road—road's subsided and the bus has slid down the mountain. Dan Macker called it in.'

'Do we know exactly where, and who's on the way?' Harry asked, looking towards the windows and knowing there was no way the rescue helicopter, based at the hospital, could fly in this wind.

'Where? This side of Dan's place. He saw the bus go past, then later heard a noise, and when he investigated he saw the landslide. Who's on the way? The fire truck, two ambulances each with two crew and the hospital's four-wheel-drive is on its way here to pick up whatever hospital staff you think you might need on site. Have you seen Grace? If we've got to set up a triage post and then get people off the side of the mountain, we'll probably need an SES crew up there as well—she can organise that.'

'I'll tell her,' Harry said, 'and head out there myself.'

Charles made an announcement aimed mainly at the hospital staff, telling them the hospital would go to the code black disaster plan, then Harry spoke, reminding people who would be taking part in the rescue on the mountain that there were open diggings and mine shafts on the slopes, legacy of the gold rush that had led to the birth of the township that had become Crocodile Creek.

He looked around the room, wondering who

he'd take, picking out hospital staff he knew were fit and active, telling them to take the hospital vehicle while he'd check on his other staff and be right behind them.

He turned back towards the shadows but Grace had gone, no doubt because she'd heard the news. More candles had been lit, but it was impossible to pick her out in the milling crowd. Joe touched his arm.

'You go, I'll organise a lift back to the cottage for Grace and Christina then go up to the hospital to see if I can help.'

Harry nodded to Joe but his eyes still searched for Grace, although common sense told him she'd be in a corner somewhere, on her mobile, starting a phone relay to gather a crew at SES headquarters in the shortest possible time. Then she'd head to the headquarters herself to organise the equipment they'd need.

As he left the restaurant, striding towards his vehicle, that thought brought with it a sense of relief he didn't quite understand. Was it tied up with the fact that Grace was safer at headquarters, organising things, than on the side of a slippery mountain riddled with old mineshafts, fighting cyclonic winds in pitch darkness?

Surely not!

Although, as a friend, he was entitled to feel some concern for her safety, so it had nothing to do with the aberration in his feelings towards her—which was purely physical.

The wind was now so strong he had to struggle to open the car door—memories of a soft body held against his chest...

Get your mind focussed on the job!

He started the car and turned out of the car park, concentrating on driving through the lashing wind and rain.

Ignoring the physical aberration? That was the voice in his head again.

Of course he was ignoring it. What else could he do? Physical attraction had led him into a terrible mistake once before and had caused pain and unhappiness, not only to himself but to Nikki as well. It had flung him into an emotional swamp so deep and damaging he'd blocked emotion out of his life ever since.

So there was no way he could allow whatever physical attraction he might be feeling towards her to touch his friendship with Grace.

If he still had a friendship with Grace. Her words before the dance had indicated she was backing away from whatever it was they'd had.

Yet she'd kissed him back—he was sure of that.

He'd have to put it aside—forget about the kiss and definitely forget about the lust he'd felt towards his friend.

Determinedly setting these thoughts aside, Harry drove cautiously down towards the town, automatically noting the level of the water beneath the bridge, forcing himself to think rescue not Grace.

He had to go, of course he did, Grace told herself as she watched Harry leave. She was on the phone to Paul Gibson, still the nominal head of the local SES, although since he'd been undergoing treatment for prostate cancer, Grace, as senior team leader, had taken over a lot of his responsibilities. But Paul's knowledge and experience were still invaluable, so Grace forgot about Harry and listened, mentally repeating all Paul had said so she'd remember.

Rolls of netting—she'd seen them in the big shed and often wondered about them—were useful in landslides. You could anchor them on the level ground and unroll them down the slope to make it easier for rescuers to clamber up and down.

'Belongings,' Paul continued. 'Gather up what you can of people's belongings. They're going to be disoriented enough, ending up in a strange hospital—if we can return things to them, it helps. And remember to search for a hundred yards all around the bus—people can wander off. As soon as my wife gets back from checking on the family, I'll get her to drive me up to Headquarters. I mightn't be much use out in the field, but I'll handle the radio calls and relays up there, which will leave you free to be out in the field.'

Through the window Grace saw Harry's big vehicle leave the car park.

'Thanks, Paul,' she said, staring out the window at the vehicle, hope sneaking in where wonder and amazement had been.

Harry had kissed her.

Surely he wouldn't have done that if he wasn't interested in her?

The sneaky scrap of hope swelled like a balloon to fill her chest.

Maybe, just maybe, she wouldn't have to get over Harry after all.

Or was she being stupid? The way she'd been with James? Thinking flowers and dinners out and a physical relationship meant love?

Not that she'd had any of that with Harry. Only one interrupted kiss.

The balloon deflated as fast as it had filled, leaving her feeling empty and flat.

One thing she knew for sure—she'd been stupid for kissing him back, for letting her lips tell him things her head knew she couldn't tell him.

She tucked her phone back into her beaded handbag and looked around the room, checking who was leaving, who might give her a lift home so she could change before going to Headquarters. Charles was leading the way out the door, Jill Shaw, director of nursing, moving more slowly to guide Susie, who was swinging along on crutches, thanks to her accident the previous day.

'Would you lot drop me home?' Grace asked, coming up to them. 'I can hardly organise my crew dressed like this.'

'No problem,' Charles told her, while Jill, who must have been running through the nursing roster in her head, added, 'You're off duty until Tuesday, aren't you, Grace?'

Grace nodded. Her month on night duty had finished at seven that morning and the change in shift meant she had three days off.

'But I grabbed a few hours' sleep this morning so I'm happy to be called in. If Willie's really heading back towards us, we'll need all available staff standing by.'

'We might need all staff back on duty, not standing by, if the bus that's come off the mountain had a full load of passengers,' Charles said, as the women ducked behind his wheel-chair to escape some of the wind that was ripping across the car park, grabbing at Charles's words and flinging them into the air. 'With this weather, we can't fly people out, and at last report the coast road was flooding. We could have a very full hospital.'

Jill confirmed this with a quiet 'I'll be in touch' as she dropped Grace at the cottage, but nursing was forgotten as Grace stripped off her dress and clambered into her bright orange SES overalls, fitted on the belt that held her torch, pocket knife and radio then grabbed her keys and headed for Headquarters. The crews would be gathering. She'd send one support vehicle straight up the mountain, and hold the second one back until she heard from Harry in case some special equipment not on the main rescue vehicle was needed.

Or…

She went herself, with the first crew, partly because Paul had arrived to handle the office but also because she knew an extra person with nursing skills would be useful in the rescue mission. This truck held the inflatable tent they'd use for triage and the generator that kept it inflated. They'd have to make sure the tent was anchored securely in this wind.

The men and women chatted casually, but Grace, huddled in a corner, mentally rehearsed the jobs that lay ahead as she watched the wind slice rain across the windscreen and cause the vehicle to sway from side to side. Willie had turned and was heading their way—the cyclone warnings on the radio had confirmed what increased velocity in the wind had already told most locals.

How much time did they have to get ready?

Who would need to be moved from their homes? An evacuation list would have been drawn up but before she, or anyone else, could start moving people to safety, they had to get the accident victims off the mountain…

'Your crews finished?'

Grace was kneeling by a young woman, the last person to be pulled from the bus after the jaws of life had been used to free her. Unconscious and with probable head injuries, she lay on an undamaged part of the road, her neck in a collar, her body strapped to the cradle stretcher on which she'd been pulled up the muddy slope. Now, as the wind howled around them, they awaited the return of one of the ambulances that had been shuttling back and forth to the hospital for hours.

About half an hour earlier, once most of the accident victims had been moved out of it and ferried down the mountain, Harry had deemed the inflatable tent too dangerous. So Grace's crew had packed it and the generator back into the SES truck prior to departure.

A makeshift shelter remained to protect this

final patient, but the wind was getting stronger every minute and now blew rain and forest debris beneath the sodden tarpaulin. Grace had angled her body so it shielded the young woman's face. She smoothed the woman's hair and removed leaves that blew onto her skin, but there was little else she could do for her—just watch and wait, holding her hand and talking quietly to her, because Grace was certain even unconscious people had some awareness.

'Are your crews finished?'

As Harry repeated his question, Grace turned to look at him. She'd heard him the first time but her mind had been too busy adjusting to his abrupt tone—and trying to work out what it meant—for her to answer.

'Just about,' she said, searching his face, lit by the last emergency light, for some hint of his mood. Disappointment because they'd failed to save the bus driver? No, deep down Harry might be gutted, but he would set it aside until the job was done.

Was his leg hurting?

It had to be, though if she offered sympathy it was sure to be rejected.

She stopped guessing about his mood, and explained, 'One of the team is already on its way back to base and the other is packing up the gear and should be leaving shortly. Why?'

'Because I want everyone off the mountain, that's why,' Harry said, his voice straining against the wind, but Grace's attention was back on her patient.

'She's stopped breathing.'

Grace leant forward over the young woman, tilted her head backwards then lifted her chin upward with one hand to make sure her airway was clear, and felt for a pulse with the other. Her fingers pushed beneath the woman's chin, and found a flutter of movement in the carotid artery.

She stripped off the oxygen mask and gave the woman two breaths, then checked the pulse again. Looked at Harry, who was now squatting by her side.

'You monitor her pulse—I'll breathe.'

They'd practised so often as a team, it seemed effortless now, Grace breathing, Harry monitoring the young woman's vital signs. Yet it was taking too long—were their efforts in vain?

'We'll get her,' Harry said, and the conviction in his voice comforted Grace, although she knew he couldn't be as certain as he sounded.

Or could he?

Grace stopped, and held her breath. The rise and fall of the young woman's chest told them she'd resumed breathing on her own.

'Yes!' Grace said, lifting her hand for a high-five of triumph, but Harry's hands were by his side, and the bleak unhappiness on his face was far from triumph.

Whatever pretence at friendship they'd managed during the wedding was gone.

Burnt away by the heat of that kiss?

Though why would *he* be upset over the kiss? Because it had broken some rule he'd set himself when his wife died?

Thou shalt kiss no other after her?

That was weird because Harry wasn't stupid and he must know that eventually nature would reassert itself and he'd want a sexual relationship with some woman—sometime.

Although as far as she knew, monks didn't…

'I want you off the mountain,' he said.

'I want us all off the mountain,' Grace retorted, battling to understand his mood. OK, he was worried about the cyclone, but they all were, and it certainly hadn't made the other rescuers go all brisk and formal. In fact, the others had made an effort to smile even as they'd struggled up the steepest parts of the slope—everyone encouraging each other.

All but Harry, who'd frowned at Grace whenever they'd passed, as if he couldn't understand who she was or perhaps what she was doing there.

'But that's hardly possible,' she continued crisply, 'without magic carpets to whisk us all away. The second SES crew will be leaving soon. The rest of the hospital personnel have gone back to deal with the patients as they arrive. I'm staying with this patient and I'll go back in the ambulance when it gets here.'

'This place is dangerous. The wind's increasing all the time. More of the road could slip, trees could come down.'

He was worrying about her safety. That was the only explanation for Harry's strange behaviour. The thought brought such warmth to Grace's body she forgot about distancing herself. She forgot about the cruel words he'd flung at her, and reached out to touch his arm.

'This is my job,' she said softly. 'We've had the risk-taking conversation, Harry, and while you mightn't like me talking about it you have to admit, as part of your job, you do it all the time. So you should understand I can't just get in the truck and go back to town, leaving this young woman with no one.'

'*I'm* here!' Harry said, moving his arm so her hand slid off—squelching the warmth.

It had been such a stupid thing to say Grace

didn't bother with a reply. She checked the oxygen flowing into the mask that was once again covering the young woman's mouth and nose, and kept a hand on the pulse at her wrist.

Harry stood up and walked away, no doubt to grump at someone else. But who else was still here? Grace had no idea, having seen the last of the SES crew heading down the road towards their truck. The first truck had taken a lot of the less badly injured passengers back to the hospital to be checked under more ideal conditions than an inflatable tent and arclamps in lashing wind and rain. The team leader of that truck would then assist in finding accommodation for those not admitted to hospital, while the other members would begin preparations for the arrival of Willie, now on course to cross the coast at Crocodile Creek.

'That you, Grace?'

She turned at the shout and saw two overalled figures jogging towards her.

'Mike! Not on your honeymoon, then?'

Mike Poulos, newly married helicopter pilot and paramedic, reached her first and knelt beside her patient.

'Could hardly leave without Em, who's in Theatre as we speak, so I decided I might as well make myself useful. I can't fly in this weather but I still remember how to drive an ambulance. Who's this?'

'We don't know,' Grace told him, watching the gentle way he touched the young woman's cheek. 'Maybe a young backpacker—there were quite a few young people among the passengers. No one seems to know for certain who was on the bus.'

'Mainly because the driver was killed and we can't find a manifest in the wreckage.' Harry was back, nodding to the two paramedics as he explained. 'This patient's the last, but we need to take the driver's body back to the hospital.'

'She's unconscious?' Mike asked Grace, who nodded.

'And though there are no obvious injuries, she's

very unstable. She stopped breathing after she was brought up from the bus,' Grace told him.

'I hate transporting a dead person with a live one, but the bus driver deserves the dignity of an ambulance,' Mike said. He looked towards Harry.

'If we take the bus driver, can you take Grace?'

Harry looked doubtful.

'As against leaving me up here all night? Taking two patients means I won't fit in the ambulance,' Grace snapped at him, aggravated beyond reason by this stranger in Harry's body.

'I'll take Grace,' he conceded, then he led the two men away to collect the driver's body, before returning for Grace's patient.

Grace walked beside the young woman as the men carried her to the ambulance, then watched as she was loaded, the doors shut, and the big four-by-four vehicle took off down the road.

'My car's this way,' Harry said, and strode off into the darkness. He was carrying the last of the lights and the tarpaulin they'd used as a shelter, and though he looked overladen he'd shaken his head when had Grace asked if she could carry something.

Still puzzling over his strange behaviour, she followed him down the road to where it widened enough for a helicopter to land—*when* weather permitted. His was the only vehicle still there.

She waited while he stacked the gear he'd carried into the back, then she made her way to the passenger side, opened the door—no chivalry now—and climbed in.

'What is with you?' she demanded, as soon as he was settled into the driver's seat. 'Is your leg hurting? Should I have a look at it?'

He glanced towards her, his face carefully blank, then looked away to turn the key in the ignition, release the brake and start driving cautiously down the wind- and rain-lashed road.

'My leg's fine.'

Grace knew that was a lie—it couldn't possibly be fine—but she wasn't his mother or his wife so she kept her mouth shut.

Between them the radio chattered—the ambulance giving the hospital an ETA, a squad car reporting on more power lines down. Yet the noise barely intruded into the taut, chilly atmosphere that lay between the two of them as they crawled at a snail's pace down the mountain road.

'Is it the bus driver? I know there's nothing worse than losing a life at an accident, but he'd have been dead the moment the bus rolled on him, poor guy. There was nothing anyone could have done, and from what the rescuers were saying, he did all he could to save the bus from being more badly damaged—all he could to save more lives.'

'So he dies a hero. Do you think that makes it better for his kids? His name was Peter. He had two kids. Photo in his wallet.'

Making him a person in Harry's eyes. No wonder he was upset.

'Someone's father,' Grace whispered, feeling the rush of pity such information always brought, but at the same time she wondered about Harry's reaction. She'd seen him bring in dead kids from car accidents without this much emotional involvement. 'No, I'm sure, at the beginning at least, the hero stuff won't make a scrap of difference to two kids growing up without a father. But all we can do is help the living, Harry. We can't change what's past.'

Harry sighed.

'You're right, and if I think rationally about it, the simple fact of having a father is no guarantee of happiness,' he said glumly. 'Georgie's Max— his father's just a nasty waste of space—and yours doesn't sound as if he brought you much joy.'

'It might not have been all his fault. I kind of got dumped on him,' Grace told him, defending blood ties automatically. 'I didn't ever know him as a small child, then, when I was seven, my mother died and my aunt got in touch with my father, who'd emigrated from Ireland to Australia, and I was sent out here.'

She paused, remembering the small sad child who'd set off on that long journey, scared but somehow, beyond the fear, full of hope. She'd lost her mother, but ahead had lain a father and a new family, a father who'd surely love her or why else had he sent the money for her ticket?

'What number wife was he on at that stage?' Harry asked, and Grace smiled.

'Only number two, but, looking back, I think the marriage was probably teetering at the time and my stepmother had only agreed to take me because she thought it might keep my father with her. Poor woman, she was kind, but she was stuck with me when he took off again, so to her I always represented a terrible time of her life. And the little boys, my stepbrothers, well, I can't blame them for hating me—I arrive and their father leaves. In their young minds there had to be a connection.'

'No one could have hated you, Grace,' Harry said, but although the words were kind his harsh voice suggested that there was more than the dead bus driver bothering him.

She listened to the radio calls, not knowing what to guess at next, but certain she needed things sorted out between them because the success of both the preparations for, and the work after, Willie's arrival depended on them working harmoniously together.

With a sigh nearly as strong as one of the wind gusts outside, she tried again.

'Is that all that's bothering you? The bus driver? His kids?'

He turned to look at her and even in the dimly lit cabin she could read incredulity.

'We're in a serious situation here,' Harry said, spacing the words as if he'd had to test each one in his head before letting it out.

'We've been in serious situations before, Harry,' Grace reminded him, ducking instinctively as a tree-fern frond careened towards her side of the car. 'Remember the time we went out to the reef in a thunderstorm to rescue the diver with the bends? That wasn't serious?'

No comment.

Grace sighed again.

Was she becoming a sigher?

Surely not. And if she considered it, being at odds with Harry could only help her getting-over-him decision. A sensible woman would welcome this new attitude of his and get on with her life. But this was, as Harry had just pointed out, a serious situation and Grace knew she wouldn't give of her best if there was added tension between the two of them.

She knew too that they'd be in some dangerous situations in the future, and if they didn't have one hundred per cent attention on the job, a dangerous situation could become a disaster.

She had to sort it out.

But how?

Bluntly!

There was only one other thing that had happened this evening that could explain his attitude.

Or maybe two things.

'Are you still annoyed about me nagging you to be careful?' she asked, thinking it was easier to bring this up than to mention the kiss.

'I apologised for that.'

More silence.

That left the kiss.

Grace's last remnant of hope that the kiss might have meant something to Harry died.

For sure, he'd started it, but the worst of it was, she'd kissed him back.

She knew it had been a mistake from her side of things, but had it also worried Harry? Had she revealed too much of how she felt?

Was that what was bothering him?

If so, she had to get around it somehow. Act as if it had meant nothing to her—pretend it had been nothing more than a casual smooch in the darkness.

More pretence!

She took a deep breath, and launched into the delicate conversation.

'Is this because we kissed? Has one kiss turned you into some kind of cold robot? If so, that's ridiculous. It was a mistake so let's get past it. We've been friends for more than two years, Harry, and friends talk to one another. We can talk about this. Isn't that easier than carrying on as if we've broken some immutable law of nature? I mean, it was a nice kiss as kisses go, but it's not likely that we'll ever do it again.'

As the flippant words spun around the cabin of the vehicle, mingling with the radio's chatter and the wind that whirled outside, Grace felt her heart break.

But this was how it had to be. She didn't want Harry thinking the kiss meant any more to her than it had to him.

He glanced her way, his face still betraying nothing.

'*Do* we talk to one another?' he asked, delving so far back into Grace's conversation it took her a moment to remember she'd made the comment.

'Yes,' she said, although doubts were now popping up in her head.

They did talk, but about their work, their friends, the hospital, the town, the price of sugar cane—Harry's father being the owner of the local mill—the weather, and just about everything under the sun.

'Not about ourselves,' Harry said, still staring resolutely through the windscreen, although, given the debris flying through the air, that was a very good idea. 'Today's the first time I've heard you mention a father.'

'Everyone has one,' Grace said glibly, but the look Harry gave her told her flippancy wasn't going to work.

'OK, you're right. We don't talk much about ourselves,' Grace admitted, though she wasn't sure what this had to do with the kiss, or with Harry's mood. 'But talking's a two-way street, Harry. Talking—really talking—means sharing small parts of yourself with another person, and it's hard to do that if the other person isn't willing to share as well. Sharing that kind of talk leads to intimacy in a friendship and intimacy leaves people vulnerable. You treat everyone the same way probably because you don't want that intimacy—don't want anyone coming that close to you. The last thing in the world you'd want to seem is vulnerable.'

Harry glanced her way, frowned, then turned his attention back to the road, slowing down as the branch of a blue fig tree crashed onto the road right in front of them. He manoeuvred the car carefully around it.

'So you start the talking,' he finally said, totally ignoring her comments about his behaviour. 'Is it just because of your father you don't like weddings?'

It was the very last conversational gambit Grace had expected.

'Who said I don't like weddings?'

'You were so tense you could have snapped in half in there this afternoon.'

Because it *was* a wedding and I was sitting next to you, and it was hard not to indulge, for just a wee while, in a pointless daydream.

Grace was tempted to say it—to tell him of her feelings. The way the wind was blowing, literally, and sending tree limbs onto the road, they could both be killed any minute.

Would it be better or worse if Harry died knowing she loved him?

The thought of Harry dying made her heart squeeze into a tight little ball, while memories of the one time she *had* told a man she loved him made her cringe back into the seat.

She could still hear James's voice—his snide 'Love, Gracie? How quaint! What a sweet thing you are! Next you'll be telling me you're thinking of babies.'

Which she had been.

No wonder she could still feel the hurt…

'Well?' Harry persisted, and Grace had to think back to his question.

'It wasn't the wedding,' she managed to say, as Harry slammed on the brakes and his left arm shot out to stop her forward momentum.

'Thank heaven for traction control,' he muttered as the car skidded sideways towards the edge of the road then stopped before plunging off the side of the mountain. 'What was it, then?'

Grace shook her head.

'I can't believe we're having this conversation,' she said. 'Any minute now a tree's going to land across us and you're worried about why I was tense at the wedding.'

She paused, then added crossly, 'Anyway, this conversation isn't about me—it's about you. I didn't change from a friend to a frozen robot in the time it took to drive from town up the mountain.' She peered out through the windscreen. 'Why have we stopped?'

'I don't like the look of that tree.'

Harry pointed ahead and, as Grace followed the line of his finger, the huge forest red gum that had been leaning at a crazy angle across the road slid slowly downwards, the soaked soil on the mountainside releasing its tangle of roots so carefully it was only in the last few feet the massive trunk actually crashed to the ground.

'Oh!'

The nearest branches of the tree were right in front of the bonnet of Harry's vehicle, so close some of their smaller limbs were resting on it.

'We'll never clear it by hand. I'll radio for a car to come and get us on the other side, but we'll have to climb around the tree. For the moment, we'll just sit here until we're sure it's settled.'

Even as he said the words Harry regretted them. Of course they were safer in the vehicle than out there in the maelstrom of wind, rain and flying debris, but out there, talk would be impossible. In the car—in the dry warm cocoon it provided—even with the radio going, there was a false sense of—what?

He shuddered—Grace's word 'intimacy' seemed to fit.

What's more, there was no excuse to not talk…

He finished his call, telling base not to send someone to clear the tree as the conditions were too dangerous and the exercise pointless because the road was cut further up at the landslide. He glanced at Grace, who was still staring at the tree that hadn't collapsed on top of them, and he felt the stirring her blue dress had triggered earlier. She'd changed into her bulky but protective SES overalls, but hadn't removed the ribbon from her hair, so it now snaked through her wet curls, slightly askew so a bit of it crossed the top of her delicate pink ear.

He'd never looked at Grace's ears before, he realised as he reached over and used his forefinger to lift the ribbon from the ear then tease it gently out of her sodden hair. He had, of course, intended giving it back to her, but when she eyed the tatty wet object and muttered, 'What a fun way to end a wedding,' he decided she didn't want it, so he dropped it into his shirt pocket, did up the button and patted it into place.

He wasn't going to accept Grace's 'frozen robot' description, but he couldn't deny anger had been churning around inside him for the last few hours. Why *was* he so cranky?

Because he was worried, sure, but if he was honest with himself it was more than that. He could only suppose it was because Grace had added to his worries. From the moment she'd appeared at the accident site, he'd felt a new anxiety gnawing at his gut, and every time he saw her, each time wetter and paler than the time before, anxiety had taken another vicious bite.

That it was related to the kiss and the new attraction he felt towards her he had no doubt, but on a treacherous mountain road as a cyclone roared towards them and trees came crashing down, this was neither the time nor the place for introspection.

Or distraction.

Although maybe if he kissed her again, it would sort itself out. He could spend the waiting time kissing her, which would also make talking impossible. His body liked the idea, but his head knew that was the worst possible way to pass the time.

However appealing it might seem.

'You didn't answer about the kiss.'

Her statement startled him. There she was, still staring at the tree, yet picking up on some vibe he didn't know he was giving out.

But this was Grace—she deserved an honest answer.

'It was physical attraction, Grace,' he began, and waited to see if she'd turn towards him. Perhaps speak and save him the necessity of saying more.

She didn't, although she did glance his way momentarily.

'Strong physical attraction—we both felt it—but physical, that's all.'

Another glance, then all he got was her profile, although he fancied now she might be frowning, so he waited some more.

'And that's bad?' she finally queried.

'I believe it is. Well, not necessarily bad in a right and wrong sense, but dangerous, Grace. Misleading. Troublesome.' There, it had been said. Now they could get back to being friends.

Or as close to friends as they'd be able to get after his comments earlier.

CHAPTER FOUR

GRACE stared out through the windscreen at the fallen tree as she ran the explanation through her head, suspecting it might be Harry's way of saying that physical attraction was all he could feel for a woman these days. Putting it like that was less blunt that telling her he was still in love with his dead wife and always would be.

And although she'd always kind of suspected this, the confirmation of the idea caused Grace pain—physical pain, like a cramp around her heart.

The hateful, hurtful words, *you're not my wife*, took on a whole new meaning.

Perhaps she was wrong, and he wasn't saying that at all. One last gulp of hope remained in the balloon. Forgetting she was supposed to be distancing herself, she turned back towards him, determined to sort this out once and for all.

'Why is it dangerous? Misleading?'

Harry was staring at her, frowning slightly as if he wasn't certain who she was, and showed no sign of understanding her questions, let alone answering them.

'You must have a reason for believing it's bad,' she persisted.

Harry, who'd been thinking how pretty her eyes were and wondering why he'd never considered Grace's eyes before any more than he'd considered her ears, shrugged off the remark, although he suspected she wasn't going to let this go. But how could he explain the still bruised part of his heart that was Nikki? Explain the magnitude of their mistake?

'We should start walking.'

'No way!' She nodded towards the radio which had just advised them the car was forty-five minutes away. 'Even if it takes us half an hour to get over or around the tree, we'd still be waiting in the rain for fifteen minutes, and that's if the road's not blocked further down.'

He nodded, conceding her point, but said nothing, pretending fascination with the babble on the radio—trying to forget where physical attraction had led once before *and* trying to block out the insidious desire creeping through his body every time he looked at Grace.

He patted his pocket.

One more kiss won't hurt, his physical self tempted, but a glance at Grace, wet curls plastered to a face that was pinched with tiredness, told him that it would hurt.

If not him, then definitely her.

And he hated the idea of hurting Grace any more than he had already.

Hated it!

Another glance her way told him she was still waiting for an answer.

Would wait all night…

'It confuses things,' he said. 'I mean, look at

us, good friends, and suddenly we're all hung up over a kiss.'

'We weren't exactly good friends when it happened,' she reminded him. 'And *I'm* not hung up over it.'

'Maybe not, but you're only pushing this kiss business because you don't want to talk about why you were so uptight at the wedding.' Good thinking, Harry, turn defence into attack. 'That, if you remember, Grace, was where this conversation started. With the fact that we don't really talk to each other. And now I know about your father, I would think you'd be as wary of physical attraction as I am. Or did he fall madly and totally in love with all four of his wives?'

It was a low blow, and he sensed she'd cringed a little from it, making him feel a bastard for hurting her. But it would be better this way— with the kiss passed off as the aberration he was sure it was and the two of them getting on with the friendship they'd always shared.

Not totally convinced by this seemingly

sensible plan, he checked the weather, acknowledged an ETA call from the car coming to collect them, waited until the wail of the three hourly cyclone warning coming from the radio stopped, then pushed his companion a little further.

'Do you know what I know about you, Grace? Really know about you?' He didn't wait for her to answer, but held up two fingers. 'Two personal things—that's all. You hate being called Gracie, and you think you're too short.'

'I think I'm too short?' Grace repeated, confused by that accusation and disturbed by the 'Gracie' echo of her own thoughts earlier. 'What makes you think I think I'm too short?'

He had the hide to smile at her! Smug smile of a man who thought he'd scored a point.

'Because of the way you throw yourself into things—especially the SES. You told me you joined the equivalent operation down there in Victoria the moment you were old enough— why? I bet it was because people had always seen you as small and cuddly and cute but in need of protection, and you had to prove to them and to yourself that you could hold your own both with bigger, taller women and with men. I see it every time we're on calls together and even when we're doing exercises—you have to go first and go highest, or deepest, or whatever. You're proving you're not only equal to other team members but better than most of them.'

'And you think that's because I'm short?' Grace demanded, hoping she sounded incredulous, not upset because he'd read her so well—although she'd got past proving her stuff a long time ago.

'I know it was, but now it's probably because you are the best—or one of the best—that you do the things you do.'

Conceding her point was definitely a low blow but, unable to refute this statement, she went back to the original bit of the 'short' conversation.

'You can add a third thing to what you know of me—I hate being thought cute!'

Harry smiled again, causing chaos in Grace's body—palpitations, tingling nerves, butterflies swarming in her stomach. Not good things to feel towards a man who'd more or less admitted he'd never love again. Not good things to feel when she was in her getting-over-him phase.

'You're especially cute when you're angry,' he teased, sounding like her friend Harry once again, although the palpitations persisted, accompanied by a twinge of sadness for what couldn't be.

Attack—that would be a good distraction for both her heart and her head.

'Well, I don't know how you can talk about always going highest or deepest—at least I don't take risks,' she told him. 'You're the one who plunges into situations the rest of us feel are too dangerous.'

'I'm not a volunteer like you guys. It's my job.'

No smile, and he'd turned away so all she could see was his profile. Hard to read, Harry's profile, although it was very nice to look at. Very well defined with its straight nose and black brow shadowing a deep-set eye. High cheek-bones with shadows underneath, and lips—

She had to stop this! She had to push her feelings for Harry back where they belonged—deeply hidden in her heart.

For the moment.

Just till she got rid of them altogether.

Returning to the attack might help…

'Oh, yes? Like every policeman in Australia would have gone down in those shark-infested waters, with a storm raging, to rescue that diver?'

'Every policeman who can swim,' he said, smiling to lessen the lie in the ridiculous statement.

'Rubbish!' Grace dismissed both smile and lie with a wave of her hand. 'If your guess—and I'm not admitting it's right, Harry—is that I went into the SES because I was short, then my guess is you do all this dangerous stuff because you don't give a damn about what happens to you. That's understandable to a certain extent, given the loss of your wife. Taking risks might have helped dull the pain at first but now it's become a habit.'

Sheesh! Was she really doing this? Talking to Harry about his wife, and his attraction to danger? The very subject he'd warned her off last night?

And how was he reacting now?

He'd turned away, the profile gone, and all she had was a good view of slightly over-long hair.

Silky hair—she'd felt it when her fingers had somehow made their way to the back of his head as they'd kissed.

Her fingers were remembering the slide of his hair against her skin when he turned back to face her.

Half smiling…

'I asked for that,' he said quietly, reaching out and touching her face, perhaps pushing a wet curl off her forehead. 'Saying that we never talked.'

Then he leaned towards her and very gently pressed a kiss against her lips.

'Time to move, my tall, brave SES friend. Where's your hard hat?'

The tender kiss and Harry's softly teasing voice caught at Grace's heart and made her vision blur for an instant. But Harry was right—

they had to move, and she had to get her mind off kisses and tenderness and concentrate on getting around the tree.

She felt around her feet for the hard hat then remembered she'd given it to the volunteer who'd climbed into the bus to tend that final passenger while others had cut her free. The helmet had a lamp on it that meant he'd been able to see what he'd been doing.

She explained this to Harry who made a huffing noise as if such an action had been stupid.

'Not that it matters now,' she told him. 'They never do much to keep off the rain.'

But Harry had other ideas, reaching behind him for the wide-brimmed felt hat issued to all police officers up here in the tropics and plonking it down on her head.

'There, it suits you,' he said, and she had to smile.

'Because it's so big it covers all my face?'

The hat had dropped to eyebrow level, but she could still see Harry's face, and caught the frown that replaced the smile he'd offered with the hat.

'That's another thing I know about you,' he said crossly. 'You're always putting yourself down. Not like some women do when they're looking for compliments, but it's as if you genuinely believe you're not smart, and pretty, and…'

Grace had her hand on the catch of the door, ready to open it and brave the wild weather outside, but Harry's pronouncement stopped her.

'And?' she asked, half wanting to know, half uncertain.

'And tonight in that blue thing you looked beautiful,' he said. 'Bloody beautiful!'

He was out the door before Grace could react. Actually, if he hadn't opened her door for her he could have been halfway to Crocodile Creek before she reacted, so lost was she in a warm little cloud of happiness.

Harry thought she'd looked beautiful…

Bloody beautiful…

Harry shut the car door, took Grace's hand and drew her close to his body. Since Grace had forced him to think about it, he'd realised his problem was physical attraction mixed with angry concern. The combination was so unsettling it was muddling both his mind and his body at a time when his brain needed to be crystal clear and all his senses needed to be on full alert.

On top of that, his inability to do anything about their current precarious situation—to protect Grace from this fury Nature was flinging at them—had his jaw clenched and his muscles knotted in frustration.

And his leg hurt…

He tried to tuck Grace closer as they followed the beam of light from his torch, clambering over the lesser boughs and branches, heads bent against the wind and rain. She was so slight— had she lost weight lately and he hadn't noticed?—she could blow away.

He gripped her more tightly.

'Harry!'

Had she said his name earlier that this time she pressed her lips against his ear and yelled it?

'What?'

'I think that way's clearer,' she yelled, pointing towards the base of the tree. 'There's a branch there we can use to climb onto the trunk, and even if we have to jump off the other side, it might be better than scrambling through the tangle of branches up this way.'

She was right and he should have worked it out himself, but the mess on the road was nothing to the mess in his head. He had to get past it—to rid his mind of all extraneous thoughts. Tonight, more than ever before, he'd need to be clear-headed in order to protect the people of his town.

She'd moved away though still held his hand, leading him in the direction she'd indicated, picking her way over the fallen branches. A sudden whistling noise made him look up and he dived forward, seizing Grace in a flying tackle, landing with her against the protective bulk of the huge treetrunk.

The branch that had whistled its warning crashed to the ground in front of them.

'This is ridiculous. I want you to go back and wait in the car,' he said, holding her—too tightly—in his arms, desperate to keep her safe.

'Are you going back to sit in the car?' she asked, snuggling up against his chest, which didn't help the mess in his head.

'Of course not. There's a cyclone coming. I have to get back to town.'

She reached up and patted his cheek.

'So do I,' she said softly. 'So maybe we'd better get moving again.'

'No thank-you kiss for saving your life?'

Oh, no! Had he really said that? What was wrong with him? The very last thing he needed to be doing was kissing Grace.

'I think kissing has caused enough problems tonight, don't you?' she replied, but the hand that was resting on his cheek moved and one finger-tip traced the outline of his lips, reminding him of the heat the kiss had generated earlier—stirring the glowing coals of it back to life.

He stood up, still holding her, controlling

breathing that was suddenly erratic, while looking around for any new source of danger. But though the wind still blew, it seemed relatively safe.

'I'm going to boost you up onto the trunk. Get over the top and into the shelter of it on the other side as quickly as you can.'

He lifted her—so light—and set her on the trunk, then heaved himself up, his leg objecting yet again to the rough treatment it was getting. Then he followed her as she dropped swiftly down to road level again. There were fewer branches to trip or slow them down on this side, so he took her hand again and hurried her along the road, sure the car would meet them before long, although driving through the storm had its own problems.

'Lights!'

Grace pointed as she yelled the word at Harry. Even if he didn't hear her, he'd surely see the lights. She couldn't wait to get to the car, not because the wind and rain and flying leaves and branches bothered her unduly but to get away from Harry—out of touching distance, where it was impossible to make sense of all that had happened during the course of this weird evening.

The thought that Harry might be physically attracted to her had filled her with joy, but his evident distrust of such attraction could only mean he still had feelings for his wife. In his mind, physical attraction to another woman must seem like betrayal—a form of infidelity—although Nikki had been dead for nearly three years.

Then there was the question of whether they were still friends.

And her determination to move on from Harry—now made harder than ever because of the kiss.

Grace sighed. If she wanted a husband and family, she *had* to move on. She may have looked beautiful in her blue dress earlier today, but what chance did she have against the memory of a woman who'd not only been tall and slim and elegant, but a former local beauty queen—the Millennium Miss Caneland—and a popular television personality?

Even when she was dying, Nikki Blake had been beautiful. Grace had seen enough photos of her to know that much.

And nice with it, according to the staff who'd nursed her.

Grace sighed again.

'Not right. The lights aren't getting closer.'

She caught the end of Harry's sentence and peered ahead through the worsening deluge. Not only weren't the lights moving, but they appeared to be pointing upwards.

'He's slid off the road.'

Harry's words confirmed her thoughts and she broke into a jog, running behind him as he dropped her hand and raced towards the lights.

Hairpin bends around the mountain—they rounded one, then two, and were on the outward curve of a third when they saw the vehicle, which had come to rest against a pillar-shaped rock, its headlights pointing uselessly into the blackness of the forest.

'Stay here,' Harry ordered, but Grace was

already picking her way carefully down the slope, testing each foothold before shifting her weight.

The torch beam cut through the useless illumination provided by the vehicle's headlights, but revealed nothing more than a cloud of white behind the windscreen. The air bags had obviously worked.

Then, as the torch beam played across the vehicle, Grace saw a movement, a hand, pushing at the cloud of white, fighting against it.

'It's Troy!'

Harry's voice held all the anxiety and pain she knew he'd feel about this, the youngest of the men on his staff.

'Sit still,' he yelled, scrambling faster down the slope, cursing his bad leg, and unheeding of the danger to himself as he plummeted towards the young policeman. 'The less you move, the less risk there is of the vehicle moving.'

Grace followed more cautiously, aware, as Harry was, that Troy wouldn't hear the warnings over the wind and through windows wound up tightly against the weather.

Harry reached the car, more careful now, not touching it—not touching anything—but circling, motioning with both hands for Troy, whose face was now visible, to be still. Grace stopped a little further up the hill, then turned to look back the way they'd come.

'Would you trust that red gum to hold the car if we wind the winch cable around it?'

She pointed towards a tree not unlike the one that had fallen close to them earlier, but this one was on the far side of the road.

'We'll have to,' Harry said. 'For a start, we'll just use it to anchor the vehicle while we get Troy out. I won't risk using the winch with him in the cabin. You stay clear of everything while I take the cable up to the tree.'

He made his way to the front of the vehicle where the winch was sited and bent to release the cable.

Grace watched the careful way he touched the winch and understood his caution. The vehicle might seem secure enough, resting as it was against a massive rock, but with all the rain they'd had, the rock could have been undermined and any change in the dynamics of the vehicle could send it and Troy plummeting into the gully.

'Damn! I can't get in the back to get a bag,' Harry muttered, looking helplessly around then focussing on Grace. 'I don't suppose you're wearing something—no, of course you're not. It'll have to be my jacket.'

He handed the hook of the winch cable to Grace to hold and for the first time she realised he was still in his dinner suit. The bow-tie was gone but, yes, that was definitely a filthy, sodden dinner jacket he was removing.

'What do you need it for?' Grace asked as he took the cable hook from her and turned towards the road.

He looked back at her and smiled.

'To wrap around the tree. We all keep bags in the back of our vehicles to use as tree protection but as I can't get at a bag, the jacket will have to do. If there's no protection the steel cable can ringbark the tree and possibly kill it.'

Grace shook her head. Here they were in the rainforest, with gale-force winds and torrential rain whipping the vegetation to ribbons, and Harry was protecting a gum tree?

She watched him clamber and limp his way back up to the road, seeing the way his wet shirt clung to his skin, defining the muscles and bones as well as if he'd been naked.

She shut her eyes, trying to blot images of a naked Harry from her mind, then turned back to Troy, using her hands as Harry had, to motion him to stillness, smiling encouragement. And something worked because although all his instincts must be screaming at him to escape the confines of the vehicle, he stayed where he was—statue still.

'I'll just hook this up—doubling the cable back to the vehicle halves the weight on the winch, although the vehicle's only a couple of tons and the winch's weight capacity is five tons.' Harry explained, returning with the hook end of the cable, which he attached to a towing point at the front of the vehicle. 'Now, I'll take up any slack in the cable then get in the cab to check the lad.'

'*I'll* get in the cab to check him,' Grace said. 'And don't bother arguing because you know it makes sense. I weigh half as much as you do so, like with the cable, we're halving the risk of the vehicle moving.'

Even in the torchlight she saw Harry's lips tighten, going white with the pressure of not arguing, but in the end he gave a nod.

This wasn't anything to do with the new physical attraction, Harry assured himself as he very carefully opened the passenger door of the cambered vehicle—the door not jammed against the rock. His anxiety was for Grace, his friend.

'You OK?' he asked, peering through the maze of white towards the young constable.

'I think I've hurt my leg.'

Troy's voice wavered slightly and Harry understood. Barely more than a kid, he'd had to drive out through the wind and rain and flying missiles, then the car had skidded and he'd thought he'd had it.

'Grace will check you out,' Harry told him, turning towards Grace so he could help her into the cabin.

Beneath his wide-brimmed hat, her face was pale and streaked with dirt, and the embattled smile she gave him tweaked at something in his heart.

Concern, that's what it was. The same concern that was making his stomach knot as she slid across the seat, cutting at the air bags with the penknife off her belt, talking all the time to Troy about where he hurt and how he felt.

'There'll be a torch snapped in grips underneath the dash,' he told Grace when she'd collapsed the air bags and pulled them out of the way.

'Thanks!'

She found the torch and turned it on, setting it down so its light shone on her patient. Then, as her small but capable hands slid across Troy's head, feeling for any evident damage, Harry remembered this was only the beginning of the salvage operation. Unless they wanted to walk the forty-odd kilometres back to Crocodile Creek, he had to get this vehicle back up onto the road.

He prowled around it, checking the tyres—all intact—and damage to the body that might inhibit movement of the wheels. The mudguard, which had taken the brunt of the collision with the rock, was pushed in, but he found a strong branch and levered it off the rubber of the tyre. Everything else looked OK, which wasn't surprising as his reading of the accident had the vehicle going into a slow slide, first across the road, then down the slope to where it had come to rest against the rock.

'Where do you keep the first-aid kit in these new vehicles?' Grace called to him, and he turned to see she'd clambered over the back of the front seat and was now searching around behind the back seats.

'It should be strapped against the back of that seat you're on,' he told her, managing to answer although his lungs didn't want to breathe while she was moving in the cabin.

'Got it. I think Troy's right leg might be broken. I'll give him a painkiller before I try to move him, then splint it as best I can.'

She turned back to her patient, the small medical kit already open on her lap.

'Actually, Troy, it might be best if you fainted when we move you. That way you mightn't feel the pain so much.'

The lad grinned at Grace and Harry shook his head. They were like two kids playing doctors, seemingly unaware that a twisted metal cable was all that held them from the very real possibility of death.

'Do we really need to get him out?'

Grace had skidded across the seat to speak quietly to Harry, while Troy's eyelids were closing, no doubt in response to the drug she'd given him.

'I don't want to try winching it with anyone inside,' Harry told her once again. 'In ordinary circumstances it's better for have someone steering, but not in this situation where we don't know if the anchoring tree will hold the weight. The winch will pull the front around this way, then drag the vehicle up the slope.'

'We hope,' Grace said, and for the first time since their adventure together had begun she sounded tired.

'The cable's holding—let me in there!' Harry said, his stomach knotting with more anxiety.

'No, I'll manage and I need you there to help Troy out and lift him down to the ground. Would there be something in the back we can wrap him in? He's already shocky from the accident and his leg. I don't want that getting worse.'

Harry pictured the gear they all carried in the back of the big police vehicles.

'There'll be a small waterproof tarp folded in the pocket behind the driver's seat and a space blanket in a pouch beside it. Get them both out and we'll wrap him in the space blanket then the tarp. It will make moving him easier as well.'

Grace found them both and wriggled across the

seat to drop them out the door to Harry, then, sat-isfied the painkiller had had time to work, she turned her attention back to her patient.

Her first examination of him had told her he was holding up well. His pulse and breathing were steady, his pupils responding evenly to light, and he was able to move all his limbs so the front and side air bags seemed to have done their jobs, protecting his head and holding his body firmly in the seat belt so his spine wasn't compromised.

But even with a painkiller circulating in his blood and blocking messages to and from his brain, he was going to be in agony when he moved his leg.

'Troy, I need to get you over onto this passen-ger seat before we can get you out. The best way I can see to do it would be for you to lie sideways across the centre console so your head and shoul-ders are on the passenger seat behind me, then if you can bring your good leg up onto your seat and use it to help you inch your way towards the door until your butt's on this side. Can you do that?'

Troy looked at her, his eyes glazed by the medication, but he nodded and turned so he could wiggle across the seat. His groan as he moved confirmed her thoughts, but she had to get him out of the vehicle before she could splint his leg and stabilise him properly.

She was squatting in the footwell on the passenger side, her body canted across the gear lever as she reached out to take a firm grip on his injured leg. She had to get it up onto the seat of the car before she could examine the damage and was concentrating on doing this is carefully as possible, trying not to hurt him, when the vehicle moved.

Troy let out a yelp, and Harry roared, 'Keep still!'

'As if I needed to be told that!' Grace muttered to herself, frozen in place with Troy's calf held gingerly in her hands.

'It's my weight coming onto this side,' Troy said.

But it was Harry's 'I need to get you both out now!' that caught Grace's attention.

She couldn't see anything from where she was

so she continued with her job, lifting Troy's injured leg up onto the seat.

He gave a whistling sigh then slumped against the seat, the pain making him pass out.

Swelling around his ankle suggested the problem was there, or at the base of his tib and fib, but there was no time to do anything but get him out, preferably while he was still unconscious.

'How are we going to do this?' she called to Harry, who now had the door propped or tied open in some way.

'You push his shoulders down towards me, and I'll ease him out. Do what you can to protect his leg as we move him.'

Back in the footwell on the passenger side, she eased Troy's body around so his shoulders slid out the door. Harry's hands caught him, then lifted him as Grace grasped the injured limb to lift it over the centre console and gently out the door.

Harry cradled the young man in his arms, holding him as easily as she'd have held a baby, then he knelt and rested his burden on the spread-out covers on the ground, so carefully Grace shook her head in wonder at his gentle strength.

'The space blanket's a bit wet but it will still keep his body warmth in,' he said, wrapping first it and then the tarp around Troy's upper body, leaving his legs unwrapped so Grace could see to his injury.

Again using her knife, she cut through the leather of his boot, wanting to ease the constriction on his blood vessels that the swelling would be causing.

'Does he need this to order a new pair?' she asked Harry, tossing the wrecked boot to one side, cutting off Troy's sock now so she could put a half-splint around his foot to hold it steady while allowing for more swelling.

The police car's first-aid kit didn't run to splints, but there were plenty of sticks which she could pad with torn strips of sock before binding them into place around his foot and ankle.

Harry watched her work—small, capable hands moving so steadily she might have been in A and E, not on a dangerous, slippery slope with wind and rain raging about her.

She was good!

'OK?'

Had she said something that he'd missed while thinking about her, that now she was standing beside him, waiting for a response?

'He's done?'

Harry looked down at the young policeman who was now fully wrapped in the space blanket and tarp.

'We just need to get him up the hill,' Grace said, nodding up the slope. 'I'll take his legs.'

For a moment Harry considered arguing but although he'd been able to lift Troy free, he knew he couldn't carry him all the way up the slippery hill when he was healthy, let alone with a bung leg. Between them they lifted the injured man and carried him up the slope, slipping and sliding, Troy groaning from time to time, but eventually they had him safely on the road.

Grace took off Harry's hat and placed it, carefully tilted, on Troy's head to keep the worst of the rain from his face, then she watched as Harry made his way back down the slope and, using a hand-held remote control, started the winch.

She heard the winch motor whirr and held her breath then, oh, so slowly, the front of the big police vehicle swung around and, with wheels churning the surface of the slope to mud, it began to move, inch by inch, towards the tree that held its weight.

Harry had placed Troy well away from where the car would reach the road, and out of danger should the tree fall, but still Grace felt her nerves tighten, fear for all of them should the tree come down, or the vehicle not make the road, clutching at her stomach.

It was nearly up, front wheels on the verge, the winch whining complaints all the way, when the back wheels skidded, sending a final flurry of slush into the air before ploughing forward onto the bitumen.

'You did it!' Grace yelled, abandoning her

patient to jump up in the air in excitement. She'd have hugged Harry if their earlier conversation hadn't suggested even friendly hugs should be avoided. 'You got it up!'

'But will it go?'

Harry's question tempered her delight, but she sensed satisfaction in his voice and knew he was fairly confident the vehicle would be drivable. He was unhooking the towing cable, then using the winch to wind it up, while Grace walked over to the tree to retrieve his dinner jacket.

'Beyond repair?' Harry asked, seeing the muddy, crumpled garment in her hands.

'We'll see,' she said, clutching the jacket to her chest, holding onto something that was Harry's, barely restraining an urge to sniff at it in the hope of picking up something of his scent.

'You're so tired you've gone loopy!' she muttered to herself, returning to her patient, who was peering out from underneath the hat, no doubt wondering if there was any chance he could be moved out of the rain.

Harry started the car then drove slowly towards them, checking the vehicle was safe to drive. He stopped beside Troy and Grace, leaping out to open the back door and lift Troy inside.

'See if you can strap him in there so he's comfortable,' he said to Grace, who scrambled in beside her patient. 'Then you hop in the front and put on your seat belt. We don't want any more patients delivered to the hospital today.'

Grace obeyed, making Troy as comfortable as she could, checking his pulse again before abandoning him to climb over into the front seat and strap on her seat belt.

'OK?' Harry turned towards her as he asked, and the smile he offered was so kind Grace felt tears prickle behind her eyelids. She knew it was relief that they were all safe, and tiredness as it had been a very long day, but try as she may she couldn't answer him, making do with a very watery smile instead.

She was exhausted, Harry realised, remembering something she'd said that morning when

they'd been called out to an accident at Wygera—
something about just coming off night duty.

'When did you last sleep?' he demanded, anxiety
making his voice more abrupt than he'd intended.

But Grace didn't answer. She was already asleep.

At least he'd got everyone off the mountain…

'Scruffy!'

Max slid and scrambled down the hill, stumbling over rocks, ducking around the ferns,
yelling until he thought his chest would burst.

The bus had been on its side, that's all he remembered. The bus being on its side and no
windows where the windows should have been.

No Scruffy either.

His dog was gone.

'Scruffy! Come on, boy. Scruffy!'

He listened for the yelp that Scruffy always
gave in answer to his name, but how to hear a
small dog's yelp when the wind was howling and
stuff was crashing in the bush all around him?

'Scruffy!'

CHAPTER FIVE

HARRY drove carefully down the road, one hand fiddling with the radio, which seemed to be the only thing not working in the vehicle. Had a wire come loose? He twirled knobs and banged his hand against it, but couldn't pick up even a burst of static.

No distraction there…

He checked the rear-view mirror. Troy appeared to be asleep as well. So he looked back at Grace, at her pale face and almost translucent eyelids, at the shadows under her eyes and the spread of freckles now dark against her skin.

Grace!

He shook his head, unable to deny the attraction that still stirred within his body.

What was happening to him? Why had his

body chosen this of all times to remind him of his physical needs?

And chosen Grace of all women?

He guessed a psychologist would tell him it was because the grieving process was finally over, but he knew what had kept him celibate since Nikki's death had been as much guilt as grief. Guilt for the pain he'd caused her. Yes, there'd been grief as well, grief that someone as young and lovely as Nikki should have to die. Grief for the child he'd lost. And grief for the friendship he'd damaged somewhere along the way in his relationship with Nikki.

He looked at Grace, knowing a similar close friendship was at risk here.

Grace! Every now and then, in the past, he'd caught a fleeting glimpse of another Grace behind the laughing, bubbly exterior most people saw—a glimpse of a Grace that disturbed him in some way.

Tonight, learning about her father—thinking about a small child flying all the way from

Ireland to Australia in search of the love she hadn't found—he'd found a clue to the hidden Grace and understood a little of the pain and tears behind the laughter.

So now, more than ever, he didn't want to hurt her…

'Did I sleep?'

Grace peered blearily around her. They were in the emergency entrance at the hospital and, outside the car, Harry was holding the rear door while a couple of orderlies lifted Troy onto a stretcher.

'Like a log,' Harry told her, his smile lifting the lines tiredness had drawn on his face.

'No, stay right where you are,' he added, as she began to unbuckle her seat belt. 'I'm taking you home. Quite apart from the fact you're exhausted, you're so filthy you're the last thing anyone would want in a hospital.'

'You're not so sprucy clean yourself,' Grace retorted, taking in the mud streaks on the wet shirt that clung to Harry's chest.

Then, remembering, she clutched his dinner jacket more tightly.

Pathetic, that's what she was, but the filthy, ragged garment in her hands had become some kind of talisman.

Though it would hardly have the power to ward off a cyclone.

'Willie?' she asked, looking beyond the well-lit area to where the wind still lashed the trees and threw rain horizontally against the building.

'Definitely heading our way.' Harry watched the orderlies wheel Troy towards the hospital, obviously torn between wanting to follow and getting Grace home. 'We're down to hourly warnings.'

'Then I've got work to do,' Grace said, unbuckling her seat belt once again. 'You go with Troy, I'll grab a hospital car, go home and change, then see what's happening on the evacuation front. I assume the SES crews started with the nursing home down by the river, so most of those people should be in the civic centre hall by now. I'll get the list and organise for all the others to be collected or chivvied into shifting under their own steam.'

She'd opened the car door while she'd proposed this eminently sensible plan, but Harry took the door from her grasp, used one firm hand to push her back into the seat and shut the door again.

'I'll take you home,' he repeated. 'Two minutes to see someone's attending to Troy and I'll be right back. We need to do the individual evacuations on our list together. We discussed this in the contingency meetings. You'll need police presence to get some of those stubborn elderly die-hards in the most flimsy of old houses to move.'

Grace acknowledged his point with a pathetically weak smile. Battling wind and rain and an approaching cyclone was bad enough, but battling all the conflicting emotions the evening had stirred up at the same time was making the job doubly— no, a hundred times—more difficult.

Harry followed Troy's stretcher into A and E, where the scene resembled something from the film set of a disaster movie.

Only this wasn't a movie, it was real.

'How's it going?' he asked Charles, who had rolled towards him as Troy was taken into a treatment cubicle.

'It looks worse than it is. I think we've got things under control, although we've some badly injured people here in the hospital. There's one young woman with head injuries. Thank heavens Alistair—you know Alistair? Gina's cousin?—was here. He's a neurosurgeon with skills far beyond anyone we have on staff. He's put her into an induced coma for the moment—who knows how she'll wake up? We lost one young girl, and that last patient…' Charles paused and shook his head. 'She died before she got here.'

He seemed to have aged, but Harry understood that—he felt about a hundred years old himself.

'How's everything out there? Did you get everyone off the mountain?'

Harry nodded then looked around again, looking ahead, not thinking back. He'd done enough of that lately.

'You've obviously cleared the walking wounded. Where are they?'

'If they weren't locals with homes to go to, they were sent to the civic centre hall. Volunteers there are providing food and hot drinks.'

Charles paused then added, 'Actually, if you're going that way and I'm sure you will be some time, you might take the belongings we haven't matched to patients with you and see if you can find owners for them at the hall. The gear's in Reception.'

Someone called to Charles, who wheeled away, while Harry strode through to Reception, aware he'd been longer than the two minutes he'd promised Grace. Perhaps she'd fallen asleep again.

Wet, squashed, some muddy, the belongings rescued from the bus formed a sorry-looking heap on the floor in one corner of the usually immaculate reception area. How was he going to ferry this lot out to the car? He'd walked through from the corridor, thinking about the belongings, and now saw the two people who stood beside it.

Georgie Turner and Alistair—the doctor Charles had mentioned. They would have been working flat out since the casualties had begun coming in, but they weren't thinking medicine now. Georgie was staring down at the small, muddy backpack in her hands. She'd emptied it—a pathetic bundle of child's clothing and a ragged teddy bear had tumbled out and were lying at her feet.

While he watched, she knelt and lifted the teddy bear. The face she raised to him was terror-stricken.

'Max was on that bus,' she whispered.

'Your Max?'

Harry found himself staring helplessly at her. Georgie's beloved Max—hell's teeth, they all loved Max.

'Harry, have you found any kids?' Georgie demanded. And then the remaining colour drained out of her face. 'He's not…he's not one of the bodies, is he? Oh, God, please…'

'He's not,' Harry said, crossing swiftly to her, kneeling and gripping her hands. 'Georgie, I've been up there. We searched the surrounding area. We found no kids.'

'His dad… Ron's on the run. They might both…'

'I know Ron, Georgie. He wasn't on the bus.'

'But he might be hiding. He might—'

'Georgie, any person in that bus would be far too battered to be thinking about hiding. And the wind's unbelievable. Ron might be afraid of jail but there are worse things than jail, and staying out in the rainforest tonight would be one of them.'

'But Max is definitely there,' Georgie faltered. She looked up at Harry. 'He is,' she said dully, hugging the bear tighter. 'This is Spike. Max has just stopped carrying Spike round but Spike's never far from him.'

Behind them the phone rang, but the pile of child-size clothes on the floor reminded Harry of something.

'There's a shoe,' he told her, looking through the mass of wet belongings and not finding it. 'I'll just ask someone.'

He left the reception area, remembering the bridesmaid, Hannah, had found the shoe. Where was it now? He tracked it down at the desk of the children's ward.

The shoe was small and very muddy, with an orange fish painted on it, the eye of the fish camouflaging a small hole.

Harry held it in his hand and hurried back to Georgie, showing her the shoe then seeing a quick shake of her head.

'That's not Max's.'

Her dismissal of it was so definite, Harry shoved the shoe into his pocket to think about later.

'We've got to go back out there,' Georgie added.

Images of young Max, a kid who'd had enough problems in his life thanks to his wastrel, drug-running father, alone in the bush, maybe injured, definitely wet, and probably terrified, flashed through Harry's mind. His gut knotted as he realised the impossibility of doing what she'd suggested.

'There's a tree across the road—we can't get

through. I'd go myself and walk in, Georgie, but I can't leave town right now.'

He could feel her anguish—felt his own tearing him apart—but his duty had to be to the town, not to one small boy lost in the bush while a cyclone ripped the forest to shreds above his head.

'Of course you can't, go but I can. I'm going out there now.'

He saw the determination in her eyes, but could he stop her?

He had to try…

'Georgie, there's a cyclone hitting within hours. There's no way I can let you go, even if you could get through, which you can't. The tree's crashed down across the road not far from the landslide. We were lucky to get the last of the injured out.'

'I'll take my dirt bike,' she snapped. She tried to shove Harry aside but he wouldn't move.

Harry ignored the fists beating at his chest, trying desperately to think through this dilemma. Georgie could throw her bikes around as competently as she wore the four-inch heels she fancied as her footwear. She'd be wearing a helmet—

As if that would help!

'Georgie, he might not even be out there. You said yourself it's not his shoe.'

'Then there are two kids. Let me past.'

Georgie shoved at him but Harry held her, and made one last attempt to persuade her not to go.

'We've got no proof he's there. It's suicide.'

'We do have proof,' Alistair said from behind them. 'We've had confirmation Max was on the bus. Suicide or not, there's a child's life at stake. I'll go with her.'

Harry's mind processed what he knew of Alistair. Gina's cousin—Harry had met him at a fire party on the beach some months ago when the American had come to visit Gina—or more to check out Gina's fiancé Cal, the locals had thought.

Stuffed shirt had been Harry's immediate reaction.

Stuffed shirt who could ride a bike?

The pushing stopped. Georgie whirled to face

Alistair, her face a mixture of anguish and fear. 'You can't.'

'Don't you start saying can't,' Alistair said. 'Harry, the tree's blocking the road, right? Who else in town has a dirt bike?'

'I've got one,' Harry told him, thinking it through. If Max *was* out there…

Maybe he had no choice but to let them go. 'It's in the shed, Georgie, fuelled up, key above the door. And be careful, keep in mind at all times that there are open mineshafts on that mountain.'

But Georgie wasn't listening. She was staring at Alistair.

'You really can ride?'

'I can ride.'

'You'd better not hold me back,' she snapped.

'Stop arguing and get going—you don't have long,' Harry told them. 'You've got a radio, Georg? Of course not. Here, take mine and I'll pick up a spare at the station. Your cellphone might or might not work. And take a torch, it's black as pitch out there. Rev your bikes, he might hear the noise.'

Harry watched them go then pulled the shoe out of his pocket, grasping it in his hand, feeling how small and insubstantial it was.

Were there two children lost in the bush?

Surely not.

But his heart clenched with worry, while his hands fondled the little painted shoe. Georgie had said it was too small for Max. Max was seven, so the shoe would fit…

A two-and-a-half-year-old?

Harry shook his head. Why did thoughts like that creep up on him at the most inopportune times?

And wasn't he over thinking back?

He tucked the shoe back into his pocket, gathered up a bundle of backpacks and suitcases and headed out to his vehicle, thanking someone who'd come out from behind the reception desk and offered to help carry things.

It wasn't until he'd packed them into the back of the big vehicle that he realised he'd lost his passenger.

'If you're looking for Grace, she went into A

and E,' a nurse standing outside in the wind and rain, trying hard to smoke a cigarette, told him.

Harry was about to walk back inside when Grace emerged from the side door, head bowed and shoulders bent, looking so tired and defeated Harry hurried towards her, anxiety again gnawing at his intestines.

He reached her side and put his arms around her, pulling her into an embrace, holding her tightly as the wind and rain swirled around them.

'What's happened?' he asked as she burrowed her head into his chest as if trying to escape herself.

'She died.' The whispered words failed to register for a moment, then Grace lifted her head and looked up into his face. 'Our woman, Harry. The last one out of the bus. I've just seen Mike. She died before they reached the hospital. Massive brain injuries, nothing anyone could do.'

'Oh, Grace!' he said, and rocked her in his arms, knowing exhaustion was adding to the regret and hurt of the woman's death. He'd felt the same extreme reaction when Charles had given him that news.

'She had a boyfriend on the bus,' Grace continued. 'He was seated with her and got out uninjured, but she had to use the bathroom and was in there when it happened. They're from Germany and now he has to phone her parents.'

'I'll do that, it's my job,' Harry said, but Grace shook her head.

'Charles is phoning now—he speaks German so he'll support the boy. But fancy someone phoning, Harry, to say your daughter's dead.'

She began to shiver and Harry led her to the car, helping her in, wanting to get her home and dry—and safe.

Safe? Where was safe tonight? Nowhere in Crocodile Creek, that was for sure.

Grace fell asleep again on the short drive to her cottage and this time, when he stopped the car, Harry sat and looked at her for a minute. He had the list and could do the evacuations himself, although that would be pretty stupid as he was likely to be needed other places or would be taking calls that would distract him.

And on top of that, she'd be furious.

He sighed, reached out to push a wet curl off her temple, then got out of the car, walked, with difficulty as the wind was far stronger here on the coast, around the bonnet, then carefully opened the passenger door, slipping his hand inside to hold Grace's weight so she didn't slide out.

Her lips opened in a small mew of protest at this disruption, but she didn't push him away so he reached across her and undid the catch on her seat belt, conscious all the time of the softness of her body and the steady rise and fall of her breasts.

She stirred again as he lifted her out, then she rested her head against his shoulder and drifted back to sleep.

But once inside he had to wake her—had to get her out of her sodden garments for a start.

'Grace!'

He said her name so softly he was surprised when she opened her eyes immediately. Was it her nursing training kicking in that she could come so instantly awake?

And frowning.

'Harry? Oh, damn, I fell asleep again. You should have woken me. You've carried more than your share of people tonight, and your leg must be killing you.'

'You don't weigh much. I'll set you down and as you still have power, I'll put the kettle on. I want you to get dry, have a hot drink then gather some things together for yourself. I'll drop you at the civic centre and you can sleep for a couple of hours.'

He eased her onto her feet just inside the door of her cottage.

'Sleep?' She looked so astounded he had to smile.

'What you've been doing in the car. Remember sleep?'

The feeble joke fell flat.

'I can't sleep now!' she muttered at him, then added a glare for good measure. 'Unless you're going to sleep as well,' she dared him. 'Then I might consider it.'

'You know I can't—not right now—but I'll be only too happy to grab a nap whenever I can. You should be, too, and now's as good a time as any.'

'So you can run around on your own, doing all the evacuations I'm supposed to be doing, fielding phone calls and giving orders and generally doing your superhero thing. Well, not on my watch,' she finished, her usually soft pink lips set in a mutinous line.

He was about to deny the superhero accusation when he realised that was exactly what she wanted. She was turning the argument back on him.

'Well, fine,' he grumbled. 'But you're not going anywhere until you've had a hot drink.'

He stalked towards her kitchen.

Joe had obviously remembered the cyclone preparations from his time working in the town because the windows were all taped with broad adhesive tape, and a note on the kitchen table told them he'd taken Christina to the hospital because he was working there and hadn't wanted to leave her at the cottage on her own.

'Also large as she is,' he'd added, 'she swears she can still be useful.'

Harry filled the kettle, banging it against the tap because his frustration with Grace's behaviour still simmered.

'Stubborn woman!' he muttered to himself, finding the instant coffee and spooning a generous amount into two cups, adding an equal amount of sugar. It wasn't sleep but maybe a caffeine and sugar boost would help them tackle what still lay ahead of them this night.

Still grumpy, though not certain if it was because of Grace's refusal to obey his orders or her repetition of the superhero crack, he was carrying the filled cups and some biscuits he'd found in the pantry through to the living room when a small mumble of frustration made him turn. Grace was slumped on the sofa. She had managed to remove her boots but was now fumbling with the press studs that held her overalls together down the front.

Grumpiness was swallowed by concern so strong he felt shaken by the power of it.

'Here, let me,' Harry said, setting down the coffee and stepping towards her, telling her at the same time about the note and the preparations Joe had made, hoping the conversation might mask the trembling of his fingers.

He undid the studs then the Velcro strips and eased the heavy, wet fabric off Grace's shoulders. His voice—in the midst of explaining that Joe had left the water bottles, bedding, radio and batteries in the bathroom—faltered and his fingers shook a little more as he saw the swell of Grace's breasts, clad only in some scraps of dark blue lace—the colour making her ivory skin seem even paler.

Reminding himself that this was Grace, his friend, he helped her stand so he could drag the clammy, all-concealing garment off her body, trying desperately to ignore his body's reaction to the matching scrap of blue lace lower down, and the surprisingly shapely legs the stripping off of the garment revealed.

'You'll have to do the rest yourself,' he told her, his voice coming out as a throaty kind of growl.

'I had better,' she said, a teasing smile illuminating her tired face. 'Although,' she added wistfully, 'I'm not so certain physical attraction is all bad.'

'Right now any distraction at all is bad, Grace, and you know it. Now, scat, and take your coffee with you. Get into the shower and into some dry clothes—I'll slip home and change, check that everything's organised at the station and come back for you in ten or fifteen minutes.'

Getting away from her—doing things that needed doing—would surely distract him from…

From what?

He couldn't find an answer, and she didn't scat. She just stood there for a few seconds with her blue lace and white skin and exhausted face, seemingly about to say something, then she shook her head and turned away, revealing the fact that the blue lace was a thong so the pert roundness of her butt had him almost agreeing that physical attraction couldn't be all bad.

Except that he knew it was…

Grace stepped over the pile of emergency supplies Joe had deposited in her bathroom, and reached in to turn the shower on. She stripped off the sexy underwear she'd bought to go with the dress, sighing as she did so. She may as well have been wearing a nursing bra and bloomers for all the effect it had had on Harry. Although if she'd been too tired to argue as he'd stripped off her gear, he'd probably been too tired to think about attraction.

She showered, cringing as noises from above suggested half the forest was landing on the roof. Joe had been right to put the emergency gear in here—bathrooms were usually the safest room in the house, but if the roof blew off, or if a large branch caused damage, anyone sheltering in the bathroom would still get very wet.

'Better wet than dead,' she reminded herself, and a wave of sadness for a woman she didn't know engulfed her so suddenly she had to rest her head against the wall of the shower for a few minutes, hoping the hot water would sluice away the pain for those they hadn't saved.

Another crashing noise outside reminded her she had work to do, so she turned off the shower, dried herself and dressed hurriedly, pulling on a light pair of cargo pants with a multitude of pockets, and a T-shirt. Both would eventually be soaked even underneath a heavy raincoat but at least they'd dry faster when she was indoors. Boots next—only an idiot would be outside on a night like this without solid boots.

They were wet and didn't want to go on, and within minutes her dry socks had absorbed water from them. She shrugged off the discomfort, knowing it would soon be forgotten once she was involved in her work.

She unhooked her two-way radio and pocket knife from her belt and tucked them into the big pockets on her trousers, then added some spare batteries for the radio to another pocket. In the kitchen she found a packet of health bars and put four and a small bottle of water into the pockets down near her knees. Finally the list, carefully sealed inside a waterproof plastic bag, completed her preparations. She had another hard hat from her days in Victoria, and with that on her head and her bright yellow rain jacket around her shoulders, she headed out to the veranda to wait for Harry.

She'd taken down the hanging baskets from their hooks beneath the veranda roof before she'd dressed for the wedding, but although she'd packed them under other plants in the garden, one look at the already stripped stems told her how damaged they were going to get.

'Plants are replaceable,' she reminded herself, leaning against the wall as all the veranda chairs were stacked inside, but now, as she waited, her mind turned to Harry. Had it been the sense of imminent danger that had prompted them to speak of things that had always been unsaid between them?

She had no doubt that her friendship with Harry had developed, in part, because she *hadn't* been on the staff at the hospital when Nikki had died. Harry was the kind of man who would have shunned the sympathy on offer from all those who knew him—the kind of man who'd have pulled away from friends to work his grief out on his own.

But everyone needed someone and Grace had filled the void, providing a friendship not linked to either of their pasts and not going beyond the bounds of good but casual acquaintances.

If anything, since her discovery that she loved Harry, she'd pulled further back from anything approaching intimacy, so they'd laughed and joked and shared coffee and discussed ideas connected with the bits of their lives that touched—work and the SES.

She was still mulling over the shift in their relationship—if one kiss and some personal conversation could be called a shift—when Harry pulled into the drive. Pleased to be diverted from thoughts that were going nowhere—she was putting Harry out of her life, remember—she dashed towards the car, ducking as a plastic chair went flying by.

'Some stupid person hasn't tied down his outside furniture,' Harry muttered as she did up her seat belt.

'It looked like one of the chairs from beside the pool at the doctors' house,' Grace said. 'I guess with the wedding and then the emergencies coming in from the bus accident, no one's had time to secure that furniture.'

Harry was already turning the car that way.

'We'll do it before we start on our evacuations,' he said. 'Imagine some poor person seeking help at the hospital and being knocked out by flying furniture before he even gets there.'

He drove up the circular drive in front of the old house that had originally been built as the Crocodile Creek hospital, and which now housed an assortment of hospital staff, parked at the bottom of the front steps and told Grace to stay where she was.

She took as much notice of this order as she had

of his earlier orders to do this or that, and followed him through the downstairs area of the big building and out to where the garden furniture was indeed still around the pool.

'Just throw it in the pool,' Harry told her. 'It's safest in there and it'll get a good clean at the same time.'

He picked up a plastic table as he spoke and heaved it into the pool, following it with a sun lounge, while Grace took the smaller chairs and tossed them in.

'This is fun!' she said, grabbing the last chair and tossing it high so it made a satisfying splash.

'You find the weirdest things fun!' Harry grumbled at her, then he took her hand. 'Come on, let's have more fun—getting Mr and Mrs Aldrich to move out of their house.'

OK, so it was a protective gesture and meant nothing, especially in the context of getting over Harry, but holding hands with Harry felt so good Grace couldn't help but smile.

They ran back through the big recreation room

under the doctors' house, out to the car. In the cove below the headland, the sea roared and tumbled, sending spray higher than the cliffs.

Willie was flexing his muscles.

CHAPTER SIX

'WHAT time's high tide?' Grace asked as they strapped themselves back into the vehicle.

'It was midnight, so it's going out now,' Harry said. 'I suppose we can be thankful for small mercies. The storm surge from the cyclone will be bad enough at low tide, but if it had coincided with a high tide, who knows how many places might have been washed away?'

They were driving past the pub as Harry spoke and Grace shivered, imagining a wave of water sweeping over the row of businesses beside it. The police station was directly behind the shops, although on a slight rise.

'Are you free to be doing evacuations?' Grace asked, thinking of the enormous task of coordination that must be going on, with the station at its hub.

'There's no room for me over there,' Harry replied, nodding towards the station. 'One of the benefits of getting a new building last year is that it's built to the stringent category five building regulations so all the staff who live in less well-constructed flats or houses have shifted their families in. It was part of our contingency plans and it works because it means I now have five trained staff there ready for emergencies and on standby for clean-up later, and also have enough people to cut down shifts on the radio to two-hourly.'

'Two-hourly shifts? Is that all they can take? Is it so tense?' Grace asked, wondering why she'd never thought about this aspect of an emergency. With the SES, all the members on duty had radios tuned to the police emergency frequency and although she and other team leaders radioed their members, they relied mainly on the police radio operator to co-ordinate their efforts.

'It's the radio operator who's under the most stress at the moment,' Harry explained. 'Taking emergency calls and relaying them to wherever they need to go, so being able to run two-hour shifts cuts down on tension and the possibility of mistakes. But having staff in the station also means I've got someone there whose sole task is to plot the cyclone's course, taking all the direction, speed and intensity readings from the Met and marking them on the map. He'll give me a call when Willie's an hour from crossing the coast and also get the radio operator to order any emergency crews off the streets. Once Willie's that close, anyone outside is in danger.'

Grace nodded her understanding. All her people had orders to return to their homes as soon as they'd evacuated the people on their lists. In times like this their families had to be their prime concern.

They were driving past the Grubbs' house and Grace nodded towards it.

'Good thing the hospital preparations included

orders for all staff in older housing to take shelter there. The Grubbs' house always looks as if it will blow down in a strong wind or slide the rest of the way down the slope into the creek. Heaven knows what Willie will do to it.'

Harry looked towards the house where the hospital yardman lived with his wife, who was in charge of the housekeeping side of the hospital. The old place had been added onto so often it was starting to resemble a shed on an intensive chicken farm. The oldest part, nearest the creek, stood on timber stumps so old they'd shrunk so the veranda on that side and the small room they'd enclosed on it were cantilevered out from the rest of the house—the stumps taking none of the weight.

'Charles has been trying to talk them into letting him build them a new house for years, but the Grubbs refuse, saying the place suits them as it is.'

'Or until it blows down,' Grace commented, then, as Harry slowed down at an even older house further along the street, she wondered how it would feel to be so attached to a dwelling you wouldn't want to change it—or leave it in a cyclone.

Was that what 'home' was all about?

Although her stepmother had always been kind, the concept of home had eluded Grace. Sometimes in her dreams she saw it as a white-washed cottage set amid green fields, but that was wrong. She knew she'd lived in Belfast and had seen enough pictures of the city to know there was nary a field nor a cottage in sight.

'You're too tired to be doing this!'

Harry's cross exclamation brought her back to the present. He was frowning anxiously at her, and his hand was warming the skin on her forearm.

'Not tired, just thinking,' she told him, pressing her hand over his. 'Thinking about homes.'

Harry shook his head and got out of the car. Why would such a simple remark—thinking about homes—get under his skin?

Because he now knew Grace had never really had a home?

But should that make him want to wrap his arms around her and hold her tight against his body?

He couldn't blame physical attraction for this urge, because it wasn't part of the equation. Not this time…

He'd parked so the passenger door was away from the wind, making it easier for Grace to get out, although walking to the front door of the old weatherboard house was a struggle, so he kept an arm protectively around her shoulders.

Mrs Aldrich greeted them with a battery-powered lantern held at shoulder height, the light good enough to show a tear-stained face *and* the attitude of belligerence written across it.

'I've got this lantern and torches and water and biscuits in the bathroom and Karen from next door has taped my windows and I'm not going,' she said, and Harry heard Grace sigh as if she understood the older woman's feelings and didn't want to argue.

'You have to, Mrs Aldrich.' Harry used his firm policeman voice. 'Your house just isn't safe. We need to move you and Bill down to the civic centre.'

'Bill's dead.'

Harry's stomach clenched. Another look at Mrs Aldrich's face told him this was true.

Floored by this unexpected development, Harry could only stare at her. Fortunately Grace had more presence of mind.

'What happened?' she asked gently, stepping past Harry and putting her arm around the elderly woman, carefully guiding her further into the house.

'He just died,' Mrs Aldrich replied, her resolute voice abandoning her so the words quavered out. 'We knew it was close. I was sitting by him and he touched my hand like he was saying goodbye then that rattly breathing he'd had earlier just stopped.'

'Oh, Mrs Aldrich, I'm so sorry,' Grace said, completely ignoring the little hurry-up motions Harry was making with his hands. 'Have you had a cup of tea? Can I get you something? I should have a look at Bill, just to be sure. Do you mind?'

She hesitated, perhaps aware she was asking too many questions, then, as Harry wondered just how she'd handle this, she added another one.

'What if Harry makes you a cup of tea while you show me where Bill is?'

Harry wondered if she'd gone mad. OK, so Mrs Aldrich was in her nineties and she and Bill had been married for more than seventy years. Was Grace thinking they had to do this carefully if they didn't want another death on her hands?

'Strong, sweet tea,' she said to Harry, as she guided the older woman towards the rear of the house where the bedrooms were.

'Cyclone warnings are now hourly, Willie's due to hit us in two to three hours and instead of evacuating people I'm making tea,' Harry muttered to himself, but he'd known Bill and Daisy Aldrich all his life and his heart ached for Daisy and the sadness she must be feeling right now.

He made the tea, still muttering to himself, knowing in his gut that this wasn't the end of the Aldrich saga for the night.

'We've got to get her to the civic centre,' he whispered to Grace, who was sitting next to Daisy, beside the bed where Bill indeed lay dead.

'I heard that, Harry Blake,' Daisy countered. 'Seventy years Bill and I have shared this house, our kids were born here, the roof's blown off in other cyclones, but it's survived. So if you think I'm leaving Bill alone here tonight then you're very much mistaken.'

For one wild moment Harry considered the possibility of taking a dead body to the safe haven of the civic centre, then he saw Grace shake her head and wondered if she'd read his thoughts.

Of course they couldn't. All their attention had to be on the living, but he knew he'd have a battle on his hands moving Daisy.

Grace was holding the cup to Daisy's lips, encouraging her to drink, while Harry stood helplessly beside her, anxious to keep moving, knowing there was so much still to do.

'Harry, would you get a thick bedcover from one of the other beds? I'll wrap it around Mrs

Aldrich's shoulders so she's got some protection should a window go. And one for Bill as well.'

Glad to have something to do, Harry went through to another bedroom where both the single beds had thick coverlets.

He brought them back and watched as Grace placed one carefully over Bill, folding down the top of it so they could still see his face.

'If the window breaks or the roof goes, you can pull it up,' she said to Daisy, now wrapping the second bedcover around the frail old woman. 'Harry and I will try to get back—or one of us will—to sit with you. But if we don't, use the cover to protect yourself, and if things get really wild, get under the bed.'

Daisy smiled through the tears that seeped down her face.

'Bill always said he'd protect me, no matter what,' she said, then she touched Grace's cheek. 'You're a good girl. If that Harry had a scrap of sense he'd have snapped you up a long time ago.'

Grace bent and touched her lips to the lined cheek.

'You take care,' she said, then she led a bemused Harry out of the room.

'You're going to leave her there? Not even argue about it? We can't just give in like that?'

'Can't we?' Grace said softly. 'Think about it, Harry. How important is her life to her right now? I know in a month or so, when the worst pain of her grief has passed, she'll find things she wants to live for, but at the moment she has no fear of death—in fact, she'd probably welcome it. And look at it from her point of view—Bill's been her whole life, how could she possibly go off and leave him now?'

Harry began to reply but Grace had turned back towards the bedroom, fishing her mobile phone out of her pocket as she went.

'Here,' she said, offering it to Mrs Aldrich. 'The phone lines are all down but the cellphones will still work. This one is programmed to reach Harry's cellphone, the one he's carrying today. Just press the number 8 and it will ring through to Harry.'

'Won't you need the phone?' Harry demanded, although what he wanted to know was who had the number one to seven positions on Grace's cellphone.

He knew she didn't have a mother…

'I've got my radio,' she reminded him, 'and just about everyone at the civic centre will be clutching their mobiles so they can report on conditions to their relatives in far-flung places or sell their phone pictures to television stations. I think I'll manage without one.'

'Because you've no relatives in far-flung places?' Harry asked, disturbed that the question of family and Grace had never occurred to him before tonight's revelations.

'Because I'll be far too busy to be phoning anyone,' Grace replied. 'Come on, we've people to evacuate.'

They ran from the house to the car, and he struggled to open the door and let her in, but even if conversation had been possible he wouldn't have known what to say. In some vague way he sensed that Grace was right about leaving Daisy where she was, but for so long his practical self had ruled his emotional self that it took a little bit of adjusting to accept emotion might have a place even in emergency situations.

Fortunately the next four couples were more easily moved, and by the time they had the last of them settled in the civic centre, everyone had been checked off the evacuation list.

Harry looked around the crowded area. Babies cried, and small children, excited by the different location and the thrill of being awake in the early hours of the morning, ran around excitedly. Somewhere a dog barked, and a cockatoo let out a loud squawk of complaint, but most of the refugee pets were as well behaved as their human owners.

'At least the majority took note of what we said, about making sure they had animal carriers for their pets as part of their cyclone preparations.'

Grace was by his side and he nodded, acknowledging it had been a good idea. The circular dropped in the letterbox of every dwelling in town had not only been an initiative of the SES, but had been delivered by the volunteers.

'Where's Sport?' she asked, looking at a small kelpie cross who was protesting loudly about his accommodation.

'He's at my parents' place. I couldn't risk leaving him in the house when I knew I wouldn't be there.'

'Bet he's furious he's missing all the fuss,' Grace said, and Harry smiled. He'd rescued the small kelpie pup from the local rubbish dump after a wild thunderstorm. Whether he'd been abandoned because of an injury to one leg, or the injury had happened during the storm, Harry didn't know. He'd paid to have the leg treated, and when that hadn't worked, the leg had been amputated. He'd intended giving the dog away, but the fiercely loyal animal had had other ideas, finding his way back to Harry's no matter where he'd been taken.

In the end, his sheer determination had persuaded Harry to keep him.

'I need to check on a few people,' Grace said,
and moved into the small corridor between
sleeping bags, mattresses and assorted padding
brought along by the evacuees.

He watched her bend to speak to a heavily
pregnant woman who should probably have
been at the hospital rather than here, then,
mindful that watching Grace was not his job
right now, he walked through to the kitchen area
where volunteers were making sandwiches and
handing out tea or coffee to anyone who wanted
it. He grabbed a cup of coffee and a sandwich,
thinking Grace was probably in need of suste-
nance as well.

She was at the far end of the hall, talking to one
of her SES crew, her arms waving in the air as
she explained some detail. And although she was
wearing plain cargo trousers and a T-shirt, all
Harry could see was a curvy figure in two scraps
of blue lace.

Muttering to himself once again, he took his coffee into one of the meeting rooms so he could concentrate on the messages coming through on his radio. Reports told him where power lines were down and where the emergency crews on duty were handling problems. The hour when the radio operator would order everyone into safe shelters, whether at their homes, at the police station or here at the civic centre, was fast approaching. Another report told him the hospital had been switched over to generator power, and even as that message came through the lights went out in the civic centre.

There was a momentary darkness, which caused the kids to scream with pretend fear, then the generators kicked in and the lights flickered back to life, but that instant of darkness had reminded Harry of the blackout earlier.

Had reminded him of kissing Grace…

'Boy, this food is good! It's the roast lamb from the wedding. Apparently, after we left, Mrs P. set the remaining guests to making sandwiches with the leftover food. Some was delivered to the hospital and the rest here.'

Grace was munching on a sandwich as she came up behind Harry. Everything had been OK between them—maybe a trifle strained but still OK—while they'd been caught up in rescuing Troy and getting off the mountain. Then, apart from a slight altercation over sleep, while they'd organised the evacuations. But now, in this lull before the storm—literally—she wasn't sure just where she stood with Harry.

Knew where she should stand—far, far away.

'We've got about ten of the less injured people from the bus here,' she said, taking another bite of sandwich and chewing it before getting back to the conversation. 'Apparently all the belongings we gathered up at the accident site were taken to Reception at the hospital. By now most of the stuff belonging to the hospitalised people will have been matched up to them, so I wondered if we could go over and collect the rest—it must belong to those who are here and I'm sure they'll all feel better if they have their own belongings with them.'

Harry shook his head, unable to believe he'd forgotten about the stuff he'd packed into the back of his vehicle.

'It's not at the hospital, it's here. I'll grab an able-bodied male and go get it from the car.'

'Get two able-bodied men and let them do it. Take a break,' Grace suggested, but Harry wasn't listening, already talking to one of the locals who then followed him out of the hall.

Grace followed him to the door, waiting until the two men brought in the luggage and handbags, then she spread it out so people could identify their belongings. The bus passengers, recognising what was going on, moved through the crowded room, then one by one they swooped on personal possessions, every one of them clutching the piece of luggage to their chests, as if they'd found lost treasure.

'It's a security thing,' Grace murmured, thinking how she'd clutched Harry's dinner jacket—remembering she'd left it in a sodden heap on her living-room floor.

Slowly the pile diminished until all that remained was a new-looking backpack.

'I wonder if the shoe belongs to that one,' Harry said, and knelt beside it, opening the fastening at the top and spilling out the contents.

'Damn it to hell!' Grace heard him whisper, as he pushed small shorts and T-shirts into one pile and some women's clothing into another. 'There *is* another child!'

'That's my dog!'

Max knew he should be pleased he'd finally found Scruffy, but the kid from the bus was clutching the dog against his chest and looked as if he'd never let him go.

All eyes, the kid. Huge eyes Max could see even though it was as dark as dark could be.

The kid was crouched under a tree fern—

stupid place to shelter 'cos the water came straight through the leaves of tree ferns.

'Come on,' he told the kid. 'We've got to find the road. Or get back to the bus so we can get out of the rain.'

The kid shook his head and must have squeezed Scruffy tighter because Scruffy gave a yelp.

'You can hold the dog,' Max offered, and watched while the kid considered this. Then he stood up and Max saw his feet. One foot—bare—the other in a sneaker, the bare one cut and scratched and probably bleeding, although it was too dark to see the red of blood.

Everything was black.

'Hang on,' he told the kid and he sat down and took off his sneakers, then his socks, then he pulled his sneakers back on over his bare feet. Hard 'cos they were wet.

'You have the socks,' he told the kid. 'Put both on your foot that's lost its shoe. I'd give you my shoe but it'd be too big. Go on, sit down and do it. I'll hold the dog.'

The kid sat and reluctantly gave up his hold on Scruffy, though when Max hugged his pup against his chest Scruffy gave a different yelp.

'He's hurt,' Max whispered, holding the dog more carefully now.

The kid nodded, but he was doing as he was told, pulling on one sock then the other over it.

The dog was shivering so Max tucked him inside his T-shirt, then he reached out and took the kid's hand.

He'd walked downhill from the bus, so it and the road must be uphill.

'Let's go, kid,' he said, hoping he sounded brave and sensible. Sensible was good, he knew, because Mum always kissed him when she said he'd been sensible.

And brave was good. All the knights he read about were brave.

He didn't feel brave. What he felt was wet and cold and scared…

CHAPTER SEVEN

GRACE watched as Harry reached for his cellphone and dialled a number, then shook his head in disgust and slammed the offending machine back into his pocket.

Whoever he was phoning must be out of range.

Now he pulled his radio out and began speaking into it, calling to someone, waiting for a reply, calling someone to come in.

Urgently!

Harry put the radio away and began repacking the clothing into the backpack, folding small T-shirts with extraordinary care. Grace watched him work, but as he pulled the cord tight and did up the catch on the top, she could no longer ignore the anguish on his face.

She knelt beside him and took the capable hands, which had trembled as he'd folded clothes, into hers.

'Are there kids out there? Do you know that for sure?'

He nodded.

'Georgie's Max we know for sure, and now this.'

He pulled the little sneaker from his pocket, poking the tip of his finger in and out of the hole that made up the eye of the fish painted on it.

'Two kids.'

Despair broke both the words.

'We can go back,' Grace suggested, urgency heating her voice. 'Go and look for them.'

'I *can't* go, and logically nor can you. You're a team captain—this cyclone will pass and we'll both be flat out sorting the damage and running rescue missions.'

He took a deep breath, then eased his captured hand away from hers.

'Georgie's gone to look—she and Alistair. We'll just have to hope they're in time.'

In time—what a dreadful phrase.

But the second child?

'If there's a second child unaccounted for, why has no one mentioned it? Why has no one said my child's missing?'

One possible answer struck her with the force of a blow.

'The woman who died? Oh, Harry, what if it's her child?'

'That's what I've been thinking,' Harry said bleakly, 'although there's a woman at the hospital who's in an induced coma at the moment, so maybe the child belongs to her. And the woman who died had a boyfriend—surely he'd have mentioned a child.'

Grace tried to replay the rescue scene in her mind—a badly injured woman *had* been rescued early in the proceedings. Susie's sister, who'd acted as a bridesmaid at the wedding, had been looking after her.

'Let's hope it's her and that she lives and that

Georgie finds both kids,' Grace said, although this seemed to be asking an awful lot.

Worry niggled at her mind—two children lost in the bush in a cyclone?

Worry was pointless, especially now with Willie so close. There were things she had to do. She looked around at the people settling down to sleep, at the two paramedics and four SES volunteers, not sleeping, watchful.

'Everything's under control here. If you wouldn't mind giving me a lift, I'll go back to Mrs Aldrich's place and sit out the blow with her.'

'Sit out the blow?' Harry echoed. 'It's obvious you've never been in a cyclone. The whole house could go, Grace.'

'So I can give her a hand to get under the bed. I had a look at that bed. It's an old-fashioned one, with solid timber posts on the corners and solid beams joining them. Safe as houses—safer, in fact, than some of the houses in this town.'

'And you talk about me taking risks?' Harry muttered, but as he, too, had been worried about

Daisy Aldrich—in between worrying about two children—maybe it wasn't such a bad idea. Only…

'You stay here, I'll go and sit with her,' he said and knew it was a mistake the moment the words were out of his mouth.

'We've already been through the hero thing a couple of times tonight! But not this time, Harry. Mrs Aldrich is my responsibility—'

The ringing was barely audible in the general hubbub of the room. Harry pulled his cellphone out of his pocket and checked the screen.

'Your number,' he said to Grace as he lifted the little phone to his ear and said a tentative hello.

'Harry, Daisy Aldrich. Karen from next door is here and she's having her baby and it's early and she can't get hold of Georgie who's not at the hospital or at home so can Grace come?'

'We'll be right there,' Harry promised, closing his phone and motioning to Grace.

'You win,' he said. 'We need a nurse. Daisy's next-door neighbour is having a baby.'

'Karen? I saw her last week when she came for a check-up. She's not due for three or four weeks.'

'Tell the baby that,' Harry said, leading the way out of the hall.

Daisy was in her kitchen, boiling water on a small gas burner when Grace and Harry arrived.

'I don't know why people boil water,' she said, waving her hand towards the simmering liquid. 'No one ever did anything with boiling water when I was having my babies.'

A cry from the back of the house reminded them of why they were there.

'We dragged a mattress into the bathroom and she's lying on that. She'd never have got under the bed, the size she is.'

Grace was already hurrying in the direction of the cry. Another battery lantern was barely bright enough to light the room, but Grace could see the shadowy shape that was Karen, hunched up on the mattress which had been placed between the wall and an old-fashioned, claw-footed bath.

Fluid made dark smears across the mattress, but before Grace could check if it was water from the birth sac or blood, Karen cried out again, helplessly clutching the edge of the bath, her body contorting with pain.

'It hurts too much,' she said. 'Make it stop. Please, make it stop.'

Grace knelt beside her, sliding her hand around to rest on Karen's stomach, feeling the rigidity there.

'How long have you been having contractions?' she asked Karen as the stomach muscles relaxed.

'This morning,' the girl sobbed, 'but I thought they were those pretend ones with the silly name. The baby's not due for three weeks. And everyone was telling me first babies are always late so they had to be the pretend contractions.'

'Have you timed them at all?' Grace asked, trying to unlock Karen's death grip on the bath so she could lay the young woman down to examine her.

'No!' Karen roared, crunching over in pain again. 'You time them!'

She puffed and panted, occasionally throwing out combinations of swear words Grace had never heard before.

Grace pulled a towel off the towel rail, then looked around to see Harry and Mrs Aldrich peering in through the door.

'Could you find something soft to wrap the baby in? And some spare towels would be good. And scissors, if you have them,' she said, then looked at Harry.

'How long do we have before Willie arrives?'

'Three quarters of an hour, according to the latest alert. He's also been upgraded—definitely a category five now.'

He looked around at the walls and ceiling of the bathroom.

'This room's too big for safety—the load-bearing walls are too far apart—although the bath looks solid enough.'

But Grace's attention was back on Karen,

who with a final shriek of pain had delivered a tiny baby boy.

He was blue, but as Grace cleared mucous from his mouth and nose, he gave a cry and soon the bluish skin turned a beautiful rosy pink.

'You little beauty,' Grace whispered to him, holding him gently in the towel.

Mrs Aldrich returned with the scissors, more towels and a soft, well-worn but spotlessly clean teatowel.

'That's the softest I've got,' she said, peering into the room then giving a cry of surprise when she saw the baby. 'It's the way of the world—one dies and another takes his place,' she said quietly, then she padded away, no doubt to sit beside her Bill.

'I'll call him William Harry,' Karen said, as Grace wrapped the baby in the teatowel and handed him to Karen, suggesting she hold him to her breast. But Karen didn't hear, her eyes feasting on the little mortal in her arms, her attention so focussed on his tiny form Grace had to blink away a tear. 'William after Bill, who was always kind to me, and Harry after Harry because he was here.'

Grace looked up at Harry who was pale and tense, shaking his head as if he didn't want a baby named after him. But even as Grace wondered about this reaction she became aware of the roaring noise outside the house and understood his lack of emotion. Another William—Willie—was nearly on them.

She turned her attention back to Karen, massaging her stomach to help her through the final stage of labour, then cutting and knotting the cord and cleaning both mother and child.

Harry returned as she tucked a towel around the pair of them. He was carrying one of the bedcovers he'd found earlier, a pillow and a couple of blankets.

'I'm going to put these in the bath, Karen, then I want you and the baby to get in there. We'll put the mattress over the top to keep you both safe from falling debris. You'll still be able to breathe and it's not heavy, so if you feel claustrophobic you can lift it up a bit.'

Karen and Grace both stared at him, Karen finding her voice first.

'In the bath?'

Harry, who was making a nest of the blankets and bedcover, nodded.

'It's an old cast-iron bath—far too heavy to move even in a cyclone. Its high sides will protect you both and support the mattress. I wouldn't do it but the house has already lost a bit of roof and the walls are moving.'

Karen stopped arguing, handing the baby to Harry to hold while she stood up and clambered into the bath. Grace helped her, leaning over to make sure she was comfortable. She turned to Harry to take the baby and the look of pain and despair on his face made her breath catch in her lungs.

'I'll give him to Karen,' Grace said gently, moving closer so she could take the little bundle. Harry's eyes lifted from the baby to settle on

Grace's face, but she knew he wasn't seeing her—wasn't seeing anything in the present.

Had there been a baby? she wondered as he stepped forward and leant over, very gently settling the baby in his mother's arms.

Then he straightened up and strode out of the room, returning seconds later with a light blanket, which he tucked around the pair of them.

Karen smiled at him then tucked the baby against her breast, murmuring reassuringly to the little boy, although Grace knew the young woman must be terrified herself.

'Here,' Grace said, fishing in her pocket for the bottle of water and a couple of health bars. 'Something to eat and drink while Willie blows over.'

Karen smiled and took the offerings, setting them down on her stomach, but her attention was all on the baby at her breast.

With Grace's help Harry lifted the mattress onto the top of the bath, leaving a little space where Karen's head was so she could see out.

'Put your hand up and move the mattress so I know you can,' he said, and Karen moved the mattress first further back then up again so only the tiny space was visible.

'You OK?' Grace asked, sliding her fingers into the space and touching Karen's fingers.

'I think so,' the young woman whispered, her voice choked with fear.

'We'll just be next door, under Daisy's bed,' Harry told her, then he put his arm around Grace's shoulders and drew her out of the room.

'I hate leaving her like that. Surely we should all be together,' Grace said, looking back over her shoulder at the mattress-covered bath.

'Better not to be,' Harry said, and Grace shivered as she worked out the implications of that statement.

Daisy met them as they entered her bedroom, and handed Grace the cellphone.

'Give it to Karen. And this torch. Tell her about pressing 8 to talk to Harry. It might make her feel less lonely.'

Grace turned, but Harry stopped her, taking both the cellphone and the torch.

'You help Daisy down onto the floor. If she lies on the mat I can pull her under the bed if we need the extra protection. And turn off your radio. I'm turning mine off as well. There's nothing anyone can do out there, so we might as well save batteries.'

He walked away, leaving Grace to put a pillow on the mat, then help the frail old woman down onto the floor.

'Cover Bill so things don't fall on him,' she whispered to Grace, and Grace did as she asked, drawing the bedcover over the peaceful face of the man on the bed. Then she sat on the floor and held Mrs Aldrich's hand while outside the house the world went mad.

'We're going under the bed,' Harry announced, returning with the second mattress from the spare bedroom. 'I'm putting this on top as extra padding.'

He arranged the mattress so it rested from the bed

to the floor, making a makeshift tent, then pulled the mat to slide Mrs Aldrich under the big bed.

'Your turn,' he said to Grace, who slid beneath the bed, leaving room for Harry between herself and the older woman.

Harry eased himself into the small space, wondering what on earth he was doing there when he could be in a nice safe police station or civic centre hall.

That it had to do with Grace he had no doubt, but he couldn't think about it right now. Right now he had to get these women—and the baby—through the cyclone.

He put his arm protectively around Daisy, but she shrugged him off.

'For shame, Harry Blake, and with Bill in the room. If you want to cuddle someone, cuddle Grace. She looks as if she could do with an arm around her, and you certainly need a bit of loving.'

Mrs Aldrich's voice was loud enough for Harry to hear above the roar of the approaching force, but would Grace have heard?

And if she had and he didn't put his arm around her, would she think—?

He had no idea what she'd think. Somehow this wild, erratic force of nature had blown the two of them into totally new territory.

Territory where he *did* need a bit of loving?

Surely not.

But just in case Grace had heard—or maybe just in case he did need loving—he turned so he could put his arm around Grace, and when she didn't object he drew her closer, tucking her body against his and once again feeling her curls feathering the skin beneath his chin.

'Cuddling me, Harry?' she said, her light, teasing voice defeating the noise outside because her lips were so close to his ear. 'Aren't you afraid? I mean, if a shuffling dance provoked the deadly physical attraction, what might a cyclone cuddle do?'

She was making fun of him, but still it hurt, and somehow, because this was Grace and maybe because Bill and Daisy had loved one another for seventy years or maybe even because within minutes they could all be dead, he started telling her.

'We'd known each other for ever, Nikki and I, our parents friends enough for me to call hers Aunt and Uncle. She left town to go to university in Townsville while I went to Brisbane for my training. Then, about three and a half years ago, her parents were killed in a car accident. She came home to see to everything, I helped her— well, my parents arranged everything for her, but I was there for comfort.'

Grace felt his arms tighten around her, and kept as still as she could. She wasn't sure if she really wanted to hear about him loving Nikki, but listening to Harry was definitely better than listening to the raging fury of the cyclone and wondering if any of them would survive.

And maybe he needed the catharsis…

'Comfort is physical, as you know, and suddenly we both felt the attraction that being close had stirred. Wild attraction, heightened most probably on Nikki's side by grief.'

He paused then added in an undertone, 'I didn't have that excuse.

'We thought it love, Grace, and married, caught in a whirl of physical delight that left no room for plans or practicality, then, as suddenly as it had come, it seemed to leave. Not the physical attraction—that was always there—but when we weren't in bed there was—I can only describe it as an emptiness. Nikki was still grieving for her parents and she also missed her job, while I spent more time than was necessary at mine.'

Grace turned in his arms so she could hold him. She told herself it was because the noise of the cyclone was as loud as an express train roaring through a tunnel, but really it was so she could rub her hands across his back, offering silent sympathy he might or might not want.

Her heart ached for him—for the pain she heard in his voice and in the silence that now lay between them. But she couldn't prompt him, knowing he had to get through this story his own way.

'We didn't talk about it—in fact, I didn't know

if Nikki felt it—but I was gutted, Grace, to think I'd mucked up so badly. Then I thought about it—really thought about it—and decided it would all be OK—that we could work it out. We'd always loved each other as friends, so surely that would remain as a solid foundation, and we had compatibility, so that had to count in building a future…'

He paused again and she felt his chest fill with air then empty on a sigh. She tightened her arms around him, offering the only comfort available.

'Eventually she told me she'd been offered a new television job in Brisbane. She'd been with the same station in Townsville but this was a promotion. Would I transfer to the city to be with her?'

Somewhere outside a tortured screeching noise suggested a roof was being torn apart. Mrs Aldrich's roof?

Grace snuggled closer, fear moving her this time.

'Go on,' she prompted, knowing Harry's story was probably the only thing holding at bay the terror that was coiled within her.

'I said I would, wanting so much to make it work, although all my life all I'd ever wanted was to be a policeman here where I belonged. We made arrangements, looked at housing on the internet, then she went to Townsville to see her old boss.'

The story stopped, and with it the noise.

'It's over?' Grace whispered, then heard how loud her voice sounded in the silence and realised she hadn't whispered at all.

'It's the eye passing over,' Harry told her as he slid out from under the bed and cautiously lifted the mattress aside. 'You two stay right where you are. I'll check on Karen and the baby and be straight back.'

Grace reached out to stop him, but it was too late, so she had to wait, fearful for his safety, having heard enough of cyclones to know that the eye was only the calm before the storm returned, only this time the wind would blow the other way.

'Both sound asleep, would you believe,' Harry reported as the howling, roaring noise drew close again. 'I guess having a baby and being born are both tiring experiences.'

He slid beneath the bed, lying between the two women, reporting to Mrs Aldrich that her kitchen roof had gone and a part of the bathroom wall had been damaged, but generally things looked OK. Radio calls to the station had assured him everything was OK there and at the civic centre.

'It's the second blow, once everything is loosened, that knocks houses about,' Mrs Aldrich told him, as they all squiggled around to relieve cramped muscles and tired bones. 'Will you go on talking, Harry?' she added. 'I can't hear the words but I like to hear your voice—it's very soothing and it makes the cyclone noise easier to bear.'

Horrified that Daisy had even heard his voice, Harry hesitated, but the cyclone was roaring again, and Grace had snuggled close, so it was easy to finish the tale he'd carried inside him for so long, locked away but probably festering because it hadn't ever been told.

He tucked Grace closer, held her tightly, and blurted out the words.

'She went to Townsville to have an abortion.'

There, it was said.

For the first time he'd actually told someone about the almost routine operation that had led to the discovery of Nikki's inoperable cancer.

He felt Grace stiffen, then her hand crept up to touch his face, cupping his cheek in her palm.

'No wonder seeing that new baby hurt you,' she whispered, her voice choked with tears.

He shook his head although he knew neither woman would see the gesture, frustrated at this situation. What was he thinking, lying under a bed—a bed with a dead body in it—in a category five cyclone, playing out his past like a series of episodes in a soap opera?

Fortunately—for his sanity—at that moment the roar grew louder and above the wild fury of the wind they heard the scream of metal sheets being torn from their anchors, nails screeching in protest as the rest of Daisy's roof peeled away.

'The weight of rain could bring the ceiling down so we stay here until we know the wind has eased,' Harry warned the two women, reaching out and drawing both of them closer, knowing they all needed human contact at the moment. 'Now Willie's crossed the coast, he'll lose his power.'

But what had that power done as it passed over the town? What havoc had it caused?

Anxiety tightened all the sinews in his body— anxiety for all the townsfolk but most of all for two small children out there on the mountain.

Had Georgie and Alistair reached them in time? Were all four safe?

Max watched the light creep into the blackness of the hole in which they huddled, turning the dark shadows that had frightened him in the night into harmless posts and odds and ends of timber.

The kid was sleeping, curled up in a puddle of muddy-looking water, Scruffy in his arms. The kid had needed Scruffy, not because he'd said anything but because the way his face had looked when Max had heard Georgie calling to them and he'd answered her.

Instead of being happy they'd been found, the kid had started crying. Not bawling loudly, like CJ sometimes did when he was hurt, but silent crying, the light from the torch Mum was shining on them picking out the tears running down his face.

Max had thought at first he was crying because Mum had said she couldn't get them out straight away because it was too dangerous and that they'd have to wait until the cyclone stopped blowing trees over. But the kid had kept crying even after Mum had thrown down her leather jacket and some chocolate bars, and Max had figured out he was crying because his Mum wasn't there.

So Max gave him Scruffy to hold because earlier, when Max had had a little cry because Mum wasn't there, holding Scruffy had made him feel really, really brave.

Max pushed the leather jacket over the sleeping kid and waited for more light to come.

CHAPTER EIGHT

IT WAS another hour before the noise abated sufficiently for Harry to slide out from under the bed. The roof had indeed gone and the ceiling had collapsed in the far corner of the room, pouring water onto the floor, but thankfully the rest of the room was, for the moment, dry.

Grace joined him, staring about her at the devastation, then heading for the door.

'Don't go,' he said, catching her hand. 'You stay here with Daisy while I check out what's solid and what isn't.'

She turned, anxious eyes scanning his face in the murky dawn light.

'Be careful,' she said, touching her hand to his

cheek, so many things unspoken in the gesture that Harry felt a hitch in his breathing.

The house was a mess. One of the bathroom walls had collapsed across the bath, so Harry had to toss boards and beams aside to get to the mattress-covered bath. Fortunately the ceiling had held so the room was relatively dry. He could hear Karen and the baby both crying, Karen hysterical when he lifted the mattress.

'Come on, I'll help you out. You can shelter in the bedroom with Daisy until it's safe enough to drive you to the hospital.'

'With Daisy and dead Bill? I can't do that. I can't take my baby into the room with a dead person.'

Harry sighed but he kind of understood. There'd been ghosts beneath that bed with him.

'All right, but I'll have to put the mattress back on top of you.'

'That's OK,' Karen said, stifling her sobs and settling back down in her nest of blankets. 'Now it's getting lighter and I know you're not all dead and that noise has stopped, it's not nearly as scary.'

He replaced the mattress—if the ceiling did come down he didn't want wet plasterboard smothering the pair of them—then did a recce through the rest of the house. To his surprise, the dining room, a square room to one side of the kitchen, was apparently unscathed, and from the kitchen he could see that the roof in that area remained intact.

Once they had tarpaulins over the rest of it, Daisy might be able to move back into her home as soon as services like electricity, sewerage and water were restored, although that could be weeks away.

Sure his charges were safe, he ducked into the dining room, sat down on a chair and pulled out his cellphone. Time to check on the damage in the rest of the town.

Unbelievable damage from all accounts, the policeman on duty at the station told him, but no reports of casualties. Harry breathed a sigh of relief.

'Just let me sort out a few problems here,' he

said, 'and then I'll do a run through town to see what's what. Expect me back at base in about an hour. In the meantime I'll be on air on the radio or you can get me on the cellphone.'

He rang the hospital. No word from Georgie but they'd despatch an ambulance to pick up Karen, the baby and Daisy Aldrich. They'd also contact the funeral home to send a car for Bill.

Grace was standing in the doorway as he ended the call.

'*Did* she have the abortion because of her career?' she asked, and the question was so unexpected he answered without thinking.

Answered honestly.

'No,' he said bleakly, remembering the terrible day he'd stared in disbelief at Nikki while she'd told him this—and then, disbelief turning to denial, added that she was dying of cancer. 'At least, she said not, but it might have had something to do with it. She said she had it because we didn't love each other. She said she knew that almost as soon as we were married—knew it was just lust between us, lust and her grief, and that I was there. She said she didn't want to bring a baby into that situation because without love we'd probably split up.'

Grace came closer and put her arms around him, holding him tightly.

'Then she told me about the cancer—that when she had the operation they found inoperable cancer.'

'She was dying of cancer?'

Harry nodded.

'Which made my anger at her—my fury that she'd gone ahead and aborted my child without discussing it with me—totally absurd. The baby wouldn't have lived anyway, but that fact couldn't penetrate the anger. I said things then that should never have been said—hard, hot, angry things, and through all that followed—her time at home and then in hospital—that was the guilt I had to carry. To have reacted with anger towards Nikki who'd been my friend for ever, to have hurt her at any time, let alone when she was dying…'

His shoulders hunched and he bent his head as if the weight of the emotional baggage he'd carried since that time still burdened his body.

'Physical attraction, Grace, do you wonder I'm suspicious of it?'

'But anger is a natural reaction to bad news,' Grace whispered to him. 'Your anger might have found an outlet in yelling about the abortion but it would have been far deeper than that—it would have been about the death sentence Nikki, your friend and lover, had just received.' She held him more tightly. 'It was natural, not cruel or unfair, Harry, and I'm sure Nikki would have understood that.'

'Would she?' he whispered hoarsely, the head-shake accompanying the words telling Grace he didn't believe her.

The wailing cry of a siren told them the ambulance was close by. Grace let him go and headed for the door, wanting to help Karen and the baby out of the bath.

She heard the vehicle pull up, the sound of

doors opening, the wheels on a stretcher dropping down.

'So now you know why he feels the way he does,' she muttered helplessly to herself, 'but what if it isn't just physical attraction?'

She understood so much more now—understood it was guilt and anger at himself that prompted not only Harry's risk-taking but also the emotional armour he'd drawn around himself.

Grace mulled it over as she led the paramedics first into the bathroom to collect Karen and baby William, then, once they were safely loaded, she walked with Daisy to the ambulance.

'Yes, I'll stay with Bill until the people from the funeral home arrive,' she promised Daisy, and was surprised at Daisy's protest.

'You'll do no such thing—you stay with Harry. Cyclone Willie shook a lot of things loose in that boy's heart. He's hurting and he needs someone with him.'

'As if Harry would ever admit to needing someone,' Grace said, but fortunately the funeral car arrived at that moment so she didn't have to make a choice.

Harry had returned to the dry refuge of the dining room while she'd been seeing the two vehicles depart. He looked grey with fatigue—or was it more than that? He looked…

Despairing?

'Georgie? You've heard from Georgie?'

He shook his head, then muttered, 'I'm thinking no news is good news out there. I told Alistair we'd left the vehicle beyond the fallen tree—they could have sheltered in that.'

But this not good but not precisely bad news did nothing to ease the knots of worry in his features.

'What's wrong?' Grace asked, walking towards him and reaching out to take his hands. Watching his face carefully, ready to read a too-easy lie.

But he didn't lie, saying only, 'It's Sport,' in a tone of such flat despair Grace thought her heart would break.

'Dead?' she whispered, then remembered where the dog had been. 'Your parents? They're OK?'

'Sport's not dead but gone. My parents are fine. Very little damage to the house, although the sheds have been destroyed and the sugar crop's flattened. But Sport's disappeared. Mum said he grew more and more agitated as Willie passed over, then, when Dad opened the door to look at the damage during the calm of the eye, Sport took off, last seen heading back towards the town.'

Grace pictured Harry's parents' place, not far from the sugar mill on the outskirts of town.

She could imagine the dog, hip-hopping his way through the fury of the cyclone.

Sport, a ragged, crippled mutt that had somehow wormed his way through the emotional barriers Harry had built around himself.

Wormed his way into Harry's heart.

She wrapped her arms around him and held him tightly.

'I love you, Harry,' she said, although it was the last thing she'd meant to say.

Bloody dog!

She was resting her head against Harry's chest so couldn't see his reaction, although she felt his chest move with a sharp intake of air.

'I know you don't want to hear that,' she added, anxious to get it all smoothed over and things back to normal between them again. 'But we've been through so much—touched by death then welcoming new life, our physical world destroyed around us—I had to say it, and it's OK because I don't expect you to love me back. I've got over love before and I'll get over this, but it needed to be said.'

One of his arms tightened around her and he used his free hand to tilt her chin, so in the rain-dimmed morning light she saw his face.

Saw compassion, which she hated, but something else.

Surprise?

Natural enough, but was it surprise?

Before she could make another guess, Harry bent his head and kissed her, his lips crushing hers with hot, hard insistence. She melted into the embrace and returned the kiss, letting her lips tell him, over and over again, just how she felt.

One corner of her mind was aware of the futility of it all, but this was Harry and right now he needed whatever physical comfort she could give him.

And *she* needed something that at least felt like love…

Perhaps a minute passed, perhaps an hour, although, looking at her watch as she pushed out of Harry's arms, Grace knew it hadn't been an hour.

Two, three minutes maybe—a short time out from all the chaos that lay both behind and ahead of them.

And if her heart cringed with shame that she'd told Harry how she felt—a confession prompted by pity that he'd lost his dog, for heaven's sake—then she was good enough at pretence by now to carry on as if the words had not been spoken.

Which, she knew, was what Harry would do…

'We've got to go. Sport will be looking for you,' she said, and Harry nodded.

'Damn stupid dog!'

'We'll look at your place first,' Grace said.

Harry turned towards her, frowning now.

Grace loved him?

'We can't go out looking for a dog,' he growled. 'I need to see the damage, talk to people, get arrangements going.'

Talk about coming out of left field! Grace, his friend, suddenly declaring love for him?

'You need to drive through town to see the damage,' this friend he suddenly didn't know reminded him, then she repeated what she'd said earlier. 'We'll go past your place first.'

And now carrying on as if she hadn't just dropped a bombshell on him.

As if love had never been mentioned.

He had to put it right out of his mind. The town and its people needed him—and needed him to have a fully functioning brain, not some twitchy mess of grey matter puzzling over love and Grace.

Grace first—he'd deal with Grace the friend and that way might not keep thinking about the Grace he'd kissed.

Twice...

'What's this *we?* I'll drop you home, that's if your cottage is still standing. Or at the hospital. You need to sleep.'

'No, Harry, we'll do a drive around town then you can drop me at SES Headquarters so I can start sorting out what's needed and who we've got to help.'

Unable to think of a single argument against this—well, not one that she would listen to—he led the way out to where he'd left the police vehicle, tucked in under the Aldrichs' high-set house. It seemed to have survived the onslaught with only minor damage.

Sadness filled her heart as Grace snapped her seat belt into place. She sent a sidelong glance at the object of her thoughts, who was talking seriously to someone on his cellphone. Now those fatal words had been said, they could never be unsaid, so things could never really be the same between them again.

That was probably just as well, because although she'd spoken lightly about getting over love, she knew this was going to take a huge effort, and not seeing much of Harry would certainly help.

Although, comparing what she'd felt for James with what she felt for Harry, maybe he was right about physical attraction giving an illusion of love.

Certainly the love she'd felt for James had never hurt like this…

It was at this stage of her cogitations that she became aware of the world around her—or what was left of it.

'I don't believe it,' she whispered, trying desperately to make some sense of the devastation that lay around them. Harry was driving very slowly and carefully, picking a path along a road strewn with corrugated iron, fibro sheeting, furniture and bedding, not to mention trees, branches and telegraph poles, the latter flung about as if they'd weighed no more than matches.

The rain poured down with unrelenting insistence, as if Nature hadn't yet done enough to bring the town of Crocodile Creek and its inhabitants to their knees.

'We'll need the army. The mayor phoned earlier. He's already asked the premier for help,' Harry said as he pulled into his driveway.

'But today?' Grace asked, staring helplessly around. 'What can we do today? Where do we start? How can we help people?'

'Food and water. I'll check Sport's not here, then drive around town. We'll stop at the civic centre first, although I've had a report that everyone's OK there. We're broadcasting messages asking anyone who needs help to get out of their house to phone the dedicated line at the police station—the number we gave out at the end of all the cyclone warnings.'

'Four, zero, six, six, eight, eight, nine, nine,' Grace repeated, remembering the trouble Harry had had getting a number so easy to remember.

The radio was chattering at them. All downed

power poles and torn lines would have to be removed before the authorities would consider turning power back on. No reports of casualties so far, apart from those lost in the bus crash. Banana plantations and cane fields had been flattened. The farmers were in for a grim year, but Willie, his violence spent, had continued moving westward and was now dumping much-needed rain on the cattle country beyond the mountains.

'So Willie moves on,' Grace whispered as she heard this report. 'But how do people here move on? How can anyone move on from something like this?'

Harry glanced towards her, and she knew he was thinking of her stupid declaration.

Well, so what if he was? Like Willie, she was moving on.

Moving on…

CHAPTER NINE

THEY stopped at the house just long enough for Harry to satisfy himself Sport wasn't there. Neither was his dirt bike, which meant Georgie and Alistair were still out in the bush.

They were both sensible people, they had his vehicle out there to shelter in—or the bus—they'd be OK.

But had they found the kids?

Worry knotted inside him and he sent a silent prayer heavenward, a plea that they and the two children were all right. Then he looked around at the havoc and wondered if heaven had given up answering prayers, because plenty of people had prayed the town would be spared a cyclone.

'Do you think the old bridge will hold?' Grace asked as they approached the bridge across the creek that separated the hospital part of the town from the main commercial and residential areas.

'The council engineers looked at it when it was forecast Willie might head this way and declared it would probably outlast the new bridge across the river, but the problem is, because it's low and water is already lapping at the underside, all the debris coming down the creek will dam up behind it, causing pressure that could eventually push it off its pylons.'

'Debris piling up is also causing flooding,' Grace said, pointing to where the creek had already broken its banks and was swirling beneath and around houses on the hospital side.

'Which will get worse,' Harry agreed, concern and gloom darkening his voice.

They were driving towards the civic centre now, Grace looking out for Sport, although the streets were still largely deserted.

Except for teenagers, paddling through floodwater on their surf-skis here and there, revelling in the aftermath of the disaster.

'I'll be in meetings for the rest of the morning,' Harry said, turning towards Grace and reaching out to run a finger down her cheek. 'You do what you have to do then get someone to run you home, OK? You need to sleep.'

'And you don't, Harry?' she teased, discomfited by the tenderness of his touch—by his concern.

'I can't just yet,' he reminded her, then he leant across the centre console and kissed her on the lips, murmuring, 'I'm sorry, Grace,' and breaking her heart one last time because the apology had nothing to do with not sleeping.

One of her fellow SES volunteers drove her home to check the cottage was all right. She'd lost a window and the living room was awash with water, her garden was wrecked, but apart from that she'd got off lightly. They drove on to SES Headquarters, passing people wandering through the wreckage of countless homes, oblivious of the rain still pelting down, looking dazed as they picked an object from the rubble, gazed at it for a moment then dropped it back.

Some were already stacking rubbish in a pile, hurling boards that had once made up the walls of their houses into a heap on the footpath. It would take forever to clear some of the lots, but these people were at least doing something. They were looking to bring some order back into their lives.

Once at Headquarters, she set up a first-aid station. Volunteers would be injured in the clean-up and would also know to bring anyone with minor injuries to the building.

What she hadn't expected was a snakebite.

'Bloody snake decided it wanted to share our bathroom with us. I had the kids in there,' the ashen-faced man told her. 'I picked it up to throw it out, and the damn thing bit me on the arm.'

He showed the wound, which Grace bandaged with pressure bandages, down towards the man's fingers then back up to his armpit.

But it was really too late for bandages. The

wound had been oozing blood, and snake venom stopped blood clotting properly.

'Did you drive here?' she asked, and the man nodded, his breathing thickening as they stood there.

'Good. We'll take your car.'

She called two of the volunteers who'd come in looking for orders to carry the man out to the car.

'The less effort you make, the less chance of poison spreading.'

'It didn't look like a brown or taipan,' the man said, but Grace had already taken the car keys from his hand and was hurrying towards the door. Even so-called experts couldn't always identify snakes by their looks.

The volunteers settled her patient into the car, and she took off, making her way as fast as she could through the hazardous streets. At the hospital she drove straight into the emergency entrance, leaping out of the car and calling for a stretcher.

'Bringing your own patients, Grace?' someone called to her as she walked beside the stretcher.

'Snakebite,' she snapped, pushing the stretcher in the direction of a trauma room. 'We need a VDK.'

Inside the trauma room she started with the basics, knowing a doctor would get there when he or she could. She slipped an oxygen mask over her patient's head, opened his shirt and set the pads for electrocardiogram monitoring, and fitted an oxygen saturation monitor to one finger.

IV access next—they'd need blood for a full blood count and for a coag profile, urea, creatinine and electrolytes, creatine kinase and blood grouping and cross-matching. Urine, too—the venom detection kit worked on urine.

She talked to the man, Peter Wellings, as she worked, hoping a doctor would arrive before she got to the catheterisation stage.

A doctor did arrive, Cal Jamieson, looking as grey and tired as Grace was feeling.

She explained the situation as briefly as she could, then was surprised when Cal picked up a scalpel and turned to her.

'Where exactly was the bite?'

Grace pointed to the spot on the bandaged arm.

'And it was definitely bleeding freely?'

She nodded.

'OK, we can take a swab from there for venom detection, rather than wait for a urine sample. I'll cut a small window in the bandages, and in the meantime let's get some adrenaline for him in case there's a reaction to the antivenin— 0.25 milligrams please, Grace. And get some antivenins ready—the polyvalent in case we can't identify the snake, and some brown, tiger and taipan, which are the most likely up here.'

Cal was working swiftly, cutting through the bandages, swabbing, talking to Peter as well as telling Grace what he required next. He took the swab and left the room, returning minutes later to go through the antivenins Grace had set out on a trolley.

'Tiger,' he said briefly, more to Grace than to Peter, who looked as if he no longer cared what kind of snake had bitten him. 'I'm going in strong because of the delay. The Commonwealth Serum Laboratories recommend one ampoule but we're going two. I've actually given three to someone who had multiple wounds. But he'll need careful monitoring—straight to the ICU once I've got the antivenin going in his drip.'

He glanced towards Grace as he worked.

'You've obviously been outside. How bad is it?'

Grace thought of the devastation she'd seen and shook her head.

'I can't describe it,' she said. 'I can't even take in what I've seen. All the photos of floods and hurricanes and even bomb-sites you've ever seen mixed into one. I don't know how people will begin to recover. And the rain hasn't let up one bit. That's making things worse.'

Cal nodded.

'We'll see plenty of post-traumatic stress,' he said. 'Hopefully we'll be able to get the staff we need to handle it—it's such a specialist area.'

He was adjusting the flow of the saline and antivenin mix, ten times the amount of saline to antivenin, and calibrating the flow so Peter would receive the mixture over thirty minutes.

Grace wrote up the notes, and the latest observations, wanting everything to be in order as Peter was transferred.

'He'll need to be on prednisolone for five days after it to prevent serum sickness,' Cal said, adding his notes. 'And watched for paralysis, which with tigers starts with muscles and tendons in the head.'

He was silent for a minute then added, 'And renal failure.'

Grace knew he was talking to himself, adding reminders as he would be the person caring for Peter in the ICU. Mistakes happened and were more likely when people were exhausted by extra shifts, and only by constant checking and re-checking would they be avoided.

'You staying?' he asked Grace.

'Am I needed?'

He shook his head.

'I think we've got things pretty well under

control. The worst of the accident victims, a young woman called Janey, is coming out of her induced coma, and everyone else is stable so, no, if you're not on duty, buzz off home. You look as if you could do with about three days' sleep.'

'Couldn't we all?' Grace said, but she was grateful for Cal's dismissal. She could walk home and look for Sport on the way. Later she'd return to SES Headquarters for another shift, but she'd be a far more effective participant in the clean-up operation if she slept first.

She tapped on Jill's office door before she left, wanting to be one hundred per cent sure she wasn't needed.

'Go home and sleep,' Jill ordered in answer to Grace's query. 'You look as if you need about a week to catch up. Go!'

She waved her hands in a shooing motion.

'We've all been able to grab a few hours— mainly thanks to all the extra staff available because of the weddings. Joe's been marvellous, and even Christina has put in a couple of shifts on the monitors in ICU. They're both safe and sleeping at my place at the moment, in case you were worrying about them.'

Grace shook her head in amazement that she hadn't given her friends a thought for the last few hours, although she *had* known they were at the hospital and so had assumed they'd be safe.

'Some friend I am,' she muttered to herself as she left Jill's office, then her weary brain remembered Georgie and the children. She poked her head back around the door.

'Georgie?'

Jill frowned in reply.

'We think she's OK. A truckie out west picked up a message that would have been sent about the time the eye was passing over. Something about finding two children, but the signal kept breaking up so he didn't catch it all.'

Jill looked worried but Grace realised there was little they could do until they heard more.

The wind had eased off, but not the rain, so she took an umbrella from one of the stands at the entrance to Reception. She'd return it when she came back on duty, although so many umbrellas were left at the hospital no one would ever notice one was missing.

The scene outside hadn't improved. The Agnes Wetherby Memorial Garden between the hospital and the doctors' house had been flattened, but the old house stood, apparently having come through the violent cyclone unscathed. Grace didn't pause to check it thoroughly—her own home was calling to her.

But as she passed the big house on the headland, she looked down into the cove, staring stupidly at the waves crashing on the shore. It was low tide, there should be beach, but, no, the storm surge had pushed the water right up to the park that ran along the foreshore so the beautifully ugly breadfruit trees and the delicate casuarinas that grew there now stood in water.

Every shop in the small shopping mall had lost its roof, while the Black Cockatoo looked as if it had lost most of its upper storey, although, from the sounds of revelry within, it was still open for business.

Grace turned down a side street, wanting to walk closer to the police station and Harry's house, hoping she'd see Sport.

Had the dog sensed Harry was in danger that it had taken off?

It seemed possible—

The scream was so loud and so fear-filled all thoughts of Harry and his dog fled. Grace turned in the direction it had come from and began to run, though to where she had no idea, until she turned a corner and saw the floodwaters. Filthy brown water swirling angrily along the street, washing under high-set homes and straight through those set lower.

Treetrunks, furniture, books and toys all rode the water, and further out something that looked like a garden shed sailed on the waters.

Another scream and this time Grace could pinpoint it. The Grubbs' house, Dora standing on her front veranda, water all around her, lapping at her feet, but seemingly safe, although she screamed and pointed and screamed again.

Grace pushed her way through shallow water towards the house, feeling how stupid it was to be carrying an umbrella with floodwaters up to her waist.

'No, no!' Dora cried, waving her arms when she saw Grace approaching. 'It's not me, it's the kids,' she yelled, pointing out into the maelstrom, towards the garden shed. 'The pantry broke off the house. I had the kids in there because it was safe and, look.'

'What kids?' Grace yelled, wondering if the cyclone had affected Dora's rationality. From what Grace had learned, Dora's 'kids' were in their thirties and living far from Crocodile Creek.

'CJ and Lily. I was minding them then Molly had the pups and the kids wanted to be there, and they're all in that room.'

Peering through the falling rain, Grace could almost imagine white, scared faces in the doorway of what she'd taken to be a shed.

'It will stop at the bridge,' she said to Dora. 'Have you got a cellphone?'

Dora shook her head.

'No matter, I've got a radio. Hopefully it's waterproof. I'll swim out to the kids and radio from there, but in the meantime, if anyone comes by, tell them to get onto the police and let them know to meet us at the bridge.'

Meet us at the bridge? she thought as she waded deeper and deeper into the murky water. As if they were going for a pleasure jaunt on the river.

Tourists went out on the river, but that was to look for and photograph crocodiles.

This was the creek, not the river, she reminded herself, but she still felt fear shiver up her spine.

'No,' she said firmly. 'Crocodiles have enough sense to stay out of flooded rivers *and* creeks.'

She bent into the filthy water to pull off her boots, then began to swim, setting her eyes on the floating bit of house, praying it would stay afloat at least until she got there.

The water fought her, pushing her one way

and then another, making her task seem almost impossible. But then she looked up and saw the children. Cal's son, CJ, and Lily, Charles's ward, clinging to each other in the doorway of the floating room. Then CJ left the safety of the room, venturing out onto what must have been a bit more veranda, bending over as if to reach into the water.

'Stay back,' she yelled at him. 'Get back inside.'

He looked up as if surprised to see her, then pointed down to the water beside him.

'It's Sport!' he called, and Grace sighed as she splashed towards them. Now she had a dog to rescue as well.

'I'll get him,' she called to CJ, then she put her head down and ploughed through the last twenty metres separating her from the children.

Sport was struggling to get his one front foot onto the decking, and Grace grabbed him and boosted him up, then, fearful that her weight might unbalance the makeshift boat and bring them all into the water, she called to the kids to stay back as far as they could and eased her body up until she could sit on the wooden boards. Then, with caution, she got on to her hands and knees so she could crawl towards them.

She looked around, realising the pantry must once have been part of the veranda because a bit of veranda was still attached, working like an outrigger to keep the structure afloat.

For how long?

With legs and arms trembling either from the swim or fear, she hesitated, breathing deeply, trying to work out what might lie ahead.

She guessed they were maybe three hundred yards from the bridge, and she was reasonably sure the bridge would stop them, but whether it would also sink them was the question.

Kids first.

She crawled forward, wondering where Sport had gone, then entered the small room, where preserves and cereal and sauce bottles were jumbled in with two small children, two dogs, and too many newborn puppies for Grace to count.

'It's like being on a boat, isn't it, Grace?' CJ said as Grace knelt and wrapped her arms around the children.

'It is indeed,' she said, realising he'd been boosting Lily's confidence with talk of boats and adventure. CJ had never lacked imagination. 'And soon it's going to dock down at the bridge and we can all get off. I'm going to radio for someone to meet us there, OK?'

She detached the children, patted the wet Sport and the only slightly drier Molly—was Sport the father of this brood that he'd come through a cyclone to be with their mother? Did dog love work that way? Like human love?—and walked outside to radio SES Headquarters and explain the situation.

'Dora Grubb's been in touch,' Paul told her, 'and we've notified the police to be ready at the bridge. Have you any idea how you're going to get them off?'

'If all goes well and we don't sink, I'll pass

the two kids over to rescuers then the pups and then the dogs.'

'Dogs?' Paul echoed weakly. 'Dora mentioned her dog Molly and some pups, but dogs?'

'Harry's Sport has joined the party,' Grace told him. 'Though what a policeman is doing with an un-neutered dog I'd like to know.'

'I guess Harry thought Sport had already lost a leg so didn't deserve to lose anything else,' Paul suggested.

Grace huffed, 'Men,' and stopped transmission.

Time to see to the kids and try to work out how to keep them all alive if their fragile craft sank.

Harry was in a meeting with local councillors, electricity officials and city engineers when he heard something different over the radio he had chattering quietly on the table beside him.

He'd been paying little attention to it, but had known he had to keep it on, half listening for any situation where he might be needed. Half listening for a report that Georgie and Alistair had returned with two kids.

But nothing so far.

Flood reports had begun to come in, but nothing serious as yet, until he heard a combination of words—flood, house, bridge, kids, and nurse from the hospital with them.

Instinct told him it was Grace and he turned the volume up a little, then, when he realised the transmission had finished, he excused himself to walk to a corner of the room and use his phone to call the station.

'No worries, Harry,' the constable who answered said. 'We've got it all under control. A bit of the Grubbs' house came adrift with a couple of kids inside, but Grace swam out to the kids and she's radioed in and reckons the room will stop when it hits the bridge. We'll have people there—'

'I'm on my way,' Harry said, anger and concern churning inside him. Grace accused him of taking risks and here she was, swimming through floodwaters filled with debris, snakes and crocodiles.

Stupid, stupid, stupid woman!

'Small crisis,' he said to the people gathered in the room as he strode out the door. Contingency plans could wait, or could be sorted without him—he needed to be on that bridge.

Which, please God, would hold.

How detailed had the engineer's inspection been? How minutely had he checked the structure?

He drove towards the bridge, passing more and more people on the rain-drenched streets, all with the bewildered expressions of disaster sur-vivors. Rebuilding houses was one thing—could you rebuild people?

Maybe…

Maybe the anger he felt towards Grace was something to do with his own rebuilding process…

He swore at himself for such inane philoso-phising when his thoughts should be centred on rescue.

Swore at the Grubbs for their ridiculous habit of adding bits and pieces to their house—bits and pieces that could break off and be swept away by floodwaters. Damn it all, he'd seen that bit of the house—it had been ready to slide into the creek without the flood.

Then he was at the bridge and one look at the people gathered there made him shake his head. It was like a party—the fishing competition all over again. How word had got around he had no idea, but there must be fifteen people on the bridge with more arriving on foot and on surf-skis. And, far off, he could hear an outboard engine.

A boat! He should have thought of that first, but then he shook his head. With the debris in the water, whoever was running their outboard was also running the risk of hitting a submerged log and being tipped into the water.

Someone else to rescue.

He stopped the car and climbed out, looking upstream. One of his men came to stand beside him, explaining they'd stopped all traffic on the bridge and were getting the volunteers to spread out across it. Beyond his car an ambulance pulled up, then the hospital four-wheel-drive, a woman tumbling out.

The constable was saying something about ropes being in place and more equipment coming, but Harry barely heard, his eyes on the bobbing, slewing apparition riding the water towards them.

The craft looked for all the world like a Chinese junk floating on some exotic harbour, but then an eddy caught it and twirled it round and round, and above the raging noise of the water Harry heard a child's shrill scream.

His stomach was clenched so tightly it was like a boulder in his abdomen, and he wanted to plunge into the waters and swim towards the now teetering room.

'It's going to hit hard—let's get some tyres ready to give it some protection.'

Harry turned towards the man who'd spoken,

recognising a member of Grace's SES team, then he saw Paul Gibson, looking grey and ill but there because a member of his service was in danger.

'There are tyres and rubber mooring buffers on the way,' Paul said, then pointed to an SES truck pulling up on the road at the end of the bridge. 'Or just arriving.'

More volunteers poured out of the truck, opening hatches to collect their booty. Soon they were walking across the bridge, mooring tyres and buffers in their arms.

'We'll wait until she gets closer,' Paul said, 'then work out where it's going to hit and use the protection there.'

Harry was glad to let him take charge. He was far too emotionally involved to be making cool decisions, and rescuing Grace and the children would need the coolest of heads.

Why he was so emotionally involved he'd think about later.

The wobbly room came closer, moving faster as the main current of the creek caught it and swirled it onward towards the bridge. He could see Grace now. She appeared to have wedged herself in the doorway of the room, and she had the two children clasped in her arms.

It made sense. All around town there were doorways still standing, the frames holding firm while the walls around them were blown to smithereens.

It looked like she was wearing a bikini, which, to Harry's dazed and frantic mind, seemed strange but still acceptable. Once he'd accepted a room floating on the creek, he could accept just about anything.

He moved across the bridge, trying to guess where they'd hit, needing to be right there to help her off.

And to rescue the children, of course.

A dog was barking.

Sport?

Harry peered towards the voyagers.

Grace couldn't have been stupid enough to swim out there for Sport?

Love me, love my dog?

His mind was going. It was the waiting. The room was barely moving now, pulled out of the main channel into an eddy. If he got a boat, they could row out to it.

The thought was turning practical when a child screamed again and the structure tipped, taking in water as it met the current once again, and this time hurtling towards the bridge.

Harry was there when it hit with such a sick crunching noise he couldn't believe it had stayed afloat. Now anger mixed with relief and his mind was rehearsing the lecture he was going to give Grace about taking risks.

He took a child, Lily, and passed her on to someone, took the other child, CJ, chattering away about his adventure but far paler than he should have been.

'I've got him,' someone said, and CJ was reefed out of his arms. He turned to see Gina, CJ's mother, clasping her son to her body, tears streaming down her face.

CJ kept talking but it was background noise. Harry's attention was on the rapidly sinking room.

'Here,' Grace said, coming out of the small room and passing a squirming sack to one of the SES men.

Not a bikini at all. It was a bra, but white, not blue.

Harry reached out to grab her but she disappeared inside again, returning with Sport, who saw Harry and leapt onto his chest. He fell beneath the weight of the dog's sudden assault, and was sitting on the bridge, comforting Sport, when Grace passed the Grubbs' dog Molly, a strange Dalmatian cross and no lightweight, across to rescuers.

Harry pushed Sport off him, and stepped around the crowd who'd emptied the sack— Grace's T-shirt—of puppies onto the bridge and were now oohing and aahing over them.

He was at the railing, reaching out for her, when the timbers groaned and shrieked, then something gave way and the little room was sucked beneath the water and the bridge.

'Grace!'

He saw her body flying through the air, registered a rope, and stood up on the railing, ready to dive in.

Paul stopped him.

'We slipped the loop of a lasso over her before she started passing the kids and dogs. She jumped clear as the timber gave way, so we'll just wait until she surfaces then haul her in.'

Haul her in?

As if she were a bag of sugar-cane mulch?

More anger, this time joining with the crippling concern he was feeling as he and all the watchers on the bridge searched the waters for a sight of her.

He grabbed the rope from the volunteer who was holding it and began to pull, feeling the dragging weight on the end of it, wondering if he was drowning Grace by pulling on it but needing to get her out of the water.

Others joined him, then her body, limply unconscious, surfaced by the bridge. Eager hands reached out to grab her, but as she was lifted from the water, Harry grasped her in his arms, vaguely hearing one of the paramedics giving orders, telling him to put her down, turn her on her side, check her pulse, her breathing.

But this was Grace and he hugged her to him, although he knew he had to do as the man had said—had to put her down to save her life.

He dropped to his knees and gently laid her on the tarred surface of the road, seeing sharp gravel from the recent resurfacing—little stones that would dig into her skin.

That's when he knew, with gut-wrenching certainty, that it wasn't physical attraction—right then when he was thinking about sharp gravel pressing into Grace's skin…

CHAPTER TEN

THE two paramedics took over, moving him aside with kind firm hands, clearing her airway, forcing air into her lungs, breathing for her, then waiting, then breathing again.

No chest compressions, which meant her heart was beating, but somehow registering this information failed to make Harry feel any better.

He loved her?

The concept was so mind-blowing he had to keep repeating it to himself in the hope the three words would eventually become a statement, not an incredulous question.

Was it too late?

He watched the two men work, saw oxygen delivered through bag pressure and a needle being inserted into the back of her hand. But mostly he just watched her face, the skin so pale it took on a bluish hue, her freckles dark against it.

One day he'd kiss each freckle, and with each kiss repeat, 'I love you.' He'd make up for all the time they'd lost, he'd—

Sport abandoned his paramour and puppies and came to press against him. Harry dug his fingers into the dog's rough coat, despair crowding his senses as he looked into the animal's liquid brown eyes and made silent promises he hoped he'd have the opportunity to keep.

'We're moving her now,' one of the paramedics said, and together they lifted Grace onto a stretcher, raised it to wheeling height, then ran with it towards their ambulance.

Running? Did running mean the situation was even more disastrous than he imagined?

Harry followed at a jog, cursing himself now that he'd sat communing with his dog, now loping unsteadily beside him, when he should have been asking questions about Grace's condition.

'What do you think?' he demanded, arriving at the ambulance as the driver was shutting the back door.

'She's breathing on her own—although we're still assisting her—and her heart rate's OK, but she's unconscious so obviously she hit her head somewhere underwater. There'll be water in her lungs, and she'll have swallowed it as well, so all we can do is get her into hospital and pump antibiotics into her and hope the concussion resolves itself.'

Totally unsatisfactory, especially that last bit, Harry thought as he drove to the hospital behind the ambulance. His radio was chattering non-stop and he really should return to the meeting, but he had to see Grace first—wanted her conscious—wanted to tell her...

But seeing Grace was one thing—speaking to her impossible.

'You're needed other places, Harry. I'll contact you if there's any change at all.'

Harry wanted to shrug off the hand Charles

was resting on his arm and tell the man to go to hell, but he knew Charles was right. There was nothing he could do here, except glare at the nursing staff and grunt when the doctors told him all they could do was wait and see.

Wait and see what, for heaven's sake?

Frustration grumbled within him, and tiredness, so heavy he could barely keep upright, blurred his senses. He left the hospital, pausing in the car park to call the station and tell them he was going home to sleep for an hour then back to the civic centre to hear the latest in the evacuation and services restoration plans.

Power had to come first—without it water and sewerage systems failed to work. It would be reconnected first in the area this side of the creek, the original settlement, where the hospital and police station were. But with the flooding…

On top of that, there was still no word from Georgie—not since the one radio transmission that might or might not have come from her. She had his radio—why *hadn't* she called in?

It was the inactivity on that front that ate at him. Until the road was cleared they couldn't get vehicles in, while the heavy rain made an air search impossible. It was still too wet and windy for one of the light helicopters to fly searchers in—if they had searchers available.

Which they didn't! Sending sleep-depleted volunteers into the mountains was asking for trouble.

So all he could do was wait. Wait for the army, with its fresh and experienced manpower, and heavy-duty helicopters that could cope with wind and rain.

Or wait to hear.

And keep believing that she and Alistair were sensible people and would stay safe…

At midnight, when exhausted city officials and the first wave of army brass had headed for whatever beds they could find, Harry returned to the hospital. Grace, he was told, was in the ICU.

'Intensive Care? What's she doing in there?' he demanded, and a bemused nurse who'd probably only ever seen nice-guy Harry, looked startled.

'She's unconscious and running a low-grade fever and has fluid in her lungs so it's likely she's hatching pneumonia, in which case the fever could get worse. And on top of that there's the chance it's something nastier than pneumonia. Who knows what germs were lurking in that water?'

And having set him back on his heels, almost literally, with this information, the nurse gave a concerned smile.

'We're *all* very worried about her, Harry,' she added, just in case he thought he was the only one concerned.

Harry nodded, and even tried to smile, but that was too damn difficult when Grace was lying in Intensive Care, incubating who knew what disease.

He strode towards the isolated unit, determined to see her, but no one blocked his path or muttered about family only.

She was lying in the bed, beneath a sheet, wires and tubes snaking from her body.

So small and fragile-looking—still as death.

Gina sat beside her, holding her hand and talking to her. She looked up at Harry and, although wobbly, at least *her* smile was working.

'She always talks to coma patients when she's nursing them,' Gina said, her eyes bright with unshed tears. 'I thought it was the least I could do.'

Then the tears spilled over and slipped down her cheeks.

'She saved my son. She plunged into that filthy, stinking water and swam out to save him. She can't die, Harry, she just can't.'

'She won't,' Harry promised, although he knew it was a promise he couldn't make come true. Gina stood up and he slipped into the chair and took the warm, pale hand she passed to him.

Grace's hand, so small and slight, Grace's fingers, nails neatly trimmed.

'Does she know?' Gina asked, and Harry, puzzled by the question, turned towards her.

'That you love her?' Gina expanded, with a much better smile this time.

'No,' he said, the word cutting deep inside his chest as he thought of Grace dying without knowing. Then he, too, smiled. 'But I'm here to tell her and I'll keep on telling her. You're right, she does believe unconscious patients hear things, so surely she'll be listening.'

He paused, then said awkwardly to Gina, 'She loves me, you know. She told me earlier today.'

It must have been the wonder in his voice that made Gina chuckle. She leant forward and hugged him.

'That's not exactly news, you know, Harry. The entire hospital's known how Grace felt for the past six months.'

'She told you?' Harry muttered. 'Told everyone but me?'

Gina smiled again, a kindly smile.

'Would you have listened?' she said softly, then she gave him another hug. 'And she didn't tell us all in words, you know. We just saw it in the way she lit up whenever you were around and the way she said your name and the way she glowed on meeting nights. There are a thousand ways to say "I love you", Harry, and I think your Grace knows most of them.'

'*My* Grace,' Harry muttered, unable to believe he hadn't seen what everyone else had. Hadn't seen the thousand ways Grace had said 'I love you'. But Gina was already gone, pausing in the doorway to tell him Cal would be by later and to promise that Grace would have someone sitting with her all the time, talking to her and holding her hand so she could find her way back from wherever she was right now.

Again it was Charles who told Harry to leave.

'I don't ever sleep late—growing up on a cattle property in the tropics, where the best work was done before the heat of midday, instils the habit of early waking.'

He'd wheeled into the room while Harry had been dozing in the chair, his body bent forward so his head rested on Grace's bed, her hand still clasped in his.

'So I'm doing the early shift with Grace,' Charles continued, manoeuvring his chair into position. 'If you want some technicalities, her breathing and pulse rate suggest she's regaining consciousness but the infection's taking hold and her temperature is fluctuating rather alarmingly.'

Harry knew he had to go. He had to get some sleep then return to the planning room. Evacuation of people who had family or friends to go to close by had begun yesterday and today they were hoping to begin mass evacuation of up to a thousand women and children. Defence force transport planes would bring in water, tents, food and building supplies and fly people out to Townsville or Cairns. Power would come on in stages, and it could be months before all services were fully operational. Getting people out of the crippled town would ease the pressure on the limited services.

He left the hospital reluctantly, and was in a

meeting when Cal phoned to say Grace had regained consciousness but was feverish and disoriented, mostly sleeping, which was good.

Harry raged against the constraints that held him in the meeting, knowing he couldn't go rushing to Grace's side when he was needed right where he was. But later…

Later she was sleeping, so he slipped into the chair vacated this time for him by her friend Marcia, and took her hand, talking quietly to her, telling her he was there.

Grace turned her head and opened her eyes, gazing at him with a puzzled frown. Then the frown cleared, as if she'd worked out who he was, and she said, 'Go away Harry,' as clear as day.

Nothing else, just, 'Go away Harry.' Then she shut her eyes again as if not seeing him would make him vanish.

She was feverish, he told himself, and didn't know what she was saying, but when she woke an hour later and saw him there, her eyes filled with tears and this time the knife she used to stab right into his heart was phrased differently.

'I don't want you here, Harry,' she said, her voice piteously weak, the single tear sliding down her cheek doing further damage to his already lacerated heart.

Cal was there, and his quiet 'I don't want her getting upset' got Harry to his feet.

But go?

How could he walk away and leave her lying there, so still and pale beneath the sheet?

'There's work for you to do elsewhere,' Cal reminded him, following him out of the ICU and stopping beside the wide window where Cal had propped himself. 'I'll keep you posted about her condition.'

So Harry worked and listened to Cal telling him Grace was as well as could be expected, not exactly improving but the new antibiotics they were trying seemed to be keeping the infection stable.

It was in her lungs and now he had to worry if pulling her through the water had made things worse, but there were no answers to that kind of question so he worked some more, and went home to sleep from time to time, to feed Sport and talk to him of love.

On the third day after Willie had blown the town apart, Grace was moved out of the ICU and two days later released from hospital, but only as far as the doctors' house, where resident medical staff could fuss over her and keep an eye on her continuing improvement at the same time.

So it was there that Harry went, late one afternoon, when the urgency had left the restoration programme and he could take time off without feeling guilty.

She was on the veranda, Gina told him. On the old couch. As he walked through the house he sensed Gina tactfully making sure all the other residents had vamoosed.

He came out onto the veranda and there was Grace, pale but pretty, her golden curls shining in the sun that had finally blessed them with its presence and what looked like a dirty black rag draped across her knees.

'Grace?' he said, hating the fact he sounded so tentative, yet fearful she'd once again send him away.

'Harry?'

The word echoed with surprise, as if he was the last person she expected to be calling on her.

A thought that added to his tension!

'Come and sit down. I'm not supposed to move about much. One lung collapsed during all the fuss and it's not quite better yet, so I'm stuck in bed or on the couch, but at least from here I can see the sea. It's quietened down a lot, hasn't it?'

Harry stared at her. This was the Grace he used to know. Actually, it was a much frailer and quieter and less bubbly version of her, but still that Grace, the one who was his friend. Chatting to him, easing over difficult moments—showing love?

He had no idea—totally confused by what he'd come to realise after that terrible moment when Grace had disappeared beneath the murky floodwaters and then by the 'go away' order she'd issued from the hospital bed.

Stepping tentatively, although the old house had withstood Willie's fury better than most of the houses in town, he moved towards the couch, then sat where Grace was patting the space beside her on the couch.

'I thought I'd lost you,' he began, then wondered if she was well enough for him to be dumping his emotions on her. 'You disappeared beneath the waters and I realised what a fool I'd been, Grace. Stupid, stupid fool, hiding away from any emotion all this time, letting the mess I'd made of my marriage to Nikki overshadow my life, then, worst of all, blaming physical attraction for the kiss. I know it's too late to be telling you all this—that somehow with the bump on your head you got some common sense and decided you could do far better than me—but, like you had to say it when I thought I'd lost Sport, so I have to say it now. I love you, Grace.'

Having bumbled his way this far through the conversation, Harry paused and looked at the recipient of all this information. She was staring at him as if he'd spoken in tongues, so he tried again.

'I love you, Grace,' he said, and wondered if he should perhaps propose right now and make a total fool of himself all at once, or leave the foolish proposal part for some other time.

'You love me?' she finally whispered, and he waited for the punch-line, the 'Oh, Harry, it's too late' or however she might word it.

But nothing followed so he took her hands in his and nodded, then as tension gripped so hard it hurt, he rushed into speech again.

'I know you don't feel the same way but you did love me once, so maybe that love is only hidden, not completely gone.'

'Loved you once?' she said, and this time the repetition was stronger, and now her blue eyes were fixed on his. 'What makes you think I'd ever stop loving you, Harry?'

He stared at her, trying to work out what this

question meant—trying to equate it with the 'go away, Harry' scenarios.

Couldn't do it, so he had to ask.

'You sent me away,' he reminded her. 'At the hospital, you said to go away and that you didn't want me there.'

'Oh, Harry,' she whispered, and rested her head against his chest. 'You silly man, thinking I'd stopped loving you. As soon stop the sun from rising as me stop loving you.'

This definitely made him happy, happy enough to press a kiss to her soft curls, but he was still confused. Maybe more confused than ever.

'But you sent me away when all I wanted was to be with you.'

She turned towards him and lifted one hand to rest it on his cheek.

'I didn't want you sitting by my bedside—not at that hospital—not again. I didn't want you remembering all that pain and anguish, and suffering for things that happened in the past through no real fault of yours.'

She pressed her lips to his, a present of a kiss.

'The fact that you talked about Nikki and your marriage suggested you were ready to move on, so I didn't want you being pulled back into the past because of me.'

'You'd have liked me there?' Harry asked, unable to believe that, sick as she had been, she'd still found this one way of the thousand to say 'I love you'.

'Of course,' she whispered, nestling her head on his chest. 'Loving you the way I do, I always want you near.'

She smiled up at him, then added, 'Look how pathetic I am—look at this.'

She lifted the black rag from her knee and it took a moment for him to recognise it as his dinner jacket.

'I brushed off most of the mud and when Gina said I had to keep something over my knees when I sit out in the breeze, it seemed the best knee cover any woman could have. Gina wanted to have it dry-cleaned but it would have come back smelling of dry-cleaning fluid, not Harry, so there you are.'

Her smile mocked her sentimentality but it went straight to Harry's heart, because it wobbled a bit as if she felt she'd made a fool of herself.

'Snap!' he said softly, and reached into his shirt pocket, pulling out a very tattered blue ribbon he'd kept with him since that fateful night.

Then he closed his arms around her and pulled her close, pressing kisses on her head and telling her things he hadn't realised he knew, about how much he loved her, but more, that he admired her and thought her wonderful, and how soon would she be his wife?

They'd reached the kissing stage when a voice interrupted them, a voice filled with the disgust that only a five-year-old could muster when faced with demonstrations of love.

'You're kissing, Grace,' CJ said, coming close enough for them to see he held a squirming puppy in his hands. 'I didn't think policemen did that kind of thing.'

'Well, now you know they do,' Harry said, tucking Grace tightly against his body, never wanting to let her go.

CJ sighed.

'Then I guess I'll have to be a fireman instead,' he said, passing the puppy to Harry. 'Mum said you were here, and this is the one Lily and I decided should be yours because it looks more like Sport than all the others, although it's got four legs.'

Harry took the squirming bundle of fur and peered into its face. He failed to see any resemblance at all to Sport, but knew once CJ and Lily had decided something, it was futile to argue.

'Do you mind if we have two dogs?' he asked Grace, who smiled at him so lovingly he had to kiss her again, further disgusting CJ, who rescued the pup and departed, making fire-siren noises as he raced away.

'Two dogs and lots of kids,' Grace said, returning his kisses with enthusiasm. 'Is that OK with you?'

Harry thought of all he now knew about Grace's background. Loving without being loved must have been so hard for someone with her warm and caring nature.

'Of course we'll have lots of kids,' he promised, and was about to suggest they start on the project right now when he remembered she was just out of hospital and very frail.

But not too frail to kiss him as she whispered, 'Thank you.' Then added, 'I love you, Harry Blake,' and made his day complete.

MEDICAL™

—/\— *Large Print* —/\—

Titles for the next six months...

May

THE MAGIC OF CHRISTMAS — Sarah Morgan
THEIR LOST-AND-FOUND FAMILY — Marion Lennox
CHRISTMAS BRIDE-TO-BE — Alison Roberts
HIS CHRISTMAS PROPOSAL — Lucy Clark
BABY: FOUND AT CHRISTMAS — Laura Iding
THE DOCTOR'S PREGNANCY BOMBSHELL — Janice Lynn

June

CHRISTMAS EVE BABY — Caroline Anderson
LONG-LOST SON: BRAND-NEW FAMILY — Lilian Darcy
THEIR LITTLE CHRISTMAS MIRACLE — Jennifer Taylor
TWINS FOR A CHRISTMAS BRIDE — Josie Metcalfe
THE DOCTOR'S VERY SPECIAL — Kate Hardy
CHRISTMAS
A PREGNANT NURSE'S CHRISTMAS WISH — Meredith Webber

July

THE ITALIAN'S NEW-YEAR — Sarah Morgan
MARRIAGE WISH
THE DOCTOR'S LONGED-FOR FAMILY — Joanna Neil
THEIR SPECIAL-CARE BABY — Fiona McArthur
THEIR MIRACLE CHILD — Gill Sanderson
SINGLE DAD, NURSE BRIDE — Lynne Marshall
A FAMILY FOR THE CHILDREN'S DOCTOR — Dianne Drake

MILLS & BOON®
Pure reading pleasure

0408 LP 2P P1 Medical

MEDICAL™

Large Print

August

THE DOCTOR'S BRIDE BY SUNRISE	Josie Metcalfe
FOUND: A FATHER FOR HER CHILD	Amy Andrews
A SINGLE DAD AT HEATHERMERE	Abigail Gordon
HER VERY SPECIAL BABY	Lucy Clark
THE HEART SURGEON'S SECRET SON	Janice Lynn
THE SHEIKH SURGEON'S PROPOSAL	Olivia Gates

September

THE SURGEON'S FATHERHOOD SURPRISE	Jennifer Taylor
THE ITALIAN SURGEON CLAIMS HIS BRIDE	Alison Roberts
DESERT DOCTOR, SECRET SHEIKH	Meredith Webber
A WEDDING IN WARRAGURRA	Fiona Lowe
THE FIREFIGHTER AND THE SINGLE MUM	Laura Iding
THE NURSE'S LITTLE MIRACLE	Molly Evans

October

THE DOCTOR'S ROYAL LOVE-CHILD	Kate Hardy
HIS ISLAND BRIDE	Marion Lennox
A CONSULTANT BEYOND COMPARE	Joanna Neil
THE SURGEON BOSS'S BRIDE	Melanie Milburne
A WIFE WORTH WAITING FOR	Maggie Kingsley
DESERT PRINCE, EXPECTANT MOTHER	Olivia Gates

MILLS & BOON®

Pure reading pleasure

0408 LP 2P P2 Medical

ten of those years I have been a satisfactorily married man—I have eight dear children, Juan. Yet in that period I have been 'discovered' to be the lover of at least eleven ladies of the nobility, most of them—so far as I know—almost as high-bred and of as impeccable virtue as the great lady you have just named, you ass. Yet they still hold their heads up in society, and so do I and my wife and family—and I am more than ever a Secretary of State."

"I have always known those stories to be true of you——"

"Indeed? That's rather generous of you, Juan! But you attribute powers to me—of every kind—which truly I don't possess. And now will you please be a good fellow and clear off to a more suitable place with your kitchen-boy's tattle?"

"You are not going to have your bluff called, I see. But that doesn't alter anything. I know that what I have said is true—and for Ruy Gomez's sake, for his honour and his children, I protest with my whole soul against such a dis-graceful situation—oh God!" he moved at last, pacing a short distance across the room. "Oh God! He was our friend and father, Antonio! He worshipped and cherished her! I was executor of his will, as you know, and he entrusted many of her and her children's affairs to me! I knew his heart in these private things. And so did you! Ah Christ, Antonio, so did you!" He paused, but Perez continued to stare at him in cool amazement. "And now—this hideous, backstairs dishonour in his house and bed!"

" 'Backstairs dishonour' is good! The lady you are traducing so effectively is an honour whom many greater men than you and I would have climbed any old stairs to reach. We've known that always, Juan. We used to debate their chances—including the king's, do you re-member?—here in this very Alcázar, when we worked together down the corridor, in the secretaries' room. With Ruy alive to be dishonoured. But you were young then, and even a touch humorous."

"Ruy was alive then, and could be trusted to manage his own wife."

"Agreed. But say this notion of yours were true—say, for the fun of the thing, that the Princess of Eboli *were* having a love-affair with, well, *you*, or me, or the French Ambassador—what of it?"

"She is having a love-affair as you call it! And not with me, and not with the French Ambassador! And I tell you it is intolerable."

"Why? Because it's not with you?"

Escovedo brushed the flippancy aside as if it were a gnat.

"Do you really require to know why? She's elderly——"

"About eight years younger than you and I, if I remember rightly——"

"She's ugly——"

"*Belle laide*," said Antonio. "Magnificently beautiful, I've always thought. But then my taste in women is extraordinarily good. I take what I can get, I grant you—but all the same, I know what I like." He laughed and stood up again. "All right, old friend, you've broken up my night's work to tell me that Her Highness of Eboli is elderly and ugly, and is therefore to be held in abhorrence for consoling her miserable life with a love-affair. If the only way of getting you to go home now is to say that you're right about all this, naturally I say it. You're perfectly right, Escovedo, and your zeal for chastity is consoling. And now—please may I get on with my work?"

"I would have done anything at any time for Ruy Gomez. He knew that. And just because he's gone I will not see his name dishonoured in intrigue, I tell you, his children rendered absurd and their fortunes squandered on a venal, climbing jackanapes whose fame and destiny were made by him!"

"Very good. Go to it—since you so conceive your duty."

There was a pause in which the two looked at each other. Antonio's face was cold and neutral; Escovedo's mottled with anger. Yet when he spoke again his voice was so steady that it might have been Perez's.

"It may be necessary for me to tell the king about it," he said.

Perez seemed to weigh this remark judicially before he answered.

"Indulging you in your hypothesis, which you haven't even *tried* to prove to me——"

"I don't have to, to you!"

"Indulging you, I say—may I remind you that Philip is still a bit in love with Ana de Mendoza? On his own peculiar terms, I grant you, but still, I'd say he's in love. Apart from that, he's very, very fond of her."

"All the more reason why he should see her as she is."

"Maybe. Only, he doesn't like bringers of bad news. Oh Escovedo, you fool—are you in love with death?"

"It comes to every man."

"No. Some men run to find it. And believe me, if just now you add to your errors with Don Juan the madness of making this grave accusation against someone so dear to the king—if you do that, you are finished."

"What matter? I shall have saved Ruy Gomez's honour."

"But he came from Portugal! He was a man of sense. He didn't have this Castilian disease about honour! Moreover, how will you have 'saved' it? By starting up an enormous and laughable scandal about his wife and family? Ah, poor Ruy! How he'd shudder at your crassness!"

"Or at your cynicism."

"Oh yes—at that too. He used to warn me against it—but one can only be oneself in the end. You, however, are being somewhat excessively yourself of late. But don't you see? If you do tell Philip what you suspect about the Princess, it will take him years, very possibly, to decide whether or not to believe you. Meantime he will torture himself, and take vengeance for his discomfort on you. It is even probable that he will have you despatched—you know how easily he does these things—before he makes up his mind to ask you for proof. But say he *does* ask you for proofs——"

"I have them."

"Aye! Against the massed oaths, threats and testimonies of all the Mendozas of Spain and all their vassals and cousins and chaplains and servants; against the iron ring of loyalty and if necessary perjury which Ruy Gomez's household could instantly form about his widow; against Madrid's immediate sympathy with any woman so preposterously singled out for censorship; above all, against Philip's vain and megalomaniac desire to have you vigorously disproved—for if he doesn't love Ana, believe me, he loves the legend of their love, he loves the gossip and the echo of it, and its reminder of gayer days, he loves to think, perhaps, that only their shared love of Ruy prevented him and Ana from giving really flagrant scandal long ago; also he loves to think that whatever he prizes no man touches save with his royal permission. He gave her to Ruy—so that was all right. But he's not giving her away again, whether or not he wants her—so you see, against all that, above all against Philip's colossal vanity, you'd bring your proofs—a bought footman or sewing maid or pantry-boy—servants too young and raw to know that you don't sell the great for a few ducats, and that if you do, that finishes you for employment by any majordomo in Spanish society henceforward. No, no—I don't care what you think you know against Ana de Mendoza—as I once loved you, I implore you now for your own sake to forget it. Don Juan of Austria has led you quite far enough into the displeasure of the king—much too far for my liking, I promise you. In sanity's name forgo this other dreadful whim. It's unbecoming anyway. It's back door stuff—and very, very shocking from you."

Escovedo smiled a little.

"That's a good speech—in difficult circumstances, Antonio. You certainly are a trained diplomatist."

"Yes. So well trained that I see diplomacy behind all this gloomy and 'honourable' fuss of yours to-night. I see your game, in fact. But you'll lose it, every way. You're on the wrong tack. Consider well, however, what I've just said. He's a brave man indeed who tampers with Philip's personal illusions."

"I have usually been as brave as the average."

"Then let that suffice. I for one like your being alive, 'Escoda'."

"Thank you. Good night."

"Good night."

After Escovedo left him, Antonio sat still at his desk for some minutes, with his eyes half-closed. When midnight rang from the chapel across the court-yard he opened his eyes and began to unfold the papers he had covered during the interview. Alert and composed, he set to work again.

III

Ana heard his quiet footsteps in the long sitting-room. The door which led from there to her bedroom was half-open.

"You may come in," she said.

Antonio entered the bedroom and crossed to her bed. He carried a tray with wine and glasses, and smiled from it to her.

"Do you mind if I drink?"

"Do I ever?"

He set down the tray and sat on the edge of the bed.

Two candles were burning in a branch-candlestick beside her. She lay low on her pillow; her hair fell cloudily away from her high forehead; the black silk patch, narrow and tragic, fitted closely along her right cheek-bone. She stretched her beautiful hand to him and he took it in his.

"You're very thin, Ana, too thin. You seem almost as if you're not there at all when you lie flat like that."

"I wasn't expecting you to-night."

"I won't stay long. But I find it almost impossible now to pass your gate. I'm bound to you." He relinquished her hand and poured himself some wine. "Are you bound to me?"

"Yes. But I can pass your gate."

He smiled.

"Well—you have to, after all."

"I think that wouldn't matter if I couldn't."

"You mean you'd go in—to Juana's house?"

"I'd have to, if I couldn't pass it."

They laughed together.

"Thank God then that you can pass it," said Antonio.

"Yes. Because I'm troublesome, really."

He mused over her, sipping wine.

"That's true, I'm certain. And yet—you've never given anyone the least bit of trouble."

She made no answer. He looked at her and guessed that she was thinking of Mother Teresa de Jesús, and the Discalced Carmelites at Pastrana.

"But no one could know you at all well," he went on, ignoring her thought, "without apprehending that. The sense of threat in you."

She laughed.

"I'm no judge, as you know," she said, "but I think you must be a superlatively good lover."

"Actually, I am," he said gaily. "But why mention it now?"

"Because you come here, weary from your old Pope and Netherlands and Bey of Algiers, at two in the morning and you sit down and start talking, as if there was nothing else in the world, about *me*."

"Silly one, ah silly, inexperienced Ana, that's why I come to you! Because you always play that trick on me, and yet never, never let me see how it's done."

"I have no tricks—truly," she said. "What's troubling you, Anton?"

"Nothing now. Your watchman welcomed me in as kindly as usual just now. I passed that young footman you like, Estéban, in the patio; and in the corridor outside your rooms one of your maids bowed to me. Is it—is it all right for you, Ana?"

"No, it's all wrong. I don't need my chaplain to tell me that. But it isn't the servants' business. It's mine. It's also yours—and your wife's. No one else's."

"You cheat—that isn't what I meant."

"But alas, it's all I mean. I wish I were sophisticated like other ladies. What do they do to help you over this worry about the watchman and so on?"

"Ah! They get up to all sorts of plans and dodges—most fatiguing!"

"That's what I thought—fatiguing. And in spite of them my *dueña* always knows everything that everyone in Madrid is doing."

"I expect so. Does she know what you are doing?"

"Bernardina knows what happens in Madrid. But she doesn't always know why things happen. However, she can be surprised without fussing. She has good sense."

Antonio leant his back against a post at the foot of the bed and looked towards her with an expression of puzzled pleasure in his eyes.

"There ought to be more light," he said. "You look a bit too tragic just now—yes, even when you smile. Shall I give you some wine?" She shook her head. He refilled his own glass, and leant back again to the silk-curtained post. "There's a foreign painter in Toledo, a Greek called Theotocopuli——"

"The king was talking to me about him the other day——"

"Oh?"

"He's considering some canvases from him for El Escorial——"

"What good luck for the foreigner!"

"But Philip isn't at all sure that he likes his work."

"Neither am I, indeed. Very hysterical, saints and ecstasies. I was in his studio not long ago, with the Archbishop. By the way, did I tell you that that good friend of yours is getting his red hat? I'm glad—aren't you? But about this Greek, Theotocopuli—the point is that a lot of his praying boys and uplifted Annunciations and things remind me of *you*. In fact, I think that perhaps he ought to paint you. However, you'll have to grow a bit saintly first—at present he's not interested in worldliness."

"I'm not either, very much."

"Ana! You are the very epitome of it!"

"Perhaps that's why it doesn't interest me."

"But aren't you interested in yourself?"

"Immensely. That's why you're here. That's why I'm your lover."

"Ah! An experiment?"

To answer that as her answer came would be pompous and egotistical. So she laughed at herself instead. "Don't be hurt—you make me talk selfishly, you are so gracious. But you know, now, that I'm in love."

She said that and knew that it was true, true in the way she had surmised it might be before she made the experiment of taking him. Yet, pronounced, the sentence always struck her as over-blown, and she always felt her soul cock an eyebrow at it. For it sounded as if it were important, as if it proved something and justified the utterer. Whereas all it did was put her in her place, among sinners.

That was well enough. She was a sinner indeed, and at present shamelessly content to discover that she could in fact pursue the fabled pleasures of sexual intercourse to that point of irrational, participatory understanding and hunger which she had awaited legitimately in marriage, but which somehow there had just evaded her. Yet it was ironic to come to it illicitly at last, and find it accompanied by no more than a conventional, almost a comedy, sense of sin. It was ironic to feel like a loose woman. The fault—or the joke, rather, of that, since she would not censure him—was in Antonio's character. She suspected now that long ago when Philip, in the full flush of his sensual arrogance and restlessness, had attracted her so strongly, she had not become his mistress simply because he could not forgo the final obligation of his personal morality. An adultery here or there was nothing to Philip the king when he was young; but the sin against Ruy Gomez was outside his courage. She would never know if it had been outside hers, because Philip, for all his love-making, had never confronted her with the final decision. Theologians would say that the present sin against Juana de Coëllo, Antonio's wife, was exactly what hers and Philip's would have been against Ruy. But neither she nor Philip would agree with the theologians; for Antonio Perez was naturally amoral, and had never, even as he uttered them, regarded his marriage-vows as more than a formality. Juana and his children would always have his duty, his kindness and his care; and she, Ana enchantingly as he loved her now, was simply another delightful and necessary loose woman. After all, Ana thought amusedly, one cannot break the sixth Commandment alone—and Antonio had never accepted its existence. So, when she said—just privately to her lover, for their joint pleasure and because it was true—that she was in love, she felt nevertheless that she was making heavy weather.

Not that she would eschew or deprecate storminess; indeed when she was young she had never dreamt that she would spend her life becalmed. She had been a spoilt and arrogant child of many tempests. She touched her black silk eye-shade now, and pressed her finger-tips against her empty eye-socket. That absurd disaster, that duel with the silly boy from Granada, her father's page—what *was* his name?—had been the first real check to her spontaneousness. The first and perhaps for ever the most effective. In her lifetime she had not become resigned—though no one had ever heard her say so, not Ruy and not her mother—to being one-eyed, *tuerta*. She was not vain in the coquettish sense, but from babyhood had taken satisfaction in the rightness, by her own standards, of her own appearance. Beauty, good aspect, in things and people, moved her very quickly; she was attracted or repelled decisively by physical attributes. So when— having challenged and punished an Andalusian jibe at Castile's claim of premiership among the kingdoms of Spain —she found herself disfigured, made grotesque for ever, the shock to her self-confidence was so profound that she understood that if she was to live with it at all it must be on terms of apparently blank dismissal. Nobody must regret or condone a misfortune which only she could measure. She wrote herself, fifteen-year-old child-wife, to tell her elderly husband in the Lowlands what had befallen her, and she was grateful to him for the unperturbed tenderness with which he replied to her letter. Thereafter, as he learnt very deftly, save sometimes to call her *Tuerta*, and once or twice to joke about her soldierly sacrifice to Castile's honour, Ruy had to leave her disfigurement entirely in her keeping, and guess or not how little or much it troubled her. Sometimes she thought that she was faithful to him and good and tame and lived as he desired her to live merely because she had lost one eye; and sometimes she thought that he also thought so. But nothing of this was said, and they grew happy together, and she wore her diamond patch with a nonchalance which the world admired.

Antonio leant along and took her hand and kissed it.

"What are you thinking about now?"

"A quarrel I was in when I was a little girl."

"I thought so," he said delicately, and she looked at him with caution. Often she suspected that his intuitions were very accurate. Yet he never betrayed more than a glint of those she did not choose to have him uncover.

She marvelled at the delicacy of feeling to be found in men, and wondered if perhaps she perceived it only because the very few she knew were overtrained in courtiership and diplomacy.

"Ah! I nearly forgot," she said, and laughed somewhat shyly as she pulled a small leather box from under her pillow and gave it to him. "See if you like it, Antón."

Giving him presents was a great delight and yet made her nervous, for he had a zest for baubles and adornments which she did not share, and so she was always afraid of mischoosing and disappointing him. In defence, she bought extravagantly and from the most fashionable dealers—but she liked, as far as possible, to like what she gave him. So, as her taste was as restrained as his was florid, every present was a hazard.

"Another present?" His eyes gleamed. "Oh but you mustn't, Ana! Is this for Christmas?"

"No, no. This is just for now."

It was a bracelet, heavy, lissom, set with large, clear topazes. It had a heart-shaped clasp of diamonds.

"You wear these things, my Frenchified *mignon*."

"Indeed I do—or shall! Oh Ana! It's disgracefully beautiful!"

"Is it? As you know, I'm never sure——"

He laughed.

"How I'm debasing you! How much I'm teaching you! And everything wrong!"

"Put it on."

"Shall I?" He clipped it round his wrist and flourished it about delightedly. "Oh, but it's lovely! Shocking, shocking, Ana!"

"It was made in Paris—but the topazes came from our own empire——"

"Spoils of the Conquistadores!"

"Yes. It seems right that our Secretary of State should have some."

"You most indulgent, wicked Ana!"

He laughed and kissed her. And she felt inevitable delight rising in them both, and she welcomed it and was glad. Yet her spirit was saying to her simultaneously that even sensuality and sin, when they were reluctantly and late allowed, should have more to expose than that one was as natural a sinner as the next woman, a vulgar, satisfactory and satisfied mistress. The spirit was saying still that the private life, however deprecatingly one chose to view it, must surely be about something more than the commonplace of any street or bed. There still must be a reason, Ana thought, for being oneself, and this is not it. Suffering perhaps, or conflict or faith or an argument or a test of some kind.

THE THIRD CHAPTER   (FEBRUARY 1578)

The Eboli children had not been in Madrid for Carnival since the year of their father's death, 1573.

"So we are not being let off the tiniest detail of pleasure-seeking," Ana told the old Marqués de Los Velez. "Bernardina and I are distracted with all their fusses and preparations."

The long, quiet sitting-room proclaimed the holiday. Masks and paper favours lay about; sugared fruits and marzipan tumbled out of boxes and little gilt baskets; and there was a wig of curly black hair—a man's wig—on a stand on Ana's writing-table.

De Los Velez pointed amusedly at this.

"But surely, Ana, you know that even *you* daren't impersonate a male character? It's against the law, dear child."

"Oh, that's not for me. Rodrigo is going to the Venetian Ambassador's masquerade to-morrow as his ancestor Santillana."

"Ah! The poet!"

"Yes. And of course Rodrigo's fair head mustn't be dyed —he's much too fond of it. So this wig has been very expensively made from study of the portrait of Santillana, at Infantado's house in Guadalajara."

"No trouble too great if Rodrigo is to look his best, eh? But what's the wig doing here, my dear?"

"Oh, I'm to see him try it on, and suggest the general make-up of his face. You see, he thinks his mother is so old that she must somehow even remember what her great-great-grandfather looked like!"

The old Marqués laughed.

"And instead of growing old to please your son, you grow young. Suddenly very markedly young. Why, Ana?"

Having left a Cabinet meeting in the Alcázar, the Marqués had called on Ana by the king's instruction to tell her that Philip would visit her informally later in the evening. Also to take his own leave of her, as he was withdrawing to his country place near Alcala de Henares for Lent. At Pastrana Ana was his near neighbour and they had many associations in common; he had served with Ruy Gomez in the Cabinet, and always stood for Gomez's policy of liberation and progress. He was fond of Ruy's wife and children.

"You're tired," Ana said.

"Yes. I'm growing too old for the king's delaying tactics. I would have liked to see a *few* decisions taken for Spain before I died."

They laughed.

"But what's this talk of dying? Are Cabinet meetings like some slow form of death, then?"

"Yes, my dear—creeping paralysis. Still, Vasquez and Perez are really energetic men, and I think that in spite of Philip they get a few things done. But the king has come back from El Pardo in a peculiarly cautious frame of mind."

"The boar-hunting should have livened him up—it always used to."

"My dear, he doesn't hunt nowadays. Even at El Pardo of all places he *prays* all the time, poor fellow! And to-morrow, he tells me, he's off to El Escorial to tackle the Forty Days in good earnest with his monks! Ah, poor Spain!"

"Poor Philip, too. He's a good king—at least, he's an extraordinarily dutiful one. Perhaps if the queen were a little more amusing——"

"I'd go further—I'd say if perhaps she were a great deal more amusing, and perhaps the least little bit attractive—still," he laughed and ran his veined old hand over his face, "that mightn't alter Cabinet methods, Ana dear."

"No. I think all this that you're talking about is *our* fault, you know—the fault of our class, I mean. I used to grumble to Ruy about that—that none of my relatives or any of the landowners ever know the least thing now about the government of Spain. He didn't think that mattered—he didn't like my class."

"He might agree with you more now—in any case, he would deplore Philip's fixed obsession with European politics and total inertia before our economic plight. We're bankrupt on paper, and Philip is always raging for money; and you've only to drive through this town or a league out into the country to see that we're bankrupt in fact—the people are starving, and nothing is being done for them. Yet we have greater possessions than any country on earth. Our empire is a sheer mystery of wealth. Some merchant ships, some system of transport, some attention to import and export, some expenditure on harbours and agriculture and roads—Oh well, I'm an old man, but younger than I will not see these simple things done for Spain, my dear!"

"Philip would attend to those things—they're the sort of things he cares about, believe me!—but he simply hasn't time. He has a million times too much to do. And it is the laziness and cowardice of all our class that make it impossible for him to get things done——"

"He doesn't want us, Ana! He simply has to rule alone——"

"But he shouldn't be allowed to! *We* own Spain; why does *he* rule it?"

"His father fooled us into letting him, and now we don't care——"

"I do—when it occurs to me."

"Exactly—when it does. And anyway you're only one, and a helpless widow-creature——"

"We've lost a principle somewhere——" Ana said.

"And a lot besides. Ah well, what talk for the eve of Carnival and with my lovely Ana! I'll be glad of my own house to-night, and the sound of the sheep coughing in the orchard."

"You're going to-night?"

"Yes—to avoid to-morrow's uproar. We'll get home for supper."

"You can give my love to the road."

"I will. You'll be at Pastrana for Easter, of course?"

"Indeed we shall. We'll have our customary feasts together, won't we?"

"To be sure, dear child. Ah, here's Rodrigo—and full of gossip, I expect, just as I have to go!"

Rodrigo Gomez y de Mendoza, Duke of Pastrana, bowed very correctly to the Marqués. He was a springy boy of sixteen, with fair hair turning now a little to brown, and with light, well-cut features. The gossips who made Philip his father were unobservant, for his fairness had none of the pallor of the king's, and the contours of his face were trim, sharp and small as had been those of Ruy Gomez.

"Telling Mother Cabinet secrets, sir? You sat all day, I believe?"

"We did indeed, my boy, and I feel unrefreshed. Tell me some town salacity, to make me laugh."

"I'd tell you plenty if Mother weren't here! May I have some wine with you?" He poured himself a drink. "Ah, there's my wig! Oh—here's a piece of news that may well blow into a scandal, and it's not salacious either, Mother—on the face of it!"

"More's the pity," said de Los Velez. "Still, let's have it. Mustn't be out of things!"

"You know Don Juan de Escovedo has been ill? Not that that matters, God knows! He's an awful bore, isn't he, Mother? But the point is—Pepe Salazar has just been telling me—that poisoning is suspected. Deliberate poisoning, I mean. I shouldn't be at all surprised. Would you, Mother? I wonder if he'll die?"

"I don't suppose so," said the Marqués lightly. "He's far too much of a worry to us all just now."

"But that's just why I think he may die, sir! He's making political enemies all the time, Pepe says. After all, this might well be one of the king's neat ideas——"

"Rodrigo——" Ana began.

But de Los Velez rose, interrupting her.

"Young man, you are so young and such a fool still that I can't be bothered to snub you as I should," he said coolly. "But don't forget yourself so idiotically again in my hearing or your Mother's." He pulled the boy's ear somewhat cruelly, and Rodrigo winced away, more from the indignity than the pain. The Marqués had not looked at Ana throughout the passage of speech about Escovedo, nor she at him. "Come now, young fool, try on this wig for me before I go. I'd like to see if you *can* look anything like a great Mendoza, when you try."

Rodrigo, who regarded de Los Velez as a *démodé* old fool and had deliberately tried his treasonous gossip on him so as to see him get excited, and also in order to annoy his mother who, he knew, adored the king—was very willing now to posture in the new wig and be admired.

"It's quite well made," he said, as he pulled it on in front of a mirror. "Ought to be, at the price. Look, Mother—how does it seem?"

"Exactly as I remember dear old great-great-grandpapa, darling! A plain old man he was!"

"I'll have to make up very sallow, alas! Oh, all you green-faced Mendozas! What an ancestry!"

"What an ancestry, indeed!" said the Marqués. "Merely the history of Spain. You're not big enough, Rodrigo——"

"Oh, it's only a masquerade—that won't matter," said Ana.

Rodrigo paid no attention. He was studying himself gravely in the glass.

"Black hair—there's something to be said for it, don't you think, Mother? I've been reading the old Marqués de Santillana—must be up to my part a bit. Do you know he was rather a good poet, sir?"

"Yes—I've read him. He's one of our glories, Rodrigo."

"He introduced the sonnet-form from Italy. That was creditable of him, I must say. I do admire Italy, and Italian ideas."

The door at the end of the long room opened and, briefly announced, the king entered.

Ana swept down the room to him, laughing as she went. But she dropped on her knee with a very correct grace as she kissed his hand.

"Your Majesty is most welcome."

"Thank you, Princess. I am earlier than I intended. I found myself suddenly free of work for half an hour—and as to-night is laden, I thought I'd come to you now."

"At any time this house and all it holds are yours, Your Majesty." Then, becoming informal again, she indicated the untidy room and Rodrigo trying to adjust his own hair with one hand and replace the wig on its stand with the other. "You must forgive us, sir. It is Carnival, and we are re-hearsing our disguises."

"So I see," said the king, taking in the whole scene friendlily and with precision. "Sit down again, old friend," he said kindly to de Los Velez. "I've given you a hard enough day; I should have known better than to interrupt your interlude of refreshment here."

De Los Velez bowed.

"Indeed no, sir. I am most happy, most happy," he murmured graciously, though in fact he was bored, and would have preferred to finish his glass of wine in peace with his "dear child", Ana.

Rodrigo, trying to forget his tousled head, made a beautiful courtier's bow, and spoke his duty.

"Thank you, boy," said Philip. He always looked indulgently on Rodrigo, Ana noticed, although the latter was not of a type normally to attract his interest. She sometimes suspected that the legend of the boy's royal paternity, amusing and half-pleasing Philip, tempted him sometimes to seem to promote it. "We have missed you from among the pages this winter, Rodrigo. However, we realise that you must study too. You'll be rejoining the Court for a part of the summer, I assume?"

"Yes, sir, indeed. I look forward to being at the Court for some weeks, before I go on military exercises."

"Ah, of course! You are to be a soldier, they tell me."

Rodrigo bowed assent. "With your cavalry, sir."

"And meantime, what do they teach you at your University?"

"Philosophy, of sorts, Your Majesty. I study French and Italian too—and I read much military history."

"Ah! He's learned, Ana, I fear. Formidably learned. How much philosophy have you, to counter his?"

"None, sir. I've never needed any. My life has lain in happy places."

The king smiled at her, seeing a compliment in what she said, and already feeling rested by the sense of her friendliness.

He sat now in a tall chair near a window, and looked about him at his ease.

"Do they behave themselves at Alcala, Los Velez, these young students?"

"Oh, not uniformly well, sir," said the Marqués lightly. "I hear grumbles from the *alcalde*. But there's nothing exactly criminal against Rodrigo at the moment. And now, if Your Majesty will permit me, and you too, my dear Princess, I shall take my leave. I have my journey to the country this evening——"

"Yes, indeed," said the king, and Ana rang a handbell. "Good gardens those of yours, my friend, but not as fertile as Pastrana."

"Ah well, Ruy Gomez was the best husbandman I ever knew—save one, Your Majesty. You certainly set us all a great example with your magnificent gardens."

He bowed low in farewell over the king's hand.

"A garden is the most grateful of earthly possessions, dear friend," Philip said. "It is very consoling sometimes."

"That is so—and I wish you all its comforts, sir, in the coming weeks at El Escorial."

"Thank you, Marqués."

The manservant was waiting, and with smiles to Ana and Rodrigo de Los Velez left the room.

Rodrigo thought the king a prig and a bore, but he appreciated passionately all that he stood for, and delighted in the familiarity with which the ruler of Spain honoured his mother's house. Ana sometimes reflected with amusement that although—short of being a reigning monarch—Rodrigo could hardly throughout all Europe hold higher rank than his birth gave him, yet the boy manifested all the signs of a social climber. Where does he hope to climb to? she often wondered— and found his snobbish antics comical. At this moment, though the actual intercourse would bore him, with its pieties and its avoidance of gossip and malice, Rodrigo would like, Ana knew, to stay and entertain Philip, so as to enjoy his own effect upon the latter, and also for the satisfaction it always so curiously gave him to be able to say that he had sat at ease for a while in a private drawing-room with the king. But he was already too good a courtier to indulge this inclination now. He knew that it was unwise, when the king came to his mother in this room, to make a third too long. He knew all the old Court gossip about them, though he did not quite know what to make of it; but he did know that they were intimate friends, and that it was not discreet to get in their way when the king came visiting Ana.

So he bent again over Philip's hand.

"Your Majesty will wish me to leave you now. This has been a very great honour and happiness. Adios, sir."

"Adios, Rodrigo."

As the boy crossed the room he picked up the wig on its stand.

"I'll take this, Mother. It's a bit incongruous here," and he laughed and bowed himself away.

"He's a pleasing boy, Ana—but he'll never be the man his father was." Philip permitted himself to smile with faint mischief as he said that.

"He has charm, I suppose," Ana replied, "but certainly he's no Ruy Gomez. I sometimes think he'd have exasperated Ruy very much—and that wasn't an easy thing to do."

"Does he exasperate you?"

"He comes near it. I dislike all this mincing social nonsense. Oh, but I'm glad to see you, after so long. May I sit?"

He laughed contentedly.

"Nonsensical woman!" She sat down opposite him. "Yes, it has been a long time, I'm sorry to say—not since just after Christmas."

Ana had taken her family to Pastrana for the Feast of the Kings which they always celebrated there, and did not return to Madrid until Candlemas. By then the king and Court were at El Pardo. So that this glimpsing visit, as he passed through on his way to El Escorial, was important to Philip. Always now when he was at the Alcázar he came to see her, without ceremony, whenever he allowed himself an hour to spare from work. Sometimes he came unannounced, sometimes he sent a servant to say that he might call—but he never named a time. Clearly he regarded her as very much his own possession, over there so conveniently across the street.

His assumption meant that, when the Court was in Madrid, Ana and Antonio Perez had to move delicately within the king's hours, which could be gambled on as being normally between noon and midnight. For herself, now that Ruy was dead, Ana acknowledged no man's lordship over her days or her actions, and Philip might enter her drawing-room when he chose, and like or not whom he found there, as he chose. As to her right to do as she pleased in her own house she no more regarded Philip's judgment than that of the youngest washer-up in her kitchen.

But, she understood that Antonio Perez's career could be ended, in fact, by Philip's least whim of jealousy or irritation against him. And she knew that his career was what Antonio really cared about on earth, and on the whole thought this a proper state of mind for a man of brains. She believed that any threat through her to his ambition would deprive her of his present love; and she was in love with him and desired him to love her as long as might be possible. So, against her nature, she was cautious when Philip was in Madrid.

Now however she smiled, leaning towards her desk to push further out of sight a note which she had received that afternoon.

"It looks as if I shall be working until dawn, if Majesty is to eat his Mardi Gras supper at Escorial to-morrow. Especially as I want to avoid having to go up there just yet myself. So put out your candles when you will, and go to sleep. Meantime, there may be a free moment when this Cabinet breaks

up, and if there is I'll cross the street for a seasonable exchange with Fernán and Anichu. I have, as a matter of fact, a
Carnival present for you also—but I don't suppose you'll like
it. Anyway, I'll not give it to you this afternoon—that
wouldn't be at all correct. I hope I shall manage to see you
before the night's labours descend. You are my refreshment.
A."

There might well be an encounter—as there had been once
or twice before. But a call by a politician on a great lady was
no more than correct—especially at this hour of the evening.
And Antonio, secretly furious at the *contretemps*, would carry
it off with grace.

Philip took a sugared grape and ate it.

"I told my people to send your children a Carnival cake
from me, Ana. I said it was to be a very pretty one."

"Ah! How thoughtful of you! They'll be enchanted."

"Not that I imagine they're going to be short of cakes!"

"Great Heavens, no! What a greedy festival it is! But a
cake from the king! My family simply revel in these special
marks of your friendship, Philip. I'm afraid they'll boast
about it all over Madrid!"

"Good children." He smiled. "How wise I was, you see,
to make you bring them back to Madrid."

"Well, certainly they think so!"

"And they're right. It's good for them to mix with their
contemporaries, and get to understand gradually what Spain
really is and how we govern. And of course it's very important that I should be able to keep my eye on them, as Ruy
desired."

He leant back in his chair and closed his eyes.

"Did you rest, at El Pardo?"

"No. I don't rest."

"That is unwise of you; it is even undutiful."

He smiled a little at the censure, and opened his eyes, which
were strained and red-rimmed.

"It might be more undutiful of me," he said, "to seek the rest I could enjoy."

She allowed herself to look baffled; his reference might, after all, be to death or abdication.

"I could rest here, Ana," he said self-pityingly. "You rest me, always."

"I'm glad," she answered, and strove to keep the mood of her speech at once truly affectionate yet innocent of provocation. "But there is so little that I can do for you—it is so seldom——"

What he needed from her now he took, for all her care; the hint of a temptation between them to which *he* would never permit them to yield. And Ana, watching him take his own cue, reflected with amusement—in love with another man though she honestly was—that Philip's game was indeed founded on fact. For it remained true that he attracted and touched her—and she thought that that was all he meant, did he but know it, when he said she rested him. His sensitive nerves felt a particular quality in her liking for him. That is restful to all of us, Ana thought, thinking of herself; and whether we are lovers or not—and Philip no longer is anyone's—can seduce us into fantasies.

"It should be never," he said gravely, believing himself master of a great desire. "Dear Ana, we must thank God that we grow old. You are somewhat younger than me, of course, but a woman ages early."

She laughed at that a little.

"Dear friend, do you know that you always pay court to me—may I call it that?—in such terms as make it seem that you are profoundly thankful to have escaped me!"

"Perhaps indeed I am. For say we had been lovers once, is it conceivable that we would sit together now, as we do, in such total trust and friendship?"

The innocence of this speech made Ana wince. Yet she told herself that her passions were her own dominion, and that the makers of naïve claims punished only themselves, if anyone.

"Can't lovers be friends?" she parried.

"What do you know of lovers?" he asked, indulgently. "And now your day is gone, and it's my fault that you have escaped all the sins your beauty entitled you to. But I was right, believe me. And you have far fewer penances to do now in your old age than I, alas! But there was one sin at least I didn't commit—I didn't rob Ruy of what I gave him."

"Between you and Ruy I was well taken care of," Ana said softly.

"I think you were," said Philip, feeling no mockery. "And I continue the work—though it's easy now."

"That's as well, seeing how incredibly busy you have become in these years, my dear friend."

"They reproach me," he said suddenly. "Oh yes, I know they do, for my method of government. But there is now no other way. There are intricacies and subtleties to be balanced in Europe now which of their nature must not be openly explained to any Cabinet. I alone can judge the full case, Ana, in all our foreign problems. Simply because I alone feel Spain's duty and destiny, and only I can be trusted with it. One man can be counted safe thus far, and another to another point—but they are only politicians—and I know therefore that they cannot judge for Spain——"

He was off on a frequent theme—self-justification. It was her belief that he was too proud to talk in this vein to anyone but her, and that therefore these wild and vaguely directed speeches for the defence which it was his pleasure to deliver to her did him more good and meant more than was apparent. They never contained any factual information; he never stated a worry, or named a significant name; he merely condescended to fret and argue with himself in her presence, and she knew that this was a relaxation normally impossible to his conceit in the presence of another.

It's like being married to him—a little, she thought.

She wondered if Juan de Escovedo was on his mind, or whether, having ruthlessly directed that anxiety to its logical end, he now dismissed it, unresolved though it yet was, in favour of other troubles.

The king's conscience, though it flourished indeed and spread rankly and eccentrically through his whole life and policy, was impossible now to separate or disentangle from his over-developed consciousness of holy privilege. Ana wondered where—if anywhere—beneath all his activities of contrition, hair-splitting, penance, debate and self-consciousness, lay Philip's plain sense of right and wrong? She wondered if ever his mind lay still, still enough to accept a moment of plain guilt, or simple doubt?

Ana took for granted the political high-handedness of her time. She had known men murdered for the king's sake, or by the king's secret wish; had known arrests made and trials conducted for false causes, simply because what was conceived to be the national good required a neat, quick putting-away. Her husband, more humane and temperate than most men of his day, had not blenched from the treacherous despatch of de Montigny and Berghen, well-intentioned envoys from the Netherlands. Common gossip had had it, when in 1568 the madness of Philip's son, Don Carlos, made his death a necessity for Spain, that Ruy Gomez counselled and promoted his murder. Ana knew that this was not true, and that Carlos had died—hideously—from natural causes. But she also knew that Ruy believed his death to be necessary, and would have compassed it without scruple had he had to.

During the winter she had learnt and guessed enough from Antonio Perez to understand that Juan de Escovedo was now become an inconvenience of whom the king intended to rid himself. He was not to be deflected from his advocacy of Don Juan of Austria's vainglorious schemes in northern Europe; and since his was the brain behind these, and he was, so far as Philip knew, the only Spaniard in government circles who was prepared to go all lengths to serve the dreams of the bastard prince, it was simplest for Spain that he should die.

The charges which Philip's secret service had now accumulated against Escovedo amounted, Ana understood, to treason. Therefore she wondered—and said so—that the king did not take the sane way of impeaching his subject, and submitting him to trial. But Perez said that that would direct public attention to a situation which did not warrant it, and might transform Don Juan's pretensions into something like a cause. Sides might be taken, animosities engendered, many lives lost and much trouble stirred up were Escovedo to be allowed a hearing. He had been warned repeatedly; he knew the king's implacability and methods; he knew he was marked for elimination; but he was a fanatic, and he went on trying to get armies and money and some kind of brotherly blessing for his very foolish master in Brussels. So he must disappear—die from natural causes, by Philip's wish, and with no comment or publicity. He was only one man, and he schemed to destroy many. He had made a fool of himself, and when he was gone Don Juan would certainly lose heart and drop his nonsensical intriguing. Which would be the last that we would ever hear, thank God, said Perez, of that foolish Enterprise against England which had wasted so many years and brains for Spain.

Ana knew—though it was never said—that Antonio had taken complete charge for Philip of this murder-plan. This troubled her, but she was not consulted or given confidences about it; she could only marvel at the apparent serenity and enthusiasm with which he continued to live, work and enjoy himself—giving no sign of his direct preoccupation with the murder of a man he had grown up with and whose friend he had been. But she had marvelled at similar examples of male detachment before—in her husband and in Philip. That passion for affairs, for government, which was so strong in the three men, must contain, she thought, the secret of how callousness can live day by day in apparent harmony with qualities humane, touching and charming which were paramount, with characteristic variations, in all three.

When she persisted sometimes in arguing the greater wisdom for Philip to have Escovedo arrested and tried, Antonio repeatedly laughed her off. "Impeachments are tricky things; might even rouse the nobility out of its long sleep——"

"That's what I mean. That would be a good thing."

"Nonsense, we've our hands quite full enough as it is! No, no. One little death—it's very easy, and we all have to die." He paused and smiled at her. "I won't mind—and *you* shouldn't—when poor Juan is under the ground. He continues to make a terrible nuisance of himself about my private life!"

"I know. But, thank Heaven, he seems to have despaired of reforming me. He doesn't call on me any more, at least."

"Oh, don't flatter yourself he's not attending to your business still, because, believe me, he is!"

"I wonder why he has taken up this—well, this extraordinarily impertinent position?"

"I've considered that, and I think that it's primarily just devotion to Ruy. You see, he *does* think it shocking of you to dishonour a great man's memory, and his children, by an intrigue with a cheap, married adventurer; he also thinks it shocking of you to spend Ruy's substance, and your children's, on that venal creature—and in both of these points, he's perfectly right——"

"I spend my own substance. The children are extremely rich—loaded with estates that I have nothing to do with——"

"I know. Still you *are* madly generous——"

"So are you."

"No, I'm not, Ana. I'm always in debt and on the make. I'm very dishonest, as you know."

"I find you honest."

"You're not a judge—you don't notice about money and things. I do, all the time."

"Well, I'm glad someone does. It makes things sound a little orderly."

He laughed at her.

"But, to get back to Escovedo. I think his indignation against us is quite sincere and natural—though I agree that it's most damnably impertinent, as expressed. But I think increasing bitterness now makes him see his scandalous secret as a powerful political weapon."

"Ah! That was what I feared from the beginning."

"You 'feared'? Is there then something that you fear, Ana?"

"Nothing, for myself. After all, what could there be? Who owns me? What crimes do I commit? But for you—yes. The king's first minister has everything to fear."

"Not really—no need for melodrama. You see, the king's first minister usually understands the king. And with Philip that's all you need. He's brainy but he's slow; I'm brainy too, and I'm quick. Now, look—Escovedo actually has a heart of gold. He respects old friendship and old times——"

"How can you say these things of him and yet seem to support Philip's intention?"

"Because I have intelligence. Because I *am* therefore first minister; because I never, never hoodwink myself. Men aren't killed because they are monsters, Ana; many most enchanting people have to be removed—and we all have to die. Well, as I was saying, Escovedo has a heart of gold. That's what has in fact betrayed his brains and training in the matter of Don Juan. Well, being what he is, he truly does not want to be informer on Ruy Gomez's *post-mortem* humiliation. He would very much rather it was never known of that great man that his widow insulted him with amorous adventures. Also, he remembers good fun with me when we were pages

and under-secretaries together; he remembers good turns I
did him, and that he always thought there was some good in
me. He'd rather not ruin me. And there I understand him
perfectly, because I would much rather not ruin him. Though
I think him as great a bore as he thinks me a cad. Quits so
far—but I shall win, and on the political issue. I wouldn't
kill a man, or have him killed—I *think*—because he was a
personal irritation. That's a dangerous tendency—leaving
morality aside. But, when the king insists on the removal,
for his high reasons, of someone who is also privately on my
nerves—then I do find it easy to see the king's point!"

"Could Escovedo 'ruin' you, as you say?"

"I wonder! He could make a situation in which I would
not have my bearings. But you, of course, might be able to
give them to me? We've never talked about this—and we
needn't now, of course. But—how much is Philip in love
with you?"

"At present he is in love with our virtue—and with the
dream of desperate temptations overcome long ago."

"What do you mean by all that?"

She paused.

"Well—all it amounts to is that we were never lovers,
Philip and I."

"Ah!"

"Do you believe me?"

"Yes. I believe you, Ana." He asked no other question
then about her relationship with the king, but returned,
reflectively, to the theme of Escovedo. "His disgust with the
private life of the Secretary of State is now becoming a part of
Juan's political passion, I think. It may seem to him that if he
can disillusion Philip about his right-hand man, and incidentally about so old a friend as you, that he will thereby
gain his personal trust, and persuade the king away from
corrupt advisers, and back to the field of Spain's traditional
honour. He would argue from the particular to the general,

and force himself into my shoes. And not for selfish reasons, mind you! Plain altruism—duty to Spain. But of course he doesn't know anything about how Philip's mind works. He doesn't know the king's dangerous way of turning against the bringers of bad news. Above all, he doesn't know that he's not going to live much longer."

The greater part of this conversation had taken place round about the New Year. That was six weeks ago. Since then it was clear that Perez had made fresh overtures to Escovedo, as if in endeavour to bring him at last to terms in the government of Don Juan. He had him to conferences at the palace; Ana saw them riding together once in the Retiro; and three or four nights ago Antonio had had the other to dinner at his house.

Now Escovedo was ill, and if, as Rodrigo said, he was poisoned, it was likely that he swallowed the poison at Perez's dinner-table. The end of the affair was in sight, might even already be here—and Antonio was in charge of it, and betraying no unusual emotion. From the manner and speech of the Marqués de Los Velez when Rodrigo uttered his careless gossip, it was evident that the old statesman was somewhat in the king's confidence as to Escovedo's fate; but not entirely, Ana surmised. No one, not even Perez, was ever entirely in possession of Philip's intentions. Perez's great strength, like Ruy's, was that he never forgot that, or forgot to reckon with its dangers.

Ana contemplated Philip now with some anxiety. He must know that Escovedo was ill; if the poisoning story was true, he knew of it. One of his subjects, a man of honour who had served him well and was still in his service, was being meanly murdered by his wish.

It occurred to her with sudden vividness that if anything went wrong, if there was investigation or outcry after Escovedo's death, it could be very, very serious for Philip. Theologians argued the divine right of kings, and a prince's claims of life and death over his subjects—and nervous old men like Diego de Chaves, Philip's confessor, could twist morality to any shape to suit their master. But no intelligent person gave the hoary idea more than a tolerant courtesy-shrug now, and Ana was sure that Philip himself did not believe it, though he would never appear to discard any conception which increased a ruler's power.

Because the people of Spain were not informed of events until they were well over and their motives blurred, and because of the lethargy now seeped through the aristocracy which, until bullied into sleep by Charles V, had been a ruling class—Philip had indeed carried off some dangerous crimes against human rights, and managed by keeping calm to steer safely past their consequences. But those actions had always been perilous, and there was no reason why the luck of his absolutism should hold.

The sudden death, here in Madrid, of a very well-known Spaniard renowned for his service with the beloved and romantic Don Juan, was bound to receive attention. If there was an inquiry—and many people would be found who, for reasons motived by principle, by family, or by private spleen, could press for one—Philip would be in a dangerous pre-dicament. Antonio Perez would also be in peril. But he would have Philip in his hand—the king, the trump card.

The plot was bad and criminal indeed. Yet Ana almost smiled now as she considered its melodramatic elements. What adventurers and dreamers, at once what savages and babes men can be! Was anything on earth furthered by their elaborate processes of cunning and criminality? Would the world ever be run by anything better than personal passion, and the scoring off each other of amoral schoolboys?

Meantime here was this man of fifty-one, highly trained king of the greatest dominions on earth, this good man Philip whom she knew and loved, plotting plain murder and protesting in perfect sincerity that only he "can judge for

Spain". And on the face of it he's right in that, she thought.
In any case Spain has only him, and he cares. And it must be
admitted that he looks at this minute like a man with an active
conscience. Which is more than one might ever say for
Antonio.

" . . . They are politicians, you see . . . I only . . ."

This was still his broad theme, while she pondered the
fixed issue of Escovedo. He would pause now and expect her
soft intervention. As always when he rested himself by
muttering at her and giving nothing away, tags of counsel
such as a wise or witty woman might give a man floated into
her mind. But she was no adviser, and no wit. Buried in her
was her own personal reserve of understanding of right and
wrong and human action, but she knew this to be so very
much, so idiosyncratically, her own that she could never
extricate any of it. Its form, in her shy manipulation, would
never apply to another's need—and in any case she detested
the idea of giving counsel. What Philip came to her for, what
he found in her nowadays she honestly did not know. She
knew, with enduring surprise, what Antonio found—sheer
sexual delight and peace. Arguing from that, but modestly
and uncertainly, she guessed that perhaps—Philip being more
imaginative than Perez, more poetic and delicate in reaction
than any man she knew—he found, irrespective of what she
said or did, an edge, a store of pleasure all his own, a symbol
for memories, an echo, a perfume from what had never been.
She thought that it hardly mattered really what she said or did
in Philip's presence—so long as she didn't offend him. Her
existence and the sight of her promoted some favourite
fantasy which he would never be so simple as to explain.

In effect she was right. She was all that he allowed himself
now of common vanity; she was all that was left of the days of
pride of life; and he was very fond of her, and very glad to
have her to himself on these easy, middle-aged terms which
asked no guilt of him. It pleased him too that she was a

widow and well past her prime, much as it had always pleased him that she was one-eyed. For he thought it eccentric in himself to be able to admire so much a woman thus afflicted; and that had always made him feel safe about her. But the surface of his consciousness did not reveal these reassurances to him. At the top of his mind she was safe and restful not because she was ageing, disfigured and too unusual-looking to appeal generally, but because she was the admired and chosen intimate of the king—towards whom therefore no other man would be so foolish as to presume.

"Spain is grateful to you, Philip," she said dutifully when he paused. "But we'd rather you didn't age yourself prematurely in our service."

He stretched for her hand and spread it out on his, admiring it.

"There are many people who *don't* think you beautiful, Ana," he said. "But your hands—well, they are just child's play."

"I suppose so. Myself, I prefer some of my more eccentric features——"

"I hope partly because I admire them?"

"That's one good reason. I've always been very proud of your admiration," she said.

"You say I age. But that's a good thing; it's necessary; I welcome it."

"I don't see why."

"One can't be a king and a man—not such a king as I have to be; not now, not in Spain." He bent his head over her hand, leant his forehead against it. "If I could take you with me to-morrow," he said softly. "Up there at El Escorial I sometimes feel like a very young man, Ana. And then I think of you." He dropped her hand. "If there were time for pleasure!"

She smiled at him.

"There's evidently time to dream of it," she said.

"Yes, barely that. And that is best, dear Ana. You and I are old now, and it is our duty not to make ourselves ridiculous."

She laughed outright, for the word "ridiculous" brought many private and wild images into her mind.

"Dear Philip, dear mentor," she said. "How firmly you guide me in virtue!"

"I have to. I always have a feeling of anxiety about you and me."

"Perhaps that's my revenge on you for being my first love——"

"Perhaps indeed," he said delightedly. "A long and true revenge." He ate another candied fruit. "Where are the children?"

"Fernán and Ana may be dashing in here any minute—they won't know you're with me. And they'll be enchanted if they meet you! Poor little Diego is spending Carnival with the Cardinas family and his very grown-up bride."

"It is a good match, Ana."

"She's rather cruel with him, I think—and he's only just fourteen. We all miss him."

"I'm sure you do. Still, you've done wisely."

"Young Ruy is out with his tutor somewhere. He promises to be learned. And Rodrigo you've just seen. They grow up and go their ways. I hear that our little Duchess of Medina-Sidonia has quite taken to matrimony now, and leads society in the south."

"That's as it should be. I have my eye on her husband for future offices. He's a promising young fellow."

"Would you say 'promising'? He's extremely good-natured and pleasant—but I always find him a little stupid."

"He may appear stupid, socially—but in public affairs I think he is observant and serious."

"Well, he and Madalena seem enchanted with each other anyway—which is a little surprising when you reflect what a bore Madalena is."

"Now, Ana, you know I hate you to talk in that cruel way about your own children."

"I suppose it *is* cruel? I wouldn't do it to the outside world, Philip."

"I should hope not! It's very shocking—and a foolish affectation, my dear!"

"Oh no, it's not an affectation. Ah! I think I hear the children! Do you mind their coming in?"

"I'll be delighted," Philip said, as a door opened and Ana and Fernando came in, followed by Antonio Perez.

The children were in their riding coats; Fernando carried a painted toy windmill with bright sails, and Ana had a wooden donkey, saddled in scarlet cloth.

They hurried to the king, and dropped on their knees to take his hand.

"Your Majesty," they said gravely, and then rose.

"Actually," said Fernando, "we knew you were here. Estéban told us in the *patio*."

"I suppose we shouldn't have come up without permission," Anichu said.

Antonio Perez, having bowed his duty, joined in now.

"I was consulted, sir, downstairs, on the point of etiquette, and as your Secretary of State I risked advising that we all come up." He turned to Ana, and bowed low. "I called, Princess, to leave these Carnival offerings——" he pointed to the toys the children clutched—"when I met the recipients coming in from a ride. So I ventured to come upstairs, to wish you also a very happy Carnival."

"I am glad you did, Don Antonio."

"Yes. Well met indeed. You're on your way to the Alcázar?" Perez bowed. "We'll be along together in a moment. Those are very fine presents you've been given, children. Have you had my cake yet?"

"Your cake, sir?" said Fernando politely.

"I told them to send you a Carnival cake. I said it was to be a very pretty one."

"Oh!" breathed Fernando. "I'm sure it will be beautiful, Your Majesty."

"I wonder *how* it will be decorated?" said little Ana.

Everyone laughed.

"When we've eaten it, sir," said the Princess, "Anichu will herself write to you, in all our names, to thank you."

"Oh!" said Anichu.

"I shall look forward to that letter," Philip said.

"I have just this moment called at the house of Juan de Escovedo, sir," said Antonio. Philip looked at him with mild interest. "I don't know if you've heard, but he hasn't been well and I was a little anxious about him. Also, I wanted to send some personal news of him in the Brussels despatch."

"Well—and how is he? Will your news be good?"

"Quite good. He's in bed still—I sat with him a while. But he hopes to be up to-morrow, and in any case whatever it was—some stomach trouble—seems to be under control now."

"I'm glad," said Philip coldly. "I had not heard that he was ill."

Antonio laughed.

"I thought you might have missed his daily letters and memoranda, sir. But they'll soon be starting again, you'll be glad to hear!"

Philip smiled.

"I haven't been reading his memoranda lately. I think I know their contents by heart. Still, I'm glad he is no longer ill. My brother will be glad to have good news of him."

Ana watched this conversation; neither speaker gave any sign of its being more than casual exchange, yet she knew that Antonio had engaged in it because of some whim of bravado before her, and that Philip in his slower way had enjoyed its cold insolence.

"How *is* Don Juan of Austria, Your Majesty?" Ana said.

Philip shrugged.

"Depressed, Princess, and petulant. He likes his own way, and a great deal of money. We don't give him either—do we, Perez?"

"No, sir; we do not."

Fernando was looking sadly at a basket of sweets on Ana's table, and then, for guidance, to his mother.

"Would it be a very great breach of etiquette, Your Majesty," she said, "if Fernán were to eat a candied fruit?"

"Not if he gives me one first, Princess."

Blushing and delighted the little boy brought the basket to the king. Philip chose a piece of marzipan.

"Anichu next, I think," he said, and the baby Ana came and chose a sweet, still holding her donkey. "Who's to ride this donkey?" Philip asked her.

"It's for Juana La Loca, Your Majesty."

"That poor old doll!" The king laughed and looked about the room for her. "But she's past donkey-riding, surely?"

"She's certainly in very poor health," the Princess said.

"Mother Teresa—you know, sir, the great Mother Teresa? —well, she rides donkeys everywhere," said Anichu.

"And Bernardina says that she's often very sick," said Fernando.

"She is, indeed," said Philip.

"But she doesn't allow herself a saddle, Anichu," said Antonio. "Do you think Juana La Loca will be so self-indulgent as to use this saddle?"

"Well, she's very thin—as thin as Mother, really," said Anichu. "I think she'd better have the saddle."

Antonio smiled. Philip stroked the little girl's head. "No, Fernán," he said. "Take that basket away from me now—or I shall have stomach trouble."

"Like Don Juan de Escovedo," said Fernando.

"Exactly. Ah, my dear friend," he said to Ana, "how you

seduce us! How I should like to spend Carnival here—with
Anichu and Fernán and Juana La Local"

"How deeply welcome you would be, Your Majesty."

"I believe that, Princess—and thank you. But come on,
Perez! What is the spell of indolence this lady casts? Beware
of it, my friend," he said, rising. "You have no time for such
delights, and neither, alas, have I."

"You warn me kindly, sir. I shall beware, believe me."

"Good-bye, Princess," said Philip. "Thank you for a
happy hour. I have few."

Ana knelt and kissed his hand. So did the children.

"God bless you all," Philip said as they rose, "and I wish
you a happy Carnival, and a holy Lent."

"And we wish you, sir, great peace and pleasure at El
Escorial."

Philip inclined his head. Antonio Perez bowed polite farewell over Ana's hand. Smiling again at the children the two
men crossed the room and were gone without ceremony.

THE FOURTH CHAPTER   (EASTER MONDAY 1578)

Ana got up and left the supper-table when the meal was
only half-way through. The children and their guests and
tutors were very gay and hardly noticed her movement. It
was an informal family meal after a long day of village
festival. Only Anichu, sleepy on her high chair, protested as
she passed.

"But you're asleep, my baby," Ana said and kissed her hair.
"Bernardina, have her taken to bed—it's after midnight."

"I'll take her myself. I'm tired of all this din," said
Bernardina, and picked up the little girl and carried her off.

Ana went into the garden, and climbed its long shelves.
She liked its furthest level, where, from a broad and quiet
terrace withdrawn and raised above her house and the town,

she could look out in many directions over the gentle lands of Pastrana and smell and enjoy their fertile peace.

This last night of March, starry and clear, seemed like a night of late April. Many of the fruit-trees were in blossom; the midnight light touched throngs of ghostly flower-faces, and the air carried a confusion of sweet perfumes.

Ana paced her favourite quiet plateau and scanned the view below her as if she sought something new from its familiarity. The village pressed about the dark mass of her house; dwellings, barns, schools and storehouses all sheltering prosperously still under the beneficence of their dead duke. Ruy's bones lay there in the *Colegiata* church, with the bones of four of their ten children—where her bones too would lie. It is much to have buried, she thought, the bones of a husband and four children. While life still burns hard in the breast, to have already ended so much means that I am old, however I forget it. It means that I have been old for these five years, since all those bones of mine rejoined each other then—to wait for me.

Further off than the *Colegiata* shone the roofs of the Franciscan monastery and convent. Ana was the patroness of these two religious houses and so had much business and many friendly contacts with their inmates, yet, secretly, she never thought of them or entered their precincts without wincing in discomfort.

When Ruy founded his dukedom and set to the work of developing the life of Pastrana, its monastery and convent had stood empty for some years, so he offered them, with endowments and generous patronage, to the new Reformed, or Discalced, Carmelites.

The gesture was wide in implication. It associated the progressive wing of Philip's government with the new cause of the rebel Mother Teresa who was then—as she was still—sweeping about Spain in search of foundations where she might exemplify with her followers, as a movement of

Counter-Reformation, the ideals of the early Christian Church. Support and friendship from Ruy Gomez were, when they came, a great political boon for Mother Teresa, and the new Carmelites established themselves happily at Pastrana.

Ana was not religious-minded, or ever disposed to examine or undergo the real rigours of spiritual progress. It was as natural to her to be a Castilian Christian as it was to have nails at her finger-ends, or an appetite for dinner. She believed, perfectly simply, the essential tenets of her faith, and was careless as to details. She said her prayers with undimmed belief and, until she had fallen through Antonio Perez into what she frankly named to herself as a mortal sin of the flesh, she had kept the major rules of Catholic life. There had been passages of dream and temptation when she was young and Philip and his desire attracted her; but otherwise she had been good, and unassailed. Now that she was by her own acknowledgment living a life of sin she did not cheat; feeling unrepentant, she did not feign repentance, and had to forgo reception of the sacraments. Very often and very honestly now she looked in dismay at this *impasse* of her soul. But it had to stand. She saw no way of clearance save to give up her pleasure in Antonio Perez. Living in mortal sin now, she knew that what she was doing did not merit eternal hell in the eyes of any human judge, and wondered—as often more detachedly she had—how theologians dared make categorical pronouncements. But she was no mystic, had no private ease of communication with God, and had to be content to take her chance, a sinner, before the tribunals of eternity. If the rules were in fact as the self-confident preachers shouted them—so be it.

But all of this had nothing to do with her discomfort before the religious houses in her village—or so she thought.

She had been pleased to have the new Carmelite foundations under her husband's wing. Less aware than Ruy of Mother

Teresa's national importance, and less attached than he was to her complex personality, character in action did nevertheless interest her, and she felt with sincerity that Mother Teresa was indeed living as the best kind of Spaniard should—and that she was a great individual and a great Castilian. And the foundations settled down, and prospered.

What happened afterwards was a large embarrassment arising from a very small and private cause.

When Ruy died, Ana, who had ended by surrendering all her will and all her forgotten, buried self to his quiet, insistent domination, became invested with panic. A sense of total incompetence, of being a cripple, swept upon her. She felt, angrily and somewhat madly in her grief, that her keeper had died either much too late or far too soon. She felt a great sense of waste in her long subjugation, and that all her life had been like an athlete's training for a course never to be run. In a chill of isolation, sick against Ruy for his bungling of everything in leaving her to have to be herself when she had been so carefully made over to be wholly his, she walked away from the whole future. She decided—in pure hysteria— to be a nun. She presented herself—scarcely remembering to ask permission of the Prioress—as a postulant of the Discalced Carmelites in Pastrana.

Had she ever been able—indulged great lady from birth— to accept the rules of a religious house, this was not the time, when she was ill, deranged, and derangedly set on doing what was unnatural.

The episode was foolish and humiliating. It was the one attempt she had ever made to express a violence from within herself, and it failed pitifully. Ana quarrelled with the Prioress, distressed the community, and caused consternation to her mother and her friends. Mother Teresa refused her the Carmelite habit, and ordered her monks and nuns to leave Pastrana. Ana withdrew to her own home, and began her widowhood in suitable seclusion. And those in Madrid who had heard of the brief *fracas* laughed and told each other that Ruy's death had unhinged her. Later, Franciscans came to teach and pray in her convents, and the life of the village went on, and the Princess's brief folly was forgotten.

By all but the Princess. The memory of it was an unclosed wound in her vanity, and it ate against courage. Before Ruy had come to her she had lost her eye; immediately he left her she acted as a madwoman; and whilst he was there, gentle, considerate, devoted, she had never been able to be anything but exactly his, as he made her. She was, it seemed, mutilated, *tuerta*—depleted in some sense she would never discover by the perfect taking over and direction of her life.

But her attempt to be a nun hurt more than her vanity. In quarrelling with Mother Teresa, in injuring the cause of reform, Ana knew she had offended against a principle important to herself; against courage and against life in action; against the best of Castile. There was no redress against that; but the oftener she considered it the more it hurt her instincts and her spirit.

It was an old pain now, and—as has been said—she often winced at it. It was like her blind eye, and both were sharp sentries over her general, surprised sense of never having managed to be herself throughout her singularly successful life. Both, she half-guessed, were answerable for the hour, the unforeseen moment in which, visited by a physical desire so precise as to be cold and shocking, she had made herself mistress of Antonio Perez. But there at least, and at last, they had not been sterile; there feeling had flowered in her, feeling entirely her own, defended and cultivated by no one. There— and let the theologians rave—she had found in pleasure that which might conceivably be allowed to be love.

But now she was unhappy. Her unhappiness was ten days old. It dated from a night three days before she left Madrid for the Holy Week ceremonies at Pastrana. Never, she thought, had she been so glad to return to the innocence and rural modesty of Pastrana. Yet now the place hurt her night and day through these very qualities she loved in it.

She looked eastwards now, towards where Alcala de Henares lay.

She and her children had spent yesterday, Easter Sunday, there—as by tradition they always did—as guests of the Marqués de Los Velez. Antonio Perez was spending Easter with the Marqués, whose neighbourliness to Pastrana, combined with his worldly suavity and indulgent love for Ana, was very useful to the lovers. The day had been brilliant and everyone light-hearted and easy, the children exacting all the sanctified customs of this outing. There was a bullfight in the town—not a very good one, but correct and exciting. Later there were feasts and fireworks.

Antonio, not having seen Ana for a week, was shamelessly enchanted with her again, and would not leave her side. He wore her Easter present, a collar of heavy, close-set rubies; he was gay and boyish, very much on holiday. But withal, she thought, secretly anxious lest she might not catch his mood. He was sensitive, she conceded—for she could feign, she hoped, but she could not feel light-hearted.

When her family were being piled into carriages for the drive home, Antonio—his mood changed now—begged her very gently to let him ride over to Pastrana to her after midnight. And for the first time in her love for him—which probably meant the first time in her life—she hesitated, worried, and declined her lover's request.

This distressed him. It touched her that, arrogant as his nature was, it did not make him cold or angry. Simply, he was distressed. He explained to her that he would have to be back at the Alcázar by Tuesday afternoon, and that on the following night, this night, Monday, his despatches would be coming from Madrid; that the courier might be late, and that he would have to await his arrival lest there was news requiring an immediate answer; that, in short, Monday night was not easy, and might be impossible.

Ana did not answer as, to her pained astonishment, the greater part of her cried out—that that would be well, and she would be glad if he did not come. She did not answer so, because she found him always very dear to her senses and she remembered what it was like to be with him in love. She loved him still, in the plain way of sensualism—and more than that, out of the gratitude, friendliness and mutual knowledge born in sensual pleasure. But her spirit had newly received a crazy shock. She knew, from the far depths of his eyes, that he was anxious about that—but he did not measure it rightly. There was no reason why he should ever do so. He thought—sympathising passionately, she knew— that the shock, the outrage was, as it must appear to anyone, to her *amour-propre*, to the sense of decency, to all the inherited rules and codes that govern civilised life. She did not discard or belittle these—and she was grateful to him for the passion with which he had reacted against their recent outraging by a madman. But she could never explain to him that her trouble was quite other—that she too was mad, perhaps, had been driven mad by the mad gesture of Juan de Escovedo, and had fantastically thereby come to share his view of herself and of her lover.

No, was all she had said to his anxiety. Cowardly and cold. No, he must not ride to Pastrana to-night. Then to-morrow night, Monday? But his despatches—he wouldn't be able to? Oh yes he might, very late. He might have things to tell her. And he *had* to be in Madrid on Tuesday, so Heaven knew when he'd see her again.

So she had driven home last night, leaving him uneasy. She felt wearily aware of her unbecoming, girlish awkwardness. She had no finesse, no style with which to meet the moods of love.

But was this a mood? She suspected that she had no style for moods because she had no moods.

Bernardina came up to her high terrace, carrying a silk cloak. "There may be frost," she said. "No need to take a chill. You're in bad enough form as it is."

Ana thanked her and put on the cloak.

"But why do you say I'm in bad form?"

Bernardina, who knew—as indeed was her duty—everything that happened to Ana, knew therefore of the shocking episode of ten nights ago in her bedroom in Madrid. It still made her sweat to consider it, and she knew that as long as she lived she would not forgive herself that such an unbelievable thing had taken place when she held any responsibility. Diego, the butler, and she had not been ashamed to weep for Ana's humiliation when they talked it out together, in hushed tones and behind locked doors. They were aghast, and would not have been surprised at instant dismissal from the Princess's service.

But nothing was said, nothing at all. Uninstructed, Diego changed the locks on all the doors, and posted night-watchmen to side-doors which had hitherto been little used and left to chance. The servants were sharply instructed—without explanation—as to admittance or non-admittance of visitors. Diego did not know what they knew or guessed of his reasons for this fuss, and in his anger and distress he hardly cared.

The Princess said nothing, and presently left Madrid with the children, as had been arranged. Only Bernardina, who knew her well, saw that she had changed overnight. Heaven knew she didn't blame her!

Still—it would be better if she spoke of the affair—to someone, once, and then no more. And this question seemed almost like a lead. Bernardina, gathering up all her affection and remorse, followed it.

"Because I'd expect you to be, even if I didn't see that you are. Ana—I shall never forgive myself—as long as I live." She raised her hand. "No, don't interrupt me.

Listen, it's better for you to let me talk—this once. That'll take some of the unnaturalness out of it."

Ana looked about the quiet landscape as if searching for something.

"It wasn't unnatural—that isn't the word," she said. "It was—like a vision of judgment, or like seeing yourself in hell."

Bernardina was very much startled.

"My dear, my dear," she said, and tears came into her voice. "Don't talk in that queer way—as if you were sleep-walking. It's over now, and it's as if it never happened——"

Bernardina's room in the Madrid house was very near to Ana's. On nights when Antonio Perez stayed very late and when she knew that he was in Ana's bedroom, Bernardina slept lightly or hardly at all. There was always a faint uneasiness—a young servant might make a mistake and go to the Princess's room, or one of the children might want her. Bernardina kept watch. Usually she heard Antonio tiptoe away in the dawn, and then she composed herself and slept soundly into the late morning.

One night, ten nights ago, dozing at about half-past three, she half-heard a man's step in the corridor. It's early for him to go, she thought sleepily; and then, it's a heavy step for him, and it's going towards her room, not from it. She became full-awake. Some idiot manservant parading where he had no business, she thought, and left her bed to look along the corridor. She was in time to glimpse a male shoulder and leg, in court dress, against the lights of Ana's room before the door closed on them. Ah, he was just wandering about, she thought—and then it struck her that the figure she had seen was larger and taller than Antonio Perez. She stood, frozen in speculation. And after some seconds of great stillness she heard a man's voice raised in Ana's room. Clear, hard and accusatory it rang—no voice of a lover in the night, no echo of Antonio Perez. It spoke again—having had no answer

that Bernardina could catch. She could not hear the angry
words, but only that they were indeed angry. She knew the
voice, yet in agitation could not name it. She kept still in a
curtained alcove, not knowing how to judge or what to do.
There was silence again—no answer to the hard, male scold.
And then the door of Ana's room opened, and Juan de
Escovedo came out. There were candles in the corridor and
they lighted his face with precision. He walked, not troubling
to tread lightly, past where Bernardina stood in the alcove.
She followed him down a small staircase and saw him let
himself out of the house at a side-door where there was no
watchman, and which was never used. He unlocked this
door with a key he produced from his belt. She heard him
lock it again on the other side and walk away. She did not
sleep when she returned to her room. She paced about, sick
with pity and anxiety. Before five o'clock rang at Santa
Maria Almudena she heard Antonio Perez tiptoe away as
usual, going by the stairs he always used.

That was all. That was all she knew, and however one
regarded the happening it was loathsome. She did not know
how to help Ana—yet she felt impelled to try.

She took her arm and drew her close to her.

"You'll forget it all, I promise you, *chiquita!* Just stay here
at Pastrana for a while and rest, and let the whole thing blow
away out of your dear head! Nobody knows a whiff about it
—except me. I swear to you! But what everyone does know
is that that poor individual is mad. We've all known that for
months! He's been piling up trouble for himself with the
king and everyone all the winter. But now! Oh well, there
was someone else concerned in this who'll know how to
make him answer for it, never you fear! You leave it all to
him, my pet——"

Ana always walked too fast for Bernardina, but the latter
did not notice this now and ran along, holding her arm and
coaxing her. And in fact Ana felt some of the comfort the

other wished towards her. It was a relief to hear this practical, kind voice lapping round the region of her shock; in some sense it distracted her from its hidden centre, made her view the event for a moment as others might, as an extraordinary piece of scandal. So that she suddenly felt a vast desire to laugh, to laugh outrageously and long—and she thought of how gloriously and salaciously this dear loyal Bernardina would in fact have laughed had the identical tale been brought to her about any other woman in Madrid save this one. She thought of the details that would have been dug from the story then, and of how crudely and unkindly they would have relished these, and added to them, together. Poor Bernardina, this time there could be no realism, no elaboration.

Yet blazingly true and crude the moment had been. So crude and true that it became of necessity, by its pure strength, a vision of sin and judgment. What would the jolly Bernardina have made of the actuality? Ana wondered. Juan de Escovedo, his dark face seared and tortured, his hands and shoulders shaking, his voice tearing like a file over iron words of rage; and she and her lover at bay in the wide, illumined bed; prone, abandoned, weary with voluptuousness, taken ludicrously in sin, unable to speak, unable to move because of the pitiful farce of nakedness in such a bitter hour. What would Bernardina make of the heaped-up minutiæ of that cartoon?

For her own part, Ana knew that it was either agonisingly funny, or serious in the mad sense in which Escovedo saw it. Indeed, it was both—and nothing in between. So therefore it might be easiest now to laugh, and make Bernardina laugh. For the other vision must remain her own. No one would ever understand her if she said—what was the simple truth— that her dignity, as they might call it or her *amour-propre* or any of those customary abstractions which constitute a lady, that none of these had taken any harm that she could recognise, and that in fact all that mattered to her outside the plain farce of that moment in her bedroom was that during it she saw that for her Escovedo was right. He was mad, and he was right.

This discovery made a problem for her which was entirely her own, and composed her present unhappiness. But the insult she had undergone was irrelevant—and she had no way of making that clear, so would not try to. All that was left was to salute the farce, and try to reassure Bernardina somewhat by that means.

She laid a hand on Bernardina's kind one that pressed upon her arm.

"Ah, you dear, true one," she said. "You mustn't worry. I'll forget it. It'll blow away! Everything does."

"That's right, *chiquita*. That's my own good girl——"

"You know," said Ana, steeling herself, "you know it's *you* I'm sorry for——"

"Me?"

"Yes, you. Oh Bernardina, how you must be ill with wanting to laugh! Yes, laugh——"

"At what, may I ask?"

"Dear saint, at the wildest piece of bedroom farce that can ever have taken place in Madrid!" As Ana spoke she laughed outright, enjoying herself. "Poor Berni! was there ever such bad luck?"

"No," said Bernardina firmly, for she felt at sea with this mood and did not think it healthy. "I admit freely that I'd laugh my guts out if it happened to someone else. But the fun of a thing depends on whom it happens to, *chiquita!* And there's something about you that *isn't* funny. No, you won't get *me* laughing over this affair. *I* feel like murder. That's what I feel like."

"Indeed, Bernardina?" said Antonio Perez's voice on the steps below them. "Then perhaps you *are* the murderer?"

The two women turned to him.

"What murderer?" said Bernardina.

He came to them and taking Ana's arm smiled at her

somewhat anxiously. When he spoke his voice was serious.

"I come with strange news," he said. "At sunset to-day in the Calle Santa Maria in Madrid Juan de Escovedo was assaulted and stabbed. Three men are being looked for. My despatch says that Escovedo is dead."

The three stood very quietly. Bernardina loosed Ana's arm and moved a step away.

"Praise God," she said coolly. "A man of Spain usually knows what has to be done."

She went down the steps then and towards the house. As she went she felt a brutal, happy impulse to laugh, and did laugh aloud, but checked herself at once, and hoped that the two she had left did not hear her.

Antonio did hear, and smiled. But Ana, in his arms, was sobbing. He felt her body wrench and shake against him. He had never known her to cry, but after the tension of recent days and as a reaction to the violent news he brought, he thought it was a natural thing. He stroked her hair and comforted her.

PART TWO: *PASTRANA AND MADRID*

I

ANA stayed at Pastrana throughout spring and summer. She sent the children to Madrid for April and May, escorted by tutors and governesses, and the whole party captained by Bernardina.

The king was disappointed. In his brief visits to Madrid he counted now upon her awaiting him at his pleasure in the long, quiet room across the street from the Alcázar. He wrote peremptorily to her to express his annoyance. But she stayed in Pastrana.

While Bernardina and the children were away she made a kind of peace with herself.

The death, by murder, of Juan de Escovedo, falling pat upon her terrible encounter with him, had driven her into a region of pain and debate for which her simplicity provided no compass. That the murder had been ordained and directed by the man who had shared her last intolerable glimpse of Escovedo and had felt responsible for her having to endure it —this was indeed a dark and unmanageable threat within her particular confusion. Yet, Spaniard, she could relegate it to a place below the plane of action. The murder had long been commanded by the king, and had already been attempted— twice, Antonio said—before the terrible private injury was offered.

She accepted the plain sense of that; she knew it was true. Yet this did not affect the visionary panic, the superstitious woe in which she felt the blow upon herself of Escovedo's death. For all she knew, men's little plans, and indeed the fore and aft of days in their designs, might even be small pieces, chessmen, in God's fingers. A sin and a soul, however small and silly both, might conceivably be at once foreseen and important in Heaven—more important than Philip's policy in the Lowlands. She laughed at her attempt to grasp God's timing of this possible intervention—laughed at her own revealed pomposity. Yet she knew what she meant—that a blade of grass might, just conceivably, by Heaven's values, be worth a planetary explosion.

She did not formulate her hysterical apprehension—indeed, she found courage to laugh at it when it came up near words and thereby suggested megalomania. But her soul was bowed, nevertheless. So it had been from the night when Escovedo stood over her bed and shouted at her. So now it was, when he lay so soon in his grave, sent there by Philip and her lover. She had not resented his admonition then, when he lived; she had only felt its truth. Now more than ever she felt that.

So through the gleaming, sweet weather she rode about the mulberry farms and the orchards, and let their tranquillity assuage her. This eastward extremity of Castile, with Aragon just over its shoulder, was not the very Spain of her heart; she understood better and admired more the land about Toledo, and the great *mesa* from Salamanca to Medina and Segovia; the people here too—Catalans and Aragonese having mixed their useful, stimulating blood with that of her own slower and more formal people, and the cross having been calculatedly bettered by Ruy, the good husbandman, by his plantation of *moriscos*, the mulberry farmers and silk-makers he wanted—the people, as she had often said to Ruy, were only by elastic courtesy Castilian. Whereat he used to laugh and gently deny the need for courtesy.

"It isn't a bar sinister *not* to have been born on a granite crag and spent ten generations starving there, Ana," he used to say. "It isn't an affliction *not* to have a brain made of granite. And I'm a foreigner too, you see, and I get on well with my fellow-mongrels. It's just that I like to see things *done*, whenever possible."

He had taken pleasure in her inbred intransigence, without ever yielding an inch to it in the conduct of life. She, however, had been perfectly gracious to his utilitarian philosophy, and obedient to it during his life and, as far as she could without his direction, after his death; while retaining her right to make the archaic, conservative observations which were native to her and which, she knew, brightened his enjoyment of her society. But she had found peace with him in his tranquil, well-governed lands, and since their early days of settlement there it had never occurred to her to desire to live elsewhere. Even in the frenzy of helplessness which had overtaken her at his death, her only idea of refuge had been the convent at Pastrana. Turned away from there in disgrace and anger, she had not even thought to seek another cloister. She had returned to her home and gathered about her the healing obscurity of the village she knew.

And now humiliated and guilty again, feeling sore and sordid, she was glad of Pastrana and desired to stay there.

I am marked for the grotesque, she told herself, as she had before, in the relentless night. And, alone, she would take off her black diamond patch. She would stare then in the mirror at her hungry, long face, so halved and split into blankness, and at the closed and dark-stained empty socket of her eye. And she would think of Escovedo in his grave, and of the cold beastliness of calculated love-pleasure, and the absurdity of sexual delight. And she would pace her room and long for the cocks to crow in daylight.

But by degrees daylight won her over somewhat. Observing, at first with resentment and forlornly, how the external process of days and pieces of work went on, how complicated all this was and how it depended upon the self-control and attention of men who were, it must be assumed, much else in their own hearts than the performers of their visible duties, she began to find patience with herself.

She watched the movements of the sky and the changes in fields; she saw how, by bell and light, men moved from work to food and from food to rest. Passion, after all, love-making, cheating and the counting of money; prayer, fear of death, the desire to know God and to have children—all these things, perilous with traps for the hasty, lay privately within the gentle, obvious surface, for every actor on that surface. If they did not the routine would have no meaning; and perhaps it derived its apparent grace, and its heavenly grace too, from the fact of underpinning dangers, private shames and snares. Sin, after all, was a commonplace; and perhaps others too felt sometimes that the most idiotic part of sin is our failure to understand our own motives within it. But a part of self-disgust must be, she thought, that we bear it alone; we have to learn to live with it in silence, and simultaneously go on being the people our fellows know and work with.

She fretted thus, riding and walking about Pastrana or looking at the open faces of villagers who smiled good-day. She looked at the lovely, changeful sky attentively, and towards the pure, high Guadarramas, and at the budding roses that Ruy had planted. And often she knelt in the *Colegiata* church beside Ruy's tomb, and wondered what he thought of her crude, blundering sins and of her love for Perez; and begged him to help her if he could, and to find mercy for her.

News came often from Madrid; from many people, but most welcomed from Bernardina and from Antonio. She had asked Antonio not to visit her for a time and he obeyed, though protesting gallantly against the ban. But she knew from his letters that he was overworked and unusually anxious and that secret journeys to the country would have been an excessive addition to his present cares.

The chief news, which came before April was half-done, did not surprise her. The family of Escovedo had not taken his murder as an act of God; and neither had Madrid society in general. Arrests and the procedure of justice were looked for, and as weeks passed and nothing happened, began to be demanded with free comment.

Antonio reported flippantly that when his wife Juana had called, in courtesy, to condole with Escovedo's widow, the latter had raised a dramatic wail upon her entrance, threatening vengeance upon unnamed enemies. Other ladies of Madrid had witnessed the curious little scene, and Juana was much surprised by it, Antonio said. "However," he went on, "the family are taking their grievance to the right quarter. My learned colleague, Mateo Vasquez—you remember him? The Andalusian cleric, my *vis-à-vis*, who controls that half of the royal mind which is not *my* territory—well, he is a family friend of the Escovedos, and so has very properly undertaken to lay a petition from them before the king, so that justice may be speeded. Speed is not, of course, what you get from taking petitions to Philip, but the Escovedos don't know that yet. And the good Vasquez is at El Escorial now, and no doubt will do his utmost. Meantime here in the town the unhappy affair is quite a topic . . ."

Ana pondered this news more gravely than she was intended to. She knew that it was thrown off carefully, as if merely to show her how the wind blew, and otherwise to indicate how pathetically blind was the appeal through Vasquez to Philip. Vasquez himself was acting with perfect correctness in undertaking the petition, and had of course no more idea than Escovedo's young son of the grim comedy of going to that tribunal.

Ana knew that Perez felt safe. Philip was bound to him by friendship and gratitude; bound even closer by shared and dangerous secrets of high politics with which Perez could do him grave harm; bound above all in this instance by his own guilt. Escovedo was killed by his royal instruction. This statement must never be made in any Spanish court of justice.

Even if it could not be proved—but Perez had the instruction
in Philip's own writing—it must not be said. It would
endanger the king and his whole policy, past and future, to a
degree Philip dared not try to measure. So, clearly, Perez felt
safe, and could not help relishing somewhat brutally the farce
of Vasquez laying the grievance of the victim's family in all
good faith before the victim's murderer. Yet she pondered
the news more gravely and more often than Antonio would
have thought necessary.

Bernardina wrote often—of the children and the house and
shoppings she had been instructed to do, and of Madrid as she
found it. She, not having the Secretary of State's powers of
sealed safe conduct for letters, was very careful in her news-
giving. " . . . to tell the truth, we are all a bit dull without
you, *chiquita*. Even the children admit that, though we do our
best with all the parties and sociabilities. And such a lot of
clothes we are having made—we'll come back to you like a
lot of dandies from the court of that fancy King Henry in
France! Many people call on us, and all are disappointed that
you stay in the country. But never mind them—you are right.
And I hope you are resting and sleeping well—and drinking
red wine at night, as I told you. La doña Beatriz de Frias
sends you her very particular love. The Escovedo family is
all in town, but naturally in deep mourning, so we do not
meet them. But they say they are in a great clamour to have
the murderers caught—which is very natural. It's said they
are appealing to the king. But Diego tells me that so far as he
can make out the police are doing nothing at all—and he
thinks that it's certain that whoever did it has got out of
Spain long ago. I expect so. I am having your bedroom
stripped, and the pictures and ornaments removed, as you
told me to. That room you want for a bedroom now is small,
chiquita, and rather far from your other rooms. However, I'll
see about hangings and all you said, and send you patterns
soon. Anichu and I were looking for something in your

sitting-room this morning and she said to me: 'I don't like the Long Room to-day. But I think it's lovely when Mother's here.' She's right—it's a dead hole without you. Fernán and Anichu are writing to you. Ruy tells me he wrote yesterday. We don't forget you . . ."

II

At the end of May the Marqués de Los Velez drove over from Alcala to see her. He had been in Madrid and at El Escorial for some weeks on government affairs, so Ana had not spoken with him since Easter Sunday.

His eyes looked worried, she thought, and he seemed somewhat guarded in his brightness. It was late afternoon when he came and he was tired. He said the drive was tiring. They sat in her drawing-room above the front court-yard, and the servants brought a *merienda* of bread and various cold dishes; Ana poured wine and pressed him to eat.

She knew he wanted to talk about Antonio, did not know how best to begin, yet would not be at ease until he had found an opening. So, after he had eaten and drunk a mouthful, she spoke plainly.

"Is there any danger for Antonio in this Escovedo situation?" she asked.

He looked at her gratefully.

"I'm not sure," he said. "I can't see any positive danger, yet it is true that the king is acting curiously. What do you know of recent news? What does Antonio tell you?"

"Nothing real, at present. His letters are gay and evasive, and as if he were very busy. Which indeed I am sure he is. And you see, I haven't seen him since—since the night of Escovedo's death."

"Ah!" De Los Velez looked at her, then took some bread and fish and chewed slowly.

He knew that Ana was the mistress of Antonio Perez, and

that she knew he knew that; he knew the shared culpability of the king and Perez in Escovedo's death, and that Ana also knew that; he knew that the dead man had lectured and interfered inexcusably in her illicit love-affair. Antonio had told him of that and of his rage against Escovedo because of his fanatical preachings. He had *not* told of the awful climax of those preachings; Ana knew that no one living would ever hear of that from Antonio's lips or hers. Still, the old Marqués knew in general the personal as well as the political shadows that hung across the grave of Escovedo.

He believed that when moving among possible dangers it was better even for trusted friends to make few, very few, plain assertions. If one has never heard a statement made, or oneself made it, then one can so swear, if need be. Thus he had never said, or heard anyone—not Ana, not Perez—say that the two were lovers; and he guessed, and rightly, that Perez had never, to Ana, verbally or in writing admitted his actual direction of the murder of Escovedo. Yet these things were known to those concerned and could be presumed upon, within the right formulæ, in the conversation of two or three close friends.

De Los Velez sought now, as he ate, for an idiom of plain statement which should be neither offensive nor dangerous. He lifted his glass.

"Let us drink to Philip together," he said with a malicious small laugh. "Do you feel loyal to him?"

Ana raised her glass at once.

"Always," she said. "Much more loyal than he needs or guesses."

They drank, and smiled at each other as they set down their glasses.

"Yes, indeed," said de Los Velez. "If only the man would understand our loyalty, how simple it is, how willing! If only he didn't have to make a sort of witch's brew every now and then of the feelings of his faithful servants. My

Heavens! Look what we do for him! Look what Perez does, and risks! Yet——"

"Yet, what? What's brewing now?"

"I wish I knew." He paused. "Perez clearly hasn't told you this—and perhaps that only means that he thinks no more of it than of any other antic of the king. Or perhaps he'll be very angry with me if I tell you. Still, I believe you ought to know. Maybe you'll reassure me?"

"What is it?"

"You know that Mateo Vasquez has taken charge—quite kindly and rightly—of the petition of the Escovedo family concerning the—assassination of their father? Now Vasquez has no access to the Netherlands files in foreign affairs, and by Philip's deviousness has had no idea at all of the king's exasperation against Juan de Escovedo. No idea at all in fact of the truth in the affair he is championing. But the Escovedos—and their advisers, many of them people in high office and well known to you, people who know their way in our politics and who, whether or not they have axes to grind, know better than to make idiotic assertions in a case like this —well, these people have assured Mateo Vasquez that Escovedo was murdered by Antonio Perez." He paused, and Ana did not move or interrupt. "They assert, Ana, that the murder was in expiation of a private grievance; that Escovedo knew of an illicit love-affair of Perez's, and was threatening to expose this secret to the king."

He waited and looked at her. Her answer surprised him.

"Escovedo did know," she said. "And he did threaten to reveal what he knew to the king. But that is accidental. The king ordained his death, and the king was obeyed."

"Yes, that is so. Well now. Vasquez wrote a despatch for the king on the death of Escovedo. In it he stated plainly this accusation. He said that Escovedo's family knew that Perez had had him murdered, because of a woman. He said that Perez feared exposure because this woman was well known, and her honour was in his hands. He presented his despatch to the king."

Ana smiled a little.

"But how do *you* know this?" she asked.

De Los Velez laughed outright.

"There's the question of someone who knows Philip!" he cried delightedly. But instantly he grew grave again, and poured more wine and drank some before he went on. "I know the contents of that despatch," he said, "because Philip did what I regard as a quite inexplicable thing with it. After keeping it to himself for some days, he showed it to Perez—and to me—and asked us how he should answer it."

"But—surely, to show it to Perez was very injudicious?"

"Outrageously—as a child could tell him. Yet Philip did it premeditatedly. And if he has a fault—and, Lord, he has many!—it is excess of judiciousness. So, you see, I can't make it out."

"What does Antonio think?"

"He hasn't told you any of this?"

"No."

"Oh! Then I wonder what that means? Well, firstly he was somewhat struck by the boldness of the accusation, and by Vasquez's audacity in presenting it. After all, Perez *is* the favourite minister and much longer in the king's close service than Vasquez is. Besides, he wields a general influence Vasquez will never command. So the despatch struck him as courageous, and *naïve*. But I think he thought that the king's showing it to him was a measure of its *naïveté*."

"And so it might be," Ana said. "After all, it shows Philip's own dismissal of it—well he might dismiss it too, seeing all *he* knows about Escovedo! And it shows his trust in Antonio."

"Maybe. I think Antonio thinks that such an apparent indiscretion from the king means that he's weary of Vasquez, on the way to getting rid of him. I don't think it means that.

But I haven't told you the *close* of the story, child—which is that Perez, by Philip's request, drafted his reply to Vasquez's despatch. That, I think, is positively funny."

"So funny," said Ana, "that I believe Antonio must be right."

De Los Velez shook his head.

"There's no real sign of it," he said. "Vasquez is too valuable—indeed, Philip's trouble is that both these Secretaries are at present irreplaceable. He has trained them to be perfectly complementary in foreign affairs, and he simply doesn't want to be inconvenienced by the loss of either. I've watched Vasquez in committee, my dear, and I often have to read his memoranda and debate his ideas. He is quite first-class—and in addition a blameless character, and a demon for work."

"So is Antonio," said Ana. "A demon for work, I mean."

They both laughed.

"Yes, I didn't think you meant a blameless character."

"I have always thought Vasquez an unpleasant sort of bore."

"Oh, he's priggish and graceless—and to the world he's just a dull, good cleric. He seems to have no personal tastes or ambitions, and no vices. He takes no bribes in office, and he steals no wives from ageing noblemen. He doesn't notice whether the pages at Court are pretty or not. You can't catch him out, and he has no enemies."

"All of which adds up, sadly enough, to having no friends," said Ana.

De Los Velez laughed appreciatively.

"That's true, indeed—in your and my interpretation of the word 'friends'. I admit that I, for instance, would take elaborate trouble at any time to escape the *ennui* of ten unnecessary minutes of the company of Vasquez—whereas his *vis-à-vis*, that scamp Antonio, may have at will my time, my house, my purse, anything of mine indeed, except perhaps my daughters—if he had ever sought them, and *if*—a long if!—I could have argued them away from his charm!"

The Marqués was growing cheerful. He had cleared a dish of anchovies and eaten a great deal of spiced sausage and smoked ham. He was fishing apricots out of syrup now and eating them whole.

"Delicious, Ana. What *is* your secret of preserving? I simply can't get them done like this by my people."

But Ana's mind was on Antonio and the king.

"What has this contrast of types to do with the Escovedo petition?" she asked.

"Nothing—just yet. But, should the present situation ever come to an open issue between the two Secretaries, don't be surprised if the man of a thousand friends and with all possible power and influence should lose his game to the man who merely has no enemies."

Ana rose and paced across the room to the great window. De Los Velez watched her kindly.

"Why should it come to an open issue between them?" Ana asked.

"It needn't, of course. But Philip's curious tactics may force it that way. He's likely to be in a bad fix himself if the Madrid gossip and outcry for the Escovedo murderers do not subside—and he sees that, and he's playing for time, as usual. Oddly enough, he seems to think that he'd gain something—or that's my guess—by setting Perez and Vasquez at each other's throats. A herring across the trail, I suppose—but honestly, I cannot see his game. Simply I think it conceals danger—for Perez."

"I can't see the danger. Philip is the guilty man, and he knows that."

"My dear—the divine right!"

They both laughed, but Ana not very happily.

"But are Antonio and Vasquez at each other's throats then?" she asked.

"Antonio is certainly in a very dangerous rage against Mateo, who, not knowing that the king has betrayed his private despatch into the hands of the man he accused in it, is touchingly bewildered! And, after all, he is only doing his duty, and will continue to do it. It is perfectly within his function to bring appeals against injustice to the attention of the king. Perez meantime has—just a little—lost his head."

Ana came back from the window slowly.

"How tall you are!" De Los Velez said. "Too tall, really."

"In what way has he lost his head?"

"Oh, he's taken to insulting Vasquez in and out of season—across the Cabinet table, and at public gatherings, and everywhere. Makes a great farce of his adoption of the Escovedo cause, and in general treats him disgracefully. A very foolish policy."

"Maybe." She paused. "You haven't told me what Philip's reply was to Vasquez's despatch. What did Antonio draft for him?"

"Oh, that was quite cunning, very neat. To the effect—I can't remember it precisely now—that Vasquez was on the wrong tack, that Philip had better information, but was awaiting a certain line of evidence before proceeding to justice; that the crime had nothing whatever to do with any woman, but that its perpetrator had a far graver reason for it; and he begged Vasquez to give no further credence to the very rash guesses and accusations of the Escovedos and their friends. That kind of thing. So far as we can make out it has quieted Vasquez down."

"Well then?"

"Oh, but only temporarily! The Escovedo party is still after him, and of course it's clear to him that a course of action must be taken when an innocent citizen is murdered. Besides, he's certain he's right about Perez, and under the stress of Perez's recent outrageous treatment of him he has begun to say what he thinks—in sheer self-defence—to this one and that one. He'll come back to the attack. And meantime it's clear that Perez isn't going to tolerate him much longer as a colleague. Which is very easy to understand. And oh, my dear, the gossip that's flying already, and the side-taking and the surmising! It's really becoming quite a bore in Madrid, this topic. You're very well out of it."

Ana sat silent awhile. A servant came in and removed the tray of food; then he returned and lighted candles.

"No, don't draw the curtains," Ana said, and he went out.

"I meant to get up and look at that picture over there before the light went," said de Los Velez. "It's a new one, isn't it?"

Ana looked with pleasure towards the small canvas he indicated.

"Yes, it's only been here a few days. You must look at it before you go. It's a Mantegna. Antonio found it somehow —through some dealer."

"It looks a beauty from here."

"Yes. It's lovely."

Ana let her eyes rest on the picture, and thought, with anxiety on many planes, of the man who had given it to her. Just when he is about to lose what he valued most between us, the surface of her mind was saying sadly, he begins to know me. This picture, for instance—but her attention was not really on it, or on the giving of presents between lovers. She was perplexed by the talk and news de Los Velez had brought; vaguely, unwillingly she felt herself trying to peer ahead and measure Philip's slow ruthlessness against Antonio's present power over him.

"Don't, Ana," the Marqués said. "Don't look like that, my dear! I've made you sad with my wretched Court gossip. Which is probably all it is—no more than gossip! In any case, what's a mere domestic side-show like this to Antonio, who spends his whole life sharpening his wits on the vast intrigues of France and Italy? He's got his hands on all the strings, my dear. He'll see the whole thing through and over without losing any sleep. In any case, what *can* Philip do, except protect him from his slanderers?"

Ana smiled a very faint question on the word "slanderers".

"It's a cold and brutal situation," she said. "Thinking of it makes one shiver a little for everyone. The poor Escovedos!"

"Well, yes, the poor Escovedos," said de Los Velez coolly. "But they're all of a sudden of major importance in Madrid—which is a novelty for them, and I don't think they are exactly disliking it."

"That's hard-hearted of you."

"I agree. I've been living too long among courtiers. Still, even I can spare some pity for poor Vasquez now. To have made Antonio his enemy—and then to have to work so close to him, day in day out!" He laughed.

"I expect Philip is already regretting that mistake of the despatch," said Ana.

"Oddly enough, I don't think so. I get the impression that he sowed this discord quite deliberately. But I wonder if he can tell what the harvest will be?"

"How does he seem, Philip?"

"Exactly as usual. Busy, tired, friendly. Immensely pleased with the new *Infante*, of course. Enormous relief to everyone that the creature was born alive and is so far staying alive!"

"Is it a healthy child?"

"Oh, no. It looks a little horror, I think."

"Poor Philip!"

"But he's ravished with it, Ana. Greatly puffed up. Full of work too, and rather boringly interested in all his building and planting up there. Impossible to assess, in fact. But I've an idea—now here is my last comment, I promise, on all this dreary news, and I only make it because I think it may be important—I've an idea that he does suspect that Perez has somehow got a woman mixed up, quite accidentally, in the

Escovedo matter. I think he'd like to verify that suspicion, and get the woman's name. So far no name has been given."

His eyes had an anxious look again.

Ana leant forward and touched his sleeve lightly, as if in reassurance.

"Thank you," she said. "I know you wanted to get that said. And there's nothing to be afraid of in it. Our private lives don't belong to the king."

"Spoken like a Mendoza," de Los Velez said, but he did not look entirely reassured. "And let's hope you don't have to test your theory about private lives."

"There isn't any way of testing it," she said amusedly. "One doesn't submit private life to public tests."

"My dear, dear Ana! Shall I have to start praying for you, you innocent? Give me a little more wine, child. It's dark now, and my coachman will be wanting to start for home."

III

Bernardina and the children returned to Pastrana early in June.

The weather unfolded into slumbrous heat. But there was water in the streams from the Guadarramas, and the gardens and farms flowered; the trees were heavily leafed for shade. The children played with their village friends. Life was timed by the *Colegiata* bell, and Madrid was far away.

Bernardina indeed spilt out her load of gossip bit by bit, and in it naturally much hearsay of the Escovedo scandal—but none of this seemed more than gossip or to carry facts as far as the Marqués had brought them.

Antonio's letters came; presents too, and luxuries from Madrid, constant tokens of his thought of her. But she did not invite him yet to visit her, and he made only joking protests against this. " . . . De Los Velez tells me that he told you of my feud with Vasquez," he wrote once. "Well!

you will understand that I have cause! The ass is quiet at present, though I hear extraordinary tales of his subterranean inquiries against me. And his clients are *not* quiet! However, that part is the king's trouble, not mine. All I need watch for are my colleague's allegations against me. I am having no more of them. Sooner or later, the king will have to choose between us, or face an enquiry. So, naturally, I'm not worrying. In any case, I'm kept at work like seven mules. And when I come out of that side-gate of the Alcázar at all hours of the night I look up in vain to the windows of the Long Room. No light ever, no one there. But to-night I drive up to El Escorial, God help me! Several days of conference, and you know how I hate the place. However, the king is being agreeable, and even considerate, at present. And Madrid isn't alluring. It wasn't so dead somehow when at least your house was open and I sometimes saw the children cantering about. But now—well, I get so bored that I almost hate you, and think of throwing stones at your detestable blank windows. Still, I *shall* see you again. You haven't vanished off the earth, have you? And when I do, how is it to be, Princess? . . ."

Summer moved on; the Escovedo stalemate slid to the background of thought; even Bernardina seemed to have forgotten it, and Antonio dropped the ominous name from his letters. Ana's days were filled, as by fixed country habit; mornings of estate and family management, either at her desk or riding about the land with bailiffs or tenants, or in conference sometimes with silk merchants from Zaragoza or Madrid; afternoons, too hot for movement, of sewing or letter-writing or indolence in her drawing-room, or with the children in the watered patio; evening rides and picnics with the children; songs in the garden with them, under the moon, and to Bernardina's guitar; and early to bed—or so Anichu protestingly called it at midnight—with music still straying up from here and there about the village street.

A suitable, conforming life, such as Philip would approve, she thought; the life, in fact, that Ruy had fixed for her and that she knew by heart.

It gave her time to think. But she did not think, or thought less and less as the days passed, of politics or of the crimes of Philip and Perez and the possible clash which these were likely now to cause between the two men's temperaments. Somehow day by day her mind withdrew from all that story, shrugging it off fatalistically until it might become necessary to consider it again.

She thought of her passion for Perez, and sought to discover whether she repented of it truly now, or whether the strange shock she had undergone—of sympathy with Escovedo's scorn and acceptance of his verdict—had been no more than hysterical, an hysterical escape perhaps from an outrage which should have been, on the face of it, unbearable.

She feared to turn sanctimonious, and therefore false, against herself; more than that, she feared to fall into the trap of seeming to judge Antonio, instead of leaving that to him. She had a horror of all such impertinence, and so should have felt, as Perez did, sheer, unadulterated loathing of their insane judge, Escovedo. But she could not. The very madness of his last gesture of condemnation attracted and held her attention, as all his former boring sermons had only made her laugh impatiently at his bad manners. There had been no question of manners at the last. It was fanaticism, right or wrong.

She missed Antonio very much in these days. He had carried her a long way in pleasure; had taught her, late, the whole art in great and little of reciprocal love. Very gratefully she had learnt to count on her delight; and now her nerves were restless; the quivering daylight, the dark-blue nights, all stars, hurt her as before she had not understood them to do.

"We're just two dull and bored old countrywomen, Bernardina, you and I," she said one evening in the garden.

"Speak for yourself," said Bernardina. "I've a perfectly good husband here at hand, may I remind you?"

Ana laughed.

"Perhaps it's well to remind me," she said. Bernardina was not faithful to her Espinosa.

"You're getting racy in your style," she said amusedly. "A year or so ago if I had said we were two dull old country-women, you'd have wondered what on earth I was sighing for. Oh, you've learnt a lot in one winter in Madrid, *chiquita.*"

"I wonder. I wonder if what I really learnt was that it's best to stay here, and be dull."

"You're sad to-day. You have a little headache. It'll pass."

Ana looked up towards the Guadarramas and thought of Antonio far away at the western end of them, with Philip in his monastery. Monasteries, convents; Philip with his monks and prayers and ceremonious barricadings against sin—but the natural answer to love and its perplexities is not in these. And Antonio in any case sought no answer, knew no perplexities. He was so much without sense of guilt in his exploitation of the senses as to be innocent. She liked this blazing pagan innocence which at once made him almost a foreigner in her eyes and a young, understandable boy.

She shrank from offending against that sweeping ease of his sensuality, that refusal of fuss, that attention to generosity and simplicity which gave style to his love-making and had been of immeasurable help to her uncertainties in the first days of their union. Was she now, because of a resolution in her breast which he could never have patience with, to hurt and strike at that in him which had meant most to her when passion was unclouded? Was she now, having taken all he gave, to be contrite at his expense, and torment him with prayers and explanations which could only appear to him stupid, medieval, hysterical, and a dull disfigurement of her?

She shrank—even if the salvation of her soul hung on it—

from thrusting her alien remorse upon his soul. She despised the unfairness, and the interference with him, of a repentance which was only hers. She had grown fond of Antonio Perez, and so she wished neither to hurt him nor, by gracelessness, to lose his dear regard. And easily now she might do both. She found herself wishing that his love had tired, as she had thought it might, in the spring just past.

One evening Anichu walked down the village with her on an errand to a woman who was weaving silk for the dining-room chairs.

They came back past the Franciscan convent as some of the young nuns, returning from work at the school, were passing in at the gate. They smiled and bowed to Ana, and one of them kissed Anichu.

The little girl beamed at them. She knew all their names and told them to Ana.

"I like our having Franciscans here, you know," she told her mother as they went on. "They're every bit as good as Carmelites, aren't they?"

"I'm sure they are, sweetheart. Certainly they are very good, nice nuns."

"Of course, I agree with Fernán that it's a pity you quarrelled with Mother Teresa."

Ana was startled. She did not know that her children knew so much about her.

"Yes, it was a pity. I'm sorry I did."

"But then of course *you* couldn't ever have been a nun! Really you couldn't! Didn't you know that?"

"Not for certain, until I tried."

"If I'd been bigger, I wouldn't have let you," Anichu said.

Ana smiled down at the little girl.

"Well, I've got you now to take care of me," she said. "Let's go in and say a prayer."

They went together out of the sun into the dark *Colegiata*

church. Ana lifted Anichu up to the holy water font, and they splashed each other's foreheads and made the sign of the Cross. Then they went and knelt side by side on the flagstones near Ruy Gomez's tomb.

THE SECOND CHAPTER (OCTOBER 1578)

It was mid-October when Antonio came to Pastrana. Officially his visit was to the Marqués de Los Velez, for two days' rest and hunting at Alcala de Henares. But on the evening of the first day he drove eastward, to have supper with Ana.

He came into her drawing-room eagerly, almost running to her and to the fire. He kissed her hands and gave a little shiver as he smiled at her and then at the warm, illumined room.

"Lovely," he said. "Lovely to be with you again—*and* to be indoors!" He dropped on his knees to get near the fire. "Forgive me if I warm my hands a minute. I love this room. And how well you shut away the howling night! Not a sound of it through your great walls!"

"Is it very wild now?"

"Horrible. I'm glad I didn't ride. I thought of doing so, as really I need exercise. But to tell you the truth, I was too tired."

Ana had never before heard him say that he was tired, but now indeed he looked it.

"What can we do for you, to rest you?"

"Let me stay here on the floor by your fire—and come and sit near me, where I can see you. Ah yes—just there." He leant his back against a chair across the hearth from Ana. "I'll tell you later how you're looking," he said gently, "what it's like to see you again."

She smiled at the characteristic, flattering ease. He might

never tell her, as he said, how she was looking, yet if he liked he would charge every other phrase he spoke with implication of her beauty.

"I wish only to obey you," she said, "but don't you think I ought to offer you something to eat or drink?"

"Nothing. You're not to move. Oh, Ana! This is rest."

"I've never heard you talk of rest before."

His face was level with the fire and at this moment turned towards it, so she could note in this exaggerating light how deep-driven were its lines of weariness. But he laughed as he turned back to her.

"I'm getting old, girl—that's all it is. Do you know that I actually dozed off and on during the drive from Alcala! Now I'm not a dozer, am I? And on my way to *you*—and after so long!"

Ana smiled.

"It's a warning."

"I'm not taking any warnings," he said, stretching himself again contentedly towards the fire. She felt a light question in his words, and let them fall into quiet.

"That was sad news from the Lowlands," she said. "Poor Don Juan of Austria. He was young to die."

"Yes. He seems to have been ill all the summer. His last letters to Philip were sad affairs."

"And Escovedo needn't have died."

He flicked a hint of hard amusement from his eyes before he answered.

"Well, no," he said. "Not for Philip's reasons."

"How did Don Juan die?"

"The pest. His wretched army has been dying of it like flies for weeks. Ah, the confusions of that whole campaign!"

"Yet he might have succeeded with the Flemings? After all, he was one of them."

"Yes. And curiously enough great numbers of them adored him to the end. But he detested them—he had none of his father's feeling for them. His letters were extra-ordinarily abusive and impatient."

"He was attractive."

"I never cared for him. But I have little use for these charming soldierly fools."

"How like Ruy that sounds!"

"Well, I am Ruy's pupil."

Ana was thinking of the early days of her marriage when Isabel of Valois was Queen, and when the two brilliant boys, Don Juan of Austria and Alexander Farnese, were the chosen companions of Philip's son, Don Carlos. Carlos was indeed already indicating then the ill-health that was to end in misery; but no one foresaw that, and the boy had an eccentric promise and originality which fed Philip's heart and, together with his pride in his beautiful new wife, made him happy, and adventurous. The court was young in character then, and owed to Isabel its light, exotic grace; Ruy was its shrewd and tactful controller; and the boys, the three royal sprigs, with their rivalries, follies and achievements, encircled the more sophisticated antics of their elders in the aura of their innocent, endearing promise.

Carlos had died, neither innocent nor endearing; and now Don Juan was coming home for burial.

"He died on the first of October, didn't he?"

Antonio nodded. "He always said October was his lucky month, since Lepanto."

"Lepanto itself was unlucky, if you ask me," said Antonio. "What are you thinking about?"

"The past—the days of Isabel. Do you remember that time?"

"Very well. I came back from Italy before the French marriage, and became Ruy's overworked assistant secretary."

"Yes. I remember. You were a vain and dandified creature."

"I still am."

"You are. Where is Alexander Farnese now?"

"The Duke of Parma? In Brussels, I hope. We're handing him the lovely tangle of the Netherlands."

"Well, *he* didn't grow up into a 'charming, soldierly fool'."

"No. He has brains. We must wait and hope. His mother didn't do so badly there, you know. At least, by comparison with what followed! Oh Christ, Ana! Don't start me off on the follies of our foreign policy! God knows I didn't come to you for that!"

Ana came to the fire to put more wood on it. Antonio scrambled to his knees to help her. They knelt side by side adjusting the heavy logs, and he watched her face attentively as the warm light caught and dramatised it. It was her left profile that he saw, and he marked how almost too delicate the fine skin seemed as it lay so spare over her narrow cheekbone; he noted the blue-brown shadow beneath and above her hollowed eye, but how golden and true the eye shone into the exacting firelight, and that her lashes were as ever, shining and childlike. It was indeed a sorrowful thing, he thought, for *her* to have lost an eye. At very close range the details of her beauty, its secret, unproclaimed treasures of delicacy, of accidental girlishness, continued, however often noted, to surprise him, to take his fastidiousness again and again by storm. Often in a side-glance, in a moment of slackness or of what he had thought to be complete inattention from her, he would be brought up sharp on an entirely unforeseen pang of appreciation of her; the edge of her eyebrow, the too-well sculptured bone of her wrist, the light, slim run of sinew from her ear to her throat—such things in her could, he found, besiege his unwary attention, and suddenly suggest themselves to him as containing all beauty. It is by these, he sometimes said to himself, by these inconsequences that I'll remember her for ever.

She leant forward, dropping pine-cones here and there among the logs of the fire. He sat on his haunches and let her do the work.

"You're unlucky," he said. "Your beauty is of a kind that only a lover or a baby can get near enough to see."

Ana rose from the hearth, and ran her hand quickly across his forehead as she did so.

"I wonder what I'm going to do without you," she said.

He sprang to his feet.

"Ah! So that is it?"

"Wait. We must talk."

"Indeed, indeed we must. Oh Ana, I've been frightened of this."

He looked about the room and back to her, and she was distressed to notice that indeed his eyes did look frightened. He moved to a table where there was food and wine, and turned to her as if in apology before he poured himself a drink.

"May I, please?" She smiled. "Oh Ana, you drink too! Drink with me! Let's drink to my power over you, that it may not fail us! Come!"

He moved towards her with two glasses full of red wine. As Ana stretched her hand to take one the great door at the far end of the room opened and her eldest son, Rodrigo, came in.

It was not correct of him to come to her drawing-room uninvited while she entertained a guest, and indeed Ana had thought that he was still at a house-party with his cousins at Guadalajara. However, she smiled at him without concern. He seemed at his ease, and was dressed in indoor clothes, so he must have got back to Pastrana a little before or after Antonio's arrival. He bowed gracefully to his mother and her guest. Ana thought there was a fraction less humour than usual in Antonio's acknowledgment of the boy. As a rule Rodrigo amused him wildly, but she supposed that the inopportuneness of this entrance was exasperating to a man already tired and overstrung. He was in no mood for courtly chatter. Well, they'd get rid of the child in a minute or two.

"I interrupt your little festivity—forgive me!" he said.

Ana raised her brows. This was insolent talk, but as she had never played a maternal role with Rodrigo she could not bring herself to call him to order now. Besides, she was more puzzled than annoyed by his tone. A courtier always, he was always excessively polite to men of power, and regarded Antonio Perez as second only to the king in Spain, and perhaps in some ways more powerful than the king. Ana had heard him make an aristocrat's mild jibes sometimes at Perez's upstart grandeur, but never in any hearing that might endanger their repetition to the Secretary of State; and always, face to face with Perez, he was—as he hoped—charm incarnate; always he seemed delighted to be in the company of this great man, and to do his best to please and entertain him. Therefore this impertinent opening gambit puzzled Ana so much that she thought she had perhaps misheard it.

Perez looked coldly at the boy.

"Yes, you do interrupt us," he said. "Why?"

Ana smiled, more bewildered than ever. It was uncharacteristic of Antonio to waste contempt on trivial people or trivial irritations. Poor little Rodrigo, she thought amusedly, and set herself to watch a scene to which she had no key.

"Because I had not heard that Your Excellency was expected, and indeed my cousin, the Duke of Infantado, told me this morning—I've been staying with him at Guadalajara —that you were due at de Los Velez's place these days, he believed, for some hunting." Ah, thought Ana with a cold shock of surprise—then that's why he came back so soon. He's here to spy on me. My children grow up indeed. Perhaps they even grow dangerous—to my friends. "But when I got here, just after dark," Rodrigo went on suavely, "I saw some men in your livery in the yard. So much smarter than ours, I couldn't be mistaken! So, as soon as I'd changed, I just came along here, to make sure. As Your

Excellency's visit was unlooked for, I take it it is—un-official?"

When this speech, so deftly embroidered with impertinence, ceased, Ana and Antonio, standing some distance from each other and without catching each other's eyes, simultaneously laughed. Two clear, grown-up and spontaneous laughs that ceased with civilised precision before the amusement they held was quite fully expressed. Each realised with pleasure, watching Rodrigo's face and refraining from looking at each other, that they could hardly have done better. There was no denying the natural enjoyment of those two laughs—and they saw Rodrigo wince and begin to look careful. Ana continued to keep her eyes on her son. She was still unable to interpret what was happening.

"How do you mean, unofficial?" Antonio asked in a bored, unanswering tone. He walked towards the fire, taking his wineglass with him. "One doesn't cart one's despatch-boxes about to supper-parties in country houses."

"No, naturally," said Rodrigo, very much a man of the world. "What I meant was that apparently at the Alcázar you are understood to be at the house of the Marqués de Los Velez."

"That is so—that's where I'm staying. May we continue our conversation now, Princess? I'm tired, and not willing to waste time on interruptions."

"I know that," Ana said, "I'm sorry. I invited Don Antonio to visit *me* to-night, Rodrigo. Had I wished you to join us in this room I would have had word sent to you. And you know that it was not correct of you to come to me here uninvited when I have a guest." She was about to add a mere word of dismissal, but suddenly—from where she hardly knew—from Antonio's eye towards which she hardly looked, or along some current of their sympathy—she apprehended, for the very first time in this scene, some real danger to Antonio, some far-concealed threat from his own wide, adult world, just hinted at, foreshadowed in caricature perhaps, by this impertinent boy, her son. So, instead of dismissing him outright, defensively for Antonio she eased her cold contempt and smiled as if indulging a juvenile mistake. "But now you're here, let us overlook that—and perhaps you'll drink a glass of wine with my guest before you leave us?"

"No, thank you, Mother." Rodrigo bowed, then drew himself up and spoke solemnly. "I came here, in fact, to utter a protest. You have not spared our honour in the past— the family should, I suppose, be used to you. Indeed, myself, I have grown up without protest under the shadow of your rumoured royal gallantry. But now Madrid is ringing with another scandal—this time a criminal one. His Excellency may indeed think the world well lost—and indeed I believe for him it *is* lost!—that is his affair, though very odd. But we, the Mendozas, have had enough of *your* legend, Mother. You are old now, you see, and a little ridiculous. And in any case your children set their name above your pitiful pleasures. So I must ask you to dismiss a guest whom I had hoped I might not again have to encounter in my house."

Ana, long trained out of anger, and totally unused to conflict with her children, heard this speech with astonishment which took her so far into surmise that she did not even consider at first that it must be answered. Indeed, though she heard it all and held its implications close, for later analysis, chiefly she attended now to this irrelevance: that though she disliked Rodrigo while he spoke, as she always mercilessly tended to dislike him, and though she thought some of his phrasing—all allowances made—objectionable, yet she saw unblinkingly the justice and right convention of his case. And she watched him with pity, and wondered what it would be expedient, for everyone's sake, including Antonio's, for her to say when he ceased speaking.

But Antonio forestalled her.

He came forward from his place by the fire, holding up a hand to her for silence, when Rodrigo's speech was done.

"Listen, Rodrigo," he said, "if it's a habit of yours to abuse your mother to her face as if she were a street whore who had overcharged you by a *real*, then let me instruct you to keep that habit to where it belongs—your private life. Because by the rules of Spanish honour—which it's time you learnt, isn't it?—any man, catching you at it, is entitled to run you through the body, as a national duty. Now, you have allowed me, for instance, to eavesdrop on one of your moments of ignobility. That's the sort of thing you mustn't do, if you want to live. Because——" Antonio's manner of speech was uniformly cold and advisory; there was no hurry and no variation of tone—"because if I call you out for this performance—and I only hesitate because you're such a baby-boy; ah yes, you are also the first-born of my friends Ruy Gomez and Ana de Mendoza—but if I do call you out, you will die within one minute of the crossing of our swords. You're a promising blade, but you know that my swordsmanship is quite simply out of your reach."

"I await your seconds, Your Excellency. Good night, Mother."

"No, I haven't finished," said Antonio. "All that was only about manners, which is the general reason why I may kill you before your seventeenth birthday. But I want to say this about the gossip you spat out so unbecomingly. I am His Majesty's Secretary of State, and it is my boring duty to know everything about such major political scandals as this with which you say Madrid is ringing. Madrid is not ringing with it—clearly you haven't been there lately. Neither has that example of provincialism, the Duke of Infantado. If either of you was just a bit in touch with events you'd know that a slightly alarmed hush has fallen in Madrid about the Escovedo petition—and that the very good reason for this discretion is that the President of Castile—Don Antonio de Pazos, whose eminence and power I need hardly stress, I think?—has examined the case which was to be offered to the High Court of Justice. His ultimate counsel to the unhappy Escovedos was clear-cut, and is known to most people of importance now. Not of course to sporting Dukes like you and Infantado. However, it behoves you if you want to save your neck and get on in life, either to keep up to date with our scandals, or if you can't do that, keep out of them. And, in conclusion, Rodrigo—I was a witness to-night of your offence of *lèse-majesté*. You're not too young to go to prison for that. So you see, I can do as I please with you—and that's all for now. Consider whether or not you've made a fool of yourself."

Antonio jerked his head in dismissal, and then turned to the table where the food was and helped himself to a handful of prawns.

Ana looked in pity at her son. It was clear that he had lost his bearings; needed time to think.

"You must go now, Rodrigo," she said gently.

"I go with alacrity," he said. "Poor Mother, what a fool you are! Good night."

"Good night, Rodrigo."

He bowed to her and left the room.

"It was a silly bluff," Antonio said. "But it did scare the little ass, I hope."

Ana was pacing the length of the room.

"Oh that!" she said, dismissing the details of the episode with a flick of her hand. "You managed him very well. And saved *me* the dilemma of answering his moral strictures! Which I couldn't very well have done, could I?" She paused in her striding in the middle of the room. Antonio noticed a faint flush rising in her cheeks—she looked excited and young. He came to her with her glass of wine.

"We were going to drink—do you remember?—to my power over you, Ana."

She took the wineglass without paying attention to it or to what he said.

"What's been going on in Madrid that I don't know about, Antonio? What does it mean, what does it come from, this amazing behaviour of Rodrigo?"

He paused before he answered her.

"Actually," he said, "I think it means a very great deal. In itself it's nothing—but it's a straw in the wind. A rather strong wind, I'd say. It surprises me a great deal more than Rodrigo guessed, I hope. There's much to be deduced from it that I hadn't known." His eyes narrowed and he spoke slowly, carelessly; it seemed that his thought was far ahead of his words, moving rapidly through obstructions and long-shot surmises. "Come, drink," he said, changing his manner. "And if you won't take that other toast, drink, girl, to my power and omniscience as Secretary of State! Ah, what a bluff it is! What a boring game we play who work with the king!"

"You are troubled. What is it? Are you in danger?"

"Troubled—no. But in danger, possibly yes. I think that we are both in danger, Ana."

"I, in danger?" She laughed incredulously. "That really couldn't be so."

He sat down near the fire.

"Perhaps you're not. Perhaps I'm thinking too fast. I often do. Coming here to-night I was in two minds as to how much to tell you—but now I see I'd better talk. Since your own son is running about to spread the news—you may need the facts at any time."

Ana came and stood beside him. She took his hand and held it lightly between both of hers. She felt very much in love with him.

"Then we were both in two minds about what we had to say to-night? That isn't like us. I suppose it means that changes are coming?"

"No. Things are happening to us from outside, happening fast and treacherously, I think—and we have to be ready for them. But nothing changes between us. I belong to you, just as I have done since that night when you seduced me so coldly. And you belong to me."

"Yes. I belong to you—in the way in which you mean it. Though not perhaps demonstrably now."

He sprang up with a sharp, protesting laugh at her odd word, "demonstrably", and took her hard and close into his arms.

"'Not demonstrably'? Ah, girl, do you want me to demonstrate this instant what I mean by your belonging to me?"

"You needn't. I belong to you far more to-night than I did on that night when I seduced you. Though that was heavenly, Antón."

"Not the best though, was it? Not the best of all?"

"No, not the best. Oh, I am grateful to you! Grateful for ever."

"That's what I mean by my power over you, Princess——"

She kissed his forehead and then moved away from him, out of his arms.

"There are other powers," she said. "Philip's power over you; Escovedo's over me."

"Escovedo's?"

She rang a silver bell.

"Wait," she said. "That must wait. There's a lot to be said to-night."

A servant entered.

"Ask Doña Bernardina to be so good as to come to me for a moment, please."

The man withdrew.

"I think I'll drink this wine now," Ana said.

"Do, I beg you. I'm tired of offering it and seeing it pushed aside. Bernardina—she is devoted, isn't she? You trust her?"

"Yes. I wouldn't expect her to face the three tortures of the Holy Office for me—why should I? But she has a good, true heart."

"She knows your secrets?"

"I assume she does. We don't discuss our private lives, but we know some things about each other."

"Ah, reciprocal blackmail!"

"Yes. Are you hungry?"

"I believe I am."

"We'll have supper early."

Bernardina came in and Antonio greeted her.

"We're very glad to see you here again, Don Antonio," she said. "It's been a long absence."

"Much too long, my friend. I'm happy to be in the Princess's house again."

"It's safer than some places, I should think, *señor*."

"It is indeed," he said, amused by her coolness.

"Listen, Bernardina," said Ana. "Supper has been ordered, of course, for Don Antonio and me? But will you tell them that we want it now, and in this room? Tell them not to fuss, and that if some things aren't ready, to give us whatever they have. That will do, won't it?" she asked Antonio.

He nodded. He was considering Bernardina and wanted to sound her friendship. Ana might need the devotion of her household soon, but would never think of playing for it.

"Oh, anything will do," he said. "I'm very hungry. Won't you drink a glass of wine with us, Doña Bernardina?"

"Do, Berni. I'll have some more please, Antón."

Pouring out the wine he smiled at Ana's casual informality. Calling him Antón before her *dueña!* Certainly she was no intriguer. He must remember that.

"Thank you," said Bernardina. "I'll just drink your health, and then fly off and tell them to hurry supper."

"Yes—do please ask them not to lay a state banquet for the

Secretary of State," Ana said. "Just let them bring a few things on trays."

"I'll do my best—but you know Diego doesn't like your slipshod notions. You're looking tired, Don Antonio. Are you overworked?"

"Naturally. You aren't, I hope?"

"Oh, she makes me earn my keep."

"She's a lazy Andalusian," said Ana. "Oh, Berni--and this is for everyone, please, including my son Rodrigo—I am supping *alone* with Don Antonio, and I do not desire to receive anyone else to-night. Make that clear, will you?"

Antonio was surprised by this stressed instruction.

"Indeed I will, *chiquita*," said Bernardina. "I beg your pardon humbly that Rodrigo came bothering you—but I didn't even know he was back from Guadalajara."

"Oh, you couldn't have stopped him. He was determined to see Don Antonio."

"So I gathered," said Bernardina grimly. "I've been giving him a piece of my mind just now. He's getting a little above himself, is Master Rod!"

"I got that impression," Antonio said, and he and Bernardina laughed together.

The *dueña* set down her emptied glass.

"You'll have supper in a very few minutes," she said. "And I promise you'll be left in peace, *chiquita*."

When she was gone Antonio looked inquiringly at Ana.

"Since we've been lovers," he said, "I've never heard you tell a lie to protect your secret, but neither have I ever—until now—heard you say anything to seem to advertise it. Why were you so emphatic about everyone knowing that you desire to be alone with me?"

"For Rodrigo's benefit—and I think Bernardina understood me. Do you mind?"

He laughed and shook his head.

"Go on. Explain."

"It's easy. If Rodrigo and the world in general are going to talk as apparently they're talking, then it has to be made crystal-clear to them that you are my very dear, particular friend——"

He laughed delightedly.

"Perverse and mad! Oh, Ana!"

"Not mad at all. I have a plan. And besides, you *are* my very, very dear, and if the wind is blowing cold for you at present, I'd like it known that you will always shelter here."

He stared at her.

"I believe you *have* a plan!" he said.

"But that's what I've just said," she answered innocently. "Of course, you have to tell me yet what in fact is happening, but still, in a general way I have a plan."

"Having a plan suits you," he said. "You look wonderfully excited."

"I am wonderfully excited."

"What is your plan?"

Servants flung open the great door and began to carry in a laden supper-table.

"To put away that very dull Pantoja de la Cruz," said Ana, waving towards a picture. "I want a clear space round the Mantegna."

"Yes—you should do that. But what will the donor of Pantoja say?"

"I doubt if he'll ever be here again to see. Doesn't the Mantegna look lovely?"

Antonio walked over to the small picture and studied it. The servants set chairs ready to the supper-table, trimmed the fire, gathered up used wineglasses and withdrew.

"Come and eat, Antón."

They sat down to supper.

"And the plan? Come on, I'm dying to hear it!"

She laughed somewhat shyly.

"Oh, I don't know what *you* call a plan," she said. "But

I have, all of a sudden, a general idea of attack."

"Attack on what?"

"*You* have to tell me that."

"It must be a splendid plan," he said, laughing at her, feeling amused and happy now as he had not felt for months. "Outline it—come on!"

"I will when I've eaten a little more," she said, for a footman came in as she spoke, to change their plates.

"Ever since my birth," she began when they were alone again, "I've been hearing that I am probably the most powerfully placed female in Spain. When I was a child I thought that that solemn fact meant something. I thought I was a pawn—a very important pawn—in the hands of our nobility!"

"How old were you when you were thinking these high politics?"

"Six, seven, eight."

"Does Anichu think in that powerful, masculine way?"

"I've no idea. But she seems a gentle character—more modest than me."

"*Your* modesty is heart-breaking, I think."

"If I have any modesty, life imposed it, Antón. Very rightly. But I was a self-important child—like Rodrigo."

"You were never the least bit like Rodrigo. He's a changeling."

"Well anyway, I just quite simply thought that I was a very important pawn in Spanish affairs!"

"Sweet child sitting among her dolls!" said Antonio. "And you were right. The Mendozas justified your faith, and sold you high."

"Not high enough, I thought at the time. I was taken aback by my marriage. I had thought that they were marrying me to the king."

"You terrible little girl," he said. "How old were you when they signed you up?"

"Eleven. I don't think I was pure politician. I had seen Philip often when I was small—and he was romantic-looking. Somehow he seemed a boy to me, even when he was twenty-four and a widower. And Ruy of course was an aged, aged man of thirty-six. I think it was Philip's fair hair had made him seem so contemporary. And then, he *was* the only fair-haired man in Spain!"

"Did you tell Ruy of your matrimonial disappointment?"

"Oh yes; he loved the story."

"No, don't ring. I'll put the plates over here. Let's just eat fruit and things now, shall we?"

She nodded.

"Philip likes that story too," she said.

"Ah! He knows it?"

"Yes, indeed. I told him—when I was older."

"When he was in love with you?"

"Yes. I told him he had mistimed—that he had been my *first* love."

"He'd like that. Does he ever remind you of it?"

"Yes. Sometimes he surprises me by jokes about it."

"Surprises you? But don't you know the length of his memory, the depth of his vanity?"

"I don't think he's much vainer than other men?"

"Perhaps not. But he has the power other men have not—to sanctify vanity, and if necessary to avenge its wounds."

"Maybe. But this about my childish fancy for him is just an old family joke, Antón——"

"But he *was* in love with you when you were grown up?"

"Yes. Yes and no. I think perhaps I was more in love than he."

"Really in love with him, Ana?"

"Attracted, restless—oh, I liked him very much. But he had given me to Ruy, and he knew that my husband had come to set store by his marriage and was determined to keep me faithful. So—give him his due—he couldn't make up his mind to the sin against his beloved Ruy. And anyway I don't honestly think he wanted me enough. He had Isabel then, and he was fairly happy——''

"So there were endless love-scenes, and again and again he tantalised you both for proof of his seductiveness——"

"You seem to know him. You talk like a woman——"

"Politics or a love-affair—oh yes, I know Philip. And so I think—from all you tell me—that you *are* in danger now."

"And I think not. That's why I've told you all this. It's part of the plan."

He laughed gently.

"If it is it's a dangerous plan."

"Plans have to be. After all, you only make plans in danger."

"Nonsense, Ana. Plans are made so that danger need not arise."

"But how do you make them then?"

"You're talking like Anichu. Lunatic, tell me the plan. Afterwards I'll tell you what to plan about."

"Perhaps it isn't much of a plan," she said nervously. "It's merely that I'm going back to Madrid. I'm going to be there, at hand, as long as you're in trouble—for all to see."

"Ana!" he said, and his eyes blazed on her. "Oh, Ana, I have nothing against that—speaking generally. But go on. I'm waiting for the *idea*."

She bent over a dish of fruit.

"I hate pomegranates," she said. "Don't you? All that spitting."

"But you don't have to spit."

"I can see no other way. These are the last figs—let's eat them."

"First or last, let's eat them."

"The idea is this. Your security is being threatened by Mateo Vasquez?"

Antonio looked at her questioningly before he answered.

"He is the instrument of the Escovedos," he said.

"Hardly. The Escovedos have a tragic grievance, but what possible reason have they to assume that you are their target?"

"They'd know about our political differences. And he probably talked at home of his disapproval of my private life. He may even have said that he and I had quarrelled about that."

"Even so—how could the poor Escovedos *dare*, all by themselves, to bring a major charge against *you*—on that much evidence?"

"Extraordinarily rash of them, I agree. Oh, certainly they are encouraged—perhaps they're just being used——"

"By Vasquez?"

"And some of his friends."

"He has friends? Who are they?"

"Oh, nobody you'd know."

Ana smiled. "Yes, but tell me."

"There's a man—Augustin Alvárez de Toledo—he's in the Treasury. And he's got a brother, a very brainy priest——"

"I've never heard of either of them."

"Well, you will hear. They are great supporters of Vasquez—live in the same house with him, I think."

"That must be charming for them."

"Then there's a man called Milio—half-Italian, and wealthy. Calls himself Dr. Milio, and frequents the aristocracy. He seems to have some hidden axes to grind. He's at present very much Vasquez's partisan. But really he's some kind of protégé of the Duke of Alba. Still, except that he would not interfere *against* any plan to ruin me, I'm certain that old egotist isn't bothering himself with courtiers' plots. Simply, his name may be used by Milio, to encourage the timid in this present affair. But mentioning Alba brings us back to that straw in the wind of a few minutes ago— Rodrigo's behaviour."

"Does Alba come into that?" Ana asked in surprise.

"I think he does. You know Rodrigo is growing up very anti-liberal?"

"Yes. He talks surprisingly about his father's mistakes. And I've heard him express disapproval of the continuing dominance of the liberal *amistad* in the Cabinet. But Rodrigo's politics, after all!"

"Oh, they may make you smile—but they're forming all the same in that pretty head. He's a reactionary, and an admirer of the soldier's way in government. Hence he admires Alba, and favours Alba's party."

"But Rodrigo's just going to be a cavalryman——"

"He's beginning to see that it would be nice to be a cavalryman with political power—as Alba has been. And he may seem silly to you, but out in the world he is the Duke of Pastrana, and could therefore count in affairs later on—if he wished to."

"I still don't see why that very remote idea should make him suddenly drop all restraint and good manners at the sight of you. He's usually only too polite to the important."

Antonio smiled.

"That's it, that's the point. Rodrigo always knows his gesture. There's going to be a gathering of the eagles against me, Ana. They think it's time."

Ana stood up.

"Not all the eagles," she said.

Centuries of assurance, Antonio thought, lay within the amused and casual phrase.

Ana rang her silver bell, and servants came to remove her supper-table. While they were setting things in order she paced up and down the room.

She wore a black dress, as always, and very few jewels. Antonio thought it a pity she was committed, as a widow, to perpetual black, for it did not in his opinion truly accord with her very black hair and Castilian pallor. Sometimes he pleaded with her for more jewellery, more ornament to challenge her distinction; but clearly she did not see any need of them. She was incorrigibly austere, and he suspected that she took far more pleasure than she recognised from her own eccentric native elegance. He pondered on how strongly it had grown on him in a few months of intimacy—his pleasure in her physical qualities. When he was a young man and she was Ruy's young bride he had simply thought her odd-looking, always too thin and in everything exaggerated; and had dismissed Ruy's delighted devotion to her as the slightly senile gratitude to a girl of an ageing man.

He smiled. Gratitude indeed it might well be, for he knew now how she bound a man by gratitude—gratitude for a way in love which was in the possession of no other woman he had known, and which indeed contradicted love's tradition. Simplicity, unpretentiousness, a tolerance which was even exasperating; lack of the impulse to change, influence or directly assist her lover; lack of claim; inability to become domesticated or proprietary in love; inability to fuss or be a bore. And supporting these negatives some complementaries more positive—reluctance to discuss herself; refusal of those intimacies which should not be given and which are the gift of a careless sensuality; caution and delicacy before that of a man's life which is not hers. Yes, gratitude might well be the word for what Ruy Gomez felt about her. It was a roomy word; it suited what she gave.

As she paced about she pressed her hand against her eye-shade. Antonio noticed that she did that when disturbed or excited. He wondered if the destroyed eye hurt her then.

When they were young and indeed always until he was her lover he had thought this disfigurement most terrible, and it had made him uncomfortable to think of any husband having to bear with it. Now, watching her tenderly and wondering if the socket ached, it struck him that if an archangel appeared in the room and undertook to touch Ana's right eye and restore it, he would probably beg her to refuse the miracle. This selfish idea made him smile, and he wished he could tell it to her. It was the sort of thing she appreciated. But one must not speak to her of her blind eye.

"What are you smiling at?" she asked him.

The servants were going now, closing the door.

"At your talk of eagles," he said. "You're not a bit like an eagle, thank God. You're just a greyhound—with all a greyhound's defects of character."

Preoccupied, she waved that off.

"I don't see what the reactionary party, and that mastermind Rodrigo, have to do with your affair. Vasquez, after all, is a liberal like you."

"Oh, it's only that they're thinking of *using* him and the Escovedo affair. They don't like him, but they could never get both of us wrenched away from Philip, and I am much the more obnoxious. I am after all the leader of the party, and by nature a dangerous man. And far too successful. Vasquez's politics may at present be wrongly tinged, but he's the pious, good kind and they know they could manage him. Anyway one of us controlling Philip is better than two—and I'm the one they fear. So they're interested in this Escovedo threat—and see that, carefully managed, it may ruin me."

"I see. They're innocent really, aren't they? And Rodrigo's moral indignation against *me*—where does that come in?"

"Rodrigo has been hearing the news, and has made up his mind. It is going to be made perfectly clear to the next group in power that he, his house and name are violently antagonistic to the fallen favourite. And that is the crux of the whole matter which—if you'll ever let me get a word in edgeways—I'll explain to you."

"I'll let you. Rodrigo must deal according to his disposition with the honour of his house. But I'm selfish, and take an interest in my own honour, which I can only manage in my own way. Now—do you want to hear my plan?"

"Haven't I heard it?"

"Not really. Here it is. Your danger comes from this cleric, Mateo Vasquez, and some people you mentioned whom I've never heard of?" Antonio laughed at her. "Well, as I've said, I'm tired of hearing all my life that I'm a person of power and privilege. At last I see advantage in the legend. You have these enemies, Antón. And you have two friends."

He looked puzzled.

"Two friends?"

"You have me."

"Yes, I have you. Who is my second friend?"

She stared at him.

"The king! The king, who asked you to embrace for him the danger you are now in; the king, who is in that danger with you. The king and you, who are in this trouble together, are at this moment—let Rodrigo squeal as he likes—the two most powerful men in Spain. And I am, they tell me, the most powerful woman. And I am the friend of both of you. Indeed, after Anichu, you are the two creatures who interest me most on earth."

"I see. So?"

"So—I'm going to Madrid. I'm going to see everybody, including Philip, naturally. I'm going to stay there and give scandal and make a fuss—and see what happens. That's all."

He came and took her hands and kissed them, laughing and moved.

"No rings? Oh Ana, where's my emerald?"

"I didn't feel inclined for it. Tell me, isn't it a reasonable plan?"

"It's utter nonsense. Oh, come to Madrid, girl! Come indeed! The place is a plague-spot without you. And your plan, Ana, your silly, silly plan will make a good last act—if you insist on it! But, it won't get either of us out of the scrape we're in."

She laughed, drawing her hands away from him.

"Come, sit down. Tell me about this scrape."

He took the invitation slowly.

"Well, you've heard things, haven't you? De Los Velez told you——"

"Oh yes! Bernardina gets the stories too. She drops hints. That you are involved with a woman—somebody of very great importance! And that Escovedo was killed because he wanted to interfere in your liaison. Dear old de Los Velez warned me very gently that Philip might be curious about that. Bernardina thinks so too, I think. I agree that he might. And say he were? Oh, they have short memories about the ineptitudes of gossip, or perhaps you haven't been the passive subject of those ineptitudes—as I have been."

"Go on. Say your say."

"I think I've said most of it before. All it comes to is that as long as I can remember the populace has tended to tell itself that I lead a life of crime. I won't bore you with all the fables you know—why, they couldn't even bury that poor child Don Carlos without saying that he was my lover, and therefore was killed in criminal concert by Philip and Ruy, who were in the habit of sharing me. From then on they've said everything they liked about me—including that I'm raving mad. I know why. It's because I was born in a vulnerable, high place—and because I'm—well—odd-looking. There was a time when these waves of malicious popular amusement against me used to worry Ruy—and Philip—but I never could see why. Fussy little men in the street I told them they were—and I was right. Gossip is natural. If you choose to live by your own light you must take it—and so long as you don't try to answer it, it won't as much as bruise you. Look at me. Have you ever known a time when I wasn't slandered in Madrid?"

"No—honestly I haven't."

"Yet here I am and no bones broken—and no ill-feeling

between me and my habitual detractors. So now—let them begin again. I can ride these little dust-storms, and so can you. We'll ride together if you like, Antón—that's the *plan!* —to enrich their trivial entertainment. And if they tell Philip the whole truth about us—well, why on earth should he *not* hear it? If it annoys him, I shall be flattered, and touched. But beyond the prick to his already half-dead vanity, it isn't his affair—our being lovers. For the rest of the story—he knows why Escovedo died."

Antonio poked the fire, and made no answer.

"So why look solemn about our 'scrape', as you call it? True or false, it is only another will-o'-the-wisp. Or are *you* a fussy little man in the street, like Ruy and Philip? I believe you are. It's curious you should all three be like that—and my three favourite men."

"Philip. He does hold his place in everything you say, doesn't he? It's odd. Ruy was your husband; I am your lover. But Philip—why must he be always so close around?"

"Because I've always been fond of him, and I have a narrow and faithful heart."

Antonio felt suddenly desperately weary.

What relation could there ever be between the loose-riding, human reasonableness of this woman and the close intrigues of the Secretaries' Rooms in the Alcázar? He had drawn her into a situation in which she would be of paramount importance and entirely at sea. He was tired of turning it over in his own mind, well-trained to its kind of intimacy. Must he really try to explain it now, to someone who would be honestly unable to apprehend its values, and who even if she did perceive them would be their victim without fuss, if necessary—but never their subscriber? He beat about his mind for a short cut through all that should be said.

"It's annoying," he said gently, "your affection for Philip."

"Is it?" She paused. "It's a strange thing to say, I know—but, I trust him."

Antonio smiled a little. Here was the short cut.

"If you're right, Ana—I mean, if in the next few months he honours your trust in him—then there's nothing to worry about. I, on the other hand, *don't* trust him. And if I'm right, well, it'll be impossible to see ahead, for better or worse."

"Explain."

Antonio straightened in his chair and drank some wine.

"I agree with you about gossip. I'm not a fussy little man in the street—can't afford to be, as I don't live like those gentry. I've always let gossip have its blow-around—and like you, though less deservedly, I'm alive to tell the tale, and no bones broken. So I'm not here to bother you with gossip. This is the true position, underneath the gossip. The Escovedo family isn't gossiping. And it's had enough of Vasquez's little petitions to the king. It's employing good lawyers now, and has captured one or two pieces of evidence on which it is certainly reasonable to found a case. So now a full brief has been drafted which they desire to present at the High Court of Justice. Vasquez informed the king recently that this *dossier* was ready—thinking no doubt that Philip would be pleased by such a show of energy! What Philip said to Mateo we shall never know, of course. But what I do know is that in fact the news frightened Majesty very much. After consultations of an incredible circuitousness—with me, with the Cardinal, with de Los Velez, with God knows who else—he instructed Vasquez to have the Escovedos submit their lawyers' draft to the private study of Antonio de Pazos, the President of Castile. You gathered that from what I said to Rodrigo?"

"Yes. What then?"

"De Pazos was shaken by what he read. The Escovedos charge me outright with the murder of Juan de Escovedo—and they charge you, naming you explicitly, with full complicity in the murder. Our reason is given, and the evidence of some witnesses is given; one or two servants—no one from your household, but some names from mine, and from the Alcázar. People I've used for errands, or who may have watched my homing steps at night."

They smiled at each other. Ana lifted her thin shoulders in expression of amusement.

"There always are these people," she said. "After all, we know that. But truly—must one go to the top of the Credos Mountains to meet a lover?"

"Uncomfortable. But please don't be frivolous. There is the evidence of a locksmith, who made a key for a little-used side-door of the Eboli palace in the Calle Santa Maria Almudena."

Ana looked at him and laughed, almost giggled like a little girl.

"So that episode's in?"

Antonio was puzzled.

"I gather it's indicated. De Pazos was—delicate in reporting it to me. Why do you laugh now? I've never mentioned that dreadful night to you because—well, because, obviously it must have been an unbearable shock——" he was still puzzled and diffident.

"Yes, it was a shock," she said, and now her face was grave and non-committal. "But not in the way you mean. It was a private shock."

He waited, not understanding, and expecting her to say more.

"Go on, Antón. We are both charged with the murder of Escovedo, because he threatened to expose our relationship?"

"Yes. There are subsidiary charges—arising from the lawyers' explanation of Escovedo's disapproval of us. His anger was not merely against our lack of sexual virtue in itself, but as an executor of Ruy Gomez's will he desired to protect Ruy Gomez's children from my venality. So, the brief charges me with living on you, with having you pay money-lenders for me, etc.—and accuses you of squandering on me in lasciviousness what belongs to your children. That is the accusation—expertly set out, de Pazos says."

"It is untrue in every word."

"Not quite in every word, Ana. You have paid debts for me; you do spend money madly on me."

"I don't spend the children's money. No, it's untrue."

"De Pazos assured the lawyers of that, warned them they were on a wrong tack and dangerous ground, and counselled them strongly to withdraw a brief which would only grievously damage their clients' case. This advice does appear to have unnerved them, and for the moment there is silence."

"Yet the Escovedos have a serious plaint against the civil authority."

"Exactly. They intend to have it heard. And Vasquez, now in full charge, is convinced of our guilt, and delighted with this new worry that has fallen on him. That brief isn't burnt."

"Very well then. When it is proffered again, let it be heard. Tell Philip so."

He laughed; then stood up and moved about the room.

"Tell Philip so! You are superb. Heaven knows where you'll land us all in this affair!"

She looked at him with sympathy. It was very well for her, she told herself, to look ahead with calm. She was innocent of the crimes with which she was charged, and for the scandal of trial hardly cared a *real*. If the world must gloat over the commonplace of a woman's having an illicit lover— that could be understood and must be borne, if it came, for the brief time the public interest lasted. She would bear it and welcome, if she had to. She knew where true humiliation lay—and that too she could bear without words said. But the world, from which she had no need to ask anything, could therefore deny her nothing that she coveted. Unfairly, it had given her all it had to give before her birth, and she had never had to make demands on it. Even did it remove all earthly power and pomp from her now, that would not matter, she knew. She had no more use for them than to enjoy their ease as they passed—but she could do without ease. Having no demands to make on life, she could face its outcries unperturbed.

But Antonio was—as Ruy had been—the servant of success. He had competed for prizes, and now he held them. Possession and responsibility *were* what he was, and in risking these he risked the forty-six full years of his life—risked everything, for himself and for his wife and children. And he, with Philip, was guilty of the death of Escovedo.

"I won't land you anywhere dangerous, if I can help it. I promise," she said gently.

"I know. And I agree with you when you say let the case be heard. You know what the risks are for me. Still, now things have gone like this, I think it would be best to have the case heard, and tell the truth."

"I'm glad. Then what we have to do is brace ourselves for a coming ordeal, you and I and Philip."

"No, Ana. Philip won't brace himself—and unless he does, you and I can't."

"But if it's coming, he must."

"He won't let it come. I see his terrible dilemma. He can't stand up in court and admit to the murder of Juan de Escovedo."

"If it's proved he'll have to. And it won't be half as bad for him as for any ordinary citizen. For one thing, they can hardly execute the king. And for another every theologian in the country will be willing to swear on oath to the divine right and the grave national necessity——"

"No—Philip will never face that. Whatever else happens about Escovedo that will not take place. Philip simply hasn't

got the decisiveness for it—and, to give him his due, he is
privately far too sceptical of the divine right to commit
himself to it on a clear issue. No, if it came to an open trial his
plight would be worse than mine—and he knows that. I,
after all, could be shown as the audacious statesman doing the
king's bidding and chancing everything in his service——"

"Which is what you are, and did."

"Yes—come to think of it," said Antonio, on a sudden
laugh. "But it won't work out that way."

"How will it work out?"

"I don't know. No one knows. Vasquez intends it to ruin
me. The Escovedos—naturally—intend to have justice.
And Philip hopes for the best. Time may resolve all, as he
says. Time and he—you know his style when he's cornered."

"Yes, I know him. But I know him in ways you don't. I
shall talk to him, Antón."

He looked at her at first as if amazed at what she had said;
but then his expression altered to surmise. He was sitting on
the edge of a table where there was a tray of wine-bottles and
glasses. He turned to these now, as if to avoid her and get
time to think, and poured wine into a glass. He sipped some
wine, and looked about the room.

"Hitherto," he said, speaking slowly, "no one in all these
plottings and gossips has mentioned your name to the king.
We all know that. It seems that even the sexless and innocent
Vasquez has had an intuition of caution about that part of
the story. A woman—as instigator—has been mentioned,
and Philip has shown, oddly, some animosity about her.
Oddly, I say, since he knows the true story of the death
of Escovedo. But he's looking for bluff, and points of
delay—so he wants to know all the twists. De Los Velez
has thought that *you* have crossed Philip's mind as the
possible woman—and that has made him nervous for you.
But I don't think you have. He regards me as a shocking dog,
and liable to have slept with every woman in sight. But I

don't think he associates me at all with—well, with his preserves."

"Why have people been afraid to name me?"

"They know that you, your husband's memory, and all that concerns you are very dear to Philip—whatever the terms of that dearness. They know the risk they take in hurting him about you—they can't be sure how thin the ice may be. Even when bad news is true, you know, Philip has a way of turning against those who bring it to him. We are all aware of that—and wary. But now—time passes, and supported by lawyers, briefs and witnesses—likewise consumed by a sense of duty and the desire to be quit of me—*now* I think Mateo Vasquez will tell the king the contents of the Escovedo brief. De Pazos and Los Velez think so too. So does your good friend the Cardinal." He looked at her, sipped more wine, and smiled. "If you *are* going to Madrid, Ana, if you are putting your plan into execution, remember that by now Philip knows that we are lovers."

"It's as well."

"I disagree. But then you trust him."

Ana thought she saw now as much as anyone yet could of the misty contours of Perez's trouble.

Philip could not face an open inquiry into the death of Escovedo, yet so long as he was defending himself from the consequences of his crime he would also loyally defend his servant who had taken the whole risk of carrying through the murder he had commanded. *But*—if a man of brains, say Vasquez, could gradually work him round to believing that he had been duped, or half-duped, by that servant—if he could be veered into suspicion that Escovedo's death was in fact desired by that servant for private reasons, and that his, the king's, wish had been used as a mere safety-device, then, pressed into panic by a demand for justice which everyone acknowledged to be the Escovedos' due, Philip might indeed take refuge in his suspicion—let it rise against

Perez, and even destroy him, while it saved his master.

Philip was capable of that. Against it stood two arguments: the one, that Perez, de Pazos and de Los Velez knew from the king's own lips that he had commanded Escovedo's death; so, Ana believed, did the Cardinal Quiroga, and the royal Chaplain, Chaves. And Perez had Philip's instruction thereto in the king's inimitable handwriting. So that a trial, unless it was faced honourably, would be both dangerous and disgraceful for the king. The second argument was that Perez was at present irreplaceable in his work, holding in his hands all the threads of relationship with Italy, France, the Pope and the Lowlands, and at a time when it was essential for the king to be free to direct his mind on Portugal and the campaign for the imminent succession. Philip would go to many lengths of trouble and deviation rather than lose at present a very sure and reliable First Secretary.

But—a dark and formless *but*—were he to be personally hurt, were his incalculable habits of self-consolation and of dream-life to be offended by this episode, were the news that *she* was Perez's mistress to sting him into secret pain and shock—then, she admitted, there was no mapping of a course. Philip would still have to protect Perez from the ordeal of an Escovedo trial—because he must; he would still have to hedge, and placate Mateo Vasquez, and search dishonestly for lies and delays and—even in despair—for some unlucky scapegoat. And he would have to behave well to Perez meantime, if the complicated work of the Foreign Office was to proceed in safety. But behind all that fixed screen—she admitted there was no guessing how Philip's inner storm, driven by vanity and exasperation, might not blow. He could be indeed as merciless and treacherous as he could be faithful. And Ruy, from the grave, could give her the long measure of his fidelity. So she understood well enough where Perez stood now, and why he looked ahead uneasily.

Yet she saw light. For she did not believe, as these men did, in the monstrousness of Philip's vanity. She did not think that his now lazy, friendly feeling for her would lead him into real dishonesty or real cruelty. It wasn't worth all that. It had outgrown its days of danger and vengefulness; it was too tired for such companions. She thought that, given all the other difficulties which Escovedo's death had heaped on him, he could be brought to compromise with a mere jab at his male vanity—could even be made to acknowledge it, and laugh. Delicate work—but worth an attempt. And if he couldn't—conceited donkey—what then? What could he do, in his dilemma? Were free Castilians to ask his permission before going to bed with this one or that?

Yes, there was plenty of light. Spain was a country of free people. And if it actually came to victimisation of Antonio because of Philip's conceit, she would enjoy asking the king how he dared intrude himself thus upon another's privacy.

"I think I know now most of what you know and think so far about the situation?" Antonio nodded. "Thank you, Antón. And don't look sad. We won't talk any more about it now—there's no need to. We'll be talking of it all the winter in Madrid!"

"In Madrid? You're really coming back there, mad-woman?" He laughed delightedly. "Then I'm not sad. Or need I be? Need I, Ana?"

He came to the fireplace and stood in front of her chair, looking down at her.

"It's been a long abstention, girl. And I know it wasn't accidental. I know you wanted me to stay away. Six months and two weeks since I've seen you; nearly seven months since I've made love to you. I think, or rather I thought, I know why."

He waited for her to speak but she did not. She was looking into the fire; her beautiful hands were folded together in her lap.

"I don't want to talk about that last time," he went on. "When I do think of it it simply makes me want to have Escovedo back to kill again, and again, and again——"

"Ah, no," Ana said. "That's not it."

"Forgive me. All I mean is that I understood—I thought— the disgust, the need to rest from it all, the distaste—that's all I can say. But that—the whole thing—must pass, must get a bit forgotten, surely?"

"I don't think so," she said gently.

"Ah! Then I was right to feel—frightened when I first came here to-night? When you said that about doing without me, you meant something?"

Ana turned her face to him, and it was haggard and very white.

"Juan de Escovedo," said Perez, "have you done this to me too?"

Ana hesitated. Anxiously now she wished for speech, speech about herself, speech that might storm out selfishly, carelessly, if it had to—driven on the gusts of indecision that blew about her brain. But she simply did not know how to make such assault on another creature, and now it was too late to learn. Juan de Escovedo haunts me, she desired to say. I have forgiven all the outrage and the madness, I think I have even forgotten our plain human discomfort, yours and mine. Indeed—and don't be hurt, she would say—sometimes I can laugh quite coarsely and calmly at the thought of our predicament that night. All that external thing doesn't matter. It's a humiliation which anyone might undergo, and be said to deserve. What I remember is how my thought fitted with his while he shouted, and how precisely I understood him. He was simply telling me what my spirit knew quite well—that love and pleasure on our terms, Antonio, are an evil thing. For me he's right—he only said what I agree with. My soul has no place in your arms. That is a dreadful, pompous thing to say, it's the word of an egotist, and I abhor

the sound of it. But I don't know any nearer way to say it.
Could you help me? Could you tell me what to do—for I
still love you, I still want you——

But she could never speak aloud like that, or claim attention
from another for mere states of mind. And as to this man, her
lover, she knew that whatever he could give her and however
acutely he searched, as he always did, to be in sympathy with
her, he could not—of his very nature—accord with her in the
inner ranges of her spirit. For there, guarded by her worldliness and by her will to feel, enjoy and behave according to
her natural law, she was credulous and simple. There she was
pure, and sought a purpose in herself which should not
merely eschew but might even contradict self-gratification.
Towards this purpose she had once made one mad, selfish
rush, and made a fool of herself. Thereafter it was more than
ever to be dismissed, and she grew shy almost to insanity of
her idea that life was not about the self. And she escaped
from it easily into normal social practices, and so by them
back to her natural curiosities and desires. But Escovedo the
madman, dead now, killed by the man who had released her
into perfect sensual freedom, who had borne her most
happily out of reach of that small, lost self that used to cry out
for a purifying explanation of itself—Escovedo had renewed
the cry, and driven her back to that place of perplexity where
she was simple and credulous and knew she had a soul which
she must save.

Her hands fell apart and she stared up almost stupidly into
Antonio's face.

He's tired, she thought. He's worried to death; he's
even within measure of disaster. I've brought him into
real danger. When all was well with him I took with both
hands all I wanted, and cared very little about my soul or
his. Now, now when the world I enjoy and know so well,
the world he works so hard for is gathering up excuses to
destroy him—is now my time to harass him with convent

metaphysics, and the entirely private, small question of my soul?

"Absurd, preposterous," she said.

"What is, Ana?"

"Did I speak?"

"Rather loudly, for you."

She laughed, and reached up to his hands. "How unattractive of me! Come here! Come down."

He fell on his knees; his face was radiant.

"But——?"

"Oh yes, there are buts! When you aren't here there's a whole theological school of them!"

"And when I'm here?"

She bent nearer to his lifted face, loving it suddenly again with some of the sharp pleasure of their winter nights together in Madrid. Grateful to him for this pang, guilty, disturbed, she searched for an answer that would please him.

"When you're here? Ah, my poor theology! Have you then a little forgotten your power over me, Antón?"

To her surprise he did not laugh. He stayed quite still at her feet, looking at her. And in astonishment she saw what she had never seen before—she saw tears flood his eyes and pour along his cheeks. Then he bent forward and buried his face against her.

She held him, and kissed his perfumed hair. She smiled. She had forgotten his sandalwood perfume. It's been a long time, she thought.

Is my poor scruple greater than what I give this man and take from him? Am I to set my little private sense of sin above his claim on me and his unhappiness? Am I cheating because I want him, and have grown tired of the unimportant fuss of my immortal soul? Am I pretending to be generous simply to escape again into his power? Well, he has power —and I, it seems, have none. Answer my questions, Escovedo.

When Antonio left her in the early morning she went downstairs with him to the stables to rouse his men.

He protested at this, but only with delight.

"It's part of the plan," she said. "You'll see. And I hope Rodrigo hears us, and is at his window."

"You're an irresponsible parent."

"I have my own precise ideas of honour—but I fear Rodrigo doesn't understand them."

They walked about the court-yard, waiting for his carriage. The world was still and cool; a cock crowed far away, and a bell rang from the Franciscan convent.

"You and I are used to convent bells," Antonio said, remembering the chimes of Santa Maria Almudena in Madrid.

Ana shivered a little and drew her cloak about her.

"You're cold? You're troubled?"

"I'm neither, as you ought to know. Ah, here they come!"

The carriage clattered through into the court.

"God bless you. I'll be in Madrid almost as soon as you."

"I wish we could stay here," Antonio said.

He got into the carriage.

"Give my love to Philip," Ana said mischievously as the door closed on him.

When he had driven away she walked through the gateway and stood in the empty square of the little town; she watched a last star fade, and the thin frost melt along the roofs. Down the street a door was banged, and a man's voice sprang up, singing. Across the square the bent old sacristan unlocked the door of the *Colegiata* church.

At last she could hear no sound at all of carriage wheels on the Alcala road.

She crossed the square and entered the *Colegiata*, to wait for early Mass. She was the first worshipper. She went and sat on a bench near her husband's tomb.

THE THIRD CHAPTER   (APRIL 1579)

I

Ana had said to Antonio that they would likely spend the whole winter in Madrid talking about the Escovedo issue. But she was wrong.

The topic faded, surprisingly; not merely from the attention of casual gossips but even out of the horizon of those whom it concerned. It seemed that the President of Castile had indeed impressed the unhappy plaintiffs with his advice. And as the world in general turned its curiosity and chatter elsewhere, the Marqués de Los Velez and Antonio, true to their diplomatic training, discouraged even the most private references to what was best left sleeping.

Ana, wondering somewhat, followed their lead, and let the whole unanswered question float out of sight. But not out of memory. From Antonio's few, quick references—always savage—to Vasquez, from the old Marqués's exaggerated discretion, and from her own observations she knew that the problem was not dead, and that Philip would yet have to solve it—at someone's expense.

Twice between All Saints' and Christmas he was at the Alcázar, yet did not cross the street to call on her.

"Then he's been told that you killed Juan de Escovedo for my sake?" she asked Antonio.

"He *must* have been. But do you know, Ana—*nobody* can find that out! The man's extraordinary. I'm with him, as you know, for hours and days together, and so is Vasquez. And he knows that I know what Vasquez has done to my repute and goes on doing, *and* he knows the truth about this situation which Vasquez had got all wrong. But whereas earlier in the summer he was a shade overplaying friendship with me—which made me very jumpy and annoyed—now he is exactly as we've always been. Perfectly natural and calm and kind, making me work like an Indian, trusting me with all kinds of dangerous information and views, and never once referring to anything outside what comes before us officially. Except to joke me vaguely, as he's always done, about my extravagance, and about women, and so on. And to make his usual kind enquiries now and then for Juana and the children. I must say I admire him—tortoise though he is, he's subtle. He can keep anyone guessing—even me—when he likes."

Antonio might advise, but Ana was hurt and surprised. Philip should come to see her. If he was angry with her he should come and say so. They were intimate enough for that, and he had a right to jealousy, if he liked to be so silly. But he had no right to cut their friendship because she had a lover.

At Christmas he sent presents and greetings to the children, and nothing to her. She let Fernando and Anichu write their own thank-you letters. She did not write. She waited and surmised. She was somewhat shaken by how much the king's silence hurt her.

But she was kept busy that winter in frivolous ways, and she took refuge—by fits and starts, and from more than her guesses about Philip—in the light preoccupations of town life.

Madrid, which as a child she had known as a small and arbitrarily chosen pleasure resort of the old king, Charles, was now growing fast, and seemed indisputably henceforward the capital of the kingdom. Philip encouraged the town in this conceit of itself, as it was conveniently near his two favourite retreats, El Pardo and the new, beloved Escorial. So now the Alcázar was the centre of government, and the ambassadors had their official establishments in Madrid. And naturally all the seekers after office, or trade, or news, or blackmail crowded in where these great ones were—so a capital city seemed established.

It was an odd accident. That Castile and the centre should rule the rest was obvious, but then Toledo, with its great cathedral, its long history, its beauty and a real river, the Tagus, might have been the obvious repository of the future; or even little Avila, with its walls, its nine towers and its pure Castilian style. But no. This dry, new place, watered only by a trickle and having no character other than that its climate was treacherously warm and that an ageing, cantankerous king had thought he felt well when he was there—this upstart place was apparently to rule, capriciously, the kingdoms of Spain.

It was amusing. All the great who formerly had been content to have their houses in the towns of their titles or estates, were now uneasily looking for establishments in Madrid—at least, the young, the pleasure-loving and the ambitious branches of the great families were doing so. Ana who, because of Ruy's constant business at the Alcázar, had long possessed her Madrid palace, felt—somewhat to her disgust—that she was a pioneer of the new, ugly town and its ugly gospel of centralisation.

However, her children were all, according to their ages, in the thick of its lively growth, taking their part in building its conventions, snobberies and rituals. And they knew everyone, were related to all the eminent, and were assiduously flattered, spoilt and cheated by swarms of place-seekers and money-makers. They enjoyed themselves, and filled Ana's house with their young friends, and her time with frivolous duties on their behalf.

As a widow and unprotected she was herself barred—to her great relief—from all full-dress ceremonies of Madrid society. She could neither be invited to banquets and dancing parties nor could she invite her acquaintances to any such formal pleasures. But her house was open, informally, and most of the aristocracy and diplomatic corps knew better than to omit to call on a senior Mendoza who was also the

widow of the Prince of Eboli. During the winter she entertained to supper, singly or in small groups, most of the
important men, Spanish or foreign, then in Madrid. Sometimes Antonio brought them; sometimes she had the Cardinal
to meet them; sometimes they brought their wives.

"But it's a funny thing," she said to Antonio, "there seem
to be no significant women in the world."

He whistled.

"Margaret of Navarre, Elizabeth of England, Mother
Teresa, the Princess of Eboli——"

"None in Madrid then——"

"The Princess of Eboli."

"God help women!"

"He doesn't, Ana. That isn't his idea."

Margaret of Valois is a poet and a notoriety, she thought;
Elizabeth has England to rule; Mother Teresa is trying to
reform the Church. But I have nothing to do. I never have
had anything to do except behave nicely and enjoy my easy
lot. It's silly, she thought—as often before through her adult
life. She did not sigh in these moods for poverty, so as to
have to wash her children's faces and cook their dinner. She
supposed that she could have done those things if necessary,
but the humble ideal had never attracted her. Still conscience, or rather personality more than conscience, fidgeted
spasmodically in her under a sense of her own pointlessness.
When she was having Ruy's babies—ten in thirteen years—
she had felt that in the world's terms at least, if not in her
own, she was being useful; and her dislike of the maternal
function and its processes had increased her reassurance.
Because at least she could say that Ruy, who loved his large
family so much, had never heard a word of complaint or self-
pity from her throughout the years during which she was
adding to it for him. It was no more than her duty, as well
she knew; but she gratified some private need in herself by
doing it gaily and as if she liked it. Yet Heaven did not allow

her a complete gratification, because her health was good and child-bearing had been easy, and had left her when it ceased almost as well as in her first bridal days, before she conceived Rodrigo.

But Anichu was rising six now, and Ruy was more than five years dead—and for long the old placatory saw, that she was doing her duty in that state of life to which it had pleased God to call her, had seemed boring and untrue. She supervised the affairs of Pastrana; but the farms, orchards and silk-works had all been so ordered by Ruy that she knew that the foremen and bailiffs, respectful and affectionate, yet regarded her authority as purely formal; and she noticed with amusement that already they paid far more heed to Rodrigo's occasional very businesslike interventions than to any suggestion of hers. She did not mind this. So long as the prosperity of the place continued, for everyone's sake and in Ruy's memory, she was content. She was not looking for great labours, or to shine in any unusual light, but simply felt a recurrent private need to feel, rather than accept, her own contact with life—to feel somehow persuaded about herself.

When she had talked a little sometimes to Ruy of this restlessness, this sense of disappointment that everything came to her and that she had always to be passive and pleased, he did not laugh or dismiss her nonsense. On the contrary, he was wise and kind, though he liked to tease her about this mood which he called "looking for a fight". "But I'm a pacifist, Ana; you live with a man of peace." She came to notice, with private amusement, that always for many days after such conversations Ruy made love to her with great increase of amorousness and assiduity. And she thought she saw his idea, and that it was good. But it did not actually bear—how could he know?—on the state of mind she had sought to examine with him.

It had been out of one of these moods of search for a personal position that she had been moved to the sudden and for her startling action of taking Antonio Perez for her lover. It was at least, as she had said to him that night, a decision of her own.

It had justified her—on one level at least, by bringing her at once into close sensual acceptance of joy. Joy which was at first so disturbing and formless, so dazzlingly luminous over the twenty-four hours of the day, as to seem silly and to be honestly enough describable, in public places, as about nothing. But her senses, though taken by storm in middle life, were not so imprecise as her heart. They had won her at last, and they made her pay. There were days in the beginning when she went hungry for Antonio Perez as a tramp for food. There were nights when she waited for him, lying in her bed and listening to the bells of Almudena, and thought of him at his desk across the street, deep in work, fully at peace with it and richly, blessedly forgetful of her—thought of him and of whether or not she might see him before dawn with an urgency which astonished her, and which sometimes seemed controllable only barely on the safe side of an act of outright folly—such as getting up and crossing to the Alcázar gate and trying to see him.

But it was this very wretchedness of joy and the press of danger, of near-lunacy, in it, that in fact made her so contentedly acceptant, and so well able to be cool and ruthless with her unhoodwinked conscience. So be it, she could say then to that monitor—I am living in sin. But I've found something that has been missing always, and that may indeed be just as important as what your voice tells me of. And I don't feel this sense of sin you warned about. No doubt I shall, but meantime—this is a battle, with rules, exactions and trials you concealed from me; this love, this sin has a morality of its own that I find I understand. I see my plight and I acknowledge still your old imperatives. But I can't obey them now—I must take a chance. This other is an imperative too—and what I like is that it seems to be my own, and not just the hearsay word of Heaven.

So she took her chance. And conscience, long-trained, did not give in and fought her every inch of the way. A ding-dong battle, but with her new-found paganism always the winner—a paganism which was learning to smile a little, in hardened amusement, at the egotism of chastity. But she knew she was too vulnerable to pursue that defence, and shelved it—marvelling only at how unsinning and un-sinned against she felt in her life of sin.

But in the ordinary human journey none of these skirmish-victories is final. So Ana found out, without overmuch surprise. Yet when Escovedo came and discovered her in her pleasure, she *was* surprised, in spite of all her own debates, to see how coldly she did in fact agree with the doctrine out of which his madness spoke. She saw with him that self-denial was a better thing, or a thing more to her taste, than self-expression; and that self-expression through the senses solely, and as practised in sterility and with accomplishment as by Antonio and her, was in itself entirely bad. She could plead very well against that judgment, and indeed again and again had buried it out of her own reach. But she knew it lived and stood—and she heard it from Escovedo with an assent which was almost solemn. For she felt while he shouted that whereas he might not be saving her soul for her, he was certainly expressing her own unadmitted judgment on this delight, sexual love.

That much was clear to her that night.

And now that she had returned, for complicated reasons, to the pleasure he had driven her from, she knew that his message stayed, as the voice of herself, and that love was henceforward what traditionally she understood it to be—a Christian passion.

So henceforward she was Antonio's lover on new and shifting terms—because of this and because of that, because he needed her, because there were moods when she couldn't do without him, because friends were failing him, because she loved him—for every stormy reason of a heart that has grown truly warm towards another; but not any longer now because she was simply in love.

The trouble of this changed temperature ran through all the movement of her life in Madrid that winter. But superficially she was gay and indiscreet. And if anyone was so uninformed as to wonder where the allegiance of the Princess of Eboli lay in the now accepted feud between the king's two chief ministers she left him in no doubt; she was Antonio Perez's friend and patroness for all to see, and at every mention of Mateo Vasquez she made it her affair to jibe, and even very dangerously, no matter who listened. When Antonio protested against this—though only with half a will, because he loved her championship—she laughed at him. It was part of the plan, she said, and she desired Mateo Vasquez to be in no doubt of what she thought of him. "Besides, you yourself say the most terrifying things about him, to all comers."

"Oh, I! That's different."

"I agree it's different."

One bright afternoon in late March she and Bernardina, returning from a ride, had to rein in their horses at a corner of the Calle Carmen, to let some market traffic cross the Puerta del Sol. As they waited she observed a tall, dark cleric on foot very near her, and bowing to her with a great show of respect and anxiety. It was Mateo Vasquez. She was astonished, and disgusted. She stared at him, her face full of recognition but implacably refusing his salute. Still motionless and close beside him, she turned to Bernardina and said in a tone as clear as ice:

"This is Mateo Vasquez trying to bow to me. What can he possibly mean?"

The tall priest shrank back instantly into the crowd, and vanished. Ana and her companion rode on.

Bernardina admired audacity, but she thought that gesture unnecessary, and she said so.

But Ana seemed pleased with herself.

"Let's hope that *now* he knows that you don't bow to the ground before those whom you're seeking to destroy! We'll teach him a little etiquette, Bernardina!"

"He looked terrified when you spoke."

"I noticed that. Poor cringing wretch."

II

Three weeks later, on an evening of April, she sat with the Cardinal in the Long Room. Antonio Perez was to join them for supper. Ana had taken the children to Pastrana for Holy Week and Easter, and had just returned to Madrid.

During March there had been stirrings in the affair Escovedo, and Ana had received some unlikely callers. And the Cardinal had views and gossip for her.

The windows of the Long Room were open and the noises of the town floated up happily; the evening was clear, and westward from where they sat they could see the shining peaks of the Gredos, immaculate against the pure sky. There were violets and early roses from Pastrana in the room.

"Well, for a woman in somewhat questionable case, I must say, Ana, that you look very splendid."

Gaspar de Quiroga, Archbishop of Toledo and now a Cardinal, was a distinguished and worthy churchman. His friendship with Ana and her husband was of old standing; and in recent years he had also become interested in Perez, and even attached to him. Antonio frequently went to stay at the archiepiscopal palace in Toledo. The friendship between these two men was odd—the venal, self-seeking politician and the detached and virtuous priest—but it was also disinterested. They quite simply liked each other.

"But *am* I in questionable case?"

He smiled at her.

"Actually, that's what no one knows. But still—we all feel that you are."

"I think you are all, in the goodness of your hearts being a little *too* intuitional! Philip knows—to his cost—why Escovedo died. And for the rest of this scandal, may I say, dear friend, that what I do with my—heart is no affair for the *Alcalde*?"

"You may, Ana. And I agree with you."

He had been standing in the window. He moved about the room now as one quite at home. He picked up a book that lay on the writing-table.

" '*Histoire Des Amants Fortunés*'. Ah, a first edition! Mine is called '*The Heptameron*'."

"Yes—I'd never read it, and Antonio found this 1558 copy for me."

"You find the stories amusing?"

"Surprisingly so. I'm lazy about reading French—oddly enough I read Latin more easily. But I find this a surprising, witty, *natural* sort of book."

"Yes, they're graceful, well-set stories. I confess I prefer them to Boccaccio. She's a woman I'd like to have talked with. She attracts me more than the great-niece, the present Margaret of Navarre."

"But *this* Margaret of Navarre is said to be so beautiful that she takes the breath away."

"So I hear." He put the book down. "I only said that the Heptameron lady attracts me more."

Ana laughed.

"You don't mean much when you say that you're 'attracted'."

"No, thank God. A dead authoress suits me well. I was born austere."

"You're a holy man."

He shook his head.

"Indeed I'm not, you foolish child. I wish I were."

"Yes—you're a holy man. So why do you continue to come to my house, and be my friend—and Antonio's? Aren't you afraid that by doing so you scandalise the little ones?"

"Yes, sometimes I worry about that. Antonio leads a bad life, and my friendship for him may indeed be misunderstood, and disturb the innocent. And you? Well——"

He looked at her in gentle surmise.

"What do you think of me?"

"I have great affection for you—which probably corrupts my thought, or rather my refusal to think. I say to myself, Ana, quite simply that I am *not* your confessor. Until I am— and for ever distant be the day!—I am under no positive obligation to answer you. And you have never sought my advice, outside the confessional."

"Were I to do so?"

"I should tell you to give up your sin, or to make certain that you are never again an occasion of sin to Antonio. You know the Christian teaching. You know that fornication is a sin; adultery is another. But the first sin is enough for your properly trained mind. And as to the adultery—I would not insult either you or Antonio, to say nothing of Juana Coëllo, his wife, by saying that she is in fact an excellent wife, a wife in a million, gentle, silent, proud and true." He paused. "It is merely emotional to advert to that. If she were a drunkard, a thief and a public whore, she is his wife, and in taking you he commits adultery. But you both know that. So what would be the good of reiteration?"

"Yes, we both know that. But Antonio knows it only as a sceptic. I know it with faith."

"Ah! Then you really are a sinner—by definition. Grievous matter, perfect knowledge, full consent."

She smiled, half-troubled.

"Not *full* consent. I sometimes think that real sin is

practically impossible to the sin-conscious on that definition, because of the loophole of 'full consent'. The terms fit Antonio better than me," she ended lightly.

"No, Ana. Because he discards the first point, 'grievous matter'. His escape is that it's all about nothing."

"Yes. It isn't mine. I'm always afraid of betraying how 'grievous' the matter seems to me."

"Then, against all appearances, you are a guilty creature?"

Ana did not answer at once. A rose had fallen from a vase, and she leant forward and replaced it with its fellows. Then she turned and faced the Cardinal.

"A year ago I wasn't, I *think*," she said. "A year ago, at least, I hoped Antonio was right."

"And now?"

"Now I wish he was. But I know he isn't."

"Then you desire to repent?"

She laughed very softly.

"No. I did repent—for seven whole months, after Escovedo's death. But this is not the time. One can't be self-indulgent even about repentance, Cardinal. I have come to love Antonio, you see, and I owe him a few sins and chances. He has taken chances for me. This is not the time for private piety. Heaven must make what it likes of my confusion. That is a risk I have the right to take."

"In other words, you are seeing him through the Escovedo affair? You are just being awkwardly loyal?"

"Oh no. I love him. And if I do, it would be unnatural to stop loving him now."

"That's a curious sentence, Ana. But I take it you are telling your immortal soul to wait on the question of Antonio Perez's earthly happiness?"

"Maybe there's a grain of that in it. But you see, don't you, that if it *were* no more, I owe him much for being able to feel like that about him? And it *is* more. I don't want to do without him."

"Well said. Yet I believe that, were you in the confessional now, you would humbly admit the burden of your sin."

"I couldn't be in the confessional now, because I have no firm purpose of amendment. I wish I needn't commit sin, but that's as far as I can go."

"And still your soul is troubled—and pleasure is not enough?"

"But there is his pleasure."

"My dear—he has a wife."

Ana laughed and threw out her hands.

"There speaks the dogmatist, the innocent priest. So had I a husband, as good and dear a man as I understand Juana Coëllo is a woman. Yet I never knew until now, at the very end of my life, what union with another can be."

"Antonio can hardly be in your case. He has had so many love-affairs that the argument would be ridiculous."

"No, he isn't in my case. He is an expert in pleasure. But I'm not arguing for his conscience. I speak for myself. All I mean is that I am his present happiness, and that is—he has known how to make it—a perilous happiness for me. And he's in danger now, and being slandered about me. But he takes great pride in the situation, and also he relies very much on my love at this time. And I am not so used to the attraction and devotion of men that I can treat that lightly."

"I see. In fact, as I suspected, you are in some trouble of soul."

"If it be trouble of soul to love a man and commit sins for him, who seems by his very faults to merit love—then I'm in trouble."

"No—it isn't as tricky as that. You're just in trouble with God. His claim is eternal and overrules your foolish, earthly time-table. And you know that. Still—God forgive me!—I admire you a little. And I must say I marvel at the subtleties which you simple creatures of the flesh can weave into your animal needs."

Ana pressed her hand against her eye-shade.

"The trouble is that the needs aren't sufficiently animal," she said.

The Cardinal smiled, but she did not see the smile.

"Maybe," he said. "I don't know." He sat down and looked about the room affectionately. "Beautiful flowers. Signs that Pastrana flourishes. And how are the children?"

"Very well. Some of them will be coming in to see you in a minute. Do you mind?"

"I should be hurt if they didn't. And we'll postpone what I'm supposed to be saying to you until Antonio is here? I do hate repeating myself."

"Then you're on a mission?" Ana laughed delightedly.

"Not very earnestly, my dear—as you can guess."

"I've had some curious, unexpected callers in the last month, but *you* now! Oh, that's really amusing!"

"I think so too."

Presently the children came—young Ruy, aged twelve, small and studious and growing in feature very like the father whose name he bore; Fernando, nine now and already saying that he desired to be a Franciscan monk; and Anichu, baby six-year-old. They did not know the Cardinal as well as the king, or like him as much, and he for his part was shy with children. But Ana watched with detached amusement as the three set to their duty of entertaining the great prelate.

III

When Antonio came it had long been dark. The windows were shut, the candles lighted in the Long Room, and the children were gone to bed.

Ana, who had seen him the night before, knew at once by the peculiar brightness of his eyes that some new, disturbing factor had arisen in his affairs during the day.

At supper conversation could be neither consecutive nor

entirely free, but Ana was able—with rapid changes of theme while servants changed dishes—to amuse her guests with accounts of visits she had been receiving from the mysterious Doctor Milio, from the two brothers, Augustin Alvárez and Pedro Nuñez of Toledo, and—funniest of all, she said, that very morning from Count de Khevenhüller, the ambassador of the Empire.

"All these people come to me," she said, "pretending of course that he knows nothing about it, on behalf of this preposterous Mateo Vasquez! Can you suppose that they are sane?"

The Cardinal demurred.

"I'm not sure that you've got their credentials quite right. However—go on!"

"What did you say to de Khevenhüller, Ana?" said Antonio. "I presume his mission was the usual one?"

"Yes. These curious, busy people seem to think it of paramount importance that I—as a leader of society, bearer of a great name, etc.—should withdraw my enmity from that good man Mateo Vasquez, and even try to be his friend!"

They all laughed very much.

"What can be the matter with their wits, Cardinal? I told our poor, bewildered German this morning to take my advice and keep well back from this very local and Castilian storm. I told him that—though he might not think so—*we* all know what we are doing in it, but that *he* never could. I thanked him for his courage and kindness, and assured him— as I assure all these eccentrics—that I shall never regard as other than an enemy whoever seeks to convict Antonio Perez of the murder of Juan de Escovedo. I then asked him to be so good as to excuse me, as my dressmaker awaited me in another room."

Antonio whistled.

"Well done!" he said.

"Poor old de Khevenhüller! The ambassador of the Holy

Roman dismissed for a dressmaker!" The Cardinal chuckled
in astonishment. "You're very good at insults, Ana. But it
isn't really an attractive talent, you know."

"No. Ruy used to say that too. I think he went in terror of
the virago in me ever getting the upper hand."

"I love viragos," said Antonio.

When they returned to the Long Room he would not sit
down when Ana suggested that he might.

"No, girl," he said tenderly, as if they were alone. And by
that mistake she knew he was indeed excited. "No, let me
fidget. I'm going to drink a great deal of wine to-night, and
you two spoil-sports must put up with it."

"Tell us why," said the Cardinal.

"Because the whole thing has broken open again. Philip is
treacherous—and I have to-day written to him to ask to be
relieved of office."

The Cardinal sprang to his feet.

"No, Antonio! Not that! Oh, this man Philip, this king,
this cheat! *What* has he done now?"

Ana said nothing. Antonio's eyes rested on her for a
second, half-absent-mindedly. When he spoke he turned to
the Cardinal.

"How can I epitomise it for you? How can I cut a way
through all the chaos of it, to make you see why I have resigned
precisely to-day, and not yesterday and not to-morrow?"

"Well, to begin with, you must have been given a superficially correct reason for resigning office?"

"I was. But that too—like everything Philip touches—is
complicated. However, here it is: as you know, the department we call the Council of Italy is my particular charge,
though directed lately for general purposes by its own
secretary. When Diego de Vargas died recently Philip and I
discussed an overhaul of this department, where there is a
great deal of waste and doubling and trebling of work. And
after the usual agonies of delay and debate and pausing for

prayer the king agreed with my wish to have *no* secretary appointed under me at present, and to leave it to me to train one or two of the young fellows in that office—on whom I've had my eye—to work it directly under me, with no go-between; as it used to be. I was pleased that he agreed to that. You remember, Ana? Over the whole thing he showed his old confidence in me, and seemed cheerful about the decision. I thought the episode was a good omen. Meantime, of course, the omens have *not* been good—but don't let me side-track myself. This morning, out of a blue sky, I receive a formal despatch from El Escorial, announcing the appointment as Secretary of the Council of Italy of a man called Gabriel de Zayas. To this document is added a chit from an under-secretary asking me to be so kind as to implement the appointment and instruct de Zayas as I may desire. No word from Philip—no explanation, no apology. And that is, superficially, why I resigned from the king's service at noon to-day. My letter is on the road to El Escorial now."

He turned aside and poured himself some wine.

"It's a sufficient pretext," said the Cardinal. "But, as you know, he won't accept your resignation."

"I've given him reasons why he must. I took my opportunity. This de Zayas is in himself of no import—he's just an under-secretary looking for advancement, and he's always been a hanger-on of Vasquez. Now that devil has nothing to do with Italy, but he found out this new arrangement of mine, and just decided to try his power against me on a small issue. He has won. And I'm having no more of these victories from a man who lives to destroy me. I said that. I said that I could work no longer for a king who allows my mortal enemy to supersede me in his confidence, and who moreover refuses to check or punish that enemy's active and public malignancies. I mean every word of this—and he can choose."

"What will you live on, if you do resign?" the Cardinal asked.

"Nothing. It's ruin."

"That's what I should have thought. Still, it's a good move, Antonio. It may be the one thing needed to bring this tragic farce to a clean conclusion. And believe me, you'll never be allowed to resign. Philip will fight against that with every trick he knows. Why—apart from the loss of you at a very urgent moment—he'd be at once completely in your power when you left his service."

Antonio laughed.

"Yes, I know that. And the point won't escape him. Well, let him wriggle!"

Ana sat leaning forward in her chair, her elbow on her knee and her fingers pressed against her black silk eye-patch. The two men looked at her reflectively.

"What are the omens you spoke of, Antón?" she asked, without moving or looking up.

"Oh, they accumulate. I had letters from El Pardo before Easter—you know de Santayo perhaps?" he asked the Cardinal. "Well, he's a Gentleman of the Household, and a reliable fellow. He wrote from there in March that the accusations against me and the Princess which were contained in the suppressed Escovedo brief of last autumn were now a matter of common discussion through the Court. Now he writes from El Escorial that the freedom of slander is infinitely worse, that the whole place is taking sides, and that everyone is waiting for the king to take some action. Meantime others write that Vasquez is going round like a cat with two tails, and that the king is as bland as cream, and perfectly unreadable. What do you make of all that?"

"I'd say it's not *quite* accurate," the Cardinal said. "I, as you know, had to visit El Escorial for two days in Holy Week—which is why I'm here to-night, incidentally ——"

"Yes—he's on a mission," Ana said with a little flick of a smile to Antonio. "Did you know?"

"Indeed! The two-faced wretch! Well, go on, Eminence. Tell us what you saw up yonder."

The Cardinal smiled.

"Naturally, as I have a reputation for saintliness, no one ventured to entertain me with views on the disedifying Escovedo scandal. Also perhaps because I'm said to be a friend of the two criminals. But Vasquez, to begin with, is *not* going round like a cat with two tails. On the contrary, he's in a very nervous, boring and obsequious state, and I'd say the man is ill."

Ana laughed.

"That's what his ambassadors tell me. The poor German this morning said that he lives in terror of me!"

"Oh yes," said Antonio. "I was sparing you that idiocy, Ana. But my informant says that Vasquez's new whine to everyone is that you are going mad and are a general danger! That you insult him, with obscene words, in public places, and that he knows that both of us plan to take his life!"

"Upon my word, it wouldn't be a bad idea!" said Ana.

The Cardinal lifted his hand in warning.

"Children, children, God knows who may be listening! And after all," he said gravely, "Escovedo *was* murdered."

Antonio smiled and bowed his head.

"True," said Ana. "And why doesn't the trial for murder begin? No one is running away from it."

"Except the king," said Antonio.

"Be quiet, both of you," said the Cardinal. "I was saying that Vasquez looks at present anything but well or sure of himself. And I think Philip is as much of a riddle now to him as to you, Antonio."

"How is Philip?" Ana asked.

"Wretched, I think. As usual he's overworking past belief, and is carrying his usual load of pompous frets. But this special thing is clearly an immense anxiety——"

"Ah, God! I'm tired of his anxieties!" said Antonio.

"I *made* him talk of it," said the Cardinal. "And his

position seems to be this—and in its characteristically tricky kind it's clear enough. He cannot and will not have a public trial of a Secretary of State for a political murder. That appears to be final. He cannot however have the standing Escovedo brief heard. He says that you, Antonio, have pressed for that, on the condition that the lady's name was never mentioned in court, and that all clues to her identity were rigidly disguised. Is that so?"

Ana looked at Antonio in surprise.

"Is it so, Antón?"

He laughed.

"Yes. I have asked him to have the brief heard on those terms."

Ana stretched out her hand and touched his.

"Madness!" she said gently. "And truly, you're as much of a sneak as Philip."

"I agree with Philip," the Cardinal went on, "that the case could *not* be heard that way. Philip, give him his due, won't have it because he says the accusation is flatly untrue; also because in the disproving it would inevitably merge into the political trial which he will not have; and because, however it went, it would be hopelessly damaging to you——"

"I like that," said Antonio. "I know, we all know, whom it would really damage!"

"Damaging to you," the Cardinal went on, "and very dangerous for someone whom we referred to throughout as 'that lady'." He smiled at Ana. "We were very chivalrous. No lady's name was breathed."

Ana was sitting straight in her chair. Her beautiful hands lay tense and long upon its arms.

"Philip didn't name me?" she asked the Cardinal.

"No. I don't think he does to anyone. Antonio de Pazos has told me of the *that lady* formula."

"But he knows who that lady is?" Antonio said.

"Oh yes. We are all agreed that he knows, that Vasquez

has certainly told him. But no one can get him to betray that, or to name you, Ana." The Cardinal paused. "I think that is a pregnant point," he said, "though pregnant of what I cannot say. But let me continue. Philip will have no trial—is that clear? But neither can he allow the present situation to continue for his perpetual shame and torment. Nor does he intend to lose either of his Secretaries of State."

"He's cocksure, for a man in a trap," said Antonio.

"He thinks that the unhappy Escovedos could be coaxed into pacification—I imagine by large damages, he thinks, with bribes, good positions for the children, etc.—vast pension for the widow, and so on. And some cock-and-bull lie about how dishonouring to the repute of the late Juan de Escovedo would be any true inquiry into the reason of his death."

Antonio laughed wearily.

"I gave him all that months ago," he said. "A fool could quiet the Escovedos."

"Well then, all that's left is merely to get Mateo Vasquez to drop his naïve campaign for justice. And Philip says he would; that he is frightened to death now of the enmities he has set up. Philip says he has it from Vasquez's own lips that all he wants, to bury everything, is apologies from you, Antonio, and from 'that lady' for recent offences—and some token of the friendship of you both."

There was an astonished silence.

"What do you think of that, confederates?"

Antonio turned, walked to where the wine was, and refilled his glass. He came back, drank a little and smiled at Ana.

"Speak, you," he said. "You say you're a virago. Come on—now is the time."

Ana shook her head at him and turned to the Cardinal.

"Do you mean that this is a message? That this is your mission?"

"It is. I just thought I'd deliver it," the Cardinal said.

"It's the same as those other missions, Ana—the German's and so on. They all really came from the king, I think."

"And he thinks that we might apologise to Mateo Vasquez for having protested against his recent public crimes against us?" she asked.

"Further," said Antonio, "you believe he thinks that I am prepared to sell my whole future into perpetual blackmail to a fool? That I am prepared to work for the State in close collaboration with a man whose mean and tattling power I shall have acknowledged, and before whom I am to go in fear as long as I live?"

The Cardinal smiled.

"You have both understood me," he said. "That is the present suggestion."

"Well, if it's the only one, it just leaves us all exactly where we were," Antonio said.

"Except that now perhaps," the Cardinal suggested, "you know a little better where you are?"

"Yes," said Antonio, "that is so. Thank you for that."

"Oh, not at all," the other said amusedly. "I just thought I'd give the curious message, as I was asked to. You must forgive me. My excuse is that it throws light a little way ahead."

"It does do that," Antonio said. "So we forgive you, you arch-plotter!" He turned to Ana. "We do forgive him, don't we?"

Ana was leaning back in her chair. She looked white and weary.

"It passes understanding," she said gently. "Where is Philip? What's the matter with him?"

The Cardinal looked at her, and then spoke with hesitation.

"You are the only one who might possibly find that out," he said.

"He hasn't come to see me in six months," she said. "He hasn't written. Now you tell me that he will not name or hear my name. So how can *I* find out what's happened to him?"

"I don't know, Ana. Still, you're the only one," the Cardinal said.

THE FOURTH CHAPTER　　　(JUNE 1579)

The Cardinal was right. Philip refused to consider Perez's resignation from office. He held it off by every device of time-marking, cajolery and affectionate concern. Notes and long letters in the king's own hand came by courier now almost every day to Perez at the Alcázar. Wait, was his burden, and trust me. I shall return to Madrid in a very short time and arrange everything. You will see how simple it is, and how my goodwill towards you will weigh like death upon your enemies. Let me pray, let me seek counsel of the Holy Spirit. I entreat you not to worry. You have no reason ever to be other than confident. Do your work as you always do and trust me. That will be enough. Everything will be arranged as you desire. I weigh all and shall decide as God directs. Only have patience a little. You know that I am not inconstant. You can be of good heart against this passing trouble, because you have me. Time and I——

Such entreaties and exhortations, as vague as Antonio saw them to be anxious, were thick now on every paper that reached him from the king. They did not reassure him but—added to what he learnt from spies and friends of the whirl of fuss and consultation into which his gesture had thrown Philip—they made him wonder if perhaps he might not yet win, by one further effort of guile and patience.

He did not give in to the king. He continued to assert in letter after letter that as His Majesty still did not deal as was necessary with his just grievances, he had no alternative but to ask him to find his successor. Until this person was appointed he would continue in his duty as Secretary of State, save only in relation to the Council of Italy, from which he was withholding henceforward his direction. But he must beg His Majesty to look with despatch for another First Minister, as he himself would have to attend very much henceforward to his own future, and would have many personal preoccupations. This firmness of tone which he preserved unbroken, coupled with his refusal ever to reply to such sentiments as for instance that he knew the king was not inconstant, had the effect he desired of keeping Philip in an unresting state of agitation.

Perez did not under-estimate himself, but he had well-founded reasons for knowing that his departure from office in this year would be a heavy blow for Philip.

The government of Spain was now more than ever, as the king aged, a closed-in, secret procedure, wherein the real facts, the true activating policies, were known only to the monarch and to the two or three ministers whom perforce he had to trust. Charles V had taken care to vitiate the ancient liberties of Castile, of which now the Cortes and Council were only perfunctory, ceremonial bodies, without power or the desire for it. The king's Cabinet, loosely divided in two parties, progressive and reactionary, was small and for the most part uncertain or uninformed of what in fact went on behind the façade of its debates. So that Philip was, as indeed he boasted, "an absolute king". But even if he were a very much faster and more penetrative thinker than he was, he could not possibly govern in the way he chose without one or two exceptionally sure and clear-headed *aides*. And these, to be effective, needed long training in and complete assimilation to his methods and his temperament. So at their best these Secretaries of State, as they were called, were not easy to find; and once found and adapted to him, they were adhered to passionately by their master.

Until their quarrel, Vasquez and Perez had functioned

perfectly together as Philip's right-hand men. Both had been trained at the Liberal side of the Cabinet table, the side honoured by the good traditions of Gonzalo Perez and Ruy Gomez. They were equal in their love for their work and in being indefatigable and quite selfless about it; equal too in their power to seize, amass and retain facts—as in their ability to keep secrets. Both were widely educated men, both were ruthless, and both were loyal in office. Both also were self-made, and from the middle class. In all these things they were ideal to Philip's purpose; and in the strong contrast they made beyond these attributes they were hardly less to his liking. For their being temperamentally antipathetic was, for the king, a great tactical advantage, as thus they kept clear of each other outside the Cabinet Room, and enabled Philip to indulge very fully his passion for concealing the work of his left hand from his right. And in broad application to principles and politics, whereas Vasquez's steadiness, incorruptibility and quiet obstinacy were excellent things, the worldly Perez brought entirely other and more vivid attributes into play. As Vasquez did not, he knew Europe, had studied and travelled in France and Italy, spoke the languages of those countries, read their literatures and liked to associate with the diplomatic corps and with all distinguished foreign visitors to Spain. And he was quick-witted and eloquent, and always able to give—what Philip himself could not—either the forceful or the subtle answer as needed, in the Cabinet or in the Ambassadors' Room. Perez could think while he talked, in two separate streams—which neither Philip nor Vasquez could do. And the king was the first to appreciate and call upon that talent.

Now at present, as Perez knew, Philip's hands and wits were even more than usually overtaxed; home, imperial and foreign affairs were piling up towards what looked like being years of massive exaction. Were the king and Vasquez left alone with the gigantic burden of temporisation and decision, they could not but flounder, both being slow men. As it was, he regarded with glee the problem he had created by his relentless withdrawal from the Council of Italy. Milan, Naples and Sicily presented extraordinary dangers of government, and although it was customary to regard the remaining Italian princes as weak, the Pope was one of them, and he was certainly as much an Italian and a temporal power as he was Christ's Vicar. Let poor green de Zayas find that out! Let him also cut his teeth on this one's and that one's crack-brained plan against the Turk, let him find his feet with Venice, and in general see what he could do with the whole question of the Mediterranean! Antonio smiled sometimes over all that. A month or two of confusion in the Italian office would teach Philip things he might be hoping to forget.

But over the rest of the globe, the range of questions requiring constant care and argument was very formidable. Parma was at the beginning of what would assuredly be a very difficult campaign of compromise in the Lowlands. Spain's relations with England and France would hang on it—and Perez was in charge of Parma's strategy. The religious war was exhausting France, and she eyed Spain therefore with increasing suspicion; but Perez, liberal, tolerant, was *persona grata* with the house of Valois, and therefore a most useful make-weight now for Philip, whose conscience was always receiving dangerous assaults from the Guises and the Pope. And as to England—it was essential to keep Elizabeth from giving full support to William of Orange, and to that end essential to sacrifice the romantic cause of Mary Stuart and the English Catholics. The Pope nagged on at Philip about this, but Perez stood imperturbable. Mary Stuart was a French princess of the house of Guise, he insisted, and therefore for everyone's sake much better left where she was, in an English fortress. Meantime, however, English pirates and buccaneers were on the seas—a man called Francis Drake had arisen and was robbing Spain of fortunes of her home-coming wealth from the western empire. And the old admiral, de Bazan, plagued Philip, for vengeance on these pirates, to be allowed to plan an invasion of England; and the Pope plagued on about the One True Faith; and the Inquisition needed perpetual vigilance, and Mother Teresa and her rivals were on the warpath all the time. And the king intended, quite rightly, to annexe Portugal at any moment now. And Alva was stirring in his sleep, and coming back into politics with his one archaic old slogan of "fire and sword".

For three men all this was work indeed. For two of them, deprived of the one who thought quickest and who had the best manner in approach, attack or retreat, it was admittedly too much, and very dangerous.

So, viewing Europe from Philip's angle, Antonio Perez decided that he could afford to mark time in his personal quarrel, while keeping up a front of cold reluctance and detachment. For the more closely he reviewed the men and talents available to Philip for his plan the more honestly could he aver that there was no one at hand who might attempt to fill it. Only names from the past came to him—his father, Gonzalo Perez, would have done, he thought; or Ruy Gomez, the perfect statesman. Or possibly, though not so good as either of those, old Cardinal Granvelle. Granvelle, though his career in the Lowlands as chief minister to Margaret of Parma had ended badly, had undoubtedly shown statesmanship of the kind Philip liked, both there and afterwards in his government of Naples. But he was old and very much an invalid now, it was said, and lived in pious retirement in Rome. So, quite simply, there was no one to take his own place, Antonio admitted—and decided therefore to be patient while playing the effective game of rash impatience.

Meanwhile since April the scandal of Juan de Escovedo's death, of Easter Monday of the year before, this scandal which in the winter had faded so consolingly from common view, was now, with all its offshoots of libel and lie and grotesque decoration, ablaze again somehow throughout Madrid. Everyone talked of it or became ominously, tactfully silent when it was mentioned; everyone had an opinion; everyone said it must be cleared up.

Even the great Mendoza family, spread richly and now in the main slumbrously across the Peninsula, from the Vizcaya and Montaña of its brave origins and across the great Castiles to Cadiz and to Malaga, began to stir and grumble vaguely in its sleep, as if it heard its name dishonoured on the wind. The Duke of Infantado began to fidget at the centre, at Guadalajara; the old Prince of Mélito blasphemed; Iñigo Lopez de Mendoza, claimant against the Princess of Eboli for some family successions, showed how he thought the tides were running for her by renewing his doubtful suit for the lands of Almenara; and the dutiful young Duke of Medina Sidonia, married to the Princess of Eboli's elder daughter, disengaged himself from his horse-breeding in Andalusia and came to Madrid to see what was afoot, and to use what he called his "influence" on behalf of his mother-in-law.

This action of the young duke made Ana, and more than Ana, smile.

Alonzo de Guzman, Duke of Medina Sidonia, now in his thirtieth year, was a wealthy man, and virtuous. He had made an apparent success of his marriage with Ana Madalena de Silva y de Mendoza, who, ten years his junior, was now a self-important matron and the leader of sporting circles in the south of Spain. But no one in Castile thought anything of what went on in Andalusia, and Madrid accounted it very suitable that society down there should be ruled by two such stupids as the good Alonzo and his boring wife. Lately however the king had taken up Medina Sidonia; he had made him a Councillor of Castile, to the immense amusement of Castilians; frequently he invited him to hunting parties at El

Pardo, and shrewd observers about the Court said that Philip really did seem to have a speculative eye on the young man. Now as Philip's normal method was to leave the aristocracy at peace with their foolish country pursuits, and as indeed he never troubled himself socially with anyone save to further a policy, it was necessary to assume that Medina Sidonia was regarded as potentially useful to the realm.

It was impossible not to smile and wonder at this idea. The stocky, steady young man knew nothing about anything except horses; he had neither learning nor wit; he had not trained for Spain either as soldier or sailor. He was unadventurous, domestic, kind, and—by Castilian standards—a provincial bore. But the king continued to flatter him. Antonio Perez said that this could only have relation to, possibly, the coming campaign against Portugal; that Medina Sidonia's estates and influence bordered Portugal on the south, and that he was wealthy and loyal. Even so, the king's attentions seemed excessive.

However, they pleased Medina Sidonia—and naturally made him a little pompous. So, as he had family feeling, and oddly enough liked his casual and eccentric mother-in-law, he came bustling to Madrid in May, to use his influence for her with the king.

Ana, though grateful to him, could not take him seriously. However, she did use him as a medium, a conveyor, of her "indiscretions".

"It's *the plan*," she told Antonio. "I want all sorts of fools to spread abroad my views on this affair, and my intransigence. I have a principle, you see——"

"Mad!" said Antonio.

Ana talked with apparent freedom therefore to the anxious and attentive Medina Sidonia. She was amused to discover in these conversations that had she confessed to him on her knees, had she sworn on the Cross that she was indeed, as accused, the mistress of Antonio Perez, he would not have believed her, but have thought it some pitiful aberration of old age, combined with exaggerated Castilian chivalry towards a man in trouble. For to her son-in-law, Ana discovered, she was an unattractive, plain old woman whom no man could possibly want now, and who must be protected for her own sake and the sake of her great name from the consequences of a slight tendency to craziness. He liked her because she was kind and generous, because she was of his own class, and because she had brought up a large family and been a good wife; he pitied her because she was thin and ugly and had only one eye; and he thought it disgraceful that the populace should be allowed to gossip so loosely and absurdly about a Mendoza, who was also a widow and old and disfigured. He was ready to do everything in his power for her and he had reason to believe that he had power with the king. This point of view saved Ana trouble, amused her and made it possible for her to talk as freely as she chose.

But her son Rodrigo took his brother-in-law seriously. Rodrigo was now openly very angry and unhappy about his mother's association with the Escovedo scandal.

"How could he be otherwise?" the Cardinal said to Ana. "He is your son. It is very painful for him, all this talk."

"I see that," Ana said.

"If you could somehow say something, do something, to withdraw yourself from it, to seem to reprove the slanderers —I think that would help him."

"I know. As for the slanderers—truly I can't be bothered to seem to reprove them. But I do see the grievance of a son. And I'm sorry." She paused. "Oh Cardinal, there are regions of my soul I would withdraw to now, regions that matter nothing to Rodrigo, but where I could rest, I promise you!"

"I believe that, Ana. Why don't you seek them, child?"

"This is not a time for self-indulgence."

"Repentance? Is that self-indulgence?"

"Repentance, like anything else, can be ill-timed."

"I've told you before that God's timing isn't yours."

"You're a prince of the Church, but—do I know you long enough to say that you're a shade cocksure about God?"

He laughed.

"Very likely you're right. It's because I haven't yet got over the surprise of my red hat, perhaps!"

"How gracious you are!" she said.

"Ana, you are contrite. You're tired of your sin, and God is grateful to you for that. Trust him to understand at least as well as you do your own dislike of repenting at what seems the timely moment. Repent when repentance is true, Ana—and chance the implications."

"It wouldn't be wholly true now—and I'm not tired of my sin. But I do recognise it and have to struggle with it—and that is tiring."

"Hair-splitter."

"Perhaps. Still—you see I chose this love-affair with Antonio. *I* made it happen—not he. And I have enjoyed it, and drunk life from it. It was a gift to me I won't attempt to explain to you. Now it matters to him, and his whole world is endangered for it, but he doesn't waver. He's every sort of profligate and sinner, but it never occurs to him that he and I might fail each other in this danger. Nor will we. It's just unlucky that before the danger rose I was beginning to be sorry for my mortal sins. I had refrained from sight of him for seven months and was fighting it out. And the night on which I had decided to explain my dull repentance to him was the night on which he told me of the danger threatening."

"So you resumed the relationship?"

"Yes. Rodrigo had his part in the decision."

"Indeed?"

"It's a complicated story. And don't think it's heroic. The night wasn't sacrificial, Cardinal. I simply saw that I was too much in love with him still, and had grown too near him, to resist his need. It was no moment for self-analysis, or for a splendid, renunciatory scene."

"You are very self-conscious. Very vain, perhaps. He'd have been angry and disgusted, and have left you—and that would have been that, and much better for both of you now. But you didn't want him to be angry and leave you."

"That's what I've just said. And anyway, parting or no parting, the damage was done to his career. No amount of austerity after the fact was going to be much good."

"H'm, I see," said the Cardinal. "Very human, local argument. But God is not mocked."

"I believe not. But neither is my conscience."

The Cardinal laughed.

"From what I read, that sounds very Protestant to me!"

"Heretical anyhow, I suppose. A shade Pelagian, do you think?"

"Ana, my dear, you can be surprisingly subtle, for a simple creature."

"I think a good deal lately, for a simple creature."

"Yet your thinking can lead you to please neither God nor Rodrigo?"

"My thinking tells me without any monstrous effort that I have a soul to save and that its salvation is paramount; my honour, which has nothing to do with thinking, tells me that no retreat is possible now, and that everything, including my immortal soul, must wait on honour. And pleasure and affection prompt me to follow honour." She smiled at the Cardinal, asking for mercy.

"Yet you know," he said, not returning her smile, "you once did try to be a nun, in a mad sort of way——" She winced. "No, I don't mind hurting you. You did try, and you did make a fool of yourself. And before that you lived thirty-three years continently, and without, I understand, the full refinements of the pleasures of the flesh?"

She smiled.

"Be sardonic if you like, old friend. You see, you are just a natural monk."

"And I have often thought, my dear, that you are just a natural nun."

She threw her hands apart.

"Oh silly!" she said. "Oh, go and make that claim for me this minute at the Puerta del Sol!"

"It would be a true claim—but it wouldn't improve the present situation, Ana."

"No. The only thing for the present situation—sorry though I am for Rodrigo—is to be true, and stand by it."

"It's never right to continue in sin."

"I know. I wasn't talking about *right*." She was bent forward in her chair, and her hand was pressed against her empty eye-socket. "Oh, believe me, I'm a battle-ground. And what's more, I'm haunted."

"I expect so. What sort of ghosts, Ana?"

"Only one. Juan de Escovedo."

The Cardinal drew in a sharp breath.

"Ana!" he said. "Ana, *you* had nothing to do with his destruction?"

There was real fear, real anxiety in the question.

"No," she answered. "I knew, but only by implication, that Philip desired him dead, and that he would die any day in the early part of last year. I knew—though this was never said either—that Antonio had charged himself to rid the king of Escovedo. But one night Escovedo, who was a little mad, behaved as if he were the Angel of Judgment. Antonio was present. And very promptly afterwards, without a word said, Escovedo was killed by unknown desperadoes."

"I see."

"Forgive me, but I don't think you do. I'm not haunted by his death. I'm reasonable. He was to die, and that wasn't my affair. Philip's business. But in fact, by a silly accident, he seems to me to have died a martyr. Secretly, accidentally, he died for the right—for what he and I know to be right."

"But you don't grant him what he died for?"

"No. At present I can't."

"This thing called honour?"

"Honour and love and goodwill, and seeing things through when you started them——"

"You're complicated. You're Protestant. But do try to get God's view of all this, Ana."

"To do so would be simple egotism just now, I think."

"But what about Rodrigo?"

"If I'm to be of any real value to my children, Cardinal, I can only be so by being precisely myself, however I split hairs, or bore or outrage the world. And some of my children would see that, I think, if they were old enough. But even if they didn't, I cannot give them the whole country of my conscience and its mistakes."

But no one, watching her talk to Medina Sidonia or to Rodrigo, would have thought that she was a battle-ground. For in general encounters at this time her manner was tranquil, light and worldly-wise.

"You see, Alonzo," she would say to her son-in-law, "it is necessary for the king to understand that we of the aristocracy will not approve this sneaking kind of injustice to a public servant. If no one else intends to express the opinion of honour in this case—*I* shall do so, for the Mendozas."

"I—er, I see. How exactly do you define the injustice, Doña Ana?"

"Dear boy! Listen. There are two Chief Secretaries of State. One of them slanders the other grievously, repeatedly and publicly. The slandered one protests with vigour. Yet the slanders are repeated, to the king and to everyone of note. The king takes no side, does nothing. Meantime, the actual crime which is the source of the slanders remains uninvestigated. No one is charged judicially with anything, nothing is done. The slanders spread, and grow worse.

Antonio Perez naturally insults and threatens his slanderer, and asks the king to adjudicate. Yet even then all Philip can do is ask him please to bury the hatchet, and shake hands with his enemy!"

"It is indeed preposterous."

"*Now*, as you know, Perez has resigned from office. It is his only course. But the king won't accept his resignation. All this shameless, autocratic torture of a free man, all this freezing of the usual channels to trial and justice is unnatural to Castile, and an insult to us all. As one Castilian, I refuse this impertinence from a half-foreign king. And you can tell him so. Tell him further, Alonzo, that he need not think to keep Perez because Perez depends on his salary and increments. I am wealthy, and there are houses on my estate to which Antonio Perez can retire whenever he likes, and I can compensate him in money, and for the honour of Castile, for any loss imposed on him by the king's extraordinary blankness and ingratitude. That is what I want the king to know. That I see the honour of Spain in this affair, and shall protect it to the extent of my possessions."

When Medina Sidonia talked over this ultimatum with Rodrigo the latter seemed awhile as if he might lose his reason.

"She's capable of it, Alonzo," he said, pacing about his study rapidly and with a hand pressed to his eyes, unconsciously reproducing his mother's signs of agitation. "She's totally irresponsible, you know! Indeed, ever since father's death I've often thought that she is insane!"

"Come, come," said Alonzo. "A little odd, I agree—but hardly insane, dear boy. And she *is* your mother," he added piously.

"Yes, alas! But have you ever heard such dishonest nonsense as this about protecting Spain's honour to the extent of her possessions! What possessions? Her possessions are ours!"

Alonzo understood money well, and he sympathised with Rodrigo's disgust at Ana's royal foolishness with it. But he had an orderly mind, and he liked facts stated correctly.

"No, Rodrigo. As you know I've had to deal somewhat with your family affairs—more or less in your place, as you've been a minor so far. And it is a fact that your mother is a very wealthy woman in her own right, quite apart from the trustee-ship she holds for the estates of her children. She can't touch any of those—nor indeed, I believe, would she attempt to. And may I say that you are all very wealthy people?"

"It looks as if we'll need to be—since we're taking on liability for Spain's honour!"

"What I'm explaining is that you're *not*. You're perfectly safe. As a Mendoza heiress and only child your mother has vast resources over which her dominion is absolute. It was because of her great wealth that Ruy Gomez was able to bequeath practically all his possessions to you children. He and she agreed upon that, and upon leaving her own estates inviolable and independent. I know all this for a fact, because your father explained it to me in connection with my wife's dowries."

"Still—as we are the children of a Mendoza heiress, we clearly have a right to our expectations from that? Surely we can be protected from her squandering her whole estate without thought of us?"

"I don't think you can be. She says—and rightly—that you are all excessively well provided for. All the Neapolitan and Sicilian estates and titles that your family holds now are very sound indeed, Rodrigo. I agree, *naturally*, that family money should stay in the family, and I sympathise with your expectations from your mother's estates after her death. But meantime you have no legal control over what she does in her lifetime with her own property."

"But, if she's mad?"

"She isn't mad, Rodrigo. I beg you not to be so brutally unfilial!"

"Oh, you try being her son before you preach, Alonzo! If she isn't mad, she's maybe something worse! I—I daren't tell you what I feel about her—her association with this bounder, Perez!"

Alonzo stared at him.

"But, my poor dear boy, you don't believe all that ridiculous talk, do you? About your own mother? And at her age, and—er—everything? Now, come, come, Rodrigo— you must try to be a little bit—well, realistic, my boy."

It was Rodrigo's turn to stare at the round, earnest, swarthy face of his virtuous brother-in-law. And what he read there made him laugh, in sudden weariness.

Poor, silly, provincial, he thought.

"I think you'll be a great help to us, Alonzo," he said sincerely. "It was good of you to come to Madrid. Still, I think the simplest thing for everyone now, including the king, would be if I ran my sword through Antonio Perez."

The Duke of Medina Sidonia bounced from his chair. He hated swords and quarrels.

"Oh no, dear boy, no, no! That would be *quite* uncalled-for, let me say!"

"I'm tired to death of him," Rodrigo said.

"That is no excuse for killing him," Alonzo answered primly. "Moreover he is a notoriously good swordsman."

"So he boasts. But when has he last fought seriously with the sword? He's getting old, and I am very young, and in training. I believe I could kill him easily—and more courageously than he disposed of Escovedo."

"My dear boy, I beg you, I beg you!" said Alonzo, looking cautiously all round him.

Medina Sidonia liked his wife's relations, but he regarded them as unstable. And, now more than ever after this conversation with Rodrigo, he saw their need of a steady man of affairs to guide them. So he went with a will to the business of arbitrator in the Perez scandal.

Philip was informed therefore, as Ana had desired him to be, that Perez need not fear poverty, and that her estates were at his disposition. Nobody, not shrewder wits than Medina Sidonia, not the President of Castile or the Cardinal, could read in the king's face or manner what he made of that insolent communication.

Vasquez continued to assert that he walked in mortal danger, that Perez and his friends made open declaration of their desire to murder him. He begged the king to protect his peace of mind, and to make it possible for him to do his work in tranquillity.

It was quite true that Vasquez's life was being made a torture to him. Perez saw to that.

The king reassured Vasquez in the same terms of royal affection that he used to wheedle Perez. And he wrote to Perez instructing him that this shameful persecution of Mateo Vasquez must cease. Perez replied that it would cease, that he was tired of the whole farce, that he apologised for all his own wrong-doing, and only begged to be released at once from office. That is all I ask, he wrote. In return I offer silence.

Philip made no direct reply.

But in conference one day he told the President and the Cardinal that he was thinking of suggesting to Perez that he go to Venice as ambassador for a time. The two men just managed not to smile; they advised the king against making so vain an offer.

So the suggestion never reached Antonio officially.

It was the Cardinal who told Ana about it.

"I almost told His Majesty not to be silly!" he said. "He really does have the most preposterous notions for getting himself out of trouble."

Ana said nothing.

At this time, when her true friends or people whom she regarded as intelligent spoke of the king, she did not take up the theme. In talk with Medina Sidonia, or Rodrigo, or even Bernardina, she made—deliberately—wild and arrogant comments on him, and sent him verbal messages as insolent as she could frame. She desired all these to reach and to trouble him. And once, having to write to him in reference to the lawsuit of her cousin, Iñigo Lopez de Mendoza, she took the occasion to reprove him daringly and proudly for allowing a criminal libel on her name to be made by a minister of State and to go unheeded and unpunished. Her letter was arrogant but phrased formally and as Court etiquette required. It could be read by anyone in Philip's entourage; she hoped that it was read by many.

Philip did not reply.

When the children, Fernando and Anichu, asked if the king was coming to Madrid and if they would see him then, she teased them and said he was tired of them, and had grown too fond of the new Infante to be bothered with anyone else. But they were unperturbed.

"The king loves you; I know that for a fact," Anichu told her mother. "He'll come to see us when he has time."

But although Ana said nothing real about Philip in these days, he was much and perplexedly in her mind. She did not believe that he was cold or treacherous, or at least, that he could be either of those things to her. She did not believe either that he was the moral coward he was now appearing to be. And she knew that his silence towards her, prolonged into many months, his silence, and his inability to pronounce her name even to her dearest friends, that these were signs of something other besides hardening of his heart. That Lady. She knew that it was not for nothing, not cheaply or cruelly that she became That Lady on Philip's lips.

If he went on sulking in his tent she would go and find him there, and speak to him freely, friend to friend, as she always could. And if he wanted then to lecture her, or to be jealous or impertinent about Antonio Perez, she could easily, whilst denying him his right to such intrusion, accord him it as the privilege of a very particular friend, and hear what he had to say, and even, for old affection's sake, go so far as to defend her love-affair against his busybody disapproval. But she would wait awhile for that. She wanted him to take full cognisance first of her public and unflinching allegiance to Antonio Perez, in the feud of the Secretaries of State. She wanted her broadcast challenges to reach him casually on any wind. She desired to make it crystal-clear to him, even spectacularly clear if necessary, that she for her part was afraid of nothing in this scandal. She knew that this—which was true and which he would certainly believe of her, since he knew her well—would work alike on anxiety and curiosity in him, would drive him at last from silence, force him to speak plainly with her. But she could wait for that. There was time yet. She guessed that she counted for very much in Philip's present weak and foolish policy of inaction. She had an idea that, if all other ways out of the *impasse* were to fail, Antonio Perez's whole future might turn upon the exact nature of Philip's feeling for her. As she had never been able to be sure of that, she was uneasy now, considering the charge that it might bear—and so was in no hurry to put it to the test. She would face it when the time came—and pray for wit and gentleness. Meanwhile she tried conscientiously to remember the king she knew, and to balance his reality or non-reality against the king who was now confounding and distracting his ablest counsellors.

One night Antonio came to her earlier than usual. It was high summer, but after the torrid day the Long Room, windows open to the west, and unlighted save by the starred, transparent sky, was cool and still.

When Antonio came into the room she was sitting there alone, straight-backed and quiet, by the upper window, on her

French day-bed. Her hands were joined in idleness in her lap; vestiges of light from the summer night fell about her, stressing her darkness, making her seem like a shadow.

He paused before he reached her, considering her.

"You look very holy," he said. "Are you praying?"

"No. I was thinking about Philip."

"So well you might."

He came and sat beside her on the couch, and she took his hand.

"Welcome," she said. "I'm glad to see you. But what is it? Are you over-excited about something?"

He laughed.

"How the devil do you know, Ana? Does my hand give off some disgusting, curious heat, or something? Or are you a witch? I absolutely *hate* witches."

"Then I'm not a witch. And I don't like them either. No. Just tell me what's the matter."

"In a minute."

"I suppose you want to drink a lot of wine first?"

"I wouldn't mind. But no—oh no, don't stir. This is all right. This is enough."

He stretched himself along the couch and laid his head in her lap.

"God! This is lovely!" he said.

She bent and kissed him.

"June—it's June, isn't it?" he said dreamily. "In September, on the ninth of September it will be two years. Do you realise that?"

"I do. I've been wondering already what to give you for an anniversary present. What do you want?"

"Anything. Everything. I love presents. Is my head too heavy? Am I hurting you?"

"Silly."

"You're so thin. It's awful, really. Do you remember we had a very good celebration on the last ninth of September?

You were a little drunk that night, I think."

"I was quite drunk."

"Oh girl, you were *so* amusing! I'll make you much, much drunker this time. Every anniversary I'll make you a bit drunker—until at last you're a dipsomaniac. That will be marvellous."

"Do you expect to love me for more anniversaries?"

He sighed contentedly.

"I'll tell you something. In the old palmy days I rarely reached a *first* anniversary. On the one or two occasions when I did, I was always far from willing to be there. But now, to be clearly in sight of a second, and talking like any sort of drivelling fool about the third and fourth and fifth—oh, it's inexplicable. It's terrifying. Perhaps it's just middle age. If it is, I'm astounded to find that I like it."

"We're beyond middle age. We're old. Medina Sidonia thinks I'm a decrepit old hag."

"I expect so. Do you remember, Ana, that first ninth of September—there were flowers on the table at supper that I had sent you——"

"Yes. Flowers from Aranjuez—I remember."

"Philip's flowers! Curious. I remember thinking before I sent them that they were a good excuse, being Philip's. I mean, it would have been a bit impertinent just to send you flowers of my own——"

"Nonsense, you weren't weighing up the pros and cons of me then. You were just manœuvring politically, and I was the not very alluring widow of the king's favourite minister of State."

"That's true, I suppose. It's a long time ago." He pulled her down to him. "I love you, girl."

Bent above him in embrace she leant on him, relaxed, at peace.

"Do you know that you never say it?" she said.

"Do you want me to?"

"Only when you do say it. Otherwise, I know."

He held her very close to him.

"Stay there. Keep still, Ana."

"But tell me what's the matter."

"Ah! That! Well, you'll have to sit up for that."

She sat up.

"So shall I, I think," he said, "to do justice to it."

"It's grave news?"

"It isn't news at all." He stood up. "I think I'll start drinking all that wine now."

"Can you see? Shall I ring for lights?"

"No. Of course I can see." And indeed moonlight was brilliant through the windows now. Antonio poured two glasses of white wine. "Come, drink with me, ascetic," he said. "Drink to my genius for finding out what *no* one knows." He sipped his wine. "Philip will miss that talent," he said.

"What have you found out?"

"You will remember, from Ruy's heyday and earlier, a Flemish churchman called Bishop Perrenot, afterwards Cardinal Granvelle."

"I do indeed. He was chief minister in the Lowlands under Margaret of Parma?"

"Yes. And a talented administrator. Afterwards he did well as Governor of Naples. In recent years he has been invalidish and living in retirement in Rome. He was a favourite of Philip's, do you remember? Very much trusted, and understood the king's very personal method of government."

Ana watched Antonio with interest. He was talking with precision and detachment, almost as if in the Cabinet Room.

"Yes," she said. "I recall all that about him. He was a friend of Ruy, was frequently with him."

"Exactly. That's one of his very strong points."

"I don't see what you mean."

"You will. I'm going to tell you something now that at present I believe only one man in Spain is supposed to know —and that man is the king. And I wouldn't know it, were it not for my uncanny knack of seeing how one improbable nothing leads to another—and the trouble I can take when these improbable nothings insist on engaging my attention. Well, I've had lately one of my curious intuitional attacks. I couldn't possibly explain to you the irrelevancies that led me along. But I was right."

"Stop boasting. Tell me the news."

"In my own time. Drink your wine and wait for what you'll hear." He paused and moved about the room. "Oh God! Oh God!" he said.

"What has happened?"

"When I wrote and asked to be released from office, I was bluffing of course, as you know. How could I want to resign? But I don't have to tell you. You know how I work, and how good I am at my work, and how I love it. Let's take all that as said. But I thought—let him try to work out how to let me go. He daren't. There simply isn't anyone, *anyone* to take my place. I thought: there was once my father, Gonzalo Perez; and there was Ruy Gomez, of course; and there was, possible, but not so good, Granvelle. Two of them, the good ones, are dead, I thought; and the other is a sick old man in retirement. So there's no one. Let him try to plan to do without me."

He paused again and drank. Ana did not speak.

"Well, he *has* planned. Nothing escapes him. Granvelle is coming back—on his personal and absolutely private invitation. I think he's on the sea this minute. Philip has secured my successor. The only catch is that he's old. But there are a few years in him—enough to see us through the annexation of Portugal—and by then he will have trained his successor. So I have lost, Ana. I didn't think I could lose. But I really believe I have."

"I don't see it. You are still in possession of the true story of the Escovedo death."

"Once he has found someone to do my work even that ugly fact loses its force. For now I can be assassinated, you see, like anyone else. Like Escovedo."

"You don't know at all why Granvelle is coming to Spain."

"He is coming in answer to a despatch and private appeal of the king. But I *know* what that means. I give you my oath he is coming to take my place."

"Or Vasquez's?"

"That's just possible. But his talents are more suited to my kind of work. He's a man of the world, a European. The correct complementary for Vasquez, just as I have been. You wait and see."

"Philip isn't like that."

"Philip is anything that he deems necessary."

"You know I don't agree."

He came and sat beside her.

"Oh girl, I'm tired! I've loved my life, I've loved my work for Spain."

She took him in her arms. Philip would have been moved by that cry, she thought.

THE FIFTH CHAPTER   (JULY 1579)

July was extremely hot. Ana sent the three youngest children, Ruy, Fernando and Anichu, back to Pastrana. Rodrigo came and went as he chose between Alcala, Madrid and the country houses of his friends. Ana hardly ever saw him; when they did meet he had only reproaches or bad news for her.

She and Bernardina lived almost exclusively in her private wing of the house, as if in retreat. It was too hot to ride or even drive unnecessarily by day, and casual visitors were discouraged. The few friends Ana would have been glad to

see were not at hand; the President of Castile was ill and the
Cardinal was directing an ecclesiastical conference in Toledo;
the Marqués de Los Velez wrote dejectedly from his Alcala
house. " . . . Philip goes much too far in deceit and
procrastination now. I despair of him. I feel when I talk
with him that I talk to a mask, or a ghost. I am tired, my
dear. Perhaps if one were to go abroad? I think of asking to
be made Governor of one or other of these new American
places. What do you think of that, Ana? And why don't you
come too? This silly Spain where we who used to govern are
reduced to puppetry—I'm tired of it. Meantime I fret
impatiently about this dreary Escovedo *impasse*, and I fear for
your friend. And, foolishly, irrationally, I fear for you. Let
me have a word of news. I am too old for Madrid in July.
Indeed, I can't understand why we've all been bullied like
this into accepting it as our chief city. I wish you were here,
or at Pastrana. Everything promises well for harvest . . ."

Antonio was melancholy and weary now. He had lost all
impulse in his fight against Vasquez, and had written once
again to the king, expressing this weariness, undertaking to
ignore the wrongs the other secretary had done to him, and
to subside for ever into silence, if only the king would do him
one last favour, instantly relieve him of office.

Philip did not answer. The official memoranda came to
Perez still, exactly as if there was no conflict between them.
So the latter was now making preparations to move his family
to his native kingdom of Aragon. "The ancient liberties of
Aragon will protect me there," he told Ana, "against any
pursuit of vengeance. And the border of Aragon is not very
far from Pastrana."

Ana still believed that Philip would find a better way than
this to end the confusion he had set up. But meantime she
helped Perez to take necessary decisions, paid debts for him
and did her best with love and fidelity to keep him from a too
profound dejection.

She was weary and uncertain herself now; tired of the disgraceful public embroilment with Vasquez and of the king's apparent stupidity; anxious very often to pray, but forbidden by her own spiritual honour to seek the balm of prayer; anxious indeed to be free to return in honesty and forthrightness to the questions of her own sins and the too long brushed-away desires of her soul. But she belonged to Antonio Perez in this preposterous external situation, and as long as she felt his need of her to be true and by his rules justified, he could be sure of her. Yet often now as she sat alone, outwardly quiet or busy, in the Long Room, she was visited, stormily, wildly inside her heart, with the old mad desire of six years ago to flee from everything and be a nun. She did not even wince from the absurdity, but let her spirit dwell on it indulgently—knowing that now she was in control of herself, and could only dream these things, while a paradoxical duty of sin kept her anchored to the wrongdoings of every day.

Philip was at the Alcázar in July, and sent her no message, gave no sign. Anxiously she turned over plans for visiting him there. If she did go, and she would, she hardly knew what she was going to say to him, save that she would tolerate no hypocrisy between them. But much lay for Antonio on that future conversation with the king, so she pondered it uneasily and often as the hot days passed.

And one evening as she sat by a window of the Long Room and thought of him, Philip came to her, unannounced.

She came across the room to him quickly. She fell on her knees, as usual, as she kissed his hand. And when she rose and looked into his weary face there was such pleasure and gratitude in hers that the king forgot himself and his knotty troubles for a minute and smiled at her as he had always liked to do throughout the years.

"Oh! This is good of you!" she said, without any etiquette of 'Majesty' or 'sire'. "Oh Philip! I've wanted to see you! Sit down. How tired you look!"

He had a small sealed packet in his hand.

"I came with this," he said. But he did not explain what the packet contained, or set it down.

He stood and looked about the room as if memorising it, or checking memory. And Ana had the impression that he was undergoing some great stress of feeling and wished for a while to avoid looking at her face. But she was so glad to see him, and so confident that his gesture in coming meant friendliness and boded well for Antonio that she decided to have no care for procedure, to let the king take his own way with what had to be said, and trust to their old sincerity and affection—Philip's for her as much as hers for him—to steer them into safety and understanding.

It was dangerous, this impulse she always had to like and find the best of him in Philip. And never more dangerous than now—if for no other reason than that somehow she always communicated to him this sense of her great liking. It had ever been a mighty charm in her for Philip, that in her presence vanity and all its unresting, self-conscious attendants could lay down arms and go to sleep. Her affection once given, a fellow-creature was safe with her. There was no sharpness in her then, no mockery or self-parade, no impulse to alter or outwit or dazzle. She could be cruel and careless to those she either did not know or did not like. She was consistently, if passively, cruel to Rodrigo; she was cruel in her casual contempt for her old father; she was notoriously cruel in her every public utterance about Antonio's enemy, Mateo Vasquez. But her affection once engaged, goodwill dominated it. So those whom she loved could rest in her, as nowhere else, from the persecutions of their egoism. She was in fact not merely passively but actively non-cruel in affection. And it was the *activity* of this principle which differentiated it from mildness; made it an intelligent and potent force, almost a peculiarity—and by no means just a condition of slumbering gentleness.

It was this active principle of goodwill in feeling, which could face conflict with other strong principles of her nature, that had made it possible for her to stay at home with Ruy for all their years, and be content and make him happy. Because he had been so lucky as to reach to the centre of her affection; and thereafter she would never be able to persuade herself that her own needs or moods were more important than his. There was no theatre and no virtue in this for her; it was her fate, because it was the way her nature worked. So it was with Antonio Perez. He could be every sort of schemer, egoist and cheat; he could commit crimes and take very long chances on honesty and even on good manners. But he had warmed her heart, he had won her goodwill, and so he was safe.

But to Philip love of any kind had never brought, could never bring, the ease it brought to Ana. For her—and she was not stupid, and had encountered and wrestled with many complications of feeling—but for her mainly love simplified life. There it was and in the midst of much nonsense one saw it to be real, and one could therefore weigh and measure it. It simplified by its positiveness, and because she, of her nature, could not haggle.

But Philip could haggle until time stood still. His curse was that he was a natural haggler. Indeed, because he and Ana were opposites in this they suited each other well. For throughout the years of his uneasy desire of her he had had, he thought, as King of Spain, to fuss and haggle all the way; and she, unacquainted with the methods of hagglers, hardly noticed what he did. For her their situation had been simple. They had a persistent attraction for each other—she never saw him in her early years without wondering what it would be like to be his mistress—but they both loved Ruy, and Ruy and his happiness were worth a great deal to anyone who loved him. So the sinful decision was not taken, though Ana in her honesty could never assure herself that had Philip been truly urgent she would have resisted him.

Yet when she was a widow he left her unmolested. He was ageing then, and crazy to save his immortal soul and have an heir, and be a virtuous king. He was haggling fiercely with heaven in these latter years, and his waning, tired desire for her was now become one of heaven's easier taxations. Ana understood this, and so did not share the vague fears of Antonio and de Los Velez that her having taken a lover would disturb him in some degree which might make his future conduct towards her incalculable. She outraged no claim of his in loving another man, and her private life was her own. And she knew him as reasonable, considerate, gentle, faithful. She knew him, through many years, as a man who could not resist any direct appeal of poverty or of little children, or of the holy, or the mad, or the sick. She knew him as a man of constant and gentle charities, and as one who was naturally attracted to painters and gardeners and scholars and monks. She knew that he liked simplicity and quietude, and cared, after holiness, for those earthly activities which can be called true and eternal. She knew him also in his plight as a politician, and as a ruler who believed himself marked by Heaven, and she knew many of the sins which he had justified within that conception of himself. But she would have said through thick and thin that, guilty, conceited creature as he was, fanatic, bully, megalomaniac—she still knew him better than his shrewdest judges, because she knew him another way; knew him in little, knew him at home as it were, knew him at rest.

This was her secret argument, and it was well-founded and in that sense true. But it did not compass the whole of Philip —and because in her innocence and mercy she thought it did, it was dangerous for her.

Because affection meant in her goodwill and a consequent dismissal of cruelty, she inclined to think that that was what affection was, the world over. That for another it might be, or have to be, power, absolutism, self-assurance, and indeed an appetite more subtle, greedy and constant, more jealous and unkind than any sensual lust, was a guess outside her compass. So Philip might, if she hurt him, be stiff, offended, difficult, sly and all the boring, slow delaying things that he could too often be. But yet affection—which was goodwill—would prevail between them, if it lived. And by his coming to her, by the way he looked about the room now, she knew that affection lived, and had brought him here. So having welcomed him with natural gladness, she was suddenly peaceful, and content to let him speak, and even be as silly and irritating as he liked.

The more fool she.

Much was indeed in the balance when Philip came into the room. But had she met him in some alien way, had she played cold or haughty, or even virago-ish with him, or in any way been false or new or disconcerting, it might have been far better. What in any case was unlucky—though neither she nor Philip could possibly feel it then—was that she gave him in their first minute together after so long the old, precious feeling of peace, of having come to where there was rest and faith. For Philip, the absolute king, the lonely, wretched, vain and hungry man, it was insufferable to feel and take this peace, this illusion, from a woman who was the declared and shameless mistress of a subject.

But Ana, clear-cut and generous, having never refused Philip anything he asked or ever suffered real unkindness from him, welcomed him back to the Long Room now with an open and uplifted heart.

"I hadn't thought to see this room again," he said.

"That is a dreadful thing to say. What do you mean by it?"

"Oh, Ana!" He moved slowly to what had been his usual chair by the lower window, and sat down. "How are the children?" he said.

"They're very well. Rodrigo comes and goes. He's very

much a man of the world now, and I hardly see him. I sent
the others back to Pastrana last week. It was so hot, and they
were getting far too frivolous. But they'll be wretchedly disappointed at missing you."

"They've wanted to see me?"

"But, Philip—of course! They love you. We all love you,
in this family."

He bit his lip and looked uneasy.

"It hasn't seemed like that," he said.

"So you appear to have thought. I'm waiting for you to
tell me why?" she said simply.

He looked at her as if genuinely surprised.

"You're very cool," he said. "You're really very, very
audacious. I suppose I must blame myself. I suppose I've
encouraged you——"

"Blame yourself! she interrupted him. "Encouraged me?
But Philip, my dear friend, what do you mean? I've only
asked you to tell me why we've been estranged?"

"Ana! Please!"

He laid his little sealed packet on the table near him, and
then laid his hand upon it as if in close protection. She
noticed how thickened and stiff his hand was. She noticed
too, now that he sat in the hard, dramatic light from the west,
that his face was green-white and older than she had remembered it, and that his eyes were weary and red-rimmed.
His once fair hair was neutral-coloured now, half-grey, half-
dun. But she liked it still, and liked the paleness of his weary
eyes. She always liked to look at him; his washed-awayness,
his curious foreign pallor appealed to her.

"Yes, Philip. Go on!"

"I fear I must," he said piously. "You have disgraced
yourself, Ana. You have dishonoured Ruy's memory and
your children's name."

She smiled a little. This was the sort of nonsense that she
well knew he could talk. It did not perturb her.

"I could pretend to be mystified," she said. "But I don't want to tease you." He looked amazed at this gambit, but she went ahead without waiting for his protest. "*I* have done no harm to Ruy's memory or my children's name. That part of me which belongs to what I associate with those phrases of yours still belongs to them. *But*, my private life *is* truly private. There have been, Philip, as long as I can remember, thoughts and even acts in that private life which, presented to the world, would seem to injure this or that. That is so, I should think, for everyone from cradle to grave. But I do not present my private life to the world. Which is not the same thing as saying that I sacrifice it to the world. I own it, Philip. If I do wrong in it, that wrong is between me and Heaven. But here below, so long as I don't try to change it into public life, I insist that *I* own it. Not Ruy's memory, and not my children's name. These are clouds I can't really see at all—I only bring them in because you did. But my private life is all that I own, and I insist on managing it myself, under God."

To Philip, the absolute king, no one had spoken like this in his lifetime. If he censured, or hinted censure as now he had, to any subject, that subject either took his censure silently or with a great flourish of submission. He had never had occasion seriously to censure Ana de Mendoza, but his habit of total authority had probably made him imagine that she too, being his subject, would be solemn and helpless under his displeasure. So the friendly coolness of her counter-censure struck him as might some astonishing foreign custom, or even a speech in an unknown language. Yet a part of him heard what she said with approval, and with envy.

"I repeat," he said coldly, "that you have disgraced yourself. This public scandal is an outrage against everything you stand for."

"I agree. And I have protested against it, and shall continue to protest. It was not *I* who made this public scandal."

He moved uneasily in his chair. Through all the honesty of her speech and in spite of her dismissal from it of forms of ceremony and care for his royal dignity, he felt the charm and kindness of her flowing towards him as it always did. He was a suspicious man and in middle life was growing pathologically so, yet now he had the restful feeling—very novel to him —that anything might be said or suffered in this room in perfect safety. He could fight here, if he liked, for the obscured meaning of his own conduct, and whatever might be exposed in such a struggle, however he might be humiliated, he would be safe.

"Ana," he said, and she did not miss a new note in his voice as he went on, a note almost of pleading, and certainly of tentative honesty. "Ana, the man who informed me and some other people about your immorality, is an honourable public servant, and had to do his duty."

She smiled.

"I know that. It began that way. But since then he has widened the scope of his duty. The whole town knows things about me now, Philip, including that I connived at the murder of Escovedo, which are quite simply untrue. This is a curious outcome of the high dutifulness of a public servant."

"It was self-defence. You have driven him far—you and another."

"Why will you have the thing upside-down? Why must you make the victim into the criminal?"

"You are all criminals now, in this public feud and cross-feud that is turning my very Council Room into something like a thieves' kitchen. I intend to put a stop to the ridiculous thing. I have work of enormous scope to do, and so have these two men, my servants, and I am tired of this disturbance of their and my efficiency."

"Everyone is tired of it, Philip. You know that. End it."

He smiled wearily at the simple advice.

"I have been trying to. Mateo Vasquez is now quite

willing to drop the whole charge," he said carefully, and watching Ana.

She laughed.

"That's very kind of him," she said. "Considering how very little trouble he has given everybody for the past nine months. But what about the poor Escovedos? It's *their* charge surely, a little bit?"

Philip frowned.

"The Escovedos will be managed. The real trouble has been Vasquez, as you know. But he has been so terrorised by—by the other Secretary of State and his partisans—that he is willing now to bury the whole argument for ever."

Ana was laughing softly in a continuous light accompaniment to Philip's careful dull words.

"I see. Oh Philip my dear, are *you* here too on that really silliest of missions?"

He looked startled.

"Silliest of missions?"

"Yes. Because if so don't please let's wade through it again! I've lost count of the people who have come to this house and told me—in the last five months—that Don Mateo is willing now to forgive himself for all his recent sins of slander and criminal libel, and that all he needs to be quite comfortable is apologies from me and from Antonio Perez for having been the awkward cause of all his crass mistakes. Just that, a public apology, a civil bow, and a promise to withdraw our threats against his life. I have repeatedly told his very odd ambassadors that never having threatened his silly life I can't withdraw a threat. And that the rest of his proposal is just plain lunacy, bearing no relation at all to life." She saw his face growing rigid with anxiety against this flow of impudence, so she rose and came near him, her hands out almost to take his, as she went on speaking. "So please, Philip, please as I love you, spare me the bitter joke of pretending, you too, that *anyone*—let alone I—owes anything but everlasting scorn to this poor Mateo Vasquez!"

She took his hands and dropped on her knees beside him, laughing and gracious. He looked in perplexity into her face and felt in spite of himself great gratitude for the warmth, vitality and trustfulness of her approach to him—after politicians, after prelates, after courtiers.

"I was not going to suggest this pacification as anything but the most cynical trick in the world," he said simply. "I don't think I could say this to anyone else, Ana—but as you know the Escovedo trouble has been mishandled. It went wrong, and is now out of hand. So we are in a fix." He looked at her, doubtful perhaps of himself for talking to her of a State affair at all, and moreover with this new, confiding freedom. She stayed on her knees by him, her hands on his, and simply waited for him to finish what he had to say. "In a fix," he repeated, still marvelling that he could say "we are" to her in such loose and almost confessional application. "So there is nothing left but to patch up a bad affair, and hope for silence and time. And the only way to do that is to pacify Mateo Vasquez. Naturally, I see your point as to the ethical absurdity. But no one could literally ask you for any apologies. Some formula is all he wants, so that he can bury the hatchet without too much loss of face—and with a sense of future safety. And so I thought that you *might*, in the painful circumstances and for—well, for many people's sakes, manage to be cynical about it, and look for a formula——"

He was so grave, and this honest speech was so complete a sacrifice of his public self, and therefore such an effort for him and so deep, so moving a tribute to her, that she could not laugh again, deliciously amusing though she found the passage about "the formula".

"I believe," Philip went on carefully, "I believe that if you could somehow, however formally, arrange to satisfy him that your enmity is no longer directed on him, he might somewhat waive similar exactions from—others. For I understand that he thinks that you exercise influence over his worst enemy—and therefore——"

Silence fell. The king had said something that was very difficult for him. It was indeed hard to believe that he had said it. We must indeed, thought Ana, be "in a fix". This is pitiful. And he is the King of Spain.

She released his hands gently. Then she rose and moved away from him. There was no use in being contemptuous or humorous now. The thing was to be literal and simple, and keep him from becoming again too soon his histrionic conception of himself.

"I'm sorry, Philip," she said gently. "It wouldn't do. It would dishonour everyone."

"I've told you it's a resort of cynicism only."

"I know." She paced along the room, backwards and forwards. "It's not cynical enough, I think. No, I'm sorry."

He watched her in silence for a few seconds, drumming his fingers nervously on the little sealed packet that lay near him.

"If I were to command you to do it, Ana?" he said at last.

She paused in her striding, and came and stood before him.

"You know that I have always been as childishly and fanatically your subject as Fernán or Anichu. You know that in everything of me that your office commands I am absolutely yours. But if you *were* to forget how to be a king, my dear—which you never could!—but if you were to command me to do this outlandishly silly thing, you know perfectly well that I'd refuse."

The conversational tone, the ease and affection she kept in this speech gave it a formidable quality. It was the quietest possible kind of comment on his wretched politician's troubles; it was suave and sweet defiance—but he knew it for what it was.

He looked away from her, looked towards the distant peaks of the Gredos.

"Then we remain in our fix," he said.

"Yet there is one clear way out. There always has been."

He looked at her almost hopefully.

"And what is that?"

"But, Philip, you know. You've always known."

"I wish I had. What is this clear way out?"

She came to the window and stood there with her back to him, looking towards her golden, fair Castile. But her thought was not on landscape. Ruy, her husband, came into her mind, and she appealed to him. Help me, she said. Give me courage now and help me to help him.

She turned and leant against the window-frame.

"Philip," she said, "Philip, my dear—as I love you, listen to me. Have the Escovedo charge heard in its proper court of justice."

He looked at her as if he had not taken in exactly what she said.

"Don't pretend to be outraged," she went on. "You know it's what must be done."

"It's what will never be done," he said harshly. And then he grew mysterious and royal. "This is, at its base, a grave affair of State. I must beg you not to plunge into it out of your depth."

"I'm not out of my depth. I know all about it," she said. "Antonio has asked you again and again to have the case heard, hasn't he?"

He looked at her without friendliness now. He loathed the free reference to Perez, and loathed answering her question. But he answered it.

"Yes, he has made that request."

"He's a good judge of lines of action."

"This instance doesn't prove him so."

She smiled. She was about to say that at least it proved he had the courage requisite to a normal man. But she decided that "for everyone's sake", as Philip would have her say, she had better let Perez be for a moment, and wheedle the king back to his fluttering mood of honesty. There was hope in that—for Perez.

"Philip, I beg you—have it heard. No, listen to me, have the brief as it stands presented. All that is untrue in it will be very easily disproved. My complicity, for instance, in the death of Juan de Escovedo. And all the minor charges brought in to prove motive—Antonio's venality, his desire to get control of my money, his fear that Escovedo could expose all that. It is every word untrue, and can be swept away in a sentence or two by any reasonable lawyer."

"Be silent, Ana, or I shall leave you."

"No—you won't do that. You know I am your friend, and you must listen to me, this once. Antonio will plead guilty to the central charge. You know he's ready to, and only waits for your permission. He will of course say why he had Juan killed. After that the rest is easy—the case will become a long argument between judges and theologians about the divine right. And very likely they may even condemn Antonio to death. But you will naturally intervene with your royal prerogative—and after a lot of fuss and pamphleteering, the air will be clear. And, as Ruy would, we'll all have learnt something, and will begin again. He never would tell me what he really meant by his 'begin again'."

She had rattled on, to help him, to give him time to see the common sense of her argument, and in general to throw out ropes and bridges. For she was startled by the staring helplessness in his tired, pale eyes, and wanted him to pull himself together. She did not like to see this abject, silly panic in his face.

Yet it did not leave it.

"What *is* it, Philip?" she said, changing tone. "Why can't you face this simple action? What are you afraid of in it?"

He rose from his chair and strode away from her across the room.

"Be silent, Ana. You are allowed great liberties. But even you must not ask me if I am afraid."

"I am compelled to," she said coolly. "And yet I cannot think you are. For say—and I suppose it's preposterous, but I don't really know the terms of your sovereignty—but say, for the fun of the thing, that a Madrid court of justice could find you, the king, guilty of murder, and say you were condemned to death——" he shook his head, almost amused at her—"I simply don't believe you'd be afraid of that. What's death? It comes once, and it comes to everyone. It's an end, a bad moment, and nothing to be what one calls afraid of. You aren't afraid of death."

"I am. I'm terrified of death, Ana. But not of dying, the physical process. Not of being condemned to it. That isn't why I refuse to have the Escovedo case examined in a public court."

"I knew it wasn't. You're afraid of moral judgments."

He wheeled about to search her face. This was an accurate observation. It took him sharply by surprise.

"I know that," she went on, "but I find it odd, in this situation. After all, you can support—I don't know how well —but still you manage to support in your own soul, and reflected in the souls of a few friends, the moral burden of your right or wrong in disposing of the life of Escovedo. Why then can't you face the breathing and blowing of the larger world on that dilemma? It might do good; it might define your powers. Certainly in any case Spain has the right to know, if she asks, why her public men are liable to disappear sometimes. And you love Spain and serve her night and day; and if you do make mistakes in that service, Spain will forgive you if you appeal to her."

"I will *not* appeal. I do not make mistakes."

"Nonsense," said Ana. "Don't be foreign, don't be German. Go to our common courts and let us hear why Escovedo died."

"I am not German," he said coldly.

"I suppose not. But what are you? Where did you get your fair head? Oh, don't try to look dignified again. You've done it far too often this evening. You know your fairness is enchanting. It must be sad for you to see it fading now."

"You are preposterous," he said, defending himself half-foolishly from the pleasure he took in all this casual impudence she flung at him.

"Half Portuguese," she said, "half Flemish, half Holy Roman——"

"Well, I can't be made up of three halves," he said angrily, "and anyway, Juana La Loca was my grandmother."

"Ah! I'd forgotten. Of course. That's a saving grace. That must be why I like you so much, Philip."

She smiled at him and stretched out a hand, and he came to her slowly, and took it.

"Listen," she said, "listen to me, a Castilian. Let your people have this story—and then, let them argue. They'll argue for ever, and they'll never decide on your conduct, but they'll understand readily—here in Castile—that your point of view is very, very important. Because every man's point of view is—in Castile. Govern us *our* way, Philip—and you have resolved your fix."

He drew back from her.

"It seems to me that *you* are very cynical."

"That's subtle. Does it mean something?"

" 'Govern us our way', you say. But I have *studied* to govern *my* way. And government is intricate and grave. It cannot be submitted to the vulgar flash-opinions of Madrid. I govern with my eyes on the real world, Ana, where they must be—Spain has a world-mission. Her king cannot submit his failures, his mistakes, to the judgment of the gypsies and thieves of the Plaza de Cebada. You seem to see Spain provincially, as something small and simple that you ridiculous Castilians have in charge. But I *know* what Spain is. And before the world and Heaven I represent that Spain I know. If, in my frailty, I have made an error for the sake of Spain, I am content to ask Heaven to judge me—but *not* the riff-raff of Madrid. Wrongly or rightly, I do not rule this nation in the light of their anarchical vulgarity, but before posterity, and Europe's destiny. And so I cannot, cannot be subject to Castile's small moral judgments. You called them moral judgments. I would not so honour them."

He was now in such a fine heat of imperial and esoteric righteousness that Ana decided that all was lost, that she had somehow thrown away a chance and done more harm than good. So she answered him straight out of her thought, without troubling at all to choose her words or deflect his anger.

"Nevertheless," she said, "you are finally subject to 'Castile's small moral judgments'. And you fear them. It is because you fear them that you have built up with so much caution this system of secret government, which now may break open in disgrace any moment, if you persist in hiding your actions from your people. No, let me finish, Philip. I love you too much not to have the privilege of saying to you sometimes what I think. This long speech you've just made— about posterity and Europe's destiny, and our local anarchical vulgarity—it seems to me to contain the truth of your error in government."

Error in government. Philip was so much astounded to find himself standing still and *listening* while a woman spoke such words to him, that when she paused for his answer he could not find one. The moment was isolated in experience, and found him unready. So Ana, surprised by his silence, went on.

"If Ruy had been listening," she said.

"Ruy?" the king asked almost eagerly, forgetting his plight of indignity because of his constant, pathetic wish as he grew older to know what Ruy might think of this or that.

"Oh, I may sentimentalise about Ruy's days—Spain wasn't perfectly directed then either. Still, I think Ruy would have been shocked by what you said just now. He'd have thought that you've got into bad habits, Philip. But, in my view anyhow, you give everything away when you jibe at the gypsies and thieves of the Cebada, and deny their right to their moral judgments. That is the end of all moral right in you, if you mean it. It's the end of princeliness, and of understanding of your place in Spain."

"I didn't know you were a thinker, Ana."

"If I am, then there are others. Many of your best friends 'think' as I do. Oh Philip, come back from inside that curious web you're weaving at El Escorial! Come back into the streets where we all are! Come back to govern us so that we can see what you're doing! Take this chance, make an instance of it. Make this gesture of having a fair trial and facing the consequences! And begin again in everything from this one awkward point. Summon the Cortés, summon the Council of Castile. Let us feel the *movement* of government in Spain again; let us throw in our responsibility with yours, and lend you those moral judgments that you fear! Oh Philip, see this! Do it! I've never seen it so simply myself before, though I've often felt it, often thought of it. But now it's clear. It can all arise from this one small entanglement. Have the trial. Make this honest gesture, which will take everyone by surprise—and see what happens! Will you do it, Philip?"

As Ana spoke, the simplicity of the solution she offered the king became enchanting to her, good in itself, and offering, by chance, an entirely new hope to Spain, a cleared horizon. She felt very happy, and almost envied Philip the opportunity he had to seize. But she reminded herself that she would have her share in it. The Escovedo trial would not be pleasant for her either; she was not urging on others an ordeal which would leave her scatheless. And she would be glad of her punishment—and think it less than she deserved, on the whole, perhaps—if it brought about between Spain and the king that renewal of co-operation, that revival of mutual trust which was so desperately to be desired.

She had surprised him beyond anger, beyond the inept refuge of imperial commands to be silent. She had surprised a whole region of his anxieties as king. Her assertion that he feared the moral judgments of his people; her appeal for what she called movement in government and letting his subjects add their responsibility to his; her casual inference that others besides her among his friends observed his methods with anxiety, observed and discussed them—all this was apt, audacious and paralysing. And at its centre was her simple, obvious answer to the festering Escovedo problem.

The whole thing lay before him now in the silent room, monumental and awkward.

Ana waited, contemplating what she had said. When Philip entered the room she had not known that she was going to say to him all that now was said. Often in their more recent days of friendship, since her return to Madrid, she had pondered his secretive way of government with dislike, had even spoken to him lightly sometimes of it, and had thought that some day she would argue it frankly with him, however angry he became. And since the Escovedo brief had come into existence in the autumn she had unswervingly advocated that it be heard in the plain way of justice. Philip had known that such was her wish, because through the Cardinal and de Pazos as well as through Perez she had sent him this advice. And always she had intended to repeat it to him, face to face, when he should give her the opportunity. But it was only whilst arguing with him now, and seeing the pitiful indecisiveness to which one single question could reduce the ruler of Spain, that she felt the connection between the Escovedo ordeal and the future of his relation to his people. She had suddenly seen that he could make it his gateway back to them.

Delight in this idea as it revealed itself had made her, she feared, incoherent, emotional and perhaps more forceful than was wise. But that could not be helped, and she knew that she meant from her heart and chiefly, in that heart, for Spain and Philip, what she had said.

But she had shot her bolt now, and could only wait.

Philip moved, with his slow, stiff gait, to his chair by the window. When he was seated and Ana could see his face again she could not read it. It was closed and weary, sealed off from expression like a death-mask. She did not wonder that his ministers so often cursed and fretted under his yoke. He could indeed be enigmatic and exhausting.

But when he lifted his eyes to her, as she stood, tall and grave, in the centre of the room, their blueness held a curious deep light.

"There's statesmanship in what you said," he said slowly.

Is it possible that I'm going to win? Ana thought. But she tried to betray no ripple of this thought.

"You would have made a good queen for Spain, maybe," Philip said.

To please him and thereby, she hoped, to help him into replying naturally to her appeal, she took this up, although it was a deviation, and therefore dangerous from one who so perpetually made use of deviousness.

"I thought that once, Philip—a long time ago."

He looked about the room, yielding himself a little, as often before, to its peace, its good effect on him. It occurred to him that if he could in fact stay here, stay here a long time protected by her presence and her restful courage, that so he might untie the Escovedo knot, and others too, by her direction; might begin again, as she suggested, to rule the people in the streets, as one of them who walked the streets in their company. If a man could have peace sometimes, and be sure he was loved. In this room he had sometimes almost begged her that, ageing and faded and belated as he was, she would take him, and in mercy give him some of that peace that flowed from wherever she lived. He had almost begged her—he, the King of Spain, who would not have her when he could.

But other thoughts pressed on him too, thoughts of a kind which all through this winter had so much sickened his *amour-propre* that he had had to train himself into a kind of false refusal, half-denial of them. Thoughts of the love and licence taken here by another man, a commoner; thoughts of the fool he had made of himself in coming here as to a refuge that was his own; thoughts of a day of Carnival, eighteen months ago, when he had sat here in blind man's innocence between the two, thinking himself almost her lover then, almost her tempter, giving them reason to laugh at him together afterwards, in their cunningly stolen delight. Two friends of his, and one his all-but mistress, and both of them knowing him their king, their ruler. In this room, this room he had used to dream about. The thoughts which all the winter he could not take, and had to take, and again had to deny, swept over him now in one strong, bitter tide.

He pressed his hands against his face, and groaned aloud.

"Philip! Philip!" Ana cried in innocent alarm, thinking him ill, and striding to his side.

"It isn't to be borne!" he said. "Go away! It isn't to be borne!"

"What isn't to be borne?"

He stopped groaning, and dropped his hands from his face.

"Ana," he said, "you have made me suffer. You have made me suffer as no man should suffer."

Ana could hardly repress a smile. And it even occurred to her to say that it seemed as if his own self-pity made him suffer as no man should suffer. Instead she went simply to the point.

"You mean—it has disappointed you to learn that—I have a lover?"

He looked at her as if he thought her a little mad.

"You choose words cunningly," he said. "Disappointed? I have not known how to speak to you! I have been shocked; I have been grieved."

"I understand that, Philip. It's not edifying. It sometimes shocks and grieves me too."

"It has undermined everything," he said. "It has poisoned all our years of—of love."

She let the word "love" go by, half-amused and half-exasperated by his use of it.

"It is *true?*" he said suddenly, on a sharp, hard note.

"Yes," she said, "it's true."

"It's still true?"

"Yes," she said, somewhat surprised.

"But, you *could* give him up?" he went on harshly.

"I don't know exactly what you mean, Philip. Or really by what right you ask me these things. Still——" she shrugged, "naturally, I *could* give him up. And naturally in any case, one of us will tire, or die, before the other."

She withdrew to the window, offended by the peevish catechising.

"I came here this afternoon to give you these," he said.

She turned back. He was holding in both hands his little sealed packet, and eyeing it as if it could wound or poison him.

"And what *are* these, Philip?"

"They are some letters of yours—to Antonio Perez."

She stood and looked at him in cold amazement.

"Where did you get them?"

"Mateo Vasquez conceived it his duty to secure them for me, so that I should have to believe what I was unable to believe."

Ana leant back against the window-pane, and pressed her right hand against her injured eye. She looked so strangely frail and white that for a moment Philip thought she might be going to faint.

"Oh, no, not that!" she said softly. "You haven't done that, Philip! Mateo Vasquez—yes—of course! But you! Oh Philip!"

She could not look at him. She stayed as she was, leaning against the window-pane.

"I have the right——" Philip began.

"You haven't a vestige of right," she said wearily, "to steal and read another person's letters."

"As head of the State——"

"Oh, don't! Be quiet!" Suddenly she was standing straight, and her voice was vibrant. "Who talks of 'rights' and 'heads of States'? It's *feeling* you offend against! The feeling I have always clung to between you and me, the certainty of something true that I could always reach in you— the kind of *goodwill* there's always been between us!" She paused, and became weary again. "But now? Oh, clumsy, clumsy ass!"

"Yes, I'm clumsy," Philip said, and his voice shook a little. "But let me speak, will you? I did not steal any letters, or ask to have them stolen, or think of such a thing. Mateo Vasquez's secret zeal drove him to the measure, unprompted. When he gave me the letters and told me what they were, I instructed him to leave them with me. He has heard and seen no more of them."

Ana was sickened, and could hardly bear to listen to this explanation. Yet she did listen because the slight shake in Philip's voice pleaded with her against her disgust, and so did his fingers, tapping on the sealed packet.

"I was shocked at his bringing them—but of course he couldn't know what he was doing, and in particular to me," Philip went on. "I was shocked at having letters from you— to another man, in my hands. I locked them away and decided not to read them. But I knew I wanted to read them. Indeed I think in a part of me I was determined to. I took them out often and held them in my hands, and tried to read them. But—Ana—I couldn't. I don't quite know why. I think I was just afraid of the pain, of the awful pain they'd be to me."

He looked up at her at last; his eyes were swimming with tears, and tears ran along his cheeks.

"So take them, will you?" he said, and held the packet towards her.

Ana came and dropped on her knees, as if receiving him ceremonially, when she took the small parcel.

She kissed his hand.

"Thank you," she said, "and forgive me."

He laid his hand on her head.

"That's a lot to ask," he said.

She rose. She was too tired to take up his implication; also too sorry for him in his weariness. Enough had been said for now. The ice of the winter was broken, and she would see him again. She felt satisfied and hopeful.

Philip brushed the tears from his cheeks.

"I am privileged," Ana said gently. "To have seen the king in tears."

"Your privilege is even greater," he answered. "Because I shed few, and many of them are for you."

"Ah, Philip!"

"But now I believe I should be in the Ambassadors' Room at the Alcázar. I don't think anyone knows that I am here."

"Well, they will soon, because I shall boast about it. And since you've come back you'll come again?"

He looked about the room.

"I don't know. I have loved it very much, coming here— in the past."

"We don't change here, Philip."

He rose, and she rang a silver bell.

Servants came at once and set the doors open for the king.

Ana dropped on her knees again and kissed hands ceremonially.

"Good-bye, Princess," Philip said, and then he turned and left the room.

THE SIXTH CHAPTER (28TH JULY 1579)

Days passed, torrid and quiet.

Philip did not come again, but Ana learnt from Antonio that he had gone to Aranjuez for a week, and would return to Madrid before the end of the month.

Antonio was reassured somewhat, as Ana had hoped he would be, by her account of the king's visit to her. The news of it surprised him greatly, and set him to fresh reflection on Philip's possible processes.

"But I gather that, on his side, the interview was at once emotional and non-committal?"

"It was emotional on both sides—and I was not in the least non-committal!"

"Oh girl, I wish I'd been a mouse under your chair! But it's Philip's feelings that make him dangerous. In politics and in things in general I've observed again and again that while you can keep him more or less cold on a problem, he will reason exceptionally well and justly, and will be sane and long-sighted, and even honest and consistent, in handling it. But let feeling blow up, let him suspect that his own person, his prestige, his inner self is related to the matter—and then the intricacies begin. Then you really have to bear in mind that you don't know him at all, that you move through virgin forest!" He laughed. "And the trouble is that so does Philip! If he'd only find out—just for his own private guidance, what he's got in his forest, and what he wants to find there!" He paced about the room. "No, Ana—*your* being in this scandal has made an emotional storm of it for Philip—and when that happens to him I for one have no clue. Still, I do think it's a good sign that he was enterprising enough to come and talk to you."

"It's a good sign that he brought me my letters."

"H'm. Maybe. But that, and his not having read them, betray emotion, much emotion. However, we'll see. And he is at present being quite endearingly fatherly and conciliatory with me. Still says that I am safe in his hands, and he will settle all my grievances for me according to God's will."

Ana smiled.

"You don't trust him when he drags in God's will, do you?"

"Well, do you?"

"No. I don't like it much."

"And I now know for certain that old Cardinal Granvelle has landed at Cartagena. He is bound to be summoned to the Alcázar during this month."

"I see nothing for you to fear in the return of that old man. After all, if Philip is going to conduct the Portuguese annexa ion himself, he probably just wants a respectable old regent to leave in Madrid."

"Yes, that's very possible. Meantime he works me to death, and flatly refuses to arrange for my withdrawal. But I'm getting my family and possessions into Aragon next month. I can argue quite easily from there—and more safely."

Ana talked of all this with no one else. Madrid was still empty of her real friends, and she began to desire Pastrana.

"I think," she said to Bernardina, "that when the king comes back from Aranjuez I'll ask if I may see him again—I want to see him—and when I've done so we'll go to Pastrana. I'd like to get there before the first of August."

So Bernardina set going their preparations for return to the country.

"There's a great deal of talk about His Majesty renewing his visits to you," she told Ana.

"Indeed? And what do they say?"

"Oh, this and that. Plenty they shouldn't, you can be

sure—but they don't try much of that on me, naturally. Some
say it's a good thing. Some say it's a scandal—with all the
other talk that's been going, you know."

Ana laughed.

"'Tell them from me, Bernardina, that it's always a good
thing for friends to be friends."

Bernardina looked at her quizzically.

"They'd agree with you," she said, "and so do I. Only it's
well to know where you are with that word 'friends'."

Madrid wearied Ana now. She sewed, wrote letters to the
children, attended to business affairs; she read; she gossiped
with Bernardina. And in the dusk when it was cool, missing
the fields of Pastrana and missing her horse-rides, she forced
the lazy *dueña* to walk with her about the streets—sometimes
towards the Retiro Wood, sometimes to San Isidor, or by the
path of the little Manzanares.

She went to Mass on Sundays and feast-days at Santa Maria
Almudena or in her own chapel; she attended Vespers too
sometimes, and she read her prayer-book dutifully. But she
did not go to Confession, and so could not receive Holy
Communion. And this half-and-half state of soul, this living
in sin while refusing to be outcast as a sinner, dragged at her
conscience.

So she thought with particular longing of Pastrana. Away
from Antonio there, safe from her inability to haggle with
him in his time of trouble, away from the attractive tenacity of
his passion and the temptation he still was to her, un-
distracted by each separate surrender, she could much better
face the whole field of her mortal sin, and try to arrive at that
decision of repentance and abstention which was as honestly
necessary to one part of her spirit as it was daily refuted by the
rest.

She did not forget her last encounter with Juan de
Escovedo. Antonio thought with contentment that it was
emotionally forgotten, and remembered only in an occasional

surface-thought of disquiet against a bad moment of mis-
chance. And they never spoke of it. She slept now in a
different bedroom in her house in Madrid. And he suspected
that when she had made that change, her intention had been
that he would never visit her there. But he made no comment,
asked no question. And she was grateful to him for that, and
despised herself for having been so melodramatic as to change
her room and yet so weak as not to complete the curve of her
melodrama. Yet often she lay awake in the new bed to which
Juan de Escovedo had driven her, and confronted him with
free and honest thought. I understood what you said, she
said to him. I had agreed with you and forgiven you before
you began. Because I have your touch of madness, or
exaggeration. I agree with madness and exaggeration. I
could have been a fanatic, but they married me young to a
sceptic. And I've never escaped from the education he gave
me. Yet I know, with my first intimations, that you are right.
For me you are right. That was really your offence against me
—your being right. Only I wouldn't have killed you for it,
believe me. But the killing is between you and him—and you
were going to die anyway, because the king wished you to die.
Don't haunt me, you don't have to. I remember—and in fact
I don't really think I needed your warning. I understood it
too well—I could have taken the words out of your mouth.
All I object to is your simplification. Because it isn't just the
thing you called it. It's that—and it's more, and less. Still, I
saw your point. Believe me, believe me, you needn't have
died for that.

But Antonio continued to be her lover. And she continued
to find pleasure in this; yet continued now to desire Pastrana
and its solitude; and to pray, and to wish she could pray from
a repentant heart. When he goes to Aragon, she told herself
uneasily, when he goes to Aragon it will all end. Yet he must
not go to Aragon, for going there was the end of his life and
career, and would be a bitter injustice to him from the king he

had served only too meticulously. Wait, wait, she said half-ashamedly to her uneasy soul. We must save him first, or at least be true to him when others are failing. Later we will argue about my salvation.

On an evening very near the end of July she walked far and, as Bernardina thought, foolishly through the south end of the town. It was a night of great beauty, with even a little movement of breeze from the west. Ana strolled through the crowds with pleasure. The Plaza de Moros and de Cebada were rowdy at night, and Bernardina grumbled against the danger she said they were in, and against the madness of being seen, the Princess of Eboli, in this quarter after sunset. Ana felt no danger among her own people, and laughed at the fussy Andalusian. She could not say that they would go unrecognised, as she supposed that she was the only woman in Madrid who wore a black eye-patch, but Bernardina must not make this point. So they went as Ana willed, skirting even the Rag Market, and going down to the Toledo road, where gypsies camped and sang all night.

Ana listened and looked about her. Madrid might be new and an unnecessary kind of accident, but it was growing out of the very heart of Spain, so it would be possible to give it some affection. How lively and real we are, she thought, outside of our solemn royal monasteries and stuffy ducal palaces. Oh, Philip, take my advice! Come back and rule us by the ordinary terms of life.

The singing of the gypsies pleased her.

"Anichu would like to hear that boy," she said.

"My goodness, don't be silly," said Bernardina. "Don't you know the *flamencos* are at it all night in the square in Pastrana at this time of year?"

"That's true. I remember. I must answer Anichu's letter to-night."

"Well, come on home then, in God's name, and do that," said Bernardina, turning implacably northward.

Ana followed her, laughing.

"I don't know why you pretend to like town life, Berni," she said. "Whenever I treat you to it—real town life, like this —you're in a perfect twitter until you're back indoors with everything bolted up."

"I like town life in respectable streets and when I can see what I'm stepping on," said Bernardina..

"Well, never mind, you'll soon be as safe as safe in Pastrana. The king is back from Aranjuez, came back yesterday. I'll write to-morrow and ask if I may see him, and say that I want to go to Pastrana on the first. Where are we now?"

"To-day is the twenty-eighth," said Bernardina.

"That leaves three days. I think I'll tell Anichu she can expect us on the first. Must we really go in so soon, Bernardina?"

But Bernardina, who dragged and dawdled on their outward walks, always led the way home and took the shortest cuts. She was almost trotting now along the Calle de Segovia. As they passed the corner of the Plaza del Cordón Ana looked up at Antonio's great palace. How he would hate to lose it, she thought—and after all, how much it means that he wrung it and all it stands for out of his own sheer brains and zest. The building looked dark and as if locked up, which was absurd, she thought idly. She was not seeing Antonio to-night. He had arranged to leave the Alcázar early and devote a whole evening to the ordering and packing of his own private papers. He was still determined to withdraw to Aragon at once when Granvelle came to Madrid.

She smiled towards his house, and thought of him affectionately—busy within it now, concentrated, by no means thinking of her. He would be amused to-morrow to hear that she had been prowling by his gate not long before midnight.

"Come on," said Bernardina. "This, if I may say so, is no place for you to loiter."

"Well, you chose the route, not I."

When she was back in the Long Room, she found a letter there from him.

"I wish I could have found even three minutes in which to see you to-day. To-morrow night is very far away. I feel a kind of pressure in the air, an anxiety. I suppose it is this decision I am taking about Aragon that makes me hyper-emotional. Silly. Because I really believe that the king regards me as essential to him now, and by doing this I shall force his hand. And anyhow secure safety for Juana and the children. Still, I do feel overwrought. I think, in a way, the king's visit to you has frightened me. I can't explain that—and it probably means nothing. Since his return from Aranjuez, where he tells me the roses are like a miracle of Our Lady, and his new fig-trees bending with promise, he is even more kind than he was ten days ago. We have said nothing in these two days—I don't like to nag!—about my imminent withdrawal from his service. But his whole manner is, I know, calculated to woo me back to patience. To-day he made some general joke about trusting him. 'You must, you see,' he said. 'Whom else can you trust?' Later, when I was leaving his room just now, he did something quite extra-ordinary. He spoke of you! Oh, not with reference to my quarrel with him, and not at all indiscreetly! But, he actually pronounced your name! He said he assumed that the Princess of Eboli was still in Madrid, and did I know when she thought of moving to Pastrana? I replied that his assumption was correct, and that I believed the Princess would leave for the country on 1st August. That was all. But it means a lot—his naming you to me. I wonder, in fact, *what* it means? In the time I've taken to write all this I could have been across the street to take one look at you, and back again. And that would have been a lifetime better than what I've done. Well, good evening, Princess—and take care of yourself until our next, faraway meeting.

"A."

Ana folded the letter and laid it aside to read again. She too was feeling some pressure in her heart to-night. So she was grateful for the letter and for the freshness of its feeling. Always, she thought, her hand on the folded sheet, always he can reach me with this *life* he's got, this power to make you feel what he is feeling without ever a protestation——

"Let's have supper here, Bernardina, you and I. Don't have servants and fuss. You just bring some things, will you?"

Bernardina smiled. She liked very much having supper alone with Ana and casually, and Ana constantly suggested it.

"While it's coming, I'll write a letter to Anichu," Ana said.

In spite of all the lighted candles, she would not have curtains drawn. Moths beat about the room, and Bernardina said that they'd have bats in their hair any minute. But Ana waved her off, and turned to her desk to find Anichu's last letter.

" . . . we spent yesterday afternoon with Sister José watching her do the bees. Fernán was a bit afraid of them, he said. Sister José is my favourite Franciscan. To-day at catechism Juliana—you know, Juliana from the shoe-making shop, not Dr. Juan's Juliana—couldn't even answer about the Unity and Trinity. And she's *seven*. Don Diego says that I can make my First Confession before Advent. Did the king say he would come to Pastrana, or what? It's a long time since we met him. Fernando and I remember when he came before. That was the first time I saw him, Fernando says. Ruy does Greek all the time. He talked Greek at supper last night. I didn't like it much. Is Bernardina very well? I hope she is. I hope you are very well. When will you be coming home? I dust your drawing-room sometimes with Paca. When I have time. Come home soon. I'll write to the king soon, I think—if you say I am to. Fernán says he will too. This is a long letter, but I must do my geography now.

                              "Your loving daughter,
                                        "ANICHU."

Ana sharpened a quill.

"Anichu, my pet,

"That's a very fine, long letter, and this won't be half as good, because it isn't worth while writing much, since I'll be home nearly as soon as you get it. I'll be home in about three days, *chiquita*. Tell all the others. I don't want you to make your First Confession yet, if you'll forgive me for interfering. Wait until you are six at least. I'll talk to Don Diego and you about it when I see you. Write to the king if you want to, pet. He'll be delighted. Oh, here's Bernardina with supper—I'm sure she sends you a kiss. I'll finish this after supper, my little daughter . . ."

Bernardina laid her tray on a table by the upper window.

"Come now," she said, "I'm hungry. All this tramping about the slums!"

Ana went to the supper-table and they began to eat. Bernardina poured out wine.

"This is beautifully cold," said Ana, sipping it.

"Did you send my love to Anichu?"

"Yes. I haven't finished the letter yet. I've told her though—and I know it will break her heart—that I don't want her to make her First Confession yet."

"Of course not. That old Diego! What nonsense!"

"Anichu's First Confession!" said Ana gently. "Poor little sins. Dear good little child."

"You make a terrible pet of her, don't you?" said Bernardina.

"I don't see how one could fail to. She's pure gold, it seems to me."

"Yes, she's a nice little child."

One o'clock rang from Santa Maria Almudena. They ate a good supper, talking or not as they felt inclined.

"I'll be glad to get back to Pastrana," Ana said.

Suddenly there was a noise of heavy feet in the corridor, and of voices raised, as if in argument.

The two looked at each other in surmise.

"Some of the footmen must be drunk," Ana said.

The door at the further end of the room was opened with noisy force even as she spoke. She saw two of her servants being pushed aside on the landing, as three armed men thrust themselves into the room.

They paused on the threshold.

Ana looked past them to the anxious servants outside.

"It's all right, Estéban," she said. "Would you just please close the door?"

The door was closed.

Ana recognised the leader of the three soldiers. He was Don Rodrigo Manuel, Captain of the King's Guard. He was a friend of Mateo Vasquez, and during the spring had come to her house as one of the latter's absurd ambassadors, asking for her friendship. She assumed that this was another such *démarche*, only more idiotically initiated.

She rose from the supper-table, but signed to Bernardina to stay seated.

"Continue to eat, Bernardina. This need not disturb *you*."

Bernardina was looking very much disturbed, but she obeyed Ana's wish that she should stay where she was.

Don Rodrigo and his men saluted Ana politely.

"This is a surprising entrance, Don Rodrigo," she said. "Only a little more surprising and ill-timed than your last. You come on your old errand, I suppose? But why do you come armed and with such a clatter to my quiet house?"

Don Rodrigo bowed again.

"I beg Your Highness's pardon for the disturbance, but your servants, not unnaturally, questioned my right to intrude upon you unannounced. Yet it is my duty to do so."

"Your duty?

It was Bernardina who spoke. By the pompous, embarrassed and excessively military aspect of the three men, and from her knowledge of common gossip she had read far more quickly into the purpose of this visit than ever would the innocent and arrogant Ana. And in the word "duty" she saw—in a sudden light that seemed to wither her heart—its end.

Don Rodrigo looked towards her. She had come to stand beside Ana. He bowed, but with less ceremony this time.

"Yes, madam, my duty."

Ana laughed.

"This is a new, funny way!" she said. "How can my dislike of Don Mateo Vasquez influence your *duty*, Don Rodrigo?"

"Your Highness, I do not come from Don Mateo Vasquez. I come as Captain of the King's Guard. I come on His Majesty's commission, to secure your person, awaiting His Majesty's pleasure."

Ana looked at him as if at first she still found his presence amusing. But almost instantly her face became grave and non-committal. If there was surprise, if there was shock in her for what he said, Bernardina, who was watching her in a painful closeness of attention, could not see either. Simply it seemed to her that Ana's face passed from amusement in one flicker to neutrality. And, masked thus, that face turned from the Captain of the Guard to her.

"I did hear correctly, Bernardina?" Her voice was still amused, unlike her face. "Then the next thing, I suppose, is to ask for the King's Warrant?"

Don Rodrigo stepped forward and with another bow presented a rolled parchment.

Ana took it and looked at it. She did not even unroll it.

"The King's Warrant," she said softly.

Don Rodrigo took it back and unrolled it. He pointed to its opening lines where she and Bernardina both saw her name, and then to the last paragraph, and the king's signature.

"From Philip to me," Ana said.

Silence fell over the room.

"Well, Bernardina, you're a practical person," Ana said. "When this happens, what do you do?"

Bernardina lost control of herself.

She snatched the parchment and flung it across the room.

"We protest!" she cried. "We raise the town! We send at once for the *Alcalde!*"

Ana looked at her admiringly.

"A very good idea," she said. "How do we send for him?"

Don Rodrigo smiled, and one of his adjutants picked up the parchment.

"You do nothing of the sort, madam," he said to Bernardina. "You prepare a small bag of necessities for this lady, and with as little delay as possible she leaves this house in my charge."

"For where?" Ana asked, still half-dreamily.

"My instructions are to convey you to-night to the Torre de Pinto."

"Where is the Torre de Pinto?"

"It is some fourteen miles from Madrid, Your Highness— on the road to Aranjuez."

On the road to Aranjuez. But Philip had just come back from there. She knew the road to Aranjuez. In the days when Isabel was queen they had often driven it together. Isabel had loved Aranjuez, and so had Philip too—planting his English elms, his English roses. She remembered the waterfall at Aranjuez, and Isabel's baby daughter playing among the fountains.

"I ought to know it," she said. "I know that road. But why am I being taken there?" she asked in wonder.

"Why indeed?" Bernardina questioned much more forcefully. "What is this farce, this foolery?"

Don Rodrigo unrolled his parchment again and brought it to Ana. Holding it so that she and Bernardina could see it also, he read aloud a turgid piece of prose. Because Ana de Mendoza y de Cerda—and all her titles were given—was at present incapable of governing her own estates and was thereby in the course of doing great wrong to her children, because moreover she was in danger of becoming an inciter to public disorder and was a threat to the general peace, and finally for her own good and safety it was necessary to remove her to a confined place to await the king's pleasure, and such alteration in the conduct of her affairs as would ensure the best interests of her family and of herself.

The sentences were long and vague. No charge was made; the whole was windy, inefficient and without any base or hold in common law. Ana listened with amazement and felt sorry for the well-trained officer who had to read aloud such nonsense to justify summary action. But Philip's signature and seal were in their proper places. And the warrant had been issued from the Alcázar, and was dated 28th July, 1579.

To-day, Ana thought, looking at the word "Philip". To-day. The day on which he was able to pronounce my name to Antonio. She turned towards her desk where Antonio's letter was lying. Philip had made a joke about trusting him to-day. "You must, you see. Whom else can you trust?" And Antonio's house had looked dark and as if locked up when she passed it an hour ago. So he won't get to Aragon, she thought.

"Thank you," she said to the still reading Don Rodrigo. "That will do. I understand it. And I apologise for having compelled a man who knows the laws of Spain to read such stuff aloud in the name of those laws."

Bernardina snatched the document and spread it on a table to read it herself.

"There's no charge in this," she said. "You can't arrest people without a charge!"

"This isn't exactly an arrest," Don Rodrigo said awkwardly. "It is a measure of safety, directed chiefly towards the Princess's own eventual benefit."

Ana smiled.

"Have you made another arrest to-night, Don Rodrigo?"

He looked at her cautiously.

"No, Your Highness, I have not."

"No? But there are other officers of the Alcázar who could be sent on such a mission as this?"

"Your Highness, I regret that it is outside my duty to answer irrelevant questions."

Bernardina pushed the warrant away.

"There isn't a word of a charge in it," she said. "You can't arrest her on it. I'm going downstairs to Diego, and we'll send for the *Alcalde* and his men!"

She moved briskly towards the door, but one of the young soldiers stepped in front of her. Don Rodrigo almost laughed.

"Do you really think we conduct affairs as amateurishly as that, Madam?" he asked. "All your servants are under strong guard downstairs, and no one can at present leave this house under any pretext whatever. We are here on the king's business. I beg you to be serious."

"We'll try," Ana said. "But you make it difficult. Bernardina, come here—sit down a minute." She drew her down beside her on to a couch. "It looks to me as if, for the moment, I must submit to this extraordinary farce. After all, I can't have everyone in the house put to the sword over it. But I shall not *stay*, I assure you, in this—where am I going, Don Rodrigo?"

"To the Torre de Pinto, Your Highness."

"Ah, Torre de Pinto. Ridiculous place it sounds. Philip can't do this to people—and he'll find that out. So don't worry now, like a good Berni. Go and pack things for me, will you?"

Bernardina looked mulish still, but after a minute she got up.

"I suppose that's the only thing," she said. "Though it's enough to make you choke! My God, I'd like to have the choking of you three!" she said firmly.

The soldiers remained impassive.

"You wouldn't be any good at it, Berni," said Ana. "Go and pack now, will you?"

"I'll pack. But it'll take a little time," she said threateningly. "I'm packing for both of us."

"My instructions relate only to the Princess of Eboli," said Don Rodrigo.

"I won't tell you, in the Princess's presence, what to do with your instructions," said Bernardina. "I'm only telling you that I'm coming with her to this Torre de Chinche!"

"And I am telling you, Madam, that you cannot."

"Berni, don't! What's the good? For the moment we're in their hands. But it won't be for long. I promise. And meantime, you'll be needed here. Your being here will be a tremendous weight off my mind."

"But you can't go off with them like this—alone?"

"Suitable female attendance will be provided for the Princess at Pinto," said Don Rodrigo.

"Oh, lovely female attendance, to be sure!" said Bernardina. "But in the meantime what's to stop these ruffians torturing—or murdering—you?"

"You mustn't call them names, Berni. And, say they do murder me, it'll be easier if I know *you* are still alive—because of Fernán and Anichu, you know."

Bernardina looked at her wildly for a second.

"Ah, those two! Ah yes!" And then she flung herself on her knees before Ana and threw her arms about her and sobbed and cried. "But I *can't* let you go like this, into the dark, into the night! There must be something I could do, and it's my duty to do it! Oh my dear, my *chiquita*, don't go with them! Refuse their nonsensical piece of paper! You're a Mendoza, you're the greatest lady in Spain! You have all those dukes and people on your side! Tell these fools to go home, Ana! Tell them to keep their noses out of what they could never understand!"

She raved, but on a theme of courage and coherency. Ana listened with respect. "I wish I could do what you say," she said. "I think it's right and it appeals to me. But all those dukes and people are at this moment scattered over Spain and fast asleep in bed, I imagine. Even my son Rodrigo is in Santander to-night. And if they were all in Madrid and wide awake, how could we get to them, Berni? No, for the moment we must do as Don Rodrigo requires, my dear. So help me now, will you? Stop crying—there, my good Berni, there! You're calmer now."

Bernardina rose, sniffing and red-eyed, but in command of herself.

"If it wasn't for the children I'd never agree to this—but we must be careful for them, I suppose. I'll go and pack for you, *chiquita*," she said, and her voice shook again on the last word..

One of the soldiers opened the door for her.

"Escort the lady to the Princess's dressing-room," Don Rodrigo said to him. "Stay with her, and see that my orders are obeyed. We take only a minimum of personal requirements."

Bernardina glared.

"Be as quick as you can, Berni," Ana said. "I shall be lonely sitting here, waiting to go."

Bernardina hurried from the room, and Ana, watching her, guessed with pity that she was crying again.

She turned to her desk.

"I may sort some letters?" she asked the captain.

He looked uncertain.

"Well, I suppose so. I have no definite instruction."

"Thank you. Would you and your lieutenant care for a glass of wine? And do sit down, won't you?" She pointed to the tray of flagons and glasses.

The men looked awkwardly grateful.

Ana turned away from them, and sat down at her desk.

She would not be able to finish her letter to Anichu. She glanced at it, afraid of it now. She could never write in that letter that she had just been arrested as a common malefactor —by the king, Anichu's dear king that she was going to write to. She picked up the sheet she had been writing, to tear it up, but she laid it back again. The baby might be glad to have it, Bernardina might give it to her, after she had explained why it was not finished. And how was that to be explained?

Ana opened a heavy inlaid box, brass-bound and with a lock and key. There were a few old half-forgotten treasures in it. She began to add to these now, carelessly, dreamily. Anichu's letter, Ruy's seal ring, a miniature portrait of her mother. Antonio's letter of that day. She looked indifferently about the desk—I suppose I might take this; I wonder if I'd miss that. Oh, better put a few things in for company, I suppose. The Torre de Pinto. It really does seem that I'm going to prison. The Arevalos used to have a shooting place at Pinto, I think. Going to prison, Antón. Are you gone too?

She leant on her elbow, pressing her fingers along her eye-shade. She sat very still and listened to the sounds of the night. She reflected that if this that appeared to be happening was happening, if in fact she was being arrested by a tyrant on no charge at all, then anything might follow. I may not come back; I may not sit here again; death may be near me; near him. For him, it can't be possible; he couldn't die yet.

The sweet, over-ripe smell of the roses on her desk made her feel tired. She heard the cautious movements of her guards as they tried to be very quiet with their glasses and their clanking gear; she heard the contented, familiar noises of Madrid, clearest of them—as it always is in the small hours— the voice of a young man singing. She thought of the children at Pastrana, asleep. Asleep. Oh Anichu, oh little child!

I'd better take some quills and ink and things, I suppose.

Or will Bernardina think of them, or will they be provided? She smiled at the absurdity of being provided for, altogether at the comic impossibility of being in prison. Oh don't bother with this silly packing. Let's see what it's like when I get there. It's quite a new experience. Philip, Philip, what is it? What have I done? What are you doing?

She stared into the darkness of a blind eye and a closed one. Smelling the roses, hearing still the sounds of her own free life, she looked into incalculable, future darkness. She was not afraid, but only sad, exhaustingly sad. Names and shadows swam in the sadness. Philip, she said, Antón, Fernán, Anichu. She felt sad, and stupefied, and a fool. I suppose I must go with these soldiers, for now? I suppose it's the only thing to do.

I'd better put this prayer-book in the box. I wish I could pray. I will, later on; I'll try to then. I'll pray for the children. Love your enemy, she thought, as she put some more things in her box. Love your enemy, do good to him that hates you.

She laughed gently.

"Yes, Your Highness?" said Don Rodrigo.

She hardly heard him, did not answer. She was thinking with amusement that she had always loved this enemy, and this very night did not see how to hate him.

"Torre de Pinto? Will it take us long?"

"We have good horses, Princess. We should be there by day-break."

Santa Maria Almudena rang out two o'clock. Ana snuffed a guttering candle. Often that two o'clock chime had rung before he came to her, from the Alcázar across the street.

She stood up straight, and locked her brass-bound box.

"Let us be going," she said sharply. "Let us be gone, in God's name."

Bernardina came in, the soldier still escorting her. She came to Ana, carrying a long black cloak on her arm. She looked calm and weary now, as if resolute to cause her mistress as little more distress as possible in this extra-ordinary hour. Ana's heart was wrung by this look of desperate composure.

"They've taken your luggage down, *chiquita*. I tried to think of everything you might need. But I couldn't find a maid, or any of our people. The house is packed with soldiery " she said contemptuously.

"Thank you, Berni. Remember, I leave it all in your charge, until I come back. And you must tell the children, tell Anichu——"

"I'll tell them," Bernardina said.

"If Your Highness will now be so good as to say good-bye to this lady——" Don Rodrigo interposed.

"I'm coming downstairs with you," Bernardina said.

"No, Madam, that is not desirable. Will Your Highness be so good as to come now?"

"I'm coming down——"

"No, Berni—leave it. I'd, I'd rather leave you here."

Ana looked longingly once about the room as she took her cloak and threw it across her shoulders. Then she turned and took Bernardina in her arms.

"Until a little while," she said. "Tell them I love them, Berni. Tell Anichu I'll be back."

Then she turned to the soldiers.

"Will one of you carry this box for me?" she asked. "I am ready now."

Escorted by Don Rodrigo and followed by another soldier she left the Long Room. She did not look back at Bernardina, whose former escort stayed with her.

She was led in what seemed to her the wrong direction down the corridor, and towards a staircase she never used.

"This is not the way," she said.

"We are using this staircase and a side-entrance, Princess," the captain answered.

"But—I wish to see my butler, Diego, and others of the household. Where are they?"

"Under guard in the patio until we have left, Your Highness."

"Then let us go through the patio and say good-bye to them!"

"It is not desirable. We go this way, Your Highness."

Ana looked at him in astonishment. But then she thought —this is what it is, this is being in prison. How extraordinary! How long could one live like this? And she shrugged and went down the unfamiliar staircase. As she went it occurred to her that it must be the one by which Juan de Escovedo had made his mad entrance eighteen months ago.

"You seem amused, Princess?" Don Rodrigo said suspiciously.

"Yes. I was thinking of an odd occurrence."

They came to a doorway Ana hardly knew about. A soldier standing by opened it, and Ana saw the street without, and carriages and soldiers waiting for her. All was brilliantly lit by the high-riding moon. She paused on this threshold of her house that she had never crossed before, and looked with love about the little street. The church of Santa Maria Almudena lay at the other side, its porch a little to the south of where she stood. She had often prayed in that church, and its bells had hour by hour admonished her. She would have liked to pray there now.

The street seemed quiet.

"If Your Highness will be so good as to enter this carriage?"

Ana got into the carriage.

While they adjusted luggage and locked doors she looked out of the window, towards the porch of Maria Almudena. Someone moved in it sharply, drew back into it as if afraid he had been seen. But the moonlight was strong, and Ana knew the fair-grey head it fell upon. Philip was watching her go, from the porch of the church across the street. She saw his face as if he spoke to her in the Long Room.

She leant back into the darkness, so as not to see him again. Love your enemy, she felt herself saying, but she was crying as she said it; she shook with sobs.

The guarded carriages drove away southward.

PART THREE: *PASTRANA*

THE FIRST CHAPTER   (MARCH 1581)

I

WHEN Ana came home to Pastrana after twenty months in prisons she came in a litter, and they carried her across the court-yard and up the great staircase to her own apartments. They laid her on a couch in the gold-and-white drawing-room and she looked about her in weary, wondering delight.

"Well, if I die now, Berni, that'll be all right. It will be good to die here."

Bernardina, bending over her to adjust pillows and coverlets, took her thin hand and kissed it lightly.

"You're not going to die, *chiquita*. You're home, and you're getting well."

It was true that she was not going to die. In January she had reached the point of death in her prison at San Torcaz, and permission had then been obtained from the king for her return to Pastrana, but only now in March was she thought strong enough for the short journey. But she had all her life been unacquainted with ill-health, and even under the crude hardships of the Torre de Pinto had remained so well that she had no way of judging gradations of illness. When she was at brush with death she was mostly either in delirium or coma, and remembered nothing of the crisis; now, getting better, she found that to move a hand sometimes exhausted her, or to look a minute at ordinary daylight, or to try to follow a speaker through one short sentence. To her this seemed a condition of dying—she did not see what else it could be, for assuredly it was not life. However they told her that she would not die, but was making a good recovery.

And she thanked them, and lay and waited.

And now they had brought her home.

She could not at present remember very clearly why she had been away so long. Nearly two years, they said. She knew she had been in prison, in two prisons; she knew the king had quarrelled with her. But she was too tired to ask anyone to remind her of what had happened. Still, it was surprising to be back in Pastrana. She wondered why that had been allowed.

She tried again to look about the room. The great window on to the court-yard was fully open; the noises of the village day came up, and sunlight poured across the floor.

"The sun. My own window," she said.

"Is the light hurting you, *chiquita*? Shall we turn the couch away from it?"

"No, please, no!"

She lay still. She could smell violets very near her; she could smell applewood burning, and could hear the crackle of pine-cones among the apple-logs. That was Ruy, that dull Dutch portrait on the wall quite near her. You were much nicer-looking than that, she said. Much more yourself. Well, I've come home, Ruy.

"Berni?"

"Yes, chatterbox?"

"The children? Fernán and Anichu?"

"Of course—but not yet, my lamb. You must rest here first after the journey, and have your milk and a little sleep. Then you'll be able to let us move you into your bedroom— and then, when you're safe in bed, you'll see them for a tiny visit."

"No. That's a bad plan."

"So *you* may think, but it's the plan, my dearie, and you've got to face it."

"No, Berni. Not in my bedroom. I want them here—I don't want any milk."

Bernardina knelt down beside her and felt her pulse. Her hands were dry and hot.

"Listen, Ana," she said, "you're talking too much. You haven't talked as much as this in an hour, during the last two months—let alone ten minutes. The doctors knew that coming home would excite you a bit, and they begged me to protect you against that. Are you listening?——"

Ana wasn't listening. She was remembering that when Anichu was allowed to come and stay with her for a little time at San Torcaz, the child told her how she used to sit in this room at Pastrana and pretend that she was there. I sit there by myself, she had said, after I've dusted it with Paca, and I have the window wide open and all the sun in, because that's how it always is when you're there. And so I pretend you're there. Ana could not find the words for this for Bernardina.

"There, there, *chiquita*—of course they can come to you here! Don't cry, don't cry. I promise you. Only first a little drink of something, lamb—and then we'll see."

Bernardina rose, and moved about the room gently adjusting things. "Josepha is bringing something warm for you to sip," she said.

"I brought it," said a small, gentle voice. "I told Josepha I'd better bring it."

Ana moved her head and smiled as if she dreamt.

Anichu stood by her couch, small and grave in her stiff silk dress. She placed a little tray carefully on a near-by table.

"Well, what next?" said Bernardina softly.

"Anichu!"

Ana stretched her arm and took the little child into its curve. Anichu swept herself in against her.

"Oh, you're home!"

"Yes, I'm home. How are you? How's Fernán?"

"We're well. But you're sick. You're very sick, are you?"

"No, not very. I'm nearly well."

Ana lay in peace, her arm about the child. Anichu leant back in the embrace and looked at her mother with attention.

"You *sound* nearly the same," she said. "But you feel very thin." She touched Ana's face and neck carefully. "I saw them carrying you in," she said. "We weren't supposed to—they said it might frighten us. But I hid in a place I know, and I saw."

"And were you frightened?"

"Yes. That's why I came now. I had to see if you were still the same. You are, I think—really."

"I'm quite the same."

Ana was beginning to feel real. Along Anichu's beloved steady voice the thread of life, of memory was spinning back.

"I'm sorry you were frightened."

"Oh, it's all right now."

"Yes. People get ill, and they get better."

"But why can't you walk?"

"I will, in a few days. We'll go for a walk, Anichu."

"Oh! Like before?"

"Like before."

"Only further ones now. Because I'm seven. I go much further now."

Bernardina intervened.

"Now truly, children, that's enough."

"Not enough," said Ana.

"You must rest, *chiquita*."

"Anichu brought my milk. I must drink it."

"Oh yes, I forgot," Anichu said, and got up and went to her tray.

Bernardina lifted Ana against pillows, and helped Anichu to feed her from a silver cup. Ana leant on her pillows and drank as they bade her, and looked at the sunlit window and at her little daughter. More and more memories came back and into place. The complicated story of all the imprisoned months before her illness began to emerge from its recent cover of darkness. So that she wondered very much, the facts re-assembling, why indeed she was here, at home. Her glance fell on the small Mantegna, caught now in full sunlight, noble, sculptural. I wonder how it is with him? I have lost touch. I wonder why I am at home. Is he at home?

"No more; no more, my baby. It was lovely."

She pressed back into her pillows. Life, her life, her world was rushing into her heart again—Pastrana, Anichu, Bernardina—and this room, its symbols, its memories, its admonitions. She was not dying, no indeed. She had returned to where she lived.

"No more."

"She's falling asleep," said Bernardina softly.

"I'll sit and look at her," whispered Anichu.

"No, *chiquita*, she must really rest."

"Stay with me, Anichu. I'm not asleep."

Anichu touched her hand.

"I'll be here—on this stool. I'll stay with you."

Ana's hand groped out and found the child's face. Bernardina moved on tiptoe between her mistress's rooms. Silence of noonday lay over Pastrana, and sunlight poured on Anichu as she sat on a footstool by Ana's couch.

II

Ana grew better rapidly at home. Within four or five days of her return she was able to walk almost unaided from her bedroom to the drawing-room; she ate solid food again, and was eager for more and more conversation, with her children and with Bernardina. There was much that she wanted to know. Many of her questions Bernardina could not answer; some of them she evaded.

Bernardina had borne a part in the troubles of the past twenty months. Two weeks after Ana's arrest and removal to the Torre de Pinto she also had been arrested, without charge, and was confined in the same cramped and filthy little prison. She was told by the officer who arrested her that she was held by the king to be an instigator of restlessness and disorder in the Princess of Eboli.

Grieved though Ana was that her *dueña* should also be victimised for her unnamed offence against the king, and furious and intractable as was Bernardina under such injustice, the two, so long used to being together, were surprised and delighted to have the alleviation of each other's company now, and they contrived often to draw comedy and even wild farce from some of the least bearable parts of their plight.

Contrasted though they were in their ways of confronting this plight, they made between them, by the force of their personalities and the impregnability of their friendship, a severe and constant problem for their guards.

The Torre de Pinto was a small square keep, built of stone. It consisted of three square rooms one above the other, and joined by a stone staircase which passed through all three. Its windows were slits, one set high in each wall, and without glass or shutter. The guards lived and slept in the top room and the bottom; Ana and Bernardina occupied the middle room. They had two truckle-beds, a table, two stools, a stone basin and pitcher and an iron bucket. Food was brought up from the lower guard-room. The decencies had to be looked after as might be; there were no screens or doors to cut the stairway off from the rooms. Neither prisoner was ever allowed to leave the middle room. The "female attendance" which the king provided was a gypsy girl who lived in a hut somewhere near, and slept most nights with the guards. "And thank God she does," said Bernardina. "It's the one useful thing she does for us." But in fact Bernardina, as Ana told her, was in no danger of rape. Don Rodrigo Manuel knew who his chief prisoner was, and went in some fear of her. Apparently it was the king's wish that she should suffer considerable discomfort, so as to break her spirit; but the

Captain of the Guard guessed what the Mendozas would do to any man who went beyond his duty in this fortress; and instructed his company accordingly. And even as to the discomforts he was not brutal, but in such a place it was impossible for two female prisoners to live other than wretchedly.

Neither woman had ever dreamt of living as in that room they had to live, nor had paused to think of the details of such discomfort and degradation. Bernardina, in her early fifties now and always comfort-loving, raged and railed therefore in protest, and made the guards' lives miserable with demands and quarrels and abuse; but she became very expert also at imposing as much order and decency as she could upon the icy-cold room and its wretched equipment, for it was by now second nature to her to protect Ana's material needs and she was domesticated and deft about a house. Her coming therefore was a vast relief to Ana who knew no more than any other great lady how to empty slops or wash an under-shirt, and whom the later arrival found sitting, patiently enough but surprisedly, in a state of outright neglect. The gypsy girl was kind and the soldiers too; but they hardly understood Ana's speech, and had no idea at all of what might or might not seem filth to her. And Don Rodrigo, the captain, did not live at Pinto, but only came on visits of inspection. Bernardina bridged this confusion, and forcibly, after she had rallied from her first shock. But her best efforts could only mean relatively less misery for two who had long taken for granted the highest attainable standard of living.

Ana cared far less than Bernardina about their physical privations. Although she was grateful to the other for her resolute attempt to keep them clean and supported her faithfully in her battles with the guard, she found all that irrelevant; useful as an amusement and for keeping Bernardina occupied and so less miserable than she might have been. But for her, Ana, if Philip had shut her up in the lovely

little summer-palace of Aranjuez the farce and the wound
would both have been what they were now.

So while Bernardina reacted against their plight by
wrangling with the guards and the gypsy girl and by talking
treason loudly and clearly, Ana treated her sojourn in the
dilapidated little keep as a fantastical episode, which almost
she had nothing to do with; almost as a bad play which she
had to sit through. And her manner with Don Rodrigo and
the guards, always polite, might be compared to that with
which we convey to actors that we do not hold them responsible for the insane conceptions of the author of their
play.

During her seven months in this prison she was allowed
only such invigilated correspondence with the world as made
it quite useless. She might write to her children and to
certain persons in charge of her estates—and to no one else.
And these letters must be handed to Don Rodrigo, unsealed,
and she need never be told how he disposed of them. The
same rule governed the letters she received. And she was
allowed no visitors. So she sat and waited, and marvelled at
her own helplessness, and wondered if all her friends and
relations in the world outside were being helpless too, and if
she might in fact be left to die in Pinto.

She came nowhere near dying. She endured the terrible
winter in that damp, draughty and heartless tower far better
than did Bernardina, whom indeed she had to nurse through
the worst of it, helped by the guards and the gypsy girl. But
except for January, when Bernardina's cough and ague made
her anxious, she cared little for their physical misery. Her
imagination was struck by Philip's mad gesture against her—
and she even took exhilaration from it sometimes, from the
effort of standing against it; so that she had bouts of high
spirits which astonished her as well as Bernardina and the
guards.

Sometimes as she sang and laughed with Bernardina, and

recalled old scandals and old jokes, and listened with amusement to the other's silly, naughty stories of her girlhood in Sevilla and her first love-adventures, sometimes as they laughed in their beds at night until the guards below or above growled at them to let them sleep in God's name—she thought of Philip's face as she had last seen it, pale and exaggerated in the moonlight, solemn, cold, hooded by the dark porch of Maria Almudena. And she wondered then how much this mad-seeming laughter, this almost schoolgirl peace, would baffle him, if he could hear it. And bitterly, sadly she wished he could.

But all she could do was wait, and help Bernardina to keep things tidy, and laugh with her like mad in the name of sanity, and write lovingly—though unable to explain where she was or why—to Fernán and Anichu; and read their baffled, loving, worried letters when they came.

After her illness in January Bernardina developed some enterprise about trying to get the gypsy girl to smuggle out letters. They tried it twice, and twice they were caught, and all three punished—the girl by a beating, they by being deprived of supper, and by having their writing materials taken away for a week. Ana found it exquisitely amusing—being punished. But it was clear that the girl was too stupid to be of any use as a smuggler—so the two waited for another idea.

Before it came they were separated.

Don Rodrigo, frightened by Bernardina's illness, advised the king against keeping the prisoners in Pinto to endure the rigours of March in mid-Castile. Also, he may have suggested that the *dueña* was more dangerous as a prison-companion for the Princess than at large in the world. One February morning therefore the two were ordered to pack; Bernardina was told that she was no longer to be held at the king's pleasure, but that a condition of her liberty was that she did not return to Pastrana, or to the Eboli Palace in Madrid. The Princess was informed that she was being moved to a small house at San Torcaz, by Alcala de Henares, not far from Pastrana.

The news surprised the two, and except in that it was to separate them—they were now close and devoted confederates—it seemed good. While they packed they formed a plan to get over Bernardina's problem of where to live. Ana had a house in Alcala which was seldom used—Rodrigo lived in it when attending university lectures—and it was arranged that Bernardina should go there, keep a close eye on San Torcaz, and work out a plan of communication.

So they left Pinto, and parted.

San Torcaz was a better place than Pinto. It was a house, and Ana was allowed a few servants, and to walk in a restricted small garden. Also, after some months, her children were permitted to visit her there.

Rodrigo came first. Ana was surprised by her pleasure in seeing him again, and touched to see that he too was moved. He gave her news. The nobility was actively concerned about the outrage the king had committed against her. Medina Sidonia and he himself never ceased to protest and petition His Majesty. Infantado, de la Ferrara and Alonzo de Leyva thought that a league should be formed, to challenge and defeat the king on this action. Meantime, the king's closest counsellor, the President of Council, and the Cardinal and others, continued to insist that Philip either release her or bring her to trial for whatever was her crime. Indeed, the king was having no peace, because her enemies as much as her friends were pressing now that she be tried for her offences. Meantime Philip was busy. The old King of Portugal was dead, and Alva was advancing the armies over the border to take possession; Philip intended to go to Lisbon too and establish a Court there. He, Rodrigo, was going at once with Alva, with his cavalry regiment. He was very much excited by this, and Ana was pleased to see that he was eager to be a good soldier.

"And where is Antonio?"

"Perez? Oh—he's been a kind of cat-and-mouse prisoner since—since you were taken. But much better treated, of course! He always gets on velvet everywhere. He was first shut up in the house of the Court *Alcalde*—quite luxuriously. Then he got ill, and his friends worked up an agitation, and he was allowed back to his own house. He's a house-prisoner there now, I believe—and he's always agitating for this and that. We're not bothering about *him*, Mother."

"I dare say not. But I am. He is in this trouble with the king because of me."

"Oh, it's not all that. He's been corrupt in office too. There's to be an inquiry into such corrupt practices now—just to catch him, I think—as there seems no other way. It's a good get-out for Philip."

"I see. And his offices?"

"Old Granvelle has his chief job—First Secretary of State. But Perez is supposed nominally still to hold some of his other offices—Secretary of the Council and so on. Anyhow no one else has been appointed, and he still gets the salaries, they say, and does some work even, in his palace-prison. It's fantastic—but trust Perez to keep on his feet. I think Philip's afraid of him somehow. I'm not surprised either. He's a dangerous cad."

Ana smiled.

"I know your view, Rodrigo. So does Antonio. But thank you for giving me all the news. I still may write no letters to my friends, you see. I still may see no visitors except you children."

"I know. It's ludicrous, and the wildest insult—to a Mendoza, my God! Really, I think the king's half-mad. But at least this place is decent. You owe it really to little old Medina Sidonia that you were moved. He's been most awfully good pushing away at the king. Between us we'll have you free soon, Mother. Don't worry too much."

"I'm not worrying. And I'm glad you're going off to the war. You look happy."

"Yes—I like my regiment, and I want to see action. But I shall get near the king from time to time during the campaign, and I'll not let him forget that I am your son. As a matter of fact he's going to have a solemn ceremony any day now before he leaves for Portugal——"

"What is that?"

"The consecration of the Infante Diego as Prince of Asturias. I shall have to do homage then with the other Dukes, and Alonso and I think that it might be a felicitous moment to remind him of the wrong he has done you—in diplomatic language, of course."

Ana nodded.

"Maybe, Rodrigo."

She felt lonely, humiliated, ashamed of Philip. She thought of all the high and solemn ceremonies of his past, in which she and Ruy had supported him, and by their presence and their friendship added, as he always told them, to his joy and courage.

Rodrigo left the next morning, riding off to the war. Ana settled down to face the summer months. There would be the alleviation—very meagrely doled out—of brief visits from her children. And—so far as she could see into the future—there would be nothing else. The dull comfort they gave her here, with a respectable aged *dueña* and with dull decent servants, would prey on her and exhaust her, she knew, far more than ever could the dramatic madness of life at Pinto, life with Bernardina and the gypsy girl and the protesting, weary guards. There were guards here, but she never saw them, and never uttered a complaint. The solitude and isolation were vast. All that comforted her in them was that she looked out eastward towards Pastrana and could almost breathe its air; that Bernardina, watchful and loyal, was under one of those roofs of Alcala that she could see from one point of the garden; and that Fernán and Anichu would come to see her soon.

As for Rodrigo's news—she was grateful for the gestures, such as they were, of some of the young nobles who were his friends; but she knew the corrupt laziness of the existent Spanish aristocracy and counted on no league of them, no organised protest. She saw much more hope in the pressure of active men of affairs on the king—and knew that Antonio de Pazos and the Cardinal would continue through all weathers to tell him the truth. And she surmised that Antonio Perez was in serious danger, and fighting hard and cunningly on a wide, treacherous field, for his life, and for the future of his children. She knew that some day, by one device or another, when he deemed it not a mortal risk for him or her, she would hear from him again, if he lived. Meantime, she prayed for him, and guessed, far more than Rodrigo could, from Rodrigo's news how constant and unpredictable was his danger now.

She grew depressed in San Torcaz. She lost her sense of the absurdity of the situation, lost detachment. The dilemma was growing stale and silly; Philip's cruelty and egotism became more apparent than his lunacy. And her guards were efficient, it seemed—for even Bernardina managed no signal.

When the children came, in midsummer, Ruy and Fernán and Anichu, she tried to be exactly herself for them. But they were worried and asked her clear, insistent questions.

"The king is angry with you, isn't he?" said Fernán. "That's why you can't come home?"

"Yes."

"I don't see why his being angry can keep you from coming home," said Anichu.

"Neither do I, pet. Neither does any sane person."

"We always thought the king was fond of you," said Fernán.

"I thought he loved you," said Anichu.

"Oh, Mother, this is awful!" said Ruy. "Your being a prisoner! Why, it's ridiculous! What is the real reason, Mother?"

"If I knew I'd tell you, Ruy. But truly, truly I don't. I've never been given a reason."

"You can't take prisoners without a reason," said Fernán.

"I'll write to the king," said Anichu. "I still think he's sane. If he wasn't he'd have to stop being king."

When the children went away again, back to the bleak care of governesses and tutors at Pastrana, summer faded. No news came, no letters.

Ana prayed and sewed and walked in the garden. She thought about her sins, and fretted about her vain, empty life, and tried not to advance with Heaven the cause of her own repentance merely because there was nothing else to do and temptation was far away and would not come again. She prayed, for her children, for Ruy's soul, for Juan de Escovedo's. She prayed for Antonio, for his safety and ultimate peace. She prayed for Philip. But she could not pray for herself, and thought this a cheap, bad time to turn to God on her own behalf.

She watched the flowers fade; she ate less and less; she grew lonely, no messages came, nothing happened. She heard, from her *dueña*, that the Portuguese campaign was triumphant, but that the king was gravely ill in Lisbon of the plague. She heard that he recovered, but that the queen, Anne of Austria, having nursed him, had returned to Spain and died.

Still there were no messages. She looked towards Pastrana across a cold sky and saw nothing. She looked towards Alcala and its roofs were blank. And then in December she became ill, and sank with contentment into death's embrace.

But now here was the spring of another year, here were the walls of Pastrana round her, here was the sun on the floor at her feet, and the *Colegiata* bell in her ears; here were Fernán

and Anichu bringing their lessons to write at her desk—and
here was Bernardina, unexplained and peaceful. She was at
home, and getting well with every minute, and there were a
hundred questions to ask, if Bernardina would but answer
them.

III

When she had been seven days at home some of her
questions were answered. Her good son-in-law, the Duke of
Medina Sidonia, arrived at Pastrana, prepared to explain
everything to her.

He came in fact from Lisbon as the king's emissary, to
explain the terms of her restoration to her own house. As, by
loyal pertinacity, he had effected this restoration, he was
concerned for the execution of its terms.

After he had changed his clothes and eaten well he came
and sat by Ana's couch. It was a bright, cold afternoon; the
window was shut and a great fire blazed in the hearth.
Alonzo settled near it gratefully. He hated the climate of
Castile and in March held it to be extremely dangerous; but
he was a dutiful man and had willingly risked it this time for
duty. However, Ana's house was comfortable, and this room
beautifully warm.

"Your gout doesn't seem to improve, Alonzo?"

He was fatter than Ana remembered him and he walked
lamely.

"On the contrary, it has recently been much worse."

"But why is that? You don't drink too much, do you?"

"Oh no, Mother—you know I don't."

This son-in-law had the domestic trick of calling Ana
"Mother" sometimes. She disliked it very much. She
understood that it was a habit formed simply from talking
of her with Madalena and Rodrigo, and also out of easy-
going affection—but it irritated her, this cosy, dull style
of address from a fat little grown-up man.

"Alonzo, you're thirty-two and I'm forty-one—and I'm *not* your mother. Please!"

"I'm sorry—I forgot. You ladies!" He smiled at her kindly. "It's very nice to see you again after so long, and to see you *here*. And you are getting better now, aren't you?"

"Yes, I'm getting better. Being at home is a good medicine. And I believe that I owe it to you?"

"Well, yes—I think so. I'm a great deal involved with the king at present, and I don't let him forget this—this stain on his record."

"Thank you, Alonzo."

Somehow he felt nervous of opening his mission to Ana. As he came here it had seemed easy and even wonderful and he was proud of himself. But now, face to face with her, he was not quite sure of how to proceed. He thought that perhaps he'd gossip a little first, and lead in to what he had to say.

"The Portuguese campaign has been a very great success," he said. "Alva has disposed of the Pretender's forces very easily. It's a pity the king's triumph had to be overshadowed for him by Her Majesty's death."

"Yes—poor Anne of Austria. She had a dull life and a dull death."

Alonzo looked somewhat shocked.

"She was a very good woman."

"I believe so—I didn't know her well."

"Rodrigo, by the way, has distinguished himself considerably in such action as he saw. He's enjoying himself in Lisbon at the moment—and sent you his love, of course. He's very keen now to get a transfer to the Netherlands to serve with Parma—things are lively there again, and promise to be more so——"

"I'm sorry to hear that. When I last heard informed conversation—which is nearly two years ago, Alonzo!— our face was set towards *peace* in the Netherlands."

"Oh well, Granvelle's policy is strong—and I must say from all I hear it seems the only one. His Ban on William of Orange has caused quite a sensation——"

"Ah! Then the work of years is set aside?"

"No, no—why should it be? But there's a time to be liberal and a time to be strong. And Granvelle after all does *know* the Netherlands."

"I dare say," she said wearily, "I'm out of touch."

"Am I tiring you?"

"No, go on. What other news is there?"

"Well, there's this rather troublesome business of Diego."

Diego, Ana's second son, not yet sixteen, had been married for two years to Louisa de Cardenas, ten years his senior. He was very unhappy, she flaunted and despised him publicly, and now was demanding an annulment of the marriage.

"I saw Diego in Madrid yesterday. He's staying with Infantado there and seeking legal advice. I also saw Louisa. She's a dreadful, shameless creature—and seems to find her matrimonial situation quite a joke. She was very rude to me, I may say."

Ana smiled. She detested Louisa de Cardenas, but she could sympathise with her need to be rude to Alonzo if he took to advising her about her love-affairs.

"Poor young Diego! It's a dreadful thing we did to him—and Philip and his uncles truly are more to blame than I, for once."

"It's a very impossible thing, a nullity suit in the family," said Alonzo primly.

Ana laughed.

"Impossible things keep happening in this family," she said. "I hope you told Diego to come home here as soon as he can, and leave the old nullity suit to Louisa and her clerics and lawyers. It's nothing to do with him. He must come back here, away from all those awful Cardenas relations. He can study at Alcala for a few terms, and forget the whole

nightmare, poor child. I'll write to him to-night and tell him
to come home."

Alonzo looked nervous.

"I wonder if that will be—er—approved?" he murmured.

"Approved by whom?"

"Well—by the king, you know."

"Why, what's Diego got to do with the king? Or is *he*
liable to arrest now, because he has failed to make Louisa a
happy woman?"

"Nonsense! But——" Alonzo fidgeted in his chair,
"rightly or wrongly, the king takes a somewhat anxious
interest in your children's future now. You see, all this
scandal——"

"He always took an 'anxious interest'. And 'all this
scandal' is of his making, and can be unmade whenever he
chooses. No, don't fuss. I'll look after Diego. That marriage
has always been on my conscience, and I'll try to make up to
the boy now for our stupidity. He'll be happy here and at
Alcala, away from all those cheap worldlings his wife trails
after her."

"Maybe. We'll see. We'll deal with Diego later."

"*We* won't deal with him at all, my dear Alonzo. There's
no dealing to be done. He'll simply agree to let Louisa have
her nullity suit, and then come home and be young again for a
while."

Alonzo got up and began to poke the fire and adjust the
logs. He looked at Ana sideways as he did so. She was lying
back on her pillows, looking weary and emaciated. She was
so thin that her long outline was only just traceable under the
silk coverlet.

This dull man was fond of her, and had not ceased to
agitate on her behalf since her arbitrary and absurd arrest in
July 1579. But he was a manager, a compromiser. He never
even tried to understand eccentricity, either the king's or
anyone else's, and he had no sympathy at all with any kind of

passion. When he met such things in the ordinary conduct of life he contrived as well as he could to work round or under them—he never met them straight. He did not know what Ana de Mendoza's life had ever really been about, nor did he wish to know. He did not know any more than anyone else why Philip had so suddenly turned against her, and expressed his anger in so unfortunate and indefensible a fashion. All he knew was the obdurate public fact that Ana, unaccused, untried and uncondemned, was the king's prisoner. And knowing the king, he believed that the only way to remove that fact was first to accept it without argument, and then to negotiate it gently away, by compromise, by shifting of ground, by realistic acceptance of the dark ways of eccentricity and pride.

But he knew enough to know that here on the couch lay no such negotiator.

He sighed and gave the fire another poke. His gouty foot was hurting him, growing hot and heavy.

Bernardina came in by the door which led from Ana's bedroom.

"Good afternoon, Your Grace," she said, and Alonzo acknowledged her greeting, but gloomily. "I am sorry to have to interrupt you, but Her Highness is still, as you can see, an invalid, and may not be left too long unattended."

She crossed to Ana's couch, lifted her under the shoulders and shook and straightened her cushions.

"I'm all right, Berni."

"Are you sure you're able for a long conversation?"

"Yes, truly. We haven't started yet. I want to hear all His Grace's news."

"Don't you think you ought to have a drink of something, chiquita?"

"No, thank you. I feel splendid, really."

"You don't look it," said Bernardina. "Try not to worry her too much," she said coldly to the Duke.

He ignored the instruction, but Ana laughed.

"If he does, I'll ring for you, Berni."

"Be sure to. But seriously, if you want anything, do ring. I shall be sewing next door in your bedroom."

"I promise. Move those jonquils more into the light, will you? Ah, that's better."

Bernardina smiled at her, bowed again to Medina Sidonia and went back to Ana's bedroom. Alonzo stared after her gloomily.

"*She* has absolutely no business here," he muttered.

"What did you say, Alonzo?" Ana asked dreamily.

He came back to his chair near the couch, and she looked at his troubled face with pity.

"You come with a message from the gaoler, don't you? Well then, deliver it."

"It's complicated."

"Trust Philip! Still, we can simplify it. Tell me this to begin with—Bernardina can't. Am I home just on sick leave, or am I free?"

"You're *home* for good, as far as I know."

"Ah! Ah, thank God."

She lay back very still, her hand pressed on her eye-shade, her left eye closed.

"Then that's all right, Alonzo. I can't say much more yet, because I might cry. But—I didn't like being in prison."

He waited, gathering his words.

"You're home, certainly. And you're free, if you choose to be free."

She turned slowly to him.

"But if I'm home, here in Pastrana——"

"Listen, Mother—ah, I beg your pardon! Listen to the king's message. Now don't interrupt with any witticisms, please. Just listen. You are to live in Pastrana, as its lady and mistress, as before—free as air, on certain conditions."

"I accept none, so save your breath."

"But don't you see, you *must*."

"*Must*? There are no conditions. Either I live as a free citizen, or I am brought to trial for whatever I am believed to have done that is criminal."

"I asked you not to interrupt me. Will you let me finish what I have to say?"

"I won't interrupt you."

"You are free if (*a*) you will desist from asking for the Escovedo case to be heard; (*b*) make a formal gesture of non-enmity towards Mateo Vasquez; and (*c*) undertake never again in life to see or communicate with Antonio Perez."

There was silence for a second.

Ana stretched out and patted Alonzo's knee.

"You got them said neatly," she said. "I could concede (*a*)," she went on thoughtfully. "It was always more of an opinion, a counsel of mine than a principle. If other people think it well to refuse to hear the case, I don't make an issue of it. (*b*) I refuse to consider. I shall not ever make that 'formal' gesture, and if Philip can find a criminal offence in that let him charge me before the justices and I will stand for trial. And since, you see, we break down on (*b*) there is no need to discuss (*c*)."

Alonzo gave a little groan.

"I beg you——"

"Don't. And don't be troubled. You are being so very good. But you see, I told you we'd simplify things—and we have, a bit. At least we've got this far, that I'm *not* free, after all—and this, this dear interlude was just a cruel mirage. When do I go back to San Torcaz?"

Alonzo was drying his eyes.

"Please, please! You're very difficult."

"You silly dear man! I hope Madalena is kind to you."

"Oh, keep to the point, dear lady! You don't go back to San Torcaz, ever! You stay here, bound or free. That at least we've wrung from him."

"I stay here, in this house, a *prisoner?*"

"Yes. A house-prisoner."

She looked about her, and then smiled at him.

"But who in Pastrana is going to keep *me* a prisoner? Who is going to stop me from going through my own open gate or across the village square? Who's going to prevent me from hearing Mass at the *Colegiata*, or say that Anichu and I are not to walk up to the Honey Farm or over to San Amadeo?" She laughed. "I don't think my Pastrana people will lock me up, Alonzo."

"That, alas, will be attended to—if you insist on it. Your servants will be changed. Persons will be placed here who will be guards as well as servants. The government of your household will be handed over to some stranger appointed by the king. You will never pass beyond the garden or the court-yard gate. Your letters and visitors will be subject to scrutiny, and all your affairs will be ordered for you by this appointed officer."

"I see."

"So think well, think well, I entreat you! If you do persist in flouting these silly, but simple conditions of freedom— honestly, I see little hope of your obtaining better."

"I expect you're right."

Alonzo got up and fidgeted lamely about the room.

"Is your foot hurting? Would you like some wine or something brought?"

"No, I'm all right. I have an idea—I've had it for some time, as a sort of last hope. But *please*, if you use it, don't say it was mine!"

She smiled reassurance at him.

"Why don't you fly, before the new imprisoning begins? You and the children—to France, or to some of your Italian estates, even? I think if you were out of Spain, Philip would forget and forgive everything. And there'd be time now. It will take me, it *can* take me a long time to get back to Lisbon with your answer. It will take time after that for the king to decide what to do about you and whom to send to govern you here. You could be safely out of reach long before his emissaries got back to you. I could help you—Rodrigo and I could arrange about your money and possessions and everything. And you'd be safe—safe and free, and with the children. Will you do that?"

"Forgive me again. But I won't. I can't run away from a guilt that doesn't exist. I have done no criminal wrong, and I won't be bullied out of my country by a nothing. Nor will I for such a nothing deprive the children of their natural home and friends. No, Alonzo, I'm sorry. But in this mad issue I have seen a principle, and I shall stay and hold it. Castile is crumbling under the curious, cautious tyranny of this king. I'm a Castilian. I've done nothing useful in all my life, and I've committed many sins. But by chance I can do this one small service for Castilian good sense before I die. It isn't even honour—it's only common sense. So I'll stay here—and you can tell the king that he can either also find some common sense and have me tried for my supposed offences, or he can turn Ruy Gomez's house into my prison. As he chooses. I'll be here when my new guards come. It'll be very curious—the oddest prison of the three."

"You're impossible. Think of the children!"

"I do think of them. It will be very bad indeed for them. Though they, I suppose, will be allowed to go past the gate?"

"I suppose so. They may be taken away. I really don't know."

"If they are, so be it. I would have had it otherwise, especially for those two little ones. But truly I can only serve them by my own light. And as things are, I think the best I can do is show them that I have regard for the free dignity of Castile."

"It's a point of view. But it's useless."

"Yes, I expect it's useless."

"You're tired now—very tired. I won't accept this as your final answer. I'm staying here until to-morrow——"

"No—I'm not very tired. And you've had my answer, Alonzo. It's my only one, and Philip knows it. He wastes your time and your good nature with these errands. Though of course I'm very glad to see you here."

Alonzo looked sadly about the beautiful room.

"If you persist in this, you won't be happy," he said.

She laughed at him.

"Did I say I expected to be happy?"

"Your servants will be changed, your habits will be checked——"

"Sing your dirge to Philip. I can sing my own, to my own heart."

"I know. I know." He came to his chair again and sat down wearily. "There's one other sma'l thing that I have to say. That woman, your *dueña*——"

"Bernardina?"

"Yes. Bernardina Cavero, isn't it? She has no business here at all. The king expressly told me that she is at liberty only on the understanding that she keeps away from Pastrana and from you."

"Ah! I wondered!" Ana smiled. "Let's have her in and question her, the criminal." She rang her bell.

"Oh no, let's leave it. Another time."

"No, no—we'll talk to her now."

Bernardina came in.

"Thank you, Berni. Come over here and get into the dock. You're in some trouble with the law."

Bernardina laughed.

"Well, I'm an old lag, after all——"

The Duke of Medina Sidonia cleared his throat and looked stern. Ana's flippancy in the bosom of her family was an aristocrat's privilege, but he felt obliged to uphold the crown against the lower classes, and wished that she might try to do likewise.

"Tell her, Alonzo——"

"Doña Bernardina, I know from His Majesty that you were given your liberty in February of last year on the condition that you did not return to Pastrana or to the service of Her Highness. That condition has not been altered. I have to ask you therefore why I find you here?"

"I'm here, Your Grace, because I thought it suitable that I should be here when Her Highness came home ill and out of sorts. She's used to me. I thought I'd be good for her."

The Duke of Medina Sidonia gasped a little.

"That explains nothing."

"Oh yes, it does," said Ana. "Go on, Berni."

"I went to live in Alcala, Your Grace, when I left the Torre de Pinto. I devoted all my time to trying to get into touch with Her Highness at San Torcaz. But she was very well guarded. Nothing worked. Then I found out she was ill. I walked down every day and asked to be allowed to see her. I might as well have been talking to The Cid's mule. I nearly went mad when they kept on telling me she was dying and still wouldn't let me in. And then I heard—from one of her doctors, a very decent poor fellow in Alcala, that they were sending her home. I gathered from him that it wasn't release, but a kind of panic, and that the idea was to get her well at home and then start arguing with her again. I gather I'm right about that?" Ana nodded. "So I abandoned the assault on San Torcaz, and two days before she came back here I drove over, and settled in. I wanted to get things ready for her, exactly as she likes them. Everyone here received me with delight—naturally. They like me here, Your Grace."

"Indeed they do," said Ana.

"But the day after I arrived the *Alcalde* came to see me. He told me—what I know—that I was breaking my parole or something. And I told him to go to blazes. And he laughed, the decent man, and we had a few drinks together. And here I am."

"It's quite a serious offence," said Alonzo.

"As serious as all Her Highness's offences, I dare say," said Bernardina.

"Well, Berni, you're a law-breaker again. But conveniently enough, and no trouble to the *Alcalde*, you're in the right place. Because after all I'm *not* free, Berni. My son-in-law has just been explaining to me that this house is to be made into a gaol."

"Ah! I thought it might be so."

Medina Sidonia groaned again.

"It needn't be so! It needn't, Ana! Not if you had a vestige of common sense."

"It's because I have common sense that it must be so."

Bernardina came over to her and lifted her up on her pillows.

"You're dead tired," she said. "It's disgraceful to exhaust you like this."

"What'll you do if they lock you up again, Berni?"

"Well, if they lock me up here—and that'd be the economical thing to do after all—it could be worse. After all, we had some fun in Pinto, *chiquita*, you and I! We make good gaolbirds together!"

"Yes, we know the ropes, Berni."

"Then I take it, Doña Bernardina, that you persist in breaking the condition of your freedom?"

Bernardina smiled at him.

"Oh yes, Your Grace. I'm staying here now until they carry me out screaming."

Ana was delighted.

"Oh Berni, this is like old times! It's like being back in Pinto!"

"Well, I've been more amused in Pinto than in many places. Haven't you, *chiquita*?"

She smiled and bowed coolly to the Duke.

"If that is all——?" she said politely.

"That is all," he snapped, and she withdrew.

"I can't manage this business at all," he said when she was gone. "Is it that you're women or is it that you're mad?"

"A bit of each, Alonzo."

Ana was indeed tired now. It was almost two years since she had had so long and difficult a conversation, and she was still under the shadow of grave illness. She hoped Alonzo would leave her. She lay still and said no more—but thought with affection and contentment of Bernardina. What a stylist she is, she thought, in her plain way. How simply and breezily she takes things as they come, and follows her own honesty. Why on earth should she lose her liberty again? But why on earth should I or any honest person? It is for the answer to those questions that I must wait in prison. So be it. It is something of my own that I can do. So be it. I'll sleep now a little while, before the children come to see me.

It was dusk in the room, and the fire glowed red and hollow. The flowers, violets and jonquils, gave up their perfume richly to the warmth. Yes, she would sleep now; she was sleepy.

But Alonzo did not go away.

He sat and stared into the fire.

"Some people think," he said, "I don't know exactly why, but they do think that the only condition that matters to Philip is the third—the one you won't discuss. They say— Rodrigo for instance—that if you could tell the king that you would never see Antonio Perez again, the whole face of things would change."

"I agree with that," she said.

"Could you send him such a message?"

"If that is all he wants, let him say so in common honesty."

"And if he said so? If he asked you just that?"

"I should be obliged to tell him that he had no right to ask it—or at least to make it a condition of my free citizenship."

"But would you answer yes or no?

"I'd answer no."

"Then you *are* in love with Antonio Perez?" The Duke's voice was full of surprise.

"Why do you always miss the point, Alonzo—just when one thinks you are seeing it? My answer would have nothing to do with being in love."

Alonzo looked relieved. He *knew* he was right about that love-affair nonsense. Really, people would say anything for scandal's sake. But what was he to do, all the same? How in God's name was he to help her now?

Ana lay in the deep shadow and thought about Antonio Perez.

Hoofs clattered in the square and into the court-yard; the children were returning from their ride. Ana heard Fernando laughing—like a little chime of bells.

THE SECOND CHAPTER   (JULY 1585)

I

It seemed henceforward as if Ana's story was told. She was shut up in Pastrana and the world forgot her.

A house-governor called Pedro Palomino was installed in the ground floor, with guards and clerks and with full authority over the whole dukedom, to direct it as he saw fit— for he was also appointed governor and chief justice of her district. Sitting at his desk in her house this stranger dismissed Ana's servants, from her devoted butler Diego downwards, without informing her of such dismissals or allowing the dismissed to see her in farewell. The children's tutors and personal servants were likewise turned away; secretaries, stewards, gardeners, all who had either worked there for Ruy Gomez or were the children of his men, left

Pastrana within a month of Palomino's arrival. A number of strangers, a much smaller number than the house was used to, were appointed in their places. The estate office, which negotiated transactions with tenants, directed the flourishing silk trade of the little town and had long been the Council Chamber of all its communal enterprises and the directing centre of its prosperity, was put in charge of a civil service clerk from Madrid, who knew no one, could not remember a face or a name from one day to another, and had seen neither a silkworm nor a loom in his life. He was a man who understood all villages to be poverty-stricken and desperate places, and saw no reason why they should not, in the order of nature, continue so.

Ana lived upstairs in her own wing. Of the personal attendants she had known Bernardina and Paca, her own special housemaid, remained. Such others as she saw about her rooms were strangers. She was allowed to use a secondary staircase which led from her suite to the children's study and dining-room, and also to a garden-door. There was always a guard, night and day, by this door and staircase.

She never saw the great staircase of her house. Outside the main door of her drawing-room an iron grill was built across the landing, with a gate which was unlocked only when Palomino came to visit her. The children were free to come and go, under the eyes of the guard, between their mother's suite and their own rooms. And they could range the house, and move as they pleased outside, with only such supervision as was needed to see that they did not traffic in illicit letters or messages. Ana's own letters were controlled as they had been in Pinto, and she had no power to spend money. She might write to tradespeople for what she required; Don Pedro Palomino decided whether or not to pass her orders.

The organisation of all this was complicated, especially with children in the house, who must not be asked to live in the atmosphere of a state prison. But no one troubled Ana with it. It was all attended to by unseen clerks downstairs; it was out of her hands.

Bernardina had been left to her—after one of Philip's long and devious struggles for decision. But she stayed as a prisoner, subject to the same restrictions as her mistress. They two were the only prisoners; and all this new machinery had to be set up in Pastrana, and everything on the vast estates must suffer great inconvenience and exasperation so that the two women might be kept under lock and key.

Bernardina's husband, Espinosa, had to leave the apartments which he and she had shared in the palace, and go to lodge in the village. He was still employed, but in a degraded standing, in the Estate Office—but as he was the only familiar person left them he was a great help to the farmers and silk-weavers as they struggled to explain their business to the civil servant from Madrid. He was allowed to speak to his wife for fifteen minutes every Sunday, through the new iron grill on the landing above the great staircase. Their son had been dismissed from his employment as bailiff of the home farm, but work had been found for him at San Lucar by the Duke of Medina Sidonia.

There was a strange chaplain now, and Ana and Bernardina were allowed to pray in the Pastrana private chapel; that is, from a tribune at the rear of it which could be entered from Ana's suite.

So everything was provided for.

As time passed Ana's sons were less and less frequently at home. Rodrigo was serving with Parma in the Netherlands; Diego, tiring of Alcala University and still waiting for the completion of his wife's nullity suit, went to Italy with a tutor to examine into his dukedom of Francavilla; Ruy, earnest boy, studied history and European languages in Salamanca and spent much time with relations in Madrid and round the Court, for he desired to go his father's way and enter the State Secretariat; Fernando lived officially at home in the first years of Ana's imprisonment, but he intended to be a priest, a Franciscan friar, and so spent whole weeks together sometimes at the Franciscan seminary on the outskirts of Pastrana.

Only Anichu was always at home. She rode about the familiar countryside as usual, and she went on her friendly errands to people she knew in the farms, and to the nuns at her dear Franciscan Convent. But otherwise she lived a prisoner's life, contentedly, with Ana.

Very few visitors were admitted now to the white and gold drawing-room, and they only after close scrutiny were passed through the iron grill. A few harmless old local bodies were allowed, if they did not come too often—the Mother Prioress, and one or two farmers' wives, and the Duke of Medina Sidonia on the rare occasions when he could travel so far from his own estates. And the old *Alcalde*, kind and jolly man still nominally in office but greatly bothered by the interferences of the new chief justice, Palomino, made many excuses to get past the grill and have a drink and a grumble with Ana and Bernardina. Diego, her butler, never came, although he was living just beyond the village. The *Alcalde* told Ana that twice Diego had tried to come to see her, but neither time could control himself sufficiently. And within the first year of his dismissal he died.

The Marqués de Los Velez was no longer at Alcala; he had gone abroad to an American governorship. There were other neighbours of his kind who tried at first to gain admittance, were turned away as having insufficient reason, and first grumbled about this, and then forgot the prisoner.

No word ever came from Antonio Perez, so Ana knew that he was still fighting his long duel with the king. She knew that he was still in danger of his life, and that he considered her life still in danger, and that while that was so to try to communicate with her and fail would be fatal to one of them, or both. She knew that she did not hear from him simply because he did not want Philip to put her to death. She supposed that she might never hear from him again.

All that she had visibly left to her therefore of her own life was whatever her rooms and garden contained of it; and two kind servants; and Anichu. These, and the view from her great drawing-room window.

The balcony of this had been filled in with blocks of stone, but she could still see her own gateway, though not much of the court-yard. But beyond the gateway she could see the western front of the *Colegiata* Church, and much of the open square, and a few roofs, houses of friends and neighbours. She could watch some of these neighbours moving about the square in the sun, and sitting by the wine-shop, or on the church steps, to talk. When the bell rang for Mass she could identify the people going into the church. This came to be a great possession, the window—for it framed life henceforward, and contained her share of the sky.

Ana had always thought, in her free past, that she led a shockingly idle and non-contributory life. It had worried her that she was pampered and purposeless. But now she looked back with almost-admiration to what seemed, in retrospect, like restless industry. She remembered the old round of her Pastrana day; the talk of meals and guests with Diego and the housekeeper, the business she transacted, or thought she transacted, in her estate office, the errands and friendly visits here and there about the village, the walks and rides with the children, the parties arranged for them, the tutors interviewed and counselled, the little local ceremonies and feasts which she directed, the letters she wrote, the plans she made, the advice she gave.

"Bernardina, are the State prisons full of useless drones like me, do you think?"

"I think they break stones in some of them. Would you like a turn of that? Shall we suggest it to old Palo, *chiquita*?"

Bernardina kept busy, because she had domestic talents, and servants were now far fewer in the house than they used to be—and she was not lowering the standard of Ana's life because of that. But Ana did not know how to polish silver or clean picture-frames, or re-cover cushions. And Bernardina would not let her try her skill at washing clothes.

"But I got quite good at that at Pinto—I liked it!"

Bernardina smiled.

"Oh yes, I did. Anyway you don't know half the filthy jobs I learnt to do at Pinto, when you were ill."

"Pinto! Those were the days! Do you remember the night old Zapo tripped on the top step, and went down backwards with the soup-pot over him?"

They laughed delightedly. Often now they caught themselves recalling Pinto as if it had been an idyllic experience.

"It isn't such fun, being a prisoner in your own house, Berni. Anyway, they're far too polite, these clerks from Madrid."

"I agree. Give me Zapo and Gypsy Rosa any time! Ah, what a slut she was, that girl!" said Bernardina appreciatively. "What a slut!"

Ana wished now, for Anichu's sake, that she had been soundly educated. When she was mistress of her own house Anichu had had—simply by convention and because she had to be chaperoned sometimes—one governess. A friendly, ageing widow who was a good horsewoman, spoke what seemed to be reasonable French, and never was unkind. But for her lessons she went to the Franciscan nuns where she had the happiness of mixing with all the other children of Pastrana, and the advantage of some good teaching.

All this was forbidden by the house-governor. The dear Viuda Maria was despatched in tears; two plain dull women were introduced to her house who undertook to teach a young lady everything she should know, and Anichu, as a daughter of the nobility, was no longer permitted to take lessons with the children of the town in the Franciscan Convent.

Ana fought against this arrangement, and the Mother Prioress fought fiercely on her side, and so did Bernardina. And Anichu fought most effectively of all by learning nothing from her two instructresses at home, and by racing off to the convent several times a day and leaving them to wonder where she was.

It was a lively battle, but it was not going to be a victory against the king's orders—and meantime Anichu was learning little of anything.

Ana burnished up her wits and tried to teach the child a few lessons. She was not a linguist, though she could smatter in French, and read Latin better than most women. But she was a naturally good arithmetician, and she was well read in the history and literature of Spain.

Anichu was enchanted to take lessons from her.

"But if you can do sums as well as this, it's absolute waste to have Doña Isabel in the house!"

"By the look of her I'd say it's waste anyway," said Ana disrespectfully—"or at any rate, it's a great increase of our trials. But perhaps that's what's intended."

The little girl chuckled.

"Anyway, I think I'll tell her I'm not doing any more arithmetic."

"Oh Anichu, I don't think you ought to say that."

"I will. After all, with you turning out to be an expert, it'd be just silly to go on with her. I suppose I'll still have to do old botany and drawing and stuff with her?"

"How does she draw?"

"Oh, I don't know. I expect it's terrible—but I'm no judge."

The lessons became a great alleviation, and interested Ana so much that she prepared them with care in advance, and became audacious and self-confident as a teacher. And friendship grew, strong and honest, between her and her little daughter, founded as it was on the deep natural sympathy that had always held them close.

One day she explained to Anichu all that she could to a child of her conflict with the king, and of his reasons for holding her a prisoner.

"I know," Anichu said. "Fernando and I have often talked it over. It's terrible—and you know we are both very fond of the king."

"So am I," said Ana.

"Yes—that's what I said to Fernando. But he and I think you're right. It may seem a bit obstinate—but really it's only just right. I don't see what else you could do."

"I'm glad you think I'm right. That's some consolation. Because it's a sad kind of life for you here now, and I sometimes think I ought to send you away——"

"Where?"

Anichu's eyes and mouth were wide open, in horror.

"To your sister's house, San Lucar, perhaps—or——"

"Oh, if you sent me away! Oh, if you did that!"

Ana gathered her up in her lap and hugged her.

"But I won't, I won't! I was only saying that if you were sad here, or thought I was wrong or anything——"

"I'm *never* sad where you are! Never! And I'd never care how wrong you were about anything!"

"Anichu, steady! Steady, pet!"

"I am steady. Only don't frighten me like that! If you knew what it was like when they took you away before, and we didn't know and they wouldn't tell us, and you'd *said* you'd come on the first of August—oh, if you knew!"

She wailed and wailed.

Ana held her in her arms.

"I knew, I knew it was like that, my baby. But I was in prison, you see—I simply couldn't do a thing—I swear I couldn't!"

Anichu stopped wailing as suddenly as she had begun.

"I know that," she said. "I'm sorry I screamed. I'll never scream again."

"Oh goodness do, if you want to!"

"I think I'd have to if—if you ever said again about, about sending me to Madalena or anywhere."

"I promise I'll never say it again, Anichu. But still, I'm glad you think I'm right about all this with the king."

"Yes, so am I glad—Fernando and I both said it would be awkward if we didn't agree with you. But we do. Still, if you were right or wrong, you'd be you just the same anyway, wouldn't you?"

"I suppose so."

"So what difference does it make then, really? I puzzle about that."

"So do I," said Ana, remembering how often she had followed that line of question about Antonio Perez, the unscrupulous wrong-doer. "But come on, child, get down off my knees. We've three more sums to do before twelve o'clock."

II

One evening of late July in 1585 a guard came to the grill outside Ana's rooms and announced to Paca that His Eminence Cardinal Quiroga, Archbishop of Toledo, was in the court-yard in parley with the governor of the house, and would shortly ascend to visit Her Highness the Princess of Eboli.

This was indeed good news and a break in loneliness. The Cardinal had only come to see Ana once before in her imprisonment, during 1581, but he wrote often, and though for her sake his letters had to be guarded in phrase he managed through them to make her understand that his concern for her was constant, that he continued to speak his mind to the king, that he sometimes saw Perez and watched as he could over him, and that one day he would visit her again, and bring her word of the world that had locked her up.

When he stood in the drawing-room and she knelt and kissed his ring she was much moved and could not speak. He murmured the Blessing softly over her bowed head and when she rose he looked first at her and then all about the room shrewdly before he spoke again.

"I've asked the gaoler if he'll be so obliging as to accommodate me for the night, Ana. I don't want to be hurried in our talk."

"And what did he say?"

It would be impossible for Palomino to refuse courtesy to the head of the Church in Spain, who was also the head of the Holy Office; yet the Cardinal was known as a frank supporter of Antonio Perez against the king, so it might be difficult for the meticulous civil servant to gauge exactly how to welcome so eminent yet dangerous a visitor to the house of Ana de Mendoza.

"He was fussed—not exactly cordial. I always thought Pastrana was a *hospitable* place, my dear?" They laughed. "However, I'm staying here to-night."

"Thank God! But I do hope they'll look after you reasonably. Isn't it strange—I haven't the faintest idea now of what goes on downstairs."

"Well, what I saw of the patio and court—it's rather like the *alcalde's* offices in any small town!"

"Oh! Oh, truly, does it look like that?"

"Yes, I'm afraid so—very much like that. I shall put it to Philip that this is a very poor way indeed of 'preserving' the family property which was so much endangered in your reign! Well come, let's sit down, let's look at you. You— you don't really look very well, my dear."

"I don't feel well. I move so slowly now, it's curious. Ever since I was ill at San Torcaz I've felt—old. I never did before."

"How old are you?"

"Forty-five. Ah, it's good of you to have come!"

"I've often tried to plan to come, as you must know. But they're working me very hard in my old age, and also things that you would want to know about have gone on being so drearily indecisive. However I had to be in Alcala this morning to confer with certain fussy ecclesiastics." He laughed. "We have our Philips and our Antonios in Christ's church too, Ana!"

"But you don't let them get to the top of the tree!"

"Oh yes we do, now and then. There's a long tragi-comedy going on just now, which was part of our business this morning." He smiled wearily. "It's about the tomb of Mother Teresa, who died as you know, and was buried at Alba de Tormes about three years ago."

"Yes, we heard that even here."

"But her native Avila couldn't have that, and recently they whisked her body off to its own place. Now Alba is appealing to Rome to have her back—and there is wild talk of miracles, and the Duke of Alba is blazing away. The young duke, thank God! It's a mercy old 'blood and iron' was gathered before this episode began. But still, we've quite the makings of a minor civil war on hand, as it is. Makes me smile, when I think of the sanity and authoritativeness of the woman they're fighting over! How easily she'd have blown their envies and jealousies to the sky! Oh well—they keep us old prelates busy."

She knew he was marking time and taking her in as he talked. She had an idea he was moved, and more saddened by sight of her than he had perhaps expected to be. He was as imaginative and kind as any man, yet she reflected that even to him the idea of six years' close confinement and deprivation of all liberties great and small, though shocking, was not in itself comprehensible—any more than it would have been to her six years ago. You have to live six such years, she thought, you have first to have accepted them from the cold and unmitigating hands of a friend you had always loved, and you have then to plod on and live them, with their dragging lifelessness, their ineptitude, their permanent mood of insult to the heart, and their blankness before the best as well as the largest of your personal attributes—you must live like that, keeping discreet and orderly in mind by means of little repetitions, invented tasks and little jokes and farces made up consciously to help out good behaviour—to be unshocked by the sum of their wear and tear.

She knew that spontaneity and health were dying in her now, that her responses were slowing down and that her mind felt dull and inelastic. She knew the efforts she made against all these deteriorations – and chiefly for Anichu's sake; but it was by measure of the effort that she understood how she was wearing out, how vitality was dying. For she, in freedom, had never known about effort in response to life.

She knew that all this inner change was in her face and movements now, and even in her voice perhaps—and she understood that they might be even crudely visible to one who had known her well in her good days, and now after this long time beheld her suddenly again.

She would have let him go on gossiping, gathering himself together—but talk of Mother Teresa still had power to make her miserable, and it was somewhat more than she could bear at this moment of joy and strain.

"Don't be sad," she said. "I'm better than I look. And I'll improve as we talk. You'll take me back to what I was!"

"Oh Ana, don't! You *are* what you were, indeed, indeed! It's only that it's a bit much, seeing you again—and we've all, all your friends, been so deadly dull without you."

"So have I been dull," she said sadly. "Have they offered you a *merienda* after your journey?"

"Yes—I'm told they are bringing some refreshment. Is the kitchen all right? Do they look after you properly?"

"Oh yes, I suppose so. Nothing is as it was, of course—but Bernardina does seem to bully some of the staff effectively."

A manservant came in with a tray of wine and cold foods, placed it by the Cardinal and withdrew.

Ana smiled.

"They're on their best behaviour," she said, looking over the food with an anxious hostess's eye. She recalled that when the house was hers she had never done that. Food was correctly offered then, it seemed, as naturally as daisies grew. It was odd to have to worry about a *merienda*-tray.

"I wonder what they'll give you for supper," she said.

"Whatever they give you, I trust."

"Oh—but I won't be allowed to have supper with you."

He stared at her.

"Either I have supper with you in this room to-night at such time as you think suitable, or I hand over that whole collection downstairs to the Holy Office, as heretics and desecrators of consecrated priests!"

They laughed.

"Oh, that'll be wonderful! Fancy having a guest to supper again—after six years! Anichu and Fernán will be ravished."

"I shall be glad to see those children."

"Bernardina will be with us too—you won't mind, will you? She always dines and sups with me."

"Of course, Ana."

The Cardinal poured some wine.

"Give me some too," said Ana.

He did so, smiling at her as she took the glass.

"Not that you need it now," he said. "You're looking wonderful suddenly."

"I told you I'd improve under your influence. Pleasure, you see—and the excitement of a supper-party!"

"Oh woman, you break my heart! Truly I didn't know I cared so much about you, you shocking, locked-up Jezebel! That's what some gentlemen in Madrid always call you now—I believe even in letters to the king!"

"Haven't they thought of anything newer? They used to call me Jezebel in Ruy's time. I know, because he told me."

The Cardinal lifted his glass.

"To Ruy's dear memory," he said.

"To Ruy."

They drank.

"I wonder what Ruy would say now of Spain's situation," the Cardinal mused. "Politics, thank God, are not my field. Yet, you know, I stare in consternation at our present paradox."

"Paradox?"

"Well, we annexed Portugal, at a loss of possibly a few hundred casualties. Our claim is doubtful, but the spoils are ours. That actually means that for all commercial purposes, Ana, we own the world. Look at the map. We now possess the two best fleets in the world. England has some good sailors, but we have two experienced and organised fleets. Pirates allowed for, we now control not only our own great western possessions, but also through Portugal the Indian Ocean. Our sailors and missionaries are everywhere. Our wealth is uncharted. This situation has been growing on us for some time, until it became fixed and inevitable. Luck caused it in the beginning, but it has been secured by the plain bravery and imaginative perseverance of our ordinary people, our sailors and soldiers and missionaries. So you'd think, wouldn't you, that there might be some sign in our national life, our home life, of this extraordinary economic strength? You'd think there might be roads and merchant ships and schools, and new houses and better shops and better wages, and more to eat and more ordinary human hope and decency? Yet there isn't. And when I talk to Philip I hear of nothing but of the inordinate expense of the Netherlands, and the mad cost of the Italian states, and this and that and this and that, as if we were beggars. And when I look about me I see that he's right, that his people *are* beggars. What's the matter? What is he doing? What would Ruy say?"

"I don't know. I'm a prisoner. I see nothing. I can only tell you that when Ruy lived and in the six years after his death that I was in nominal charge of Pastrana, this estate and its people were prosperous. Now it's being run by the government, and I can tell from looking out of that window, from walking through my own garden—even if none of the people ever came to see me—that, for some reason which no one can quite fix on, that is no longer true. The people here are worried now, and beginning to get into debt. And some of the best of them, some of the really skilled silk-workers, *moriscos* from Valencia and Alicante, have already gone away."

"Yes. I can believe it. I think the reason, both for Spain's paradoxical plight and Pastrana's, lies in reach of our understanding. But sentiment does not sound orthodox in economics—so we waive it. Still—Spain is mistress of the world, Ana, and she is in hopeless decay."

"Hopeless?"

"I think hopeless. I wouldn't mind that if, say like Rome, she had ever, her people had ever had one brief phase of enjoying the achievement. But what annoys me is that we have become great and are now ceasing to be great, while still at the top of our power, in two generations. Let greatness, anyway let absolute mastery go, by all means—if meantime you have pulled some of its lasting advantages, its advancements out of the fire for those, and their children, who earned you that passing glory. If Spain, the people of Spain, were to have a residue, in civic and trade development, in training, in education, in ordinary hope and comfort, the decline could come and welcome. But what maddens me is to hear Philip and his sycophants exulting now over this magnificent double empire, and then to look about the

country that gave it to them—and then to go back to the
secretariat's wails about debts and extravagances and in-
solvency. I can't see why we tolerate such crass mismanage-
ment."

"We deserve it. Don't think I talk now just as a victim of
absolutism, which I am. But when I was free, in the blind,
foolish days when I looked on, and thought that no tyrant
ever born could tyrannise over me, a Mendoza—even then I
feared Philip's tyranny for Spain. But we accepted it. We
who had the power, who owned Castile and governed it by
the free wisdom of our people, we sold ourselves to his old
father—and we have allowed him to be such a tyrant as
Charles never was. I know Philip and I—I have always
loved him, oddly enough. But he is a dangerous tyrant, and
we have been bullied, and here we are, in chaos. The decaying
mistress of the world, as you say."

"It's curious. Because there have always been men, and
men in power, to speak their minds."

"Yes, yes—there have been men, and I've known how
they've cared and worked—oh, don't sadden me too much
to-night!"

"I don't want to."

"You haven't really. Only I'm out of the habit of talking
about what matters, and it is perhaps too exhilarating." She
turned the glass in her hand and looked at the gleaming wine.
"Wine is good. I've come to understand that in prison."

"Have you become an addict, Ana?"

"Well, no. But Bernardina's always liked to drink it, and
sometimes here at night I drink with her. It makes me sleep—
it even makes me think I'm happy."

"That's a good service," the Cardinal said.

"I remember," said Ana, "that I used to smile at Antonio's
wine-drinking. He'd come from the Alcázar often, very tired;
and then he'd start talking, and he'd walk up and down the
Long Room filling and refilling his glass, talking, talking,

talking. But he never seemed to be drunk. I used to wonder at that."

"Poor fellow! How much he'd give to walk the Long Room now, and talk and talk and talk."

"Oh!" said Ana. "How is he? What is happening?"

"Much, very much is happening. But he's fairly well. Whenever I see him he sends you his—love."

Silence fell for a moment.

"Is he in prison always?"

"Yes. Ever since you were arrested he too has been under arrest. Sometimes he's seemed to be under easier terms than you. Philip makes extraordinary variations in his treatment. But all the time he has been, I think, in danger of death. He has told me that he constantly explores means of writing to you, but that he knows interception might mean your death as well as his. I think he's right about that."

"Tell me what has been done to him."

"I can't possibly tell you *all* he's been through. He's been under house-arrest, then in state prisons, then practically released to normal life, then seized again and in a dungeon, then back to house-arrest. The thing is an idiotic scandal."

"How shameless Philip can be, for a prim, respectable man!"

The Cardinal laughed delightedly.

"Exactly! That's the whole thing in a nutshell. But let's not begin on Philip's psychology, Ana! I have simpler fish to fry."

"Tell me about Antonio."

"I must cut the story to essentials. While Philip was still in Lisbon he was worked upon to settle the Antonio Perez question once and for all—and so he ordained that an investigation be held into corrupt practices among high state officials. A commission went to work—about three years ago. In the autumn of last year, on its findings, Perez was brought from one or other of his prisons to trial. He was accused of taking bribes in office, and of tampering with state papers. He declared in court that he could not defend himself against the second charge without producing private files which His Majesty might not wish exposed. This caused a halt. Our long-suffering friend Antonio Pazos—who, by the way, if this affair drags on much longer will most certainly put henbane in all our wine, poor fellow!—was sent to look at these files. His advice to Philip was for his own sake to drop that silly charge!"

Ana laughed.

"However, the bribe-taking accusation was pursued, and Perez offered no defence. He was condemned to pay a fine of 30,000 ducats—half to the Crown and half to the Mendoza estates——"

"What?"

"Yes. You are supposed to have cheated the family funds to that amount on his behalf——"

"But——"

"Oh, leave it. The arguments were nonsense, and all promoted by your vindictive cousin Almenara and his gang. But further, Perez was condemned to two years' hard labour in Segovia State Prison."

"When did this happen?"

"Last January. I was in Madrid and heard the trial and the sentence. I can safely say that, apart from my standing sympathy with Perez against the king, my sense of equity was outraged by the proceedings. Perez was only under house-arrest then and on parole until he should be moved back to prison. I went to him that evening and told him that justice and law had been flouted in his trial, and counselled him to seek sanctuary at once. Then, you see, he would be immune, in any civilised country, from the temporal power, his case would become the affair of the Holy Office and—in a word— he would be safe. He took my advice, and I went home with a quiet mind."

"Well then?"

"Ana—have you heard anything of the father of Elizabeth of England? That Henry VIII whom we all, good anti-Reformationists, comminate against in all our prayers?"

"Yes indeed, I've heard plenty about him."

"But I don't think you've heard of his breaking sanctuary—which is what the servants of His Most Catholic Majesty did that night."

"Philip did that?"

"Yes. Oh, but Philip will pay for it! The Nuncio is already under threat of dismissal for his eloquent protests, but he has Rome's support and he has mine, and the matter isn't being dropped. Meantime, however, Perez is in a filthy prison, and what's more his heroic wife and his children are in another wing of the same prison. And Juana is being put to everything but the torture to try to make her say where his private papers are. And she'll never say. And Philip the king is in Arágon, seeing how he can best set about imposing absolutism there, and improving the hour—I hear from my spies—by collecting one or two witnesses now living there who might be used in a possible trial of Antonio for the Escovedo murder. That is the news up to the present. It's not very novel—it's only ugly and cowardly and a disgrace to a king I used to admire."

"Oh God! How slow he is! How deadly! Will he never *act* in this thing? Will there never be a decision?"

"Never, I think. But any minute there'll be another change of plan, naturally. Philip, as you know, by his nature hates all Popes, and this new Pontiff just elected, Sixtus, looks like being intolerably masterful. But the temporal lord of the world is, after all, a Catholic, so he *has* to be the ally of the Papacy. And already this little affair of breaking sanctuary has received the attention of Sixtus V. I imagine that means that Perez and his family will come back from Segovia any day now, and have another spell of house-arrest. Oh the wearisomeness of it!"

The Cardinal laughed a little as he ended.

"What are you laughing at?"

"You know poor old Don Diego de Chaves, Philip's patient, honest chaplain? No man of imagination dare try to measure what *he* must have endured on this Escovedo-Perez-Eboli affair during the past six years! God help him! Well, he—who is sent everywhere at all seasons to do all Philip's dirty work with this one and that one—do you know what he is reported to have said to Juana de Coëllo herself in her prison-cell the other day?"

"Poor man! I truly can't imagine."

"He said to her that if a decision wasn't come to and action taken within the next three months, he would go into the Puerta del Sol, call a meeting, and tell the truth, on oath, to all the people, about Escovedo's death. And then, he said, he'd go home and die quietly."

"One can only sympathise."

"It's very funny though—His Majesty's distracted confessor!"

"Let's drink more wine," said Ana.

The Cardinal filled their glasses.

"You know," he said, "that all kinds of mystification and side-taking still go on among the so-called informed about this scandal of your and Perez's arrests. But I believe you accept my simple reading of it? That Philip loved and trusted Antonio and intended to see him quite safely through the Escovedo trouble, and that he has always been a bit, not entirely but a bit in love with you. Am I right so far?"

"I think so."

"Am I right in assuming that you were never Philip's mistress?"

"Yes. He never really asked me to be. He's always been, as you say, only a bit in love with me."

"Exactly. Well then he heard of your—love-affair. For

some reason hidden in his own dreams it maddened him. He had no claim on the private life of either of you—but as your king, on his own terms, he has power over you. Since he learnt that you were lovers, he has not been able to be quite quit of the thought of either or both of you. And he has got his miserable personal emotion entangled with the Escovedo problem—because somehow hidden in that may be, if he can find it, the destruction of your lover. And it isn't that he's in love with you. It's that he has long been in love with the idea of your being in love with him."

"Yes—all that is right, I think."

"So far so good. I saw that from the beginning. And I know too how oddly and slowly his mind works when pain or self-defence of any kind is controlling it. But *why* those sudden, savage arrests? I have never been able to understand the motive for that curious, wild decisiveness."

"They were my fault, I believe. He came to see me in that July—about a fortnight before we were arrested. I was very happy to see him and we talked, as I thought, frankly. He was moved and upset, and so was I. He asked me if it was true about my relationship with Antonio and naturally I said it was. I begged him to have the Escovedo case heard, and to let us all take the consequences of one piece of honesty, and he seemed as if he might consider that. He was kind and weary, and he cried. And I thought that we had got back to real association. I was glad of all we'd said that evening—and I thought he'd come again. But then he sent them to arrest me. And when I was driving away from my house in Madrid that night, I saw him standing in the porch of Maria Almudena, watching them take me off."

"Ah! I see."

"I think that visit to me was merely a test of himself. He wanted to see whether or not he really felt affronted by my having a lover who wasn't he. Somehow it seems he found that after all he was. He tests everything, you know, before he decides. He tested that—and decided that it was an outrage to him, as in fact he had suspected it to be! So here we are! Am I right?"

"I think so. I think that, outside of his ceaseless care for Spain, and his desperate hope to keep his one sick little son alive, his chief personal passion now is to know that somehow—without incriminating him—Antonio Perez is safely dead. And as a rider to that, to be certain that you are never again within hand's reach of Perez or any other man. And this isn't love, even at love's crudest. It's self-love, insanely indulged by a lonely and unbalanced man."

"What you say makes me wonder again what I've often wondered. Seeing how little it is—forgive me, dear ascetic—but seeing how little it need matter to a woman of brains—sexual intercourse I'm talking about—should I, for Antonio's sake and in the name of all our peace, should I have forced poor Philip into a belated love-affair that he didn't want?"

The Cardinal laughed delightedly.

"Has ever a priest been asked so amusing a question, Ana? The moral answer is of course no. But the diplomatic answer coincides, in my opinion, for once. Any kind of perjury is always to be avoided, on politic grounds. I think such a false step might only have made bad worse."

"Well then—since our imprisonment, I have frequently been told that if I would promise Philip never to see Antonio again, all would be well. My soul cannot admit his right or anyone's to ask such things of me, let alone put me in prison until I answer them to his liking. But am I being self-indulgent there? It isn't that I expect or even now especially desire to see Antonio again. It's that I cannot countenance blackmail. But should I perhaps? Should I bear that indignity—rather than what I do bear—in the hope of lessening Antonio's danger?"

"Again the moral answer is no. Indeed, child, this stand of yours against blackmail is one of Spain's few good deeds at present—and I for one am glad to witness it. Antonio, and good luck to him, is fighting, and not quite honestly all the time, for his life, and his family, and prestige and money, and everything he has worked for. But you, differently placed, are fighting quite simply for your idea of human conduct. If you've done wrong in the past—and you have—you are now doing something that is hard and right and cold and even disinterested. Moreover, you are acting in character."

"You haven't told me if diplomatically I am wrong."

"No, because I don't know. But anyway, it is too late for your diplomacy now; and you and Antonio have had your pleasure and your sin. If one of you can balance that feeble self-indulgence by accepting an impeccable principle, making it your fate and your penance, and even dying for it, it will have been a good deed, Ana. And I for one shall know why I have always admired you—even in your recent Jezebel days."

"I wonder. You haven't answered me."

"I can't. I can only repeat that I know that in this conflict with Philip you have been morally as right as in committing adultery with Antonio you were morally wrong."

Silence fell. Ana looked out towards the sky and the *Colegiata* tower. Night was descending. To-night would not be as lonely as evening customarily was—for the children and Bernardina would be enchanted by the novelty of a guest for supper, and the guest was worthy of his rarity. There would be wine-drinking and gossip and laughter, and the breath of the world. Indeed, a great break with loneliness, which would make her hidden heart shiver, so lonelily would the simple pleasure ring there. And meantime Antonio would pace his cell in Segovia alone, with everything he valued lost and gone.

"I gather that you think that Philip is actually now considering a trial of the Escovedo brief?"

"My answer to that can only be surmise—and it is

dangerous. But it is a fact that some new Escovedo relations have started up a new agitation, and the impossible Vasquez is again encouraging them. Now—here is my uncharitable and bitter guess—if Philip's agents can find among Perez's captured papers the fifty or sixty letters on that affair which could incriminate the king, those papers will be destroyed, and Philip will throw conscience to the winds at last and let Perez be tried—and of course condemned to death. If those papers cannot be found—and I don't believe they will be— the pressure is now so insistent in all classes for a trial of you two criminals that I think the king will *have* to risk it. He so much desires to destroy Perez that I fear it may come to that— and to corruption of the Court in favour of the king. But such a risk would take Philip a long time—and so long as you are both in gaol he won't rush it."

"It breaks my heart," said Ana.

"But I thought it would have done that long ago?"

"No. That's the curious thing. I *keep* on hoping he'll have the courage of his good feeling. I'm simple about affection, you see—and I keep on crazily hoping that before the end he'll prove to me that he is too."

"Oh Ana, he isn't and he won't prove it. In feeling, in feeling most of all he's insane."

"I've never seen it. Always he was easy to like, easy to trust. Vain and sensitive and touchy, and like a living man. That night when I saw him in the porch of Maria Almudena watching them take me away, I was shocked, and thought that he *must* be unnaturally cruel. But even so—anyone might have that sort of awful mood. Still, I've said to myself since that Philip *is* good and grateful—I *know* that. And by nature I'd say that he *couldn't* do what he's doing to Antonio, who has given him a lifetime of work and love."

"It is his nature to distort and worry nature. But he isn't a natural brute. That's why his brutalities take years, and are so hideous."

"I never knew him brutal."

"Yet in these six years he has been brutal to you."

"It's terrible to have reduced him to all these dishonours of his soul."

"That's generous—but goes too far. You have sins enough to carry, Ana—don't be officious about Philip's sins."

"Yes, I have sins enough."

"Do you repent of them?"

"I would do so more easily if the occasions of my sin were not now in so much guilt and trouble."

"That isn't your affair. You are only asked for your own soul."

"Oh you theologians! Try *living* before you counsel! Find out what it is to have sinned in twos before you start lecturing in ones!"

The Cardinal smiled.

"Your advice comes late—my hair is white, dear Ana. But God may be amused, I venture to think, by the obstacle-race you make of approach to His love."

She looked at him in honest wonder.

"But surely—for sinners—it *has* to be an obstacle-race? I mean, you can't *assume* an unimaginable thing like the love of God?"

The Cardinal pressed the fingers of his two hands together.

"That question leaps over many others," he said. "I'll examine it with you to-morrow morning, if I may. It brackets all that I really want to know about you—and so I can't have Bernardina or the children charging in on it."

"There's nothing to examine in it," said Ana, a shade wearily. "I have been six years alone now with the idea of God and the question of my own sins—and I cannot yet see how you go hat-in-hand to Him, when you know yourself."

"May I say that you are sometimes very unlike a woman, Ana? And now—you are looking perilously tired, and I must go and read my office. No, don't stir, don't move. I'll be back here in an hour—and for the rest of to-night we'll talk gossip and nonsense—and even a little bawdry, if that's what Bernardina likes."

He rose and was gone before she could decide to get up and be ceremonious. So she lay back in her chair and covered her blank right eye with her long, nervous hand. And weariness and hopeless sorrow and a sense of failure overswept her, and tears of weakness and ill-health poured down her face.

III

In the morning she walked with the Cardinal in the garden.

"You see what I mean," she said, pointing to this and that untidiness. "They're strangers to it, of course. But you did know this garden? You remember it?"

"Indeed I knew it. Many's the hour I walked it with Ruy. Don't you remember how he argued me into all kinds of expensive plants and bulbs from Holland?"

"Yes. It was his years in Holland that made a gardener of him."

"Indeed it was! I wish I had the money back that he made me spend on tulips! Tulips in Toledo!"

Ana laughed.

"We lost a few small fortunes here too on his tulip-craze. Ah, but I hate this garden now! I only walk here because I suppose I must walk somewhere in the air." She looked about her sadly at the weeds and the general tangle of neglect.

"Its condition relates to the main part of the house," the Cardinal said. "I mean, it's like a neglected park in a sordid country town. I'll describe it to Philip. Preservation of the family property indeed!"

"In a few years Pastrana will be a ruin," Ana said.

"I think so," said the Cardinal. "That's what happens when you lock up life."

"Well, Ruy is safely dead. And I'll be gone soon."

"Do you feel that you are dying?"

"It's a long time since I felt that I was living. Look at how slowly I walk."

Anichu came running up the terrace to them.

"I only wanted to tell you that I'm going down to Sister Antony for my geography lesson," she said. "Please don't tell Doña Isabel where I am if she asks, as she'll only come pestering, and they all laugh at her, and it's awkward."

"All right, pet, I won't tell."

"Then I'll say good-bye, Anichu," said the Cardinal. "I fear I shall have to be gone any minute now."

"Oh! Oh, I am sorry, Your Eminence." Anichu dropped on her knees and kissed his ring. He blessed her and she rose and bowed and ran away again down the terrace steps.

Ana looked after her.

"I constantly wonder if I ought to keep her here," she said.

"Why? Where else should she be? She looks very well."

"Still, a child shouldn't live in a prison."

"That child isn't living in prison, Ana. She's happy, she's where her heart is."

They were on the highest platform of the garden.

"Let us sit down," said Ana.

The fair-bleached land, waiting for harvest, lapped away from them eastward and westward. At their backs far off the Guadarramas rose, ridged with green-black pines; the sky was immaculate, thin, insubstantial blue, of glittering, terrible purity. Near them, below them, homely-seeming, lay the heavy quiet house of stone, with crowded about it the other roofs and towers of Pastrana.

"Does it hurt you ever," Ana asked, "to look at a scene you knew very well and consider how it will lie there happy and unchanged the day you die, and the next day, and hundreds of years after you're forgotten?"

"Yes, indeed. Our attachment to those things our senses

apprehend may be our silliest part, philosophically—but it is also, alas, our strongest."

"Ruy used to sit on this bench very often the summer before he died, and sometimes I came to him here and I knew by his face that he was saying good-bye."

"You weren't in love with him?"

"No. Only because he was too old for me, I think. He was very much worth love."

The Cardinal studied her, considering sadly that he might never see her again, for he was old and she was losing hold on life, though not yet old. She looked very distinguished and ascetic, he thought, like a very good nun who has been worked too hard. I can see why she appeals to me, he reflected, a man who has long ago mastered and forgotten all the hungers of sex. But the strength of her appeal to Perez, though indeed æsthetically, fastidiously one can apprehend it, is yet a very unexpected and arresting fact.

"Your injured eye," he said gently, "has that distressed you much in your secret life?"

She turned and looked at him in astonishment.

"I am an old man, and I may never see you again on earth. So I say what I wish to say. I have often wondered how much or little it has meant to you."

"I—I never speak of it."

"I know. Speak now."

"There's nothing to say now. I too am old. But I think it decided everything in life for me."

"Hardly," said the Cardinal. "At least, by rule of thumb one would say that it did not decide your becoming Antonio's mistress."

Ana looked away across the fair horizon.

"Yes, that too."

"How, Ana?"

"Can't you understand? A sort of belated challenge. The glove a panicking coward may at last decide to throw down."

"I see."

She clutched his hand, and he felt with surprise and pity that she was trembling.

"No more, no more!" she said unsteadily. "I haven't the control I used to have, I'm tired and shaky! Say no more of that!"

"I'll say no more, you foolish child. But as to the challenge —it justified itself?"

"Oh, I can't tell. How could I? But I was happy as his lover. With him I learnt and forgot many things." She had withdrawn her hand, and now was calm again and laughed a little. "Nothing is more embarrassing than an old woman talking about her love-experience," she said.

"Last night," said the Cardinal, "you asked a rather wide, loose question about the love of God. And you called it 'unimaginable'. Now I should call it 'indefinable', rather. That is—I can't tell you what it is, yet I have spent my life in dim, poor apprehension of it, in seeking symbols and reflections of it in the work and thought of man, and in my own most weak and sinful soul. And in those apprehensions— such as they are—lies all the best of me and of what life reflects to me. And in you, my dear, in your foolish, sinful life I have sometimes thought I caught reflections, intimations of what I apprehend by God's love."

"In me? Oh no—there's none of that grace in me. I have always had faith, a plain, hard, infantile faith, the unimaginative faith of all my ancestors, and I have too their plain and childish sense of right and wrong. I've been glad of that in a way—because at least for good or ill I've always known in every action where I stood and I have sinned or not with all my wits about me."

"What advantage was there in that?"

She laughed.

"Well, it keeps you from self-pity and from putting the stresses wrong; and it prevents the kind of regret that blames other people. Besides, it keeps memory clear. You'll forgive me if I say that when one has sinned—in the sensual sins, the sins of pleasure—in full private cognisance of guilt, one does not afterwards forget, as sentimentalists do, how sweet the pleasure was and how much it gave you. You buy it high, you see."

"This is a kind of epicureanism."

"Yes, you could call it that. It gives an edge to gratitude. It also makes repentance difficult."

"Why?"

"Because you know that you were as clear in your mind at the time of your sin as you are now that it was an offence against God's law, and you know that you were as sorry then as you are now to commit that offence. Yet you took your pleasure and your chance. And you can't without falsity, it seems to me, be retrospectively repentant—for that would be like trying to have it both ways."

"Oh, Ana, no! How prim you are! My child, that's where the love of God comes in."

"I dare say. I'm only saying that I find it difficult to—to assault the love of God. Because I persist in being grateful for the love of man—and the best of that that I had was forbidden fruit. But I understood what Escovedo meant——"

"What did Escovedo mean, and when?"

"Did I say that aloud? Lord, am I getting senile, do you think? Oh never mind, that's an old story."

"It haunts you a bit?"

"Yes. But all I mean is that I accept, from the teaching I never discarded, my guilt. And I have repented long ago in that clear-cut sense, and returned to the usual religious practices. And I accept these years and all this empty loneliness and forsakenness as a part perhaps of my purgatory. But as this purgatory was forced on me, I cannot seek to derive merit from it in heaven—and in general I can't, with any honesty, turn to God, as holy people say. Because while accepting His ruling, I shall always be glad of Antonio."

"God doesn't ask the impossible of you, you conceited woman. He only asks what you are giving, your honest repentance, and acceptance of His Will as higher than your own. He doesn't ask you, while still clothed in human flesh, to see your sins through superhuman eyes."

"The trouble is that sometimes, in a calm kind of way, I think I do!"

The Cardinal laughed.

"Arrogant, self-deluding creature! Dear Ana, stop all this hair-splitting. You are lonely here and punished and weary—and all that you accept with excellent Christian fortitude, may I say. For the rest, open your heart to the sweets of Heaven, child. God isn't all made of tiny rules and calculations, and it is presumptuous of you actually to invent these games and graphs for Him. Pray, child, and love Him. It's not such a very long journey from the love of man to the love of God."

"I do pray. I pray a great deal."

"Pray more—and more freely. And since you *are* so rigidly orthodox, I take it you believe in the communion of saints?"

"Oh yes, indeed I do."

"Then *I* shall pray for *you* a very great deal henceforward, and so will many others. And our prayers will find you out here in your loneliness, and teach you how to imagine the love of God."

"Yes, pray for me. Pray for my empty heart."

"Do you pray for others?"

"For everyone imaginable. For the children, for you, for the repose of many souls. For Philip, very much. Constantly for Antonio."

"I shall tell them that—both of them."

"Do. And give Antonio my love."

A manservant came up the garden to say that His Eminence's coach was ready now.

The two rose.

"No, Ana, don't come back to the house. I'll leave you now; I'll like to remember you standing here in sunlight."

So she went on her knees and kissed his ring and he blessed her.

THE THIRD CHAPTER   (1585-1590)

The Cardinal's prayers may have reached Ana as he said they would, for as the years deepened, as ill-health increased and the silence and neglect of the world, rising now as a great sighing forest between her and all that she had been, immured her past hope as the king's life-prisoner, she escaped further and further from the spiritual desolations which had wearied her in the first years of her entombment.

This was the more consoling and lucky as the external conditions of her life were made harder by her keeper as time went on.

Not long after the Cardinal's visit, Pastrana's house-governor was changed. Don Alonso Villasante was sent to take over the duties of Palomino. Bernardina, fat and ageing now and considered jolly and harmless by some of the guards, managed to get gossip and comment out of them sometimes, and was told that the idea of the change was reform; that the king was dissatisfied to learn that the dukedom was losing its trade and prosperity and that the Princess's palace was slipping into disorder. Under Don Alonso there was to be efficiency and a fresh start.

But so far as Ana, Bernardina and Anichu could judge, this efficiency only meant a great multiplication of the rules governing the life of the whole parish, and a great increase of severity and callousness towards the prisoners. The material comforts which he found these enjoying were considered excessive by Don Alonso; so henceforward their food became less attractive, requests for renewals of clothing or of household requirements of any kind were questioned and usually refused; firewood and candles were issued on a dole and to the accompaniment of warnings against self-indulgence. Visits from friends in the village were cut until at last they were totally forbidden; Ana's doctor from Alcala was hardly ever allowed to see her; neither she nor Bernardina was permitted to pick a flower or an apple when they walked in the garden; and Anichu's free movements through the village and the countryside were censured and curtailed.

They learnt too—Bernardina became almost supernaturally successful in getting news—that in the estate office, whence Bernardina's husband Espinosa was dismissed by the new governor, chaos had been imposed upon chaos, and that the old easy farming and trading methods of the prosperous days were now lost for ever under a confusion of regulations which no one understood. Sadly Ana heard that first this farmer sold out and went away, and next that one, less lucky, was sold up; silk-weavers one by one were setting off eastward to look for work in Valencia; the craft-schools at the monastery and convent were less and less well attended. Poverty was coming back to Pastrana.

All this, Ana thought in wonder still, all this, affecting the peace and work of hundreds of people, merely because a woman he did not want took a lover who was not he.

The drawing-room grew shabby. The gold-painted acacia-leaves, flaking off the white walls, could not be restored, even by Bernardina's amateur hand, for the house-governor would give her no gold paint. The silk curtains were frayed and dusty and the dark velvet on the chairs had faded; but the looms just beyond the gate, that had woven these were allowed to weave no more for the Princess of Eboli, and half of them indeed had ceased their shuttling. No flowers came up from the garden now, no fruit lay about in dishes, and it was many years since any new books had reached Pastrana from Ana's bookseller in Madrid. There were at last no silks left for needlework, and the tapestry-frames stood idle.

But Anichu came and went contentedly with her lesson-books and whatever talk or news there was, graceful, sweet-faced, serious and true—every day more precious in Ana's sight. And Bernardina still laughed in the teeth of her keepers, and fished up jokes against all weathers, and bullied jugs of wine from the kitchen-men. And the window still looked out to the *Colegiata* doorway and the sky.

When Fernando was fifteen, in the winter of 1585, he went away to a Franciscan house of novices at Salamanca, and to begin his university studies there. Anichu cried very much when he left, and for long afterwards was quieter and whiter of face than seemed good for her. She herself was twelve then and growing tall, promising to be as slender as Ana and more correctly beautiful in face. Ana lay on her couch often, watching Anichu bent over her books, and marvelled at her contentment in this mad, unnatural life, and pondered anxiously her future. Her own health puzzled her. She was growing almost a rheumatic cripple; headaches were savage and frequent, and she was for ever fighting against waves of nausea and giddiness. She assumed therefore that she would not live much longer, and she deplored, somewhat remorse-fully, the passion of Anichu's devotion to her, its undeviated-ness and its great content.

"You *ought* to go to Madrid sometimes, my pet," she said once or twice. "You really ought to stay with friends and get to know your cousins again, and live like other girls."

"Don't say it. I entreat you not to say it. I don't *want* any cousins. I want to stay here, with you."

News from the world—whether true or false they could not be sure—came in sometimes to Bernardina. They heard, for instance, that Antonio Perez continued the king's prisoner; that the Escovedo murder trial was being heard, then that it was abandoned, then that it was to be heard again. Bernardina found out somehow that the Escovedo letters that the king's men had searched for so earnestly had not been found, and likely never would be found. They heard that the king was being urged again, by the Duke of Guise and the Pope, to the old mad idea of invasion of England, and that Santa Cruz, his great admiral, had gathered an Armada and was straining hard for action.

One evening of February in 1587 Bernardina came upstairs with the news that in England they had beheaded the Queen of Scots.

Ana prayed for her a minute, saying nothing. Anichu sat up, her face very white and her black eyes burning.

"How long was she in prison, Berni?"

"Oh, ages, *chiquita*—about twenty years, I'd say."

"Well, she'll have been glad of this," said Ana.

"But why?" said Anichu. "It's better to live! You know it's better to live!"

Ana saw an unpronounceable fear racing through Anichu's brain.

"Of course it is," she said. "But she wasn't lucky like me. She didn't have you and Berni with her always."

"Tyrants can go very far, can't they?" said Anichu.

"Well yes, they go far, as we know. But she was a very important queen. *Her* tyrant probably thinks it was necessary to behead her, for reasons of state. You have to have reasons of state to behead people, Anichu."

Anichu said no more, but she did not return to her book. She sat and stared into the fire.

"We'll pray for the peace of her soul, Anichu. Poor queen, poor Mary of Scotland."

In the spring of 1588 Bernardina constantly had news of coming war, of ships and alarms, of English pirates in Cadiz Bay, and of this one and that one gone to be a sailor. Once or twice there were brief letters from Rodrigo in the Netherlands, and although he spoke of overtures of peace and of Parma's conferences to that end, it was clear that he was excited about some new campaign in the air, and he did not talk of coming home just yet. But early in the spring all Spain heard of the death of the old Admiral Santa Cruz, and Ana as well as others who knew his warrior-spirit breathed more freely again for the young men newly pressed into naval service, and assured herself that now the Armada could not sail.

This relief was short-lived.

But when, a week or two after the old sailor's death, Bernardina brought in the most curious piece of public news that she had ever collected—grave though it might be for Spain—it raised a wild, incredulous laugh in the Pastrana drawing-room.

The Duke of Medina Sidonia, she told Ana and Anichu, was to command the Great Armada and lead it against England.

Ana was feeling ill that evening, in pain all through her body, but this most exquisitely tragi-comic piece of news, which she refused to accept as more than some travelling man's fantasy, roused her to a mood of mockery that was rejuvenating and even analgesic. She and Anichu laughed and questioned Bernardina in a rapture of non-belief, and all three excelled themselves in inventing dilemmas, fusses and disasters for their important relative, when he should take his ships to sea. They had great fun, and drank his health.

"I give you my brother-in-law, that great sailor!" said Anichu, waving her glass above her head. They laughed until they cried, and were merrier over this *canard* of Bernardina's than they had been for many an evening.

That night, unable to sleep, Ana let herself wonder if such an utterly frivolous rumour could by any disastrous chance be true. And at the thought that it might her heart lurched in fear for the men in the great ships at Cadiz and at Lisbon. But she shook the nightmare away and returned to her prayers, the many, many prayers that took her now with increasing kindness through the nights of loneliness and pain.

Spring passed; May opened and spread its beauty on Pastrana; and they learnt that the Great Armada was to sea, and commanded indeed for good or ill by their unhappy Alonso, Madalena's husband, who had never directed as much as a sardine-boat in his life, and who would be honestly terrified, Ana knew, of his appalling honour.

It sailed, and with it sailed, as occasional letters told them, many, many that they knew—cousins and friends and neighbours, and Bernardina's son, her only child, in the flagship of his new employer, the new Great Admiral.

By the end of September its tale was done—what was left of it was back in Santander, and Ana's unhappy son-in-law was hurrying south to hide himself in San Lucar from the anger of the people. Bernardina's son did not come back, and there were many others, friends of Rodrigo's, young men Ana had seen christened, who never returned from the Enterprise against England. Spain, even to two lost, forgotten women-prisoners in Pastrana, writhed in anger and grief, and Ana sometimes thought with bitter embarrassment of the February night when she had laughed so enchantedly at Bernardina's rumour and drunk the health of Medina Sidonia, "that great sailor".

During the winter Bernardina became gravely ill, with inflammation and congestion of her lungs such as she had had in Pinto. But now she was older and fatter, and the years of imprisonment had weakened her; she grieved for her lost son too, and talked to him in her delirium.

Ana, with a breaking heart—for life would now be harsh indeed without Bernardina—wrote to Philip, breaking the silence of nine years, and asked him to pardon her *dueña*, pleading her ill health, the loss of her son in the Armada, and that her ageing husband was ill too, and needed her in

Madrid. She never knew if the letter got to Philip, for she received no answer.

She moved now only by leaning on two sticks; her long, beautiful hands were distorted by swollen joints; she coughed continually, and almost everything she tried to eat except bread made her feel sick. Her hair was grey, and her face was darkened by the long deep grooves of age and pain. Sometimes, if she caught sight of herself in her long mirror, as she tried to move with her sticks across her bedroom, she was taken aback, even astonished by her own image. For well though she knew her own pain and disabilities, yet somehow she did not, could not visualise herself, Ana de Mendoza, as just a creeping ruin, an ugly, broken invalid. But that was what the mirror showed her; that was what she was.

She joked about this awful decay, half-bitterly, half-lightly, to Anichu.

"Would I have got like this in any case, do you think, Anichu? Prisoner or not, was I just bound to be an old freak like this at forty-nine?"

"Are you forty-nine?"

"Yes, indeed. But I feel a hundred."

"Somehow, I never dream you're anything like forty-nine. Oh yes, I know you can't walk very well—but that's probably because of all that ill-treatment in those awful places—and because of the way you've been cooped up here too. But—otherwise, you don't seem to me to change."

"Oh pet! Don't be so unkind! Anichu, I'm hideous now—and I wasn't, or I thought I wasn't, once."

"I always thought you very beautiful," Anichu said. "You're beautiful now. You're the sort of person—there are hardly any of them, I imagine—who is beautiful, for those who think so, once and for all."

Ana bit her lip, afraid of the weak tears that so often defeated her now.

"Child," she said gently, "I must be somehow good, to have so perfect a daughter."

Bernardina recovered in the spring, and Ana too revived, and they often made their slow way together to the topmost terrace of the now neglected garden, and sat in the sun and looked about over the dear, free stretches of Castile, and laughed at their ludicrous life, and at finding themselves turned into two feeble, plain old fogies whom the world had agreed to forget.

And sometimes there in the sun Ana thought of the Armada and of Spain and of all the disastrous mistakes of a great reign, and of the dismal failure and weakness throughout it of her own caste. And she talked in that vein to Bernardina and Anichu.

"I wish I'd been a man," she said one day.

"I wish you had," said Anichu. "You'd have been a great one."

"Some people might say, *chiquita*, and I'm one of them, that you're a great woman."

"Ah no, Berni. I've been of no use at all."

"You've set a good example," said Anichu.

"I had no choice. I mean, no choice in my heart. You can't say black is white."

"Everyone does but you, *chiquita*, when it suits them."

"Well then, it suits them. But it would never suit me. Still, being like that hasn't anything to do with being great."

"You're the only subject of Philip's who hasn't compromised with his dishonesty—in my day anyway," said Bernardina.

"Nor has Antonio Perez."

"Ah, that's different. You just stood by an idea. He's fighting for himself."

"And he's still fighting. He may win."

"I doubt it, *chiquita*," said Bernardina, looking troubled.

"But, Philip," said Ana dreamily, following another

thought, "whoever wins or doesn't win, he loses. He's losing everything, I fear. Poor Philip!"

By the autumn of 1589 the Duke of Medina Sidonia, having licked his wounds in luxury at San Lucar and been forgiven by his king for failing to do what was completely beyond his capacity, found time to worry again about family affairs. He was too out of sorts and gouty now to make a journey from Andalusia to mid-Castile, and in any case having lost heart in his battle for Ana's right to be free, saw no sense in depressing himself by the spectacle of her present life. He knew that its conditions were bad and that her health was wretched, and his heart was soft, so he had to spare it a vain ordeal. But he was concerned for the future of the child Anichu. and so—his letters showed—was Rodrigo, and so were other relatives. Anichu must be fourteen now, he calculated, and would be a wealthy woman. Her mother must by all accounts die soon; Anichu's brothers were scattered, and she would need a protector and a comforter when she was left alone. It was necessary, in fact, to arrange a betrothal, possibly even a marriage for the girl.

After consultations with the king and with many Mendoza cousins including the head of the family, the Duke of Infantado, Alonso selected the young Count of Tendilla for his sister-in-law. It was a good choice, considering that so many of the young flower of Spain had recently been lost in the English Channel or on the rocks of western Ireland. The Count was a Mendoza and a cousin, young, gentle and pleasant to the eye; he had known and played with Anichu's brothers from babyhood; he was sufficiently wealthy, and his parents were good people and approved of this design for him.

So Medina Sidonia wrote of it in detail to Ana. And Ana read his letter and thought it over, and read it again, and with a little shiver of sorrow realised that she approved of it too. She remembered the boy in the old Madrid days and had liked him. And it was true that Anichu would be vulnerable and desolate indeed on a day that could not now be far removed.

She did not answer her son-in-law at once.

"Do you think of marrying ever, Anichu?"

Anichu looked very much surprised—even amused.

"No! Good heavens, no! Well, not for centuries yet, I mean."

"But what do you mean by centuries?"

"Oh—ages. When I'm a real grown-up, I suppose I'll marry. Everyone does, after all."

"In any case, I wouldn't let you marry until you are at least sixteen."

"Sixteen? But that's only two years off! I'm not going to marry in two years. In any case," she laughed, "I'll probably have to marry one of these guards or someone."

"Why, my pet? They're dreadful-looking creatures."

"Yes, I know. But it'll have to be someone who lives here, you see."

"Oh no, Anichu, what nonsense! You can't marry a man and expect him to live in a prison."

Anichu smiled.

"Then I can't marry. Because I'm never going away from here. Not while you're a prisoner. Not for fifty husbands."

"There won't be fifty of them, pet. But you'll have to go away when you marry."

"Well then, I've told you—it's quite simple. I won't marry. I prefer to stay with you."

"I see. But you won't always. A little later on you'll want to love a man. You'll want children."

"I'm not so sure. What I love is being with you."

"That's only because you think I'm wrongly treated, and you feel fanatical about my ill-usage."

"Oh yes, that too. I simply wouldn't leave you now for any reason on earth. But it's easy to say that—because I *want* to stay with you. What's put all this into your head so suddenly about marriage, of all things?"

"Well, you're growing up. And you have, as a matter of fact, a suitor, a very suitable suitor." Anichu stared at her. "Someone who desires to be betrothed to you."

"Who is it?"

"Your second cousin, Diego de Mendoza, Count of Tendilla. You remember him? He used to fence rather well, with Rodrigo."

Anichu looked thoughtful.

"Yes. I remember him. He was nice. He was very quiet, but he always looked nice."

"Well, there it is. Will you think it over?"

"No, I don't think so. I don't want to be betrothed. You wouldn't really like me to be, would you?"

Ana looked at the girl.

"I think I would. It would be a comfort. I'm old, pet, older than my age, and you know as well as I do that I'm ill. When I'm gone, you'll be very lonely——"

"When you're gone," said Anichu very steadily, "being betrothed or not to my cousin will make no difference to me at all."

"Oh yes, it will—believe me."

"Please, don't say any more of this, I beg you. I'm very grateful to my cousin, and I think I liked him when I knew him. But please excuse me from being betrothed. Let us stay here, just as we are—it isn't much to ask."

"That's true," said Ana. "Very well, I'll say no more."

And she wrote to Medina Sidonia thanking him for his project and saying that she approved of it. But she said that there could be no betrothal yet, as Anichu was still too young in spirit and asked to be excused. But that she liked her cousin and spoke kindly of him, and that if he was not impatient—and he was young enough to wait—she believed that the contract might be arranged within another twelvemonth.

So it was left at the close of 1589. But Ana felt less bleak, less guilty now when she contemplated her youngest child. I will go, she thought, I will go soon, and she will still be very young and susceptible to comfort, and our kind Alonso will see that this good plan for her happiness is secured. And then she will grow up and grow wings and be happy and normal, and forget these years and forget her grief.

This relief to her heart was timely, for in January and February it began to be clear that she must no longer attempt any greater effort than the now very great one of creeping from her bedroom to her couch in the drawing-room. She knew now that she would never see the garden again, never sit on its topmost terrace with the Guadarramas at her back and the fields of Castile spread out golden in the sun. The end was beginning. And she was powerless to spare Anichu its sorrow. But afterwards the young life would begin. Ana folded this assurance into her heart, and said her prayers more peacefully, and lay with her couch so placed that she could always see the sky and the *Colegiata* tower. And she thought of Ruy's tomb awaiting her beneath the tower, and reflected peacefully on death.

THE FOURTH CHAPTER   (18TH APRIL 1590)

I

During March Ana was so ill that she was unable to leave her bedroom, a sign in her that pain was indeed in the ascendant over her will. But one morning towards the end of Lent she woke and told Bernardina that she was feeling well again. And so indeed she seemed; and she got up and dressed herself slowly, very slowly—but still refusing help, as all her life she had refused it.

Bernardina fretted sometimes now for Ana, about this privacy of her dressing-room. She knew it was because of her disfigured eye that she had all her life brushed and washed her own hair, and she washed her face and took her bath unattended. Even at Pinto, when they had lived together in slum-proximity, Bernardina had never seen Ana's right eye without the black silk shade. But now the day was coming when those once-quick and authoritative hands would no longer be able to reach to Ana's head, or reaching there do her will. Already for many months it had hurt Bernardina to see the dressing-room door close on that weary, pain-ridden figure, and to count how long, how very long it was before it opened again. Ana, austere in personal taste and impatient of the delays and follies of elaborate adornment, had always dressed and undressed faster than any woman Bernardina had ever known or heard of. Now that was over, but by long pride and shyness of habit she still dressed and undressed alone.

However, on this April morning after a whole month in bed she seemed indeed most touchingly recuperated, and came from her dressing-room, slowly on her sticks indeed, but seeming not too much exhausted, and looking groomed and slender and even elegant in her old black silk dress. And she came back to her couch by the great window, and looked with greedy pleasure towards her view again.

"I think April is a lucky month, don't you, Anichu?"

Anichu, radiant to see her well, agreed indeed.

"This is a lucky April anyway," she said. "We must have a happy Easter."

"When is Easter?"

"On the twenty-second. Only about a fortnight off."

"Oh, goodness—nearly all of Lent is gone, and I spent it cosseting myself in bed! I must make up for lost time. I think I could crawl as far as the chapel for Mass to-morrow."

"You'll do nothing of the sort, let me tell you," said Bernardina. "That chapel is a death-trap, it's so cold and draughty."

Ana looked out at the radiant day.

"There are no draughts in weather like this," she said. "This is spring."

Every day that month she got up and came to her couch and was well, and read and did sums and puzzles with Anichu, and at supper drank wine rashly.

For Holy Week Anichu went, as she went every year, to stay at the Franciscan convent and make a retreat.

"I hate being away when you're so well," she said to Ana before she left her on Palm Sunday. "But of course it's much better than leaving you when you're ill."

"And you'll be home on Saturday—early, mind! Immediately after all those endless ceremonies. Promise!"

Anichu kissed her.

"I promise. You know I'll come flying. Keep well now—please!"

"I will. I'll always be well now, perhaps?"

"No need for 'perhaps'," said Anichu, and kissed her again and was gone.

The lovely days lengthened.

In spite of Bernardina's protests Ana did manage to edge her way across the landing to the tribune of the chapel to assist at some of the great and sorrowful rites of Holy Week. And on her couch she read the Offices of the Church and prayed and sought in recollection and silence to identify herself with the Passion of Christ. Time passed gently. There were no arguments with Don Alonso Villasante, and Ana, a prisoner now to her own health, almost forgot that she was Philip's prisoner too.

On Wednesday evening in Holy Week Bernardina came into the drawing-room as dusk was falling. Ana lay propped against pillows on her couch; her head was relaxed as if she slept, and in profile to the evening light which gleamed about her greying hair. Her hands lay still on the coverlet.

Bernardina looked at her as if in perplexity, and for a moment did not speak or move to disturb her. She looks so peaceful. She's ill and old, and it's all over. I don't think the message ought to have been sent. It's too dangerous. All very well for him, but it might mean death for her——

Ana stirred, and smiled at her.

"What are you doing, standing there staring at me, you old sneak?"

"Admiring you, my beauty. I thought we might have a drink?" She set down a tray.

"But am I allowed one at this hour?"

"Well, it's Holy Week, and we really are rather overdoing the penitential business, in my opinion. I'm exhausted."

"Poor Berni. Let's have a lot to drink."

"It's seven o'clock anyhow. *Merienda*-time in the good old days." She poured their wine, and set Ana's where it would be easiest to her stiffening hand.

Ana was watching her face, on which the evening light fell fully.

"Come on, Berni—what's happened? What are we drinking about?"

"Honestly I don't know whether to tell you or not. Still, I think you might not forgive me if I didn't. I think that, if I were you, I'd wish to be told."

Ana stared at her.

"But of course I'd wish to be told! What *is* it, Berni?"

Bernardina took a careful, steady drink, and set down her glass.

"You know old Jorge?"

Old Jorge was the retired *Alcalde* of Pastrana, and the only person from the village who nowadays managed sometimes to get further inside the house than the Estate Office. He invented pretexts in *alcalde* jargon for these entries. He was not supposed to see either of the prisoners, but one or two of the guards who liked him and liked Bernardina sometimes arranged for them to have a few words in the children's apartments or some safe place downstairs. In any case, to let him do so could not be regarded as a major crime, for he was a fat and simple old villager, not to be suspected of intrigue.

"Yes. Has he been calling?"

"I've just been talking with him in the children's study. He sent you his most devoted respects."

"And then? Go on, Berni!"

"A man passed through Pastrana to-day and called on Jorge. Jorge didn't know him and he gave no name. He said he was from Zaragoza and was on his way home."

"Ah! An Aragonese!"

"He gave this message to Jorge, which Jorge was to try to get to us. He said that Gil de Mesa wished you to know that a traveller will be making for the Aragon frontier to-night and may seek entrance here, from the top of the garden, as he passes."

"Ah!" There was silence a moment. "Thank you, Berni."

"Do you know the name, Gil de Mesa?"

"Yes. He is a friend of Antonio's."

"An escape is evidently planned for to-night. It's very daring of them—because, from what I've been hearing, it might well be expected."

"What have you been hearing?"

"Nothing much for the past two or three weeks. But then I did hear that the trial was going against Perez, that witnesses were betraying him. And that he was in rigorous solitary confinement again, in some house in Madrid. It didn't sound hopeful. But of course—by the time a rumour gets to a village——"

"When did Jorge's visitor come?"

"About four o'clock. And went on at once towards Guadalajara."

"It is about a hundred and fifty miles, isn't it, from Madrid to the frontier of Aragon?"

"About that—a little more, I think."

"An escape from a place like Madrid couldn't be started

until well after dark." Ana looked out at the twilight and its handful of stars. "With changes of horses, and good horses, I suppose a man could be near the border by daylight? That is necessary, I'm sure—to use the cover of the dark."

"Yes. In this empty countryside you could get a long way in safety in the first night. But by morning rumour will have spread and may have got ahead of you, or you might even be recognised. But I don't think, with the best horses on earth, he could be in Aragon until after midday to-morrow. It's a very dangerous scheme, for him," said Bernardina. "Because the moment he is missed they'll know there is only one road for him into safety—or possible safety."

"He shouldn't come here. It's an absurd addition to the risk."

"But we've no way of stopping him."

"No, thank God," said Ana with a smile.

"You're glad? You'll be glad to see him?"

Ana leant back into her pillows and looked out towards the sky.

"Glad?" she said dreamily. And then she laughed outright. "Berni, you're ridiculous, ridiculous!"

Bernardina felt tears sting her eyes.

"You incorrigible old rip," she said lovingly.

"Give me more wine," said Ana.

They drank, and sat in silence awhile.

"He will have planned this to the very last nicety, if I know him," she said. "He even found the means to send that message here, and took the risk."

"Remember now, he may not get this far—it's a very mad thing he's doing—if he's doing it."

"He'll get here—and get to Aragon."

"If he gets as far as here, but not to Aragon, it will probably mean death without further delay for both of you."

"And for you."

"Yes—and for me."

"He mustn't die. He doesn't want to."

"Even in Aragon they may well give him up to the king.'·

"No, I think they'll stand on their ancient rights, and protect their man against the foreign king."

"Castile didn't do as much for you."

"But we Castilians sold our rights to Charles V. The Aragonese have clung to theirs. No, if he gets to Aragon he has a chance of life and freedom. Berni, did you really think you wouldn't tell me he was coming?"

"Not really, I suppose. But God in His High Heaven forgive me, *chiquita*, if it all goes wrong!"

"It won't," Ana said. "And if it does—well, it's a better ending than I'd thought of. I wonder why he's decided to do this at last?"

"He may be looking ill—or changed, you know."

"Ah, well!" Ana laughed sadly. "But why do you say it like that, Berni? Have you heard then that he's ill?"

"No, I haven't heard anything of that."

Bernardina got up and began to light candles and draw curtains.

"What time is it fully dark in Madrid, Berni?"

"Same as here. It should be full night at about eight o'clock."

"He's getting ready now."

Ana made the sign of the Cross and so did Bernardina. The latter went to the fire and piled it recklessly with wood. She was thinking of devices for getting more wood brought up, and also of how to steal candles for all the candelabra. He would be cold, maybe; and Ana would not wish him to find the room very different from his memory of it.

"If he leaves Madrid say at half-past eight, he should be here about half-past ten, Berni."

"Yes. As far as here will be the first lap. He has all his real travelling to do afterwards."

"We must get ready. We haven't got a lot of time. I'll go

and change out of this shabby dress——" She felt for her sticks and began to raise herself from the couch. "Ah, how he'll be shocked at me!" She stood leaning on her sticks and looked about her. "What an odd and terrible meeting this will be!"

"You're sure you want it?"

"Perfectly sure."

She moved as she spoke towards her bedroom door.

"It'll tire you to change your dress, *chiquita*. Won't that one do?"

"No, I don't think so. There's an old black velvet that he used to like——" She stopped and turned suddenly. "But, Berni—the guards, the garden wall! How is he to get here, ever?"

Bernardina smiled.

"I'm thinking that out," she said. "I'll manage it, *chiquita*, if it's the last thing I do. Now away with you to your dressing-room, and I'll see to everything. And first I'll furbish up this room a bit."

Whilst Ana was dressing she prayed for Antonio. It's good of him to come to me, her heart was saying peacefully. Good and true. She faced her mirror without cheating herself, and considered what this man would see who was risking so much to pause and salute the past, as he rode away from it for dear life's sake. Yet he is right to do it; he is right to have courage and come here. God, God speed him now! Oh God in Your dear mercy protect him——

II

The *Colegiata* bell rang out eleven o'clock. After it had ceased the silence all around seemed absolute. Ana strained her ears, and tried not to, for a sound of hoofs. But better, far better that she should not hear them, for then others also would not hear.

He won't ride through the village. He'll turn north up the
track at Holy Tree. Half a mile along there he should
dismount, leave his horse with whoever's with him, and cross
the Valdez orchard to the top of the garden. I'm sure he
knows all that. He is so curiously observant. The wall is
shallow on our side, and steep into the orchard. But Bernardina will be there; she'll know what to do. The night is
clear, too clear. Oh God, have pity on him now! Grant him
this one good fortune! Let him get home to Aragon! Let
him be lucky just to-night, to-night and till to-morrow, Lord!
Oh Lord, dear Christ, be with him!

She lay on her couch, looking like a composed and ageing
invalid lady. She looked aristocratic and cold; her face was
very white, her hands were still. Her only ornament was a
narrow gold chain on which was slung a ring of one fine
emerald set in pearls. It was the last jewel Antonio had ever
given her, and she had hurt him by her disinclination to wear
it. To-night she would have worn it, but her finger-joints
were swollen, and it would no longer fit even her little finger.
So she wore it on her breast.

She fingered it now and then, and lay still and looked about
the room.

Bernardina had done well. Candles flamed in all their
former places, and the fire smelt of pine-cones and applewood. A table was set with cold food and with silver jugs of
wine. The shabbiness and sorrows of the years were visible
indeed in the room, but its old elegance was astir to-night
nevertheless, over-riding time and pain; and the pictures
looked down as they had done in the good days—Ruy,
smirking dully as he never smirked, and she herself, austere
and expressionless as Sanchez Coëllo had seen her; but the
lovely Giorgione too and the Clouet head and the Holbein
drawing, and the noble, small Mantegna he had found for
her. Once more we light you up, she said—once more,
before I turn to everlasting darkness. And still she listened

for the hoofs she wished no earthly ear to hear, and she stroked her emerald and prayed.

He came into the room by the door which led towards her bedroom.

He stood and they looked at each other, and for half a second she would have said it was not he. And simultaneously she thought she read the same doubt in his face.

Then he came towards her, smiling a little, and walking on tiptoe, not making a sound. He was in dark riding clothes, but wore no weapons or spurs. Nothing that clanked. His hair was grey like hers. She noticed that he held his hands somewhat awkwardly, away from himself. She stretched her own hands out, wondering if he would notice at once how they were changed.

He came and stood beside her, looking down.

She laid her hand on one of his, and noticed that it was red and hot, and that he winced. She took her hand away.

" 'The Question', the torture?"

He nodded.

"The mildest form. And I gave in. I told them I had had him killed, on the king's instruction."

"Thank God."

He dropped on his knees and laid his head against her breast. She held him and stroked his hair, wondering with sad pleasure that it too should be grey, like hers.

"You look old," she said. "Nearly as old as me."

"I'm eight years older than you, girl."

He smiled upward to her boyishly, wearily—and memories of many, many other nights when he had smiled exactly thus against her breast came back and lighted her face.

"You haven't forgotten?"

"I haven't forgotten anything, Antón."

He closed his eyes. She noticed more exactly then the aged, weary texture of his skin, a weariness grooved in below the dust and heat of to-night's hard ride.

"But you've made your soul now? You've repented and are in the state of grace?"

"Ah, yes! It's been easy. When you're ill and a prisoner, it's easy to be virtuous."

"I know. I've thought of that. I've been virtuous too."

She smiled. He lay as if he might fall asleep. His head was very heavy.

"How long can you stay?"

"Gil says not more than forty minutes. Bernardina will come and tell me."

"Did she meet you at the garden wall?"

"Yes. I saw her as I came across the orchard. It gave me a heavenly sense of long ago—to see her there, the dear good lump, just as if we were all at peace and happy and this an affair of every night. Ah! Then you have it still?"

He had the emerald in his hand.

"I'm wearing it for the last time to-night."

"The last time?"

"Yes. I want you to take it with you—you'll need money, and I have none to give you now. But I've packed together here—you see that little leather roll—I've packed all the jewels you gave me, and some others that are my own and need not descend to the children. You'll take them, and this emerald, and use them as you need them, for love of me."

"Ana—the things I gave you——"

"It's a good way for them to serve me now. No one else should have them anyway, after I'm gone. And I'll be gone soon."

He lifted his head and turned and looked at her closely.

"Are you *very* ill, Ana?"

"I don't feel very ill now, but I have done so most of the last two years. At least, I feel that I'm dying, in a dull way."

"Why? What do the doctors say? Why are you dying?"

"They don't say much. I had a fever of some kind when I was imprisoned in San Torcaz, and since then my bones have hurt me more and more, and my heart hurts—and in general I know I've been dying slowly. I don't mind—except for Anichu. Especially now if you are safe."

"You look old, you look tired. Oh girl, how beautiful you always are!"

"Remember me, will you? Try to remember me clearly when I'm dead."

He smiled, but tears came into his eyes.

"I'll try. May I have some wine?"

"It would be strange if you didn't."

He managed the wine-jug by tilting it with the third and little fingers of both hands. She watched him with pity.

"I'll come and fetch mine," she said. She found her sticks and came to him with her crippled walk. He watched her gravely.

"I always used to think you moved too fast," he said.

"Well, he's made us pay, hasn't he? But it was worth a price."

She took her glass, and he picked up his with difficulty.

"What shall we drink to, Antón? To Aragon?"

"No, because you won't be there. I'll give you a better toast. We'll drink to the chime of Santa Maria Almudena."

He drank, delighted with this memory of lost pleasures, lovers' nights; and she smiled back into his mischievous smile. But she thought also, with a reminiscent shiver, of Philip's face under the porch of Maria Almudena.

"How do you manage to ride, with these poor hands?"

"It's torture—but I have to. Gil straps the reins up on to my elbows—you see, they used their devices on my wrists and thumbs—and then I manage to control things with these other fingers and my elbows. I was beginning to get the knack of it just about at Alcala."

"When will you be safe?"

"I don't know about *safe*—they mayn't want me in Aragon, but it's worth trying. We hope to get to Calatayud some time after midday to-morrow."

He took her gently by the arm and drew her near the fire.

"Sit down," he said, and when she did he dropped beside her on the floor. "Oh God, oh God, to stay here! Just to stay here, Ana, and be forgotten, and sleep and sleep—and die some day, when you die!"

He looked about the room with love.

"It's shabby now," she said.

"Yes, I can see that."

"When you confessed—would it not have been all right? I mean, since Philip is now known as your accomplice?"

"No, they were instructed to ignore that. The judge was shameless—everyone saw that all they were taking of my confession was the admission of my own guilt."

"And your letters?"

"They wouldn't accept them as evidence—they said they had enough. And I don't know whether perhaps I couldn't have borne the torture longer—but I was sick of the farce; so I spoke. In any case——" he laughed, "it *was* most damnably painful. And it was only the first degree."

"Eat—you'd better eat something."

"No—I can't. I had food in Madrid, and we have some with us, I believe. But more wine, Ana—oh, more wine!"

He went and refilled their glasses.

"Our time is nearly gone," he said, "and I'm saying nothing. But really I only wanted to look at you again."

"Yes. There's nothing to say, I think, that we both don't know."

"Why did you take me for a lover?"

"On a kind of cold speculation. And you didn't really want me that first time."

"No, I believe I didn't. At any rate, I could have done without you. Yet, it brought us to this—to years and years of pain."

"Yes, it brought us a long way."

"Oh girl, remember me."

"I remember you and pray for you every day of my life. Do you pray?"

"No. I've never prayed, I think."

"Well, I'll be praying for you—here and hereafter. What do you expect from Aragon?"

"A small civil war, at least—which ought to annoy Philip a great deal, I hope. And if the right side wins—there's no knowing! If we lose, I shall have to think again. But do you know who is Governor of Aragon now?"

"No, indeed."

"Your cousin of the lawsuit—Iñigo de Mendoza, now Marqués de Almenara on the titles and lands he filched from you."

"That's not a good omen. He hates me."

"So he's not likely to favour *my* cause. However, I'm appealing to the Aragonese—not to our foreign Castilian governors."

"Are your family safe?"

"The children are already in Zaragoza, I hope. And Juana will leave Madrid to-morrow and join them. Without her complicity I couldn't have arranged this escape. She has been a tower of courage all these years."

"So I should expect her to be."

Antonio smiled a little.

"I've never before made the mistake of talking about my wife to my mistress——"

"But now you *have* no mistress, and you can talk of anything to an old friend."

He came and knelt before her.

"I wish I could embrace you," he said. "These wretched hands! Girl, you're no 'old friend'. You are for ever in my heart my mistress."

She took his head into her hands and kissed his mouth.

"You're a very, very good lover, Antón."

It was a phrase from their past, and he smiled and gave her the old answer:

"If you'd perhaps let me have it in writing?"

There was a soft, steady tap on the door by which he had come in. They both heard it.

"Ah! Then it's time?"

"Yes. Bernardina said she'd knock."

They rose and stood together, looking desolately about the room. Ana took the little leather roll of jewels and said:

"Where can I put these for you? Don't take it in your poor hands?"

She found a pocket in his tunic and slipped the packet in. Then she took the chain and ring from her neck.

"No, not in my pocket, that. Round my neck, Ana."

She put the chain over his head, opened his tunic at the throat and put the ring inside his shirt against his breast.

"Thank you," he said. "It's warm from you."

"Have you no cloak, no spurs or sword or anything?"

"I left them all with Gil and the horses—so as to make less noise."

There was another gentle knock.

"Yes, Berni," Ana said.

Antonio took her in his arms.

"You'll hurt your wrists."

"Oh silly, and why not?"

He drew her hard against him, and kissed her mouth as if in first desire. Ana thought—this is the last embrace of my mortal life; people can't often know when they have reached the last. But I do know. Good-bye, she answered him now with her whole self, with all of strength and gratitude in her possession—good-bye to you, and also to that long-assuaged and quieted me that you alone commanded. Good-bye, dear past, dear sin, and go from me in peace. I loved you and I have atoned and will atone.

Antonio leant back from her to look into her face.

"I don't need to look," he said. "I know it. I've carried it with me a long time."

"Is it the same face, now it's old?"

"It's the same face, and now as then it's young and old," he said and laid his mouth gently against her black silk eye shade, into the hollow of her lost right eye. Then he released her from his arms.

"God speed you," she said. "Let me hear that you are safe."

"There'll be a message." He looked swiftly about the room again and then back to her face. "I must go."

"Yes, you must go, Antón."

He gave a little bow, and walked to the door, but there he turned, smiling.

"I've suddenly thought of Juana La Loca—do you remember, Anichu's old doll?"

She laughed.

"Yes, I remember her. I think she still exists."

"Well, give her my love then—and to Anichu."

They smiled at each other for the last time.

THE FIFTH CHAPTER   (MAY 1590)

I

Anichu came home on Holy Saturday, emaciated from the austerities of the retreat, but very happy. She found Ana well and Bernardina also in good spirits. The three had a happy Easter, not even too much overclouded when they recalled other Easters of Anichu's babyhood; the great processions around Pastrana, the dinner-party for the whole village on the top terrace of the garden, the Monday bullfight at Alcala, supper with the Marqués de Los Velez, and the long drive home and everyone singing all the way. Anichu liked to hear these tales of the splendid, family days she had hardly known.

Ana had told her at once on her return of Antonio Perez's escape from Madrid to Aragon, and of his visit to her on his way.

She looked grave at the news.

"Did he get to the frontier safely?"

"We don't know yet. There'll be a message."

"You must be anxious."

"Oddly enough, I'm not. I'm certain he's safe."

"We'd better pray though."

"Oh yes, I'm praying. You pray, my pet. God will listen to you."

Anichu looked at her thoughtfully

"You *were*—his mistress?"

"Yes, Anichu, I was."

"For how long?"

"For not quite two years before we were imprisoned."

She saw Anichu's look of relief. No doubt she was thinking of the father she had never known, who had died just after her birth.

"Forgive me for asking you this," the young girl went on anxiously, "but did you have other lovers?"

"No, pet," Ana said. "There was no one else. Only your father while he lived—and then Antonio Perez."

"Thank you—thank you for telling me. I've no right to ask you——"

"You have, Anichu."

"—But, I've heard things said about—the king, and I couldn't help wondering sometimes, he's been so terrible to you——"

"I agree—there's matter for wonder. We were devoted friends, Philip and I, but he never asked me to be his mistress, and the grave things that were said about us were untrue."

"I see. It's all the more puzzling, isn't it?"

"I've given up that riddle long ago."

She seemed now, Anichu thought, as if she had given up most riddles.

On Easter Tuesday a stranger riding west from Aragon called on Jorge, the former *Alcalde*. After he had gone on his way, Jorge, setting out laboriously for Ana's house, met Anichu and gave her the stranger's message. He said that the traveller from Madrid had reached Calatayud in Aragon on the afternoon of Holy Thursday, that he was well and had taken sanctuary in the Dominican house of San Martin. Great trouble was rising in Aragon, he said, and he sent his love to Pastrana. Anichu ran home with the message.

Nunc dimittis said Ana's heart as she received it; and henceforward she composed herself secretly and contentedly for death, which she hoped might tarry now as little as might be. And not because she turned from life in desolation or disappointment any longer, as she had done at earlier periods of her imprisonment. But her sole earthly care now was for Anichu, and for Anichu she desired her death to be hurried forward.

Antonio was gone. While he was in Spain and in the troubles and dangers his love for her had brought upon him, her heart had still tugged back towards life a little, even in bitterest hours of emptiness and loss; she had still desired, against all likelihood, to see him again and also to see some conclusion, for better or worse, put to their story. Now this had come to pass, and he was gone for ever from what was left of her life—gone indeed into danger and inconclusiveness still, but with hands freed at last to fight these, and with a real chance of evading Philip's final vengeance. Antonio's life, divorced from Castile henceforward, was entering a new, strange phase, and her part in it was played and done with.

So there only remained Anichu; and to be with the child in these sweet years of her early girlhood, to have her companionship, so steady, so comfortingly optimistic and young, to love her and enjoy her love, was indeed a poignant consolation and almost a stronger attachment to life than any other she had ever felt. But Ana knew that she took this one great grace of her latter days at a price to Anichu; she knew that the longer they lived together as now, with the child so unself-consciously and generously sacrificial in her love, the wilder and more wounding would be her grief when Ana died, and the harder her return to normal life and to the ways and friends of her own generation. There would be grief indeed—in pity for which Ana shuddered many times each day—whenever death took her from this single-hearted child. There was now no evading that; Anichu had been allowed, unwisely, to devote herse'f to her one great love, her one fanaticism almost it might be called, and it was no longer sane or kind to talk to her of going away from Pastrana. Their situation as it had grown must now be seen through, and Anichu must be prepared as firmly as love could devise for the slow pain of watching it end. But Ana believed that the younger she was when that end came so much the better. She desired that the child's approaching ordeal should be short, at least, since it could not be escaped. And when it was over, she could still go out young and curable into the sun of the world, able to take its natural comfort again, and forget Pastrana and prison and grief. Ana thought with gladness of the young Count of Tendilla, and sometimes spoke of him lightly to Anichu, who did not repudiate his name, and indeed spoke of him with a gentle interest and goodwill. So watching her and reflecting on her, Ana saw that the best thing she could do was to die very soon. And therefore it pleased her to feel, with Antonio's going, that she was at last completely ready to welcome death.

With the beginning of May she began to feel that she was getting her wish.

The days were exquisitely fair, and she always managed to get to her couch by the great window and lie where the sunlight fell and where she could hear the sounds of life come up from her forgotten village. And because her heart was composed and at peace, because indeed she felt almost gay sometimes, she did not think that Bernardina and Anichu perceived at first the relapse she felt all through her body. She would be glad if they, and especially Anichu, did not. So she lay on her sofa, and said as little as possible about aches and pains; and prayed, and reflected on her life and sins, and watched her daughter's delicate beauty opening to the early summer; and in the sunlight and quiet sometimes almost caught herself being grateful to Philip for having brought her perforce to this readiness and detachment, this calm which saints might envy, she thought, and in which, no saint at all, she did not merit to depart from life.

"I owe the king a great deal," she said to Anichu. "Because I really think he has saved my soul for me!"

"You'd have managed that for yourself," said Anichu. "But he *has* made you something of a philosopher."

"I suppose I've heard the last of him now. I suppose he has in fact forgotten me."

"Does that make you sad?"

"No, not any longer. And I have forgiven him, Anichu. Truly I have. I pray for him every day."

II

On the morning of the twenty-second of May Ana woke early, feeling very ill. But, restless, she got up and dressed, very slowly, more slowly than ever, she noticed; and at seven o'clock made her way in pain to the tribune of the chapel to hear Mass and receive Communion. Anichu and Bernardina were already in their places, and the latter frowned and shook her fist at Ana as she helped her to settle in her *prie-Dieu*.

It was a radiant morning, loud with bird-song, and as the sunlight streamed in on the altar and the priest Ana forgot her aching bones and the feeble thudding of her heart, and prayed in peace and praised God for the beauty of the day.

She stayed in her *prie-Dieu* for a little while when Mass was over and the others were gone. The empty chapel pleased her, so hushed and quiet, and holding many simple and good memories of Ruy and of her married life. She supposed she would find Ruy again after death—the Church taught her that she would, and so though it was difficult to imagine how such meetings might be, she accepted the teaching. Well, if it was true, it made death even easier to welcome, for indeed it would be good to see Ruy again, after all her mistakes and troubles.

She rose with her sticks, dipped her fingers in the holy water font and made the sign of the Cross. And with the morning song of the birds filling her ears she made her way back to the drawing-room.

The morning collation was there, of milk and bread and fruit. Anichu was eating hurriedly, as she had some early classes at the convent. Bernardina looked fussed, Ana thought—even agitated.

"What is it, Berni? Let's sit down and have some milk. I feel quite hungry."

Bernardina looked at her, helped her to sit down and poured her some milk. Anichu smiled at her mother and then glanced at Bernardina.

"Yes—what is it, Berni?" she said sharply.

Bernardina sat down.

"There's something the matter, *chiquita*," she said. "There's something very queer happening—I don't know what it is."

"Go on," said Anichu.

"Well, everyone's disappeared! I had to go to fetch this tray myself, and there's no sign anywhere of old Paca, and it was handed to me at the kitchen door by a soldier! A soldier I've never seen here before. I can't find either of the two usual kitchen-men. And Doña Isabel is nowhere to be seen, and neither is the other governess, Josepha. None of them is downstairs—and the silence, well, the silence is uncanny, *chiquita*."

"There'll be an explanation," said Ana.

"I dare say," said Anichu dryly.

"I don't like it," said Bernardina. "I don't fancy the explanation."

"I'll send for Villasante presently," said Ana, who could hardly bear the look of anxiety in Anichu's eyes. "But let's have some of this lovely breakfast first. We'll need it perhaps," she said with a little laugh.

"I can't," said Bernardina. "I'd choke if I tried. I'm frightened, *chiquita*. It isn't nice—that silence down there."

Bernardina has had too much of all these sinister prison ways, Ana thought in pity. She's breaking up, dear soul. They've almost broken *her* courageous spirit. It's probably nothing—some silly change of plan about the staff.

"Dear Berni! Drink some milk at least."

At that moment they heard the squeaking locks being turned in the iron grill beyond the great door of the drawing-room; they heard the heavy gates scream open, and heard them closed again. In another moment the house-governor, Villasante, was in the room, escorted by four armed soldiers. He looked very grave and self-important.

He bowed coldly to Ana. He had some papers in his hand.

"Your Highness was recently so ill-advised as to abuse the terms of your detention here. Evidence has been received by His Majesty that you admitted an enemy of the state illicitly to your presence, and aided and abetted his flight from justice. In view of this crime, His Majesty is now compelled to alter your house-detention to total imprisonment, and I must request you to offer no resistance whilst we proceed with the necessary arrangements, as instructed by His Majesty."

He bowed again and handed Ana one of the papers he held in his hand.

She glanced at it, saw Philip's signature and laid it down. Anichu took it from her hand and read it. Bernardina sat and stared at Ana. For once, it seemed, she had nothing to say to her gaoler. Neither could Ana think of much to say.

"Are they elaborate, these arrangements?"

"They are, madam. They will include some heavy work by masons and builders in these apartments."

"Masons and builders?"

"Yes, madam. You are to be allowed to occupy this room and your bedroom, and to have access to the chapel. But all outlets beyond that limit, all unnecessary doors and windows are to be built up and barred. And the rooms are, of course, to be stripped of these valuable pictures and furnishings, which would only come to harm in prison conditions. But we hope to have accomplished the work in two days. The masons will not disturb you long."

"I see."

Bernardina roused herself.

"Where are Her Highness's usual servants?" she asked Villasante. "Where is Paca? Where are the governesses?"

He smiled a little.

"They are dismissed, and at present on their way to Madrid, where you will also be, madam, before evening."

"I?"

"Yes. It is the king's stringent instruction that I dismiss you, and all your possessions to-day, and deliver you safely to your husband's lodging in Madrid. You are free and pardoned henceforward, but you return to the district of Pastrana only under penalty of instant death."

He bowed, and handed Bernardina a paper which bore Philip's signature.

Bernardina glanced at it, and stood up.

"I shall not go," she said. "You can tell the king to do what he likes about it, but I'm staying here."

"Berni——"

"No, madam—you are going. You shall not force us into making a martyr of you. You will go this morning under strong escort. You have long been a difficulty and a bad influence here. And in view of your share in the recent outrage of regulations, His Majesty's clemency in setting you free is, may I say, astonishing. Your personal possessions were packed whilst you were assisting at Mass, and they now await you in a coach in the court-yard. Will you therefore be so good as to bid adieu to Her Highness? We shall then, when you are despatched, be able to begin our work on these apartments."

Bernardina looked wildly about the room. She was over sixty now, and unhealthy and tired and fat. Ana thought that she might be going to have a stroke. With difficulty she rose and went to her. She put an arm about her shoulders.

"Berni, Berni! Don't look like that. It's all right, and it can't be helped. We've had a good life together, in spite of all these gaolers. And it's over now and we're both old women anyway, and won't be troubling the king and his servants much longer. So say good-bye, and take my gratitude and a great deal of my heart with you, my dear, to Madrid. And to Heaven, where I'll meet you soon."

"I won't say good-bye! I can't! It's murder, plain, slow murder, to do this to you now! And what *are* they going to do? I'd go mad, I tell you, if I had to leave you to their devilries now! No, I won't say good-bye, I won't, I won't!"

Villasante signed to two soldiers who slipped forward and laid hands on Bernardina. But Ana waved them off.

"Just a moment, please. Berni, for my sake go, and go in peace. After all, you owe it to your poor husband, who has had to suffer so much because of your loyal duty to me. Think of the consolation it will be to him to have you back again for his old age. And——" she put both arms round the *dueña* now, and spoke softly, turning away from where Anichu stood rigid, with the king's order still in her hands—"you know very well that for me it won't be long now, so whatever they're going to do, just bar me in a bit, I suppose, will matter very little. You know I'm near death, and very glad to be. So make it easy for me now. It will be a real comfort to know that you are back with poor dear Espinosa, whom I have wronged so much in taking all your years of loyalty. Do you hear me, Berni? Are you listening?"

"Yes, I hear you, *chiquita*." Bernardina spoke dully, slowly. This last shock was too much and she knew it was. She knew there was no way of resistance for her now, a fat old woman, against armed men and proclamations from the king. Yet she turned once more on Villasante.

"How is she to be looked after? She is, as you know well, a very ill woman. She simply cannot be left without me now! I've taken care of her for years—indeed, it seems like all my life!"

"A female has been engaged who is competent to perform the necessary offices of a wardress."

"A wardress!"

Ana laughed.

"Ah, Berni, what does it matter? Why not a wardress? Perhaps she'll be as amusing as Gypsy Rosa! Do you remember Pinto, and Gypsy Rosa?"

Bernardina broke into helpless, desolate sobbing. Ana held her in her arms, and Anichu came to them, and tried to help her fragile mother to support the dejected weight of her.

"Mother is right, Berni. And it will comfort her to know that you're at home again with Espinosa."

Bernardina was past further speech. She sobbed and shook in Ana's arms.

"Good-bye, my dear, dear friend," Ana said. "Good-bye, my Berni, and God bless and keep you. Pray for me, and I will pray for you."

She signalled to the soldiers, and they came and took

Bernardina gently by the arms. She went with them, blind with shock and desolation. She did not look back, and after the iron grill beyond the door had opened and shut on her and the guards, her choked and formless crying could still be heard—but dying away as she descended the great staircase.

Ana stood leaning on her sticks and looked at Anichu. She wondered with terror what instruction there might be about her.

Villasante looked from one of them to the other.

"What arrangement does Your Highness wish me to make for the young Countess?" he asked politely.

Ana and Anichu looked at each other quickly. Evidently the king had sent no ultimatum about the latter.

"If you wish, we can have her sent under careful escort to the house of her sister, the Duchess of Medina Sidonia, at San Lucar. Or is there any other relative you would prefer her to be sent to?"

Anichu smiled. Ana could see something like radiant happiness taking possession of a face that a moment ago had been rigid with fear.

"Thank you, Don Alonso," Anichu said with a politeness which almost sought to be ingratiating. "Thank you, but I don't wish to be sent anywhere. I am staying here."

It was clear that she understood from his manner that he had no instructions about her, and that therefore he would be unable to force her away.

Villasante looked perplexed. He spoke to Ana.

"I cannot advise such a course," he said. "The Countess is not under arrest, and your conditions here henceforward will be total imprisonment. If she were to stay here, she would have to suffer those conditions also. I can allow no traffic whatever between these rooms and the outer world. And no comforts, nothing more than the standard of life in state prisons, will be permitted. I believe therefore that I shall be obliged to arrange to send the young Countess to her Grace, her sister."

Ana looked at Anichu. The girl intended to stay with her, she knew. And she knew that this time Philip was in earnest, and for her sin in seeing Antonio again, she was to pay the full penalty, and drag out the remainder of her days in the deprivation, filth, darkness and neglect which was the portion of Spain's worst criminals in the crudest prisons. She hardly cared for herself—but it terrified her for Anichu. It would only hurry death to her, which would be good; but it might undermine the young girl's health for ever, and it would leave a great scar of bitterness and sorrow on her soul. And she would have to be alone, more or less, with the ordeal of her mother's death. It was a very dark, dangerous way for a young imagination to have to tread. Yet she believed that for Anichu, who knew so well how to love, the alternative might be far worse. To be sent away by force now into the sun and freedom with nothing to do but try to imagine what was happening in Pastrana—Ana shuddered for what that might do to a spirit like Anichu's.

"You heard what Don Alonso said, Anichu?"

"Yes. And I thank him again. But I am staying here. I understand the terms, Don Alonso, and shall abide by them."

Don Alonso bowed, and frowned.

"I regret your decision, Countess."

Ana sat down again. She suddenly felt most desperately ill and weary. She sat with her elbow on the table and her fingers pressed against her eye-shade. Anichu had chosen the right way for herself, but this strange burden that her fate had laid upon her child was going to be heavier and harder than had ever been foreseen. Oh Philip, Philip, must I forgive you this as well?

"Then, with Your Highness's permission, I will send for the workmen and instruct them. And meantime, we must start on the removal of these pictures and books."

Ana looked up and nodded vaguely. The men began to move about the room. Anichu stood at the other side of the table where breakfast still lay untouched. She sat down now, and leant across and stroked Ana's hand.

"Come, let's have breakfast," she said.

They sat and tried to eat and drink.

Outside the peerless day spread in brightness. The square stirred with its usual gentle, easy signs of life, and the façade of the *Colegiata* threw a peaceful shadow.

"Do drink some milk," Anichu said.

One of the men was taking down the Mantegna. Ana watched him in wonder. They were quick; already the pictures were gone from the long wall. Ruy was gone, and the Clouet head that Isabel of Valois had given her.

There was a clattering sound below—a coach driving out of the court-yard; they could not see it from here. They looked at each other, and said good-bye again to Bernardina in their hearts. Ana listened to the wheels until the sound vanished for ever along the Alcala road.

By the evening of that day they had grown used to the sound of hammering, the clang of iron bars being driven into place, and the tramp and noise of several men working at great pressure all about them.

When they sat eating the mess of supper which their new wardress brought to them, the drawing-room was bare of everything save Ana's couch, two tables and two chairs. The curtains and carpets and desk and all the accustomed furnishings cf a whole life were gone with the pictures, and the white walls with their fading and peeling acacia-leaves of gold looked absurd, dishonoured and sordid.

A great wall had been built to cut them off from the staircase which led to the garden. A small iron door was inserted in this, through which the wardress would come to them henceforward, unlocking and locking it with her every move. The landing now where this wall had been built, and Ana's bedroom and dressing-room, where the windows had been built in, were entirely deprived of daylight and ventilation.

After supper they did not light their one candle. The great window was open, and they sat and looked at the rising stars, and smelt the sweet May night. They could see the *Colegiata* door open and shut as people went in and out to say their evening prayers.

Anichu sat on the floor by Ana's couch.

"Talk to me," she said. "Tell me about when we were all little. Tell me things about when you were little."

Ana stroked her shining, dark head.

They stayed very late by the window, and talked of a great many things.

On the second evening of this new imprisonment they had no window by which to sit and talk. The masons had done their work within scheduled time, and the king's instructions had been carried through. There was no light any more in the drawing-room at Pastrana. The great window had been built up, and Ana would never again see the sky or the tower of the *Colegiata*. Nor her daughter's face, save by the light of one candle. Philip's work on her was done now. She could compose herself and wait. Contentedly she realised that she felt very ill indeed. It won't be long, Anichu, her heart said passionately. I promise you, my darling, it won't be long.

EPILOGUE

PHILIP was tired, and having worked without pause all
day at his desk was tempted, when he recognised its
handwriting, not to open the last letter of the afternoon's
great collection.

It was from the Duke of Medina Sidonia, a loyal man and
virtuous, so well-meaning indeed that Philip had had no
heart to be other than forgiving and considerate with him
over the catastrophe of the Armada. And after all, Philip had
acknowledged to himself, that was chiefly his own fault. Yet,
though bearing no grudge, he could not bear the sight of
Medina Sidonia's writing, for it reminded him of Ana de
Mendoza.

He was sixty-five now, gouty and stiff and full of ill-
health. His eyes hurt him constantly and were watery and
red-rimmed; his once-distinguished fairness of hair and skin
had long been a blur of desiccated, neutral grey. But he cared
little for his own disabilities and infirmities, so long as he
could still work, work for Spain, work with the caution,
closeness and tenacity that were all he could give his country
in place of brilliance or decisiveness. He was much dis-
heartened now, and pondered questioningly the past for its
mistakes. But still he must work, because now he knew of
nothing else to do, and because he must keep on trying to
redeem some of the failures he had brought on Spain, and on
his own reputation as a king.

He had sacrificed Spain's integral greatness to his zeal for
Catholicism in Europe—and now it appeared even to him
that that cause was lost. The threat of the Armada and its
brilliant defeat had roused all England, and settled for ever
the Catholic hope in that island; France, with which he was at

war, had now a Protestant king, and the Duke of Guise was dead, assassinated; the Netherlands, though William of Orange was long since gone, assassinated also, fought and wrestled eternally still, divided and confused, but intransigent in their refusal to impose Catholicism; they drained his resources and his wits. At home, with Mother Teresa's reformers divided and quarrelling since her death, with the Holy Office as arrogant as always and with Jews and *moriscos* everywhere, he saw the Faith often disgraced and frequently threatened; and overseas the *conquistadores*, though spreading God's message indeed, were doing so at a cost of blood, ships, men, piracy and crime which often made Spain's empire seem to him instead of a glory the source of all her present poverty and decline.

He viewed this picture with realistic depression and regret. He had intended to be a very great king, and had never been less than a conscientious and a serious one. And he had sought God's Will in prayer and self-denial—more and more with every year—and as he thought he read that Will, he had obeyed it without shrinking. But the great scheme had gone wrong somewhere and he knew it, and knew that a vast measure of the blame must lie with him. Yet he could not see how other he could have acted, for he could only be himself and give what he had to give to his high vocation. And that he had done—and the rest was with God, and meantime he must continue, against heavier and heavier odds, to work by his light for Spain and for Heaven's great cause. The thought of Heaven's great cause reminded him now of Granvelle's long memorandum of the war in France which still lay unread and must be discussed within an hour. He turned to look for it—he had better read it. It was undoubtedly dangerous for Spain that Antonio Perez was at the French court, and apparently high in favour with this Protestant, Henry IV. Perez always *had* been liked by the French liberals; Henry III had liked him, and now this Bourbon had taken him up, the renegade. And Perez knew a very great deal, and never forgot anything. It was regrettable that he had escaped from Aragon—and all the more bitter that he did so on the very day that the province yielded unconditionally to Castilian arms. Ironic for Aragon to have lost its ancient liberties in such an unworthy cause, and ironic for him, Philip, to have lost the prey he went to war for. He smiled coldly. He had desired the death of Antonio Perez. Well, it had not been granted. The wrong people died; he had a way of removing the wrong people. Yet it was much to have subdued Aragon at last, to have brought her stubborn nobles as irrevocably to heel as his father had the aristocracy of Castile. The Peninsula was one now, and ruled by one man. Yet the accomplishment had failed of Philip's real purpose— and Perez was the protégé of a Protestant king in France. Ironic. Philip smiled patiently. He was growing used to failure.

He looked about his workroom. It was the end of a very hot day, and he never felt well in Madrid. He did not like the Alcázar, and thought gratefully that at nightfall he would be driving back again up the Guadarramas to El Escorial. There, if anywhere on earth, he found some peace now, and there he saw rising about him—in the library, the schools, the experimental farms, the hospital, and in that great church with its perfect choir and perfect adherence to liturgical symbolism—there in all of these things at least he saw a happy achievement, a carrying-through of his desire. There were his dear children too, Isabel's daughters and the one sickly, precious son who alone survived of poor Anne of Austria's attempts to give him a male heir. Young Philip was fourteen, and it looked as if he would survive and reach the throne. That at least was a comfort.

Philip would be glad to drive home to-night. To-morrow he might have a few hours off and take the boy fishing, to that trout-pool just beyond Carreño Wood. The gardens would be lovely now—he had been away from them for fourteen days, and that was too long in June. He looked distastefully about him, and through the window where across the courtyard and the roof of Santa Maria Almudena he could see Madrid, baking defencelessly in the late afternoon light.

This was the hour when in former days he had liked to rest awhile from work, to leave this cramping room, and be himself awhile and not the king. This was the hour when he had sometimes allowed himself to leave the Alcázar by that gate which he could see from where he sat, and go and idle in the Long Room in the Eboli Palace. The Eboli Palace was closed and empty now.

This memory had overtaken him unawares, and he winced from it and turned back to his table. He thought of Ana seldom and never by his own choice. He had enough discomforts in his consciousness; this, his most private, which he had never understood, he buried at its every stirring under the rubble of a long life of anxieties and regrets.

He had loved her, after his fashion. And his love had had much that was tender and brotherly in it, and only in rare moments of impulse to throw off kingship had become desire. And in later life he had been able the more to enjoy those moments for knowing that he would never yield to them. They were a delicate sensuality and sentimentalism of his secret moods, a very private, untroubling grace in a life that had slowly stripped itself of decoration. And he loved her company—rarely though he allowed himself to taste it— and loved with greedy jealousy the flattery of her love, and the hint, the more-than-hint in it that if he had so willed he could have taken her when they were young. She was his preserve, his very private tenderness, and he rested in its reassurance. He liked even to hear her tell how she had thought when she was a little girl that she was to marry him; he liked to think that he had given her some heartache, that she had sometimes been made impatient by the non-finality of his desire for her; he liked to think that he, the king, was what this great and spoilt princess had coveted and never had. It was a day-dream, it was a feather in his cap—and because she gave it to him he gave her great affection. And he admired her, and all the more because he knew that she admired him.

The discovery therefore that in her middle age, while still his friend and dear illusion, she had a lover; right under his blind eyes, and out of his palace, and his closest friend—this shock worked in him slowly and creepingly, like an illness. It wrought effects in him that he could never manage and never face. And he never would face now all that retrospective misery. Against it he had acted, or not acted, by blind, frightened instinct, and in a series of struggles with himself; in a succession of sins against his heart and indulgences of his aching, cancered vanity. There was no law in his reaction, and he had no clue to it. Simply she had disillusioned him, and thereafter he could not, however he sought to, desist from vengeance. And when, regretful, ashamed and weary, he kept the whole tale buried in himself, only hoping that she was at peace in Pastrana and out of mischief and saving her soul—when then, in their old age, the news was brought to him that she was by no means at peace, that she still had her lover, that he had come to her in her prison in his flight into Aragon, perhaps only for the last of many visits, and that she had helped him in his escape—then a last fever of savagery against her invaded him. It was too much gall, this ultimate, unlooked-for opening of an unhealed-wound. He could not resist the passion, the old man's passion of self-pity that invaded him. He could not and he did not. Almost without consulting himself, almost without thought and as if he acted in his sleep, he answered her last flippancy against him, answered it for ever.

But he could not let himself think of her. He hated her dear name. It was carved beside Ruy Gomez's now on their tomb in the *Colegiata* Church of Pastrana. There it must stand, but in his soul would Heaven in mercy bury it, and let him never come on it again?

But Heaven was not considerate. Here was this letter from Medina Sidonia, which could not fail to stir the one forbidden woe.

Ana was now dead five months. She had died on the second of February, the Feast of the Purification of Our Lady; for all that they had told him of her desperate ill-health, she had lived twenty months in darkness and incarceration. But she was at peace now in her grave. And in the absence of her son Rodrigo with Parma's armies, her son-in-law was attending to the family affairs. Every now and then he deemed it his duty to report on these to Philip.

Philip opened his letter reluctantly, and read it through without letting himself concentrate, as if by too close attention he would receive more hurt from it than he could bear.

It was businesslike and gave details of the disposal of certain pieces of property. It lamented, as Alonso's other letter had done, the great depreciation in the value of the Pastrana estates, the almost-disappearance of its silk trade and the depression on its farms. Rodrigo would be worried by the figures, he said, and was pressing for money. Rodrigo, had His Majesty heard?, was not well. He was developing a serious weakness of the lungs, and might have to give up soldiering. The Princess's other sons were well, he understood, and Fernando would soon be receiving Holy Orders. Alonso heard from his superiors that he was a very promising cleric. One sad piece of news, however, he had to impart to His Majesty about this family in which he had always taken so much interest. His Majesty would recall that a betrothal was to be arranged this summer between the late Princess's younger daughter, the Countess Ana de Silva and her cousin, the Count of Tendilla. This had not been arranged earlier as the Countess had asked for a little time in which to meditate and, no doubt, recover from the grief of her mother's death. But, alas, in April the young man had had a fall from a horse, and only a week or two ago had died of his injuries. This was very regrettable in the already sad circumstances, but he the Duke, would have found no difficulty in arranging another equally suitable match for his beautiful and wealthy young sister-in-law. But he heard from her now—and he hastened to communicate the news to His Majesty—that she had returned to Pastrana, and had entered the Franciscan convent there as a postulant. She had said in her letter that this decision made her very happy—so perhaps if it was God's will it would be for the best. What did His Majesty think? . . .

Philip laid down the letter.

He rose painfully from the table and moved without purpose about the room. He came to rest at the window and looked across the court-yard at Madrid outside his walls. A bell was ringing from Santa Maria Almudena. He remembered how much more clearly one heard that bell in the Long Room of the Eboli Palace. Anichu, she used to call the little one, Anichu who did not leave her until the end, and had gone back to her now, gone back to Pastrana.

Philip stood a long time by the window and listened to the bell. His foot was hurting him, but he could not move to return to his chair. It was as if by keeping very still awhile he might master the leaden, deadly pain in his breast. He looked out at the sunlight towards her empty house, and the glare hurt his eyes, and the bell seemed to toll for his loneliness, and the sins that drove him on, for ever further into loneliness.

But he would be at El Escorial by morning, where his children were.

October 1945.   Clifden, Corofin.

Lightning Source UK Ltd.
Milton Keynes UK
12 October 2010

161122UK00001B/7/A